THE ARX

....

JAY ALLAN STOREY

JAY ALLAN STOREY

Non Sequitur Publishing

Vancouver, BC

Copyright © 2015 by Jay Allan Storey.

July 9, 2020

Jay Allan Storey/Non Sequitur Publishing
190 - 1027 Davie Street
Vancouver, BC V6E 4L2
jayallanstorey@shaw.ca

- 1 -

The Arx/Jay Allan Storey. – 4th ed.
ISBN 978-0-9917912-2-4

Dedicated to my brother, Ross, the first author in our family.

ONE

....

TWO UNEXPECTED GUESTS

I t was Friday afternoon. Dinner was at 5:30. At 5:35 Frank Langer pulled up in front of his sister Janet's house in the suburbs. At 5:40 he stood fidgeting in front of her door. At 5:42 he finally rang the doorbell. A few seconds later he was turning to leave when the door opened behind him.

"Frank! It's so good to see you!" It was Janet's voice. "I was afraid you wouldn't show."

Frank turned back and attempted a smile. "Hi, Sis. Long time no see."

After a quick hug he stepped across the threshold and the door slammed shut behind him. It was hard to breathe; the air was thicker than outside, like the house had been pressurized. He tugged on his tie, trying to get his breath. Janet took his coat and he plodded after her down the hallway to the living room.

He glanced over at the couch and the hair on the back of his neck stood on end. Seated where he'd expected to find Janet's husband

Chuck, was a woman. She smiled and brushed back a lock of impeccably coiffed hair. Her skin was as smooth and immobile as a department store mannequin, and the colour of her eyelids matched her purple dress exactly.

He turned, hunting for an escape route, but his sister was blocking the hallway.

"Gloria," Janet said, turning to the woman. "This is my brother, Frank. Frank, this is my friend Gloria Hanon. Gloria works with me at Garland Cosmetics."

Gloria rose and presented her hand. "Pleased to meet you."

"Hi," Frank said, shaking the tips of her fingers.

Janet headed for the kitchen. "I've got to check on the roast," she said. "You two get acquainted."

Frank excused himself and followed her.

"What the hell is this!" he whispered when they were out of hearing. "You said dinner."

"Don't be mad, Frank. She's just a friend. She's lonely, like you..."

"I'm not lonely."

"Sheila's been gone for six months," she said. "You've got to move on – get out there – start a new life. Gloria's a single mother and..."

"You're setting me up with a single mother!"

"Please don't call it 'setting you up' – I'm just introducing you, that's all."

"What did you tell her about me?" he said. "Did you happen to mention that I'm a loony?"

"You're not a loony, Frank. I wish you wouldn't say things like that. I told her the truth – that you were on stress leave from the force."

"For a year?"

She turned away and grabbed a dish towel off a rack by the stove. "What happened to you would be enough to drive anybody a little crazy. Then Sheila leaves you. You just need time, that's all."

"Why didn't you say anything about this before?"

Janet stared at the tiles on the kitchen floor.

"You knew I wouldn't come, right?"

"Sometimes you have to help people help themselves," she said to the tiles. She turned back and looked up at him. "I know I should have told you. But please stay. You don't ever have to see Gloria again if you don't want to." She smiled. "Just relax and we'll have a nice time together."

Frank glared down at his sister. She was trying to help him, as she always had.

"Okay," he finally said, placing a hand on her shoulder. "Forget about it. Let's eat."

There were four of them at the table: Janet across from Chuck, Frank across from Gloria.

"So how've you been doing?" Chuck said, digging into his mashed potatoes. "Any news about getting back with the squad?"

Chuck winced as Janet kicked him under the table. "Well, what do you *want* me to talk about?" he said.

"It's okay," Frank said to Janet.

He turned to Chuck. "I'm not thinking about that right now. But who knows? Maybe I'll make it back there someday."

"Gloria's District Sales Manager at Garland," Janet said, changing the subject. "We've been through some brutal marketing campaigns over the years."

"That's very interesting," Frank said. He wanted a smoke.

Janet and Gloria talked about work. The pressure from before intensified, as if he was sliding underwater. The lights in the room started to buzz and flicker. Gloria's voice became muffled then faded away completely. He stared at her, hypnotized by the bare curve of neck connecting her head to her shoulders, and the movement of her silent lips. He laid down his knife and fork.

"Frank," he heard somewhere far in the distance, and began to surface. He shook his head to clear it.

"Frank?" It was Janet. He scanned around the table. The others were staring at him. His clenched fists were trembling on the place mat in front of him.

"Frank, are you alright?" Janet said.

"I'm fine," he said, warmth rushing to his cheeks.

All through dinner Gloria chattered on about her baby, Ralphie – how cute Ralphie was, how he was moving his head already, the lovable sounds he made. Frank half expected her to start in about Ralphie's adorable upchucks or bowel movements.

Frank had forgotten what a good cook Janet was, especially when it came to their mother's favourites – comfort food from his childhood. He and Gloria had nothing in common, but beneath her paint job and annoyingly nasal voice, he could see that at heart she was a good person, who deserved love. It was sad, because he knew that she would never get that love from him. Anyway, he wasn't even close to being ready for a relationship.

To Frank's relief, they had no sooner finished an after-dinner drink when Gloria checked her watch. "My, it's almost seven-thirty already. I'm sorry, but I have to be going."

"Oh, what a shame," Janet said.

Frank did his level best to look disappointed.

"Ralphie likes to be home and in bed by eight o'clock," Gloria said. "He's very particular."

As if in response to her statement, an ear-splitting wail erupted behind the door of the spare room.

"Oh, Frank, you haven't seen Gloria's baby!" Janet said. "Here, come with us."

Janet stood in the doorway, while Frank followed Gloria into the tiny room. A baby carrier rested on the bed. Frank moved next to the carrier and peered inside.

Ralphie had been screaming a few seconds ago, but now showed not the slightest hint of distress. It was as though he'd literally been calling for his mother, and now that she'd come there was no longer a need.

The child's face shone like yellow wax in the halo of the table lamp. His eyes, strangely alert, scanned Frank up and down as if compiling a record for future reference. The eyes glowed with an inner fire, like a cat sizing up its prey.

"How old is he?" Frank asked.

"Three months," Gloria answered.

"He seems very precocious."

Her eyes opened wide. "Oh, yes! He surprises me every day with the clever things he does. I think he might be one of those 'gifted' children they talk about. The doctor said it's too early to tell, but a mother knows..."

Frank caught a flash of white, as the glow from the lamp illuminated the child's open mouth. He bent down to look. He could clearly make out two tiny stubs like white flower buds emerging from the top gum.

"Teeth," he said, half to himself.

"Oh yes, two are coming in already," Gloria said. "That's very unusual. See – he's special in so many ways."

For some reason he couldn't explain, the baby made Frank nervous.

"Well, that's a beautiful baby you've got there," he said, straightening up.

"Thank you, Frank," Gloria said. "I sure think so."

☼

After Gloria and Ralphie had gone, Frank and Janet stood in the alcove at her front door. He grabbed his coat from a peg on the wall.

"I'm so glad you could make it, Frank," Janet said. "I hope you had a good time. I'm sorry for springing Gloria on you."

He smiled. "No offense, but I don't think we'll be strolling down lover's lane any time soon."

He shrugged on his coat and turned toward the door.

Janet touched his elbow. "Frank, you've quit going to Dr. Sampson again."

"Those sessions were a waste of time," he said, without turning around.

"Look, Frank, you can't just let this go. If you don't like Dr. Sampson find someone else. You can't just live in denial."

He turned to face her.

She put a hand on his sleeve. "I'm sorry. I don't mean to nag. You're my brother – I care about you. If I didn't care, I wouldn't bother saying anything."

"I know."

"Please, just think about it," she said. "Anyway, aren't you glad you came?" She stepped forward and gave him a long hug.

"Yeah, sure I'm glad," he said. He stepped back with his hands on her shoulders and smiled. "It was nice spending some time with my kid sister – even if she *is* annoying the shit out of me trying to set me up."

☼

On the way home Frank stopped for cigarettes at a convenience store. He was the only customer. A nervous looking blond kid with acne took his money and handed him the pack.

On the way to his car he glanced back over his shoulder at the vacant lot next door. The glare from the store window spilled out onto crumbling pavement dotted with weeds. His eye caught a trace of movement behind the store's dumpster. He turned and stared into the blackness, his hands absently tearing at the plastic wrap on the cigarette pack. He extracted a smoke and put it to his lips, then fished through his pockets for his lighter. The black shape of a rat squeezed through a gap under the wall of the store.

A finger of shadow flowed across the lot like black oil, drifting past the dumpster. As quickly as it had appeared it shrank back and faded away. A puff of wind rustled a discarded plastic bag on the ground and he caught a whiff of rotting garbage. The reflection from a stray hubcap cast a pool of light in a distant corner.

Frank's hands shook as he flicked the lighter. Suddenly the darkness was a physical presence, descending on him like a smothering blanket. His body began to collapse under the weight. He couldn't breathe. He shut his eyes and clenched his fists, fighting to drive away the memory, but it swept through his mind again like a tsunami.

The convenience store melted away. Suddenly it was a year earlier and Frank lay on the filthy pavement of a vacant lot in the Downtown Eastside, his ears ringing, his vision blurred. He staggered to his feet and his hand explored the large blood-soaked lump on the back of his skull.

Thick fog swirled around his toes. Traffic from the next block sent silhouettes undulating like giant sea creatures across the pavement beneath his feet. They morphed into freakish geometric shapes as they tracked over discarded boxes and overturned trash cans. A nearby street lamp cast a purplish halo over a fence crowned with razor-wire. The place stank of rotting garbage and another sickly-sweet odour he didn't recognize. He paced slowly toward the light, intensely aware of the tap of his heels on the pavement.

Just beyond the street lamp a figure stepped from behind a dumpster. Frank tensed and thrust his hand inside his jacket, unbuttoning the strap on his shoulder holster. The figure approached and stopped a few meters away. Only the glint of light from a pair of glasses stood out from features blotted with shadow, but Frank knew who it was without seeing the face. He went to draw his gun, but for some reason his arm was paralyzed. He started to shake violently.

Something monstrous was about to happen.

"Hey!" a voice above him called in the darkness.

Frank's mind resurfaced as a bright light flashed in his eyes. He found himself on his knees back in the convenience store parking lot. He glanced around him. A car was pulling into one of the spaces. The kid from the counter stood in the glare of the entrance with a cell phone in his hand, staring at him. A squad car, its red and blue beacon still flashing, sat a few meters away.

Standing over him was a cop with a flashlight.

"Hey, buddy," the cop said, shaking his shoulder.

Frank blinked his eyes.

"You okay?" the cop said.

Frank shook his head to clear it. "Yeah, I'm fine," he finally said.

"You sure?" the cop said. "You had anything to drink tonight?"

"No. I'm fine," repeated Frank.

"Maybe I should call an ambulance."

Frank staggered to his feet and brushed off his clothes. "Just tired – I've been losing a lot of sleep lately."

"That your car over there?" asked the cop.

Frank nodded.

"Well you're not driving it anywhere tonight. Better call a cab. You can pick up the car tomorrow."

"I'm okay," Frank said.

The kid from the store shrugged and went back inside.

"Can I see some ID?" the cop said.

Frank handed him a card from his wallet. The cop's eyes widened and he shook his head slowly as he played his flashlight over the name. He walked over and showed the ID to his partner in the car.

They called Frank over and gave him a ride home.

At exactly five AM several days later, the big hand of the old mechanical alarm clock on Frank's nightstand ticked the hour, and the metallic clatter of its bell echoed off the walls of his bedroom.

Frank sat bolt upright in bed. After a moment of confusion, he smashed his fist down on the clock and it went silent. He sat for a moment shaking, his head in his hands. There was no going back to sleep now. It was almost morning anyway.

Downstairs, still in his pajama bottoms, he ran some hot water from the tap into a Styrofoam cup of instant coffee, swirled the cup to mix it, and lit his first smoke of the day. He collapsed into a chair at the kitchen table and plowed aside a collection of empty beer bottles, unread mail, used paper plates, and pizza boxes to clear a space for his cup. Running a shaking hand through his hair, once jet black, now peppered with strands of gray, he slouched and smoked, tapping the ashes into one of the bottles.

Three hours later he was passed out where he sat, his fallen cigarette staining yet another black smudge on the linoleum beneath his dangling arm. A scraping sound from outside shocked him awake.

The mail had come.

He shuffled to the front door, treading on discarded newspapers covering the floor and scratching at several days' growth of beard. He tossed the stack of bills, final payment notices, and fliers on the kitchen table with the others, gratified to note his latest disability check lying on top.

After sweeping last night's paper plate off the counter into a black plastic garbage bag hung there for that purpose, he hoisted a new packet of plates onto the counter beside the sink full of dirty dishes, and began picking at the seam of the shrink-wrap.

"Shit," he said, unable to get a grip with his trembling fingers and bitten-down nails.

The theme from 'Dragnet' blasted from somewhere on the kitchen table. He dropped the package and rummaged through the debris, finally emerging with a cell phone in his hand. Janet was at the other end.

"Frank," she said. "You're not answering your home phone. Is it off the hook or something?" There was a quiver in her voice.

"I don't know – maybe they disconnected it again. Something wrong?"

"It's Gloria. It's terrible."

"What?"

"Her baby – Ralphie's been kidnapped."

"What!"

"They took him from right under her nose. Ralphie sleeps in a crib in her bedroom. Two days ago, she was in the bathroom taking a shower. When she came out she looked in on the baby and the crib was empty. Whoever it was stole her car, too."

Frank scratched his stubbled chin. "I take it the cops are involved."

"Your old buddy Grant Stocker's leading the investigation."

"Great," he said sarcastically.

"I don't think he believes her story. It sounds like he suspects her of doing something to the baby."

"Is it possible he's right? No offense, but she did seem a bit off..."

"Gloria would never hurt Ralphie! She adored him." Janet's voice started to break. "Why? Why would anyone do such a thing?"

"Don't get upset. The baby might still be alright. So, where's Gloria now?"

"She's at home. She's devastated. They made her promise not to go anywhere. I'm worried about her. If anything's happened to Ralphie..."

Frank held the cell phone with his chin and picked up the package of plates.

Janet spoke. "Frank?"

"Yeah."

"Do you think you could go and talk to her? I don't think she trusts the police."

He groaned. Once again he tugged, frustrated, at the seam. The whole package slipped out of his hands and landed on the floor.

"Frank?"

He bent down and picked it up.

"Frank?"

"I'm busy."

"Busy? Busy doing what? Sleeping?"

"I'm not a cop anymore, Janet. Let them handle it. That's their job."

"Who? Grant Stocker? You've told me how you feel about him. What kind of investigation is it going to be with him leading it?"

"It's going to be the official investigation conducted by the guy they chose to do the job."

"You could talk to him," she said. "He might listen to you."

Frank closed his eyes and took a deep breath.

"I know you don't really know Gloria," Janet continued, "and you don't owe her anything…"

"I'll think about it."

"Well, don't think too long. If Ralphie doesn't turn up soon, she may be in jail, charged with murder."

Janet hung up. Again the package slipped out of Frank's hands.

"Shit!" he said, kicking it across the room.

TWO

....

FRANK, GLORIA, AND
CONSEQUENCES

Early in the afternoon the next day, Frank stood on the fifteenth floor of an aging West End high-rise, outside the door of Gloria Hanon's apartment.

He fought to stamp down the rising terror that threatened to paralyze him. For fifteen years he had dedicated his life to seeing justice done; he couldn't turn his back now on a woman who might be innocent. He was still one of the good guys, even if he no longer wore a badge.

He stared back down the hall at the elevator door sliding shut, pumping the air pressure in the building up a notch. The closing door flung a shadow across the hallway. He shuddered, fighting to hold it together. Shaking out his arms and shoulders, he relaxed a little.

According to her story, he thought, *somebody snuck up fifteen floors, broke in, stole her baby, and left again without making a sound and without being seen? All in the time it takes to have a shower?*

No wonder they don't believe her.

He knocked on the door and heard shuffling footsteps on the other side. Finally it opened, and Gloria appeared.

"Sorry about the way I look," she said.

She was no longer the perfect Barbie doll he'd met at his sister's house. Her eyes were red and puffy, supported underneath by large bags. Tufts of hair pitched wildly from her head. She wore an old sweat shirt and sweat pants. She was a mess, he thought. But at least now she looked human.

"You look fine," he said. "I'm sorry about what happened."

"Thank you," she said, running her sleeve under her nose. "Would you like to come in?"

The apartment mirrored her appearance. Dishes and clothes were scattered everywhere. She flopped down on the couch and he sat in an armchair across from her.

"Are they still out there?" she said.

"What? Oh – the reporters? Yeah, I had to push through them to get in."

She ran her shaking fingers through her hair.

"Do you feel up to talking about it?" Frank said.

"I guess."

He pulled a small notebook from his jacket.

Just like the old days, he thought. *Why don't you just describe to me what happened, ma'am. When did you last see your husband? Is this door usually locked? Who was the last person that talked to your sister?*

"Why don't you just describe to me what happened," he finally said out loud.

Her eyes were sunken and hollow. "Janet probably told you. I went for a shower. Ralphie was in his crib. I wasn't out of the room for more than ten minutes. When I got back he was gone." She hunched forward with her face in her hands. "It's like some horrible nightmare..."

"Did you notice anything out of place when you first got home?"

She stared up at him. "What?"

"Whoever did this must have been in the apartment already."

"You mean – they were here all night?" She scanned around them.

"Probably – how else would they know when you were going to be out of the room?"

A wave of horror passed over her face. "No – I didn't see anything."

"Was there a note? Anyone call demanding ransom?"

"No. I don't know what they'd get from me anyway."

Frank got up and studied the door lock. Gloria followed him.

"They kept asking how I thought anybody could get in here without me knowing," she said to his back, "and harping at me about what happened even though I told them already. It's like they're trying to catch me in a lie."

Frank turned to face her. "They *are* trying to catch you in a lie. If you haven't got a lawyer you should probably get one."

He turned back to the lock. "No sign of tampering," he said. They returned and sat in their original positions.

"What about the father?" Frank said. "Were you in some kind of custody battle?"

"He died in a construction accident eight months ago."

"I'm sorry."

Frank flipped through the pages of his notebook without really seeing them. Her story was weak. So far, the only person in a position to harm Ralphie was his own mother.

"Are you sure you're telling me everything?" he said, searching for the truth in her eyes.

"You don't believe me either."

"I want to believe you. It's hard to explain all the facts. There's no sign of forced entry, no sign that anyone else has been in the apartment. No ransom note. What about outside? Have you noticed anybody suspicious hanging around the entrance – or driving by?"

"No," Gloria whispered.

"Can you think of any reason why anybody would want to take Ralphie? Has anyone shown interest in him? Anyone been acting in an unusual way toward him?"

Gloria shook her head. Her trembling hands rubbed together between her knees like they were consoling one another. Her eyes drifted over Frank's shoulder and stopped. Suddenly they sparkled with light, as if the morning sun had risen behind them. Frank turned his head. On a bookcase behind him stood a picture of Gloria holding Ralphie in her arms. He turned back. Just as quickly the light died and her eyes were dark and hollow.

"Look, I believe you," he said. "You understand that I'm not a cop anymore – there's not much I can do."

She nodded.

"I'll see what I can find out. I'll call you in the next day or so and give you a status report."

He stood up and headed for the door. Gloria tugged at his sleeve. He turned back to face her.

"It's kind of you to help me," she said. She held out a business card. "I hope you're not offended, but Janet told me what happened to you. My sister Rebecca is a counselor with Community Development Services. She might be able to help..."

"Thanks," he said as he took the card without reading it and stuffed it in his shirt pocket. "I'll think about it."

He opened the door, then turned to face her and awkwardly put a hand on her shoulder. "Keep your chin up."

Shit, I'm bad at this, he thought.

The panic attack started just as Gloria's apartment door thudded shut. The walls and ceiling were already pressing in as he rushed along the hallway. Unable to face the elevator, he flew down fifteen flights of stairs, his anxiety ratcheting up with every step. The knot of reporters on the sidewalk outside her building stared as he doubled over and hyperventilated for several minutes.

Help Gloria? Who was he kidding?

On the way home, he stopped at the liquor store and bought a case of Lucky Lager and a bottle of Alberta Rye. After the fourth beer the hollow stare in Gloria's eyes as she turned away from Ralphie's photograph had started to fade. After a few more, chased by shots of Rye, it was almost gone, and his crushing sense of inadequacy and helplessness had been replaced by a familiar and comforting numbness.

He woke the next morning lying on the kitchen floor, his shirt soaked with spilled beer, the overturned rye bottle lying beside him. He staggered upstairs to the bedroom. As he peeled off the filthy shirt he felt something solid in the pocket. He reached in, pulled out a business card, and stared at it blearily:

Rebecca Hanon, M.Sw.
Community Development Services BC
Community Support Officer

Underneath was an address and phone number.

He tossed the card on the dresser beside him, set the alarm – two hours in the future, and collapsed on the bed.

It was the same dream. He stood in the vacant lot near the street lamp. Again, a figure stepped out from behind a dumpster. It was holding something in its right hand. Again, Frank reached for his gun, but was paralyzed. Again, the figure approached and again Frank knew who it was. The face pushed out of the shadows, which stretched over its contours like black shrink-wrap. The blackened lips twisted into an insane leer.

"We're going to play the crazy game. I've got a present for you..." the lips sang.

A clattering bell demolished the scene. He swatted at the alarm clock and it was silent. He sat up and sat shaking for several minutes, then swiveled around, put his feet on the floor, and tried to stand. His legs gave out. He lost his balance, staggered sideways, and bashed his knee against the dresser.

"Shit!" he yelled, rubbing his kneecap. Suddenly he felt sick. He stumbled toward the bathroom, again lost his balance and fell to the floor. It was too late – he threw up on the bedroom carpet. Rising shakily to his knees, he put his head in his hands. His mouth tasted of acid and metal; a throbbing ache jackhammered the inside of his skull.

He turned and peered into the mirror over the dresser. Only his head and shoulders were visible. Squirming floaters swam across his line of sight as he blinked at his reflection: his hair caked with dried beer, his face lined, drawn, and clouded with stubble, the corners of his mouth specked with vomit.

He glanced at the dresser. The business card Gloria had given him lay there upside down. He staggered to his feet and stuffed the card in his wallet.

THREE

....

REBECCA HANON

After two aborted attempts and two panicked retreats back outside for a smoke, Frank dragged himself for a third time down the brightly lit hallway of an aging brick building in Yaletown. The polished floor reminded him of a hospital corridor. The meshed glass in the windows reminded him of a prison.

His stomach churned as he opened a door marked *Community Development Services BC* and stepped inside. The reception area was furnished with institutional-looking couches and a metal and glass coffee table strewn with aging psychology magazines. To his relief, nobody was waiting.

Behind the receptionist's desk sat a cute blonde with glasses, studded nails, and lots of rings on her fingers.

"Can I help you?" she asked, smiling.

"I want to speak to Rebecca Hanon."

"Do you have an appointment?"

He felt himself blush. He wanted a cigarette. "The name's Langer," he said. "I'm sort of a friend of her sister Gloria."

The receptionist pressed a button on the intercom and talked to somebody at the other end.

"You can go in," she said. "First door on your left."

He headed down a short hallway lined with office doors. Muffled voices droned behind a couple of them as he passed by. The target door had a frosted glass insert on which was stenciled:

Rebecca Hanon M.S.W.
Community Support Officer

He scoured his memory for the number of instances that, with the exception of his sister Janet, he'd spent time alone with a woman in the past six months.

Zero, he concluded as a willowy form appeared behind the glass.

The door opened and the rope around his gut tightened a notch. The face of the woman in the doorway was cute rather than stunning, with a turned-up nose, a smattering of freckles, a small mouth with full lips. There was only the tiniest resemblance to her sister. Wavy brown hair tumbled over her shoulders. Her gray eyes hunted constantly, boring into him with questions before they had even spoken.

She smiled, and her face took on a warmth and charm that paralyzed him. He wanted to run, but it was too late now.

"Hi, Frank," the woman said. She reached out her hand, which he shook limply. "Gloria mentioned you. I'm Rebecca."

"Yeah," he said. She looked at him expectantly. He stood there like a moron as several uncomfortable seconds ticked by.

"Gloria said…" he stammered, "y-you might be able to help me…you know, with…"

She smiled again. "Gloria's got an outdated impression of what I do. I haven't been a counselor for several years now."

Shit, he thought. *This was a mistake.*

"Come in," she said.

He turned to leave. "No, that's okay. I shouldn't have bothered you…"

"It's okay, come on in." She stood aside and swept a hand into the room. "We can talk."

He stepped in, at a loss what else to do.

The window behind her antique wooden desk offered a pleasant view of downtown and, in the far-right corner, a tiny glimpse of False Creek. The two closest walls sported posters from opera performances: La Boheme, Aida, The Magic Flute, Lohengrin.

On the far wall were Rebecca's credentials: her framed degrees and society memberships. His level of anxiety jumped. She sat down behind the desk, and motioned for him to sit in a chair facing her.

"I'm sorry about what happened to Gloria," he said, reluctantly taking a seat. "I don't know her very well, but she seems like a nice lady."

"She told me you're looking into her case."

He tensed, remembering the interview with Gloria and its aftermath. "I think she's a little confused there," he said. "I'm on stress leave from the force. She probably told you. I said I'd do a little digging, that's all. There's not much I can do. In fact, officially, there's nothing I can do."

"I'm sure it'll boost her morale just knowing someone with your credentials is on her side."

Frank laughed nervously. "Hey, it's not like I've got a lot else to do." He picked up a paper clip from the desk and twirled it between two fingers.

"Anyway," Rebecca said. "We're here to talk about you. You understand that I'm not a therapist anymore. I don't mind talking to you as a friend, in return for your helping Gloria, but all I can really do is refer you to someone. From what Gloria told me, you should be getting in touch with a professional."

"I've had it with shrinks," Frank said, his hands moving nervously on the table. "They've never done anything for me. They've just made things worse."

She gave an almost imperceptible shrug. "If you like we can just talk. Then maybe I can recommend a course of action, or suggest someone who would be compatible."

Frank nodded.

She slid a pad of paper in front of her, and picked up a nearby pen. "What is it that's bothering you?"

He wanted to get up and walk out, but he felt trapped.

"I can't sleep," he finally said.

He unfolded the paper clip, straightening the outer wire into an 'L' shape, then folded it back up, then unfolded it again.

She scribbled something. "So what is it that's keeping you awake?"

"Well, I guess technically it's the alarm."

"The alarm?"

"Yeah," he said, concentrating on his paper clip sculpture, "I set it to go off every two hours."

"You're having recurring nightmares."

He looked up, surprised at her perceptiveness. "Y…Yeah. It usually wakes me up before they get too bad."

"Any other problems?"

He shrugged, and went back to work on the paper clip. "Headaches – but that could be from not sleeping, I guess it could also be from the drinking. And I think I zone out sometimes. Time passes and I don't know what happened in the interval. But that hasn't happened for ages."

"Are you sure?"

He looked up. "What do you mean?"

"Would you actually know? If no one else was around?"

He tensed again. "Yeah, sure…sure I'd know."

"Gloria mentioned a horrific experience you had on the job. Is that what the nightmares are about?"

"Yeah."

Her eyes moved to his hands. He noticed, set the paper clip sculpture down and laced his fingers on the desk in front of him.

She leaned back in her chair. Her hair fell away, exposing the curve of her bare neck and shoulders. "It was one of your cases…"

"I've been through all that already."

"You can take it slow," she said in a soothing tone. "Start from the beginning. How did you first get involved? It was what – about a year ago?"

Frank nodded.

He picked up the paper clip again and twisted one prong into a ninety-degree angle. "We were after a serial killer."

He paused, focusing on his sculpture.

"Go on," she said. "You were after a serial killer. It was a difficult case?"

Frank blew out a puff of air. "Difficult – yeah, that would be one word to describe it. The guy was making us look like bozos. We were under a lot of pressure."

"We?" she said.

His work on the clip stopped. "You know," he said, looking up, "the team."

She studied him with those penetrating gray eyes. "But it wasn't just you," she said. "You had a partner?"

His body began to tremble and beads of sweat rose on his forehead. The blood hammered through his veins and roared across his eardrums like a freight train. The light faded and the room closed in around him. He shut his eyes. A monstrous shape loomed above him in the darkness. The stench of rotting garbage permeated the air, and shadows swam beneath his feet. The lurid purplish light splashed over the pavement. It was coming... he began to shake violently.

"Frank!" he heard a voice far in the distance.

The floor heaved up like he was in the midst of an earthquake. He opened his mouth to scream but nothing came out.

"Frank!" the voice was much closer now.

He opened his eyes. Rebecca was leaning over him, her hand on his shoulder.

"Frank!" she shouted. "You're bleeding!"

He shook his head to clear away the darkness and stared down at his hands. His fists were clenched and trembling. A trickle of blood ran down the edge of his right palm. He felt pain in his right fist. He opened it. It was covered in blood – the sharp point of the paper clip had been driven deep into his flesh.

"Here," Rebecca said, snapping a tissue from the box on her desk and handing it to him.

He extracted the end of the metal clip from his palm and pressed on the wound with the tissue.

"Are you okay?" she asked.

"I'm fine."

She left the room and came back with a bottle of antiseptic. She swabbed the wound and applied a Band-Aid, then walked back around the desk and sat down.

"Where were you?" she said.

"What?" He opened and closed his injured hand.

"Just now. Where were you? What were you thinking?"

"What do you mean?"

"I think you were in what's called a 'dissociative state'. You were re-living something that happened to you."

"What are you talking about? I was just sitting here."

"Then what happened to your hand?"

"I'm just nervous or something, I guess."

Rebecca leaned forward on her desk and looked directly into his eyes.

"Frank," she said, "Based on the amount of time we've spent I can't draw specific conclusions, but I've seen cases like yours before. You

30

need to come to terms with what happened to you. As long as you keep your problems bottled up you'll never be rid of them. They'll manifest themselves as mental and even physical health issues. It's been more than a year since the incident – and you're still having nightmares about it? It seems to me that you need to talk to somebody about what happened."

His fists clenched again in front of him as he stared at the desktop, "I can't do that." The pressure was building.

"Let's come at this from a different angle," she said. "Just tell me what you're feeling right now."

It was too much. "I've had it with this crap," he said, his voice rising. "Talk about your feelings – tell me about your childhood – why did you hate your mother – how did you feel about your dog – it's a waste of time."

"Frank, we don't-" she started to speak.

"This was a mistake," he interrupted, rising from his chair. He pushed it back. It tipped over and landed on the floor. He bent down and righted it, then started toward the door.

"Frank," Rebecca called after him. "Wait – I could refer you to someone. I know some excellent therapists…"

"I gotta be going," he said.

Rebecca rose and followed him.

"Frank," she said as he reached for the door handle, "this will never be over until you deal with it."

He opened the door and strode out of the office. The receptionist glanced at him from one of the other doorways. Rebecca followed him back through the waiting room toward the main door.

"Come on, Frank," she said. "Don't give up so easily. I thought you cops were supposed to be fighters."

Frank turned on her. "I'm not a cop anymore, remember? And maybe I'm not a fighter anymore."

He rushed through the door and down the hallway.

"Take some time and think about it," she called after him. "You have my card. Call me if you change your mind."

He waved his hand without turning, then passed through the front doors and out onto the street.

FOUR

....

A TRAGIC EVENT

T wo days later, in the depths of a dream, Frank was startled awake by the ring of his cell phone. He found himself sitting in a kitchen chair in the dark, with his forehead lying on the kitchen table. The ring repeated, rattling the phone on the Formica table top.

"Shit," he said, fishing through the debris. He flipped open the vibrating phone.

"Yeah," he said.

"Did you follow up on the stuff you were going to do for Gloria?" It was Janet. Her voice was distant and impersonal.

"Oh yeah – I'll do it today," he said, running a hand through his unwashed hair.

"Save yourself the trouble," she said curtly. "Gloria's dead. She hanged herself last night."

A jolt raced up Frank's spine like an arc of electricity on a high voltage line. It tore into his brain, which suddenly seemed to go blank.

"W…What?" was all he could think to say.

"Don't sweat it, Frank," said Janet, in a tone he'd never heard from her before. "Don't put yourself out worrying about somebody else's problems. She's dead now. You're off the hook."

"I'm s...sorry," he said, now feeling like a fool as well as an asshole.

There was silence at the other end of the line. He fought desperately for something to say.

"How did it happen?" he finally blurted out.

"Her sister called early last night and told me Gloria had been arrested. I offered to go down and see her, but she said they weren't allowing any visitors. They found Gloria's car. It was torched, and they found Ralphie's body inside."

"Oh, God..."

"She said Gloria was out of her mind with grief. I thought they were supposed to put a suicide watch on people like that."

"They should have... sounds like they really screwed up."

"I tried to call you, but you weren't answering. I guess you were off somewhere crying in your beer. I'm disappointed in you, Frank," she said, breaking down. "Maybe there's nothing you could have done, but at least you could have tried. I wouldn't wish what happened to you on my worst enemy, but..."

Frank said nothing.

"I'm sorry," Janet finally said. "I know it's not your fault. I'm just upset, that's all. It's not your fault, Frank. I shouldn't have accused you." She was sobbing. "I'm sorry – I have to hang up now."

The line went dead.

Frank set the cell phone down on the kitchen table and sat trembling, staring at the wall.

☼

For several days Frank spiraled downward, circling like a leaf caught in a storm drain, toward a black abyss the depths of which he hadn't experienced even in the darkest nights of the past year.

He was burning through what was left of his stores of alcohol, but it no longer provided the anesthetic power he'd valued so much before. Even his nemesis, his recurring nightmare, was now spiked with images of Gloria: taking the final desperate step to break the cycle of anguish and despair, the light fading from her eyes the way it did after she looked away from Ralphie's picture.

He was uniquely qualified to understand Gloria's pain, but, given the chance to help her, he'd turned his back and retreated into his usual pattern of depression and self-loathing.

His rational mind knew he couldn't have saved her. The point was that he hadn't even tried. He was impotent, useless. His emotional mind stood in judgment and found him guilty, a pathetic loser pursuing oblivion in a bottle while an innocent woman was driven to suicide.

For a while he considered following her, letting go and erasing his own pain forever. But that wasn't an outlet he was built to pursue. He was baptized and raised Catholic, but that wasn't it. The fact was that some people were capable of making that leap and some were not. Maybe that was his curse, condemned to sink ever lower into despair while being denied the option of ending his torment.

35

One day, a memory that hadn't surfaced for years crowded into his psyche. Seventeen years old, called to the principal's office at school and told to go home. His mother sobbing on the living room couch. A stoic cop, the bearer of bad news, staring at the floor.

Frank's father, a beat cop, had been blown away when he stopped to check a stolen car.

He remembered the question that had haunted him from that day forward. How could the world tolerate such a senseless crime...?

When he opened his eyes, he was once again at the kitchen table. He sat up and shook himself awake, trembling, with his fists clenched. Gloria was dead; there was nothing more he could do to help her. But if she was innocent, he *could* use his knowledge and experience to find out the truth about the tragedy.

If he no longer had the option of saving her life, at least maybe he could redeem her memory.

☼

Just before noon several days later, having staked out the building long enough to learn her routine, Frank stood waiting for Rebecca Hanon to emerge from the doors of her workplace and head out for lunch. She appeared on schedule, her long legs moving sensually under a pale yellow dress. Unexpectedly he felt his heart race. She was alone. She glanced around, but didn't notice him. She headed south toward the restaurant district.

"Rebecca," he called. She turned, startled.

"Oh," she said, recognizing him. "Frank, – hi."

It was hard to look her in the eye, remembering how he'd failed her sister. He stared down at the pavement under her feet.

"Can I do something for you?" she asked.

"I'm sorry about Gloria," he said. "I feel like shit about it. I should have done more to help."

"There's nothing you could have done. If anyone's to blame it's the police, for not putting a watch on her. What did they think would happen after the most precious thing in her life was taken away...?" Her voice began to break.

"Sorry." He looked up. "I didn't mean to upset you."

"Thank you for your concern." She fished a tissue from her purse and dabbed at her eyes. "I'm glad you came back. I'm sorry we got off on the wrong foot in our first meeting. I hope you understand that my only interest is in helping you. Why don't you go on in and make an appointment with Judy? I can recommend somebody—"

"I'm not here about that."

"Then what—?"

"Would it be okay if I walk with you for a minute?"

"I don't feel comfortable talking to you like this, Frank. Make an appointment."

"Look, I know I've got a few problems, but I'm not crazy. I want to try to get to the bottom of what happened to Gloria. I feel like I owe her that much."

She glanced over his shoulder. He turned to look. A beat cop was crossing the street headed toward them.

"Everything okay, Ms. Hanon?" the cop asked on arrival.

Frank understood the situation. "I'm harmless," he said to Rebecca, with what he hoped was an innocent-looking smile. "I just want to ask you a couple of questions."

The cop raised an eyebrow and looked at her. She hesitated. "Everything's fine," she finally said. "Thanks."

The cop nodded and walked away.

She started walking and Frank joined her.

"Have the press finally quit hanging around?" he asked.

"It doesn't take long for them to latch onto something new," she answered. "Especially once the story's been nicely wrapped up in a bow."

"They tell me Stocker's planning to close the case."

Her face hardened. "I've been trying to decide how to fight that decision."

They walked in silence for half a block.

Finally Rebecca spoke. "Look, Frank. I hope you won't take offense. I appreciate you wanting to help Gloria, but you have your own issues. They should be your priority right now."

"Hey, investigating crime is what I did for a living for fifteen years. It's what I am. Who knows?" he smiled. "It might even be good therapy for me."

Rebecca studied the pavement as she walked. Finally she stopped and faced him. "I don't believe for a second that Gloria had anything to do with Ralphie's death. He was her reason for living. She would never have done anything to harm him." She turned back and continued walking.

"I guess once a cop, always a cop," Frank said. "When I was on the job they always said I had a nose for the truth. When I interviewed Gloria my nose told me she was innocent."

They turned onto Mainland Street. The west side of the block featured a raised brick sidewalk that was crowded with cafes. The boulevard bustled with the lunchtime crowd.

They reached a sidewalk café called the *Downtown Bistro*.

"Why don't you join me?" Rebecca said.

The sun was shining. They sat down at an empty table. Frank fished a pack of cigarettes out of his shirt pocket, saw Rebecca's expression, and put it back. A waiter brought them both coffee and took Rebecca's order.

"You should eat," Rebecca said. "I'll even buy."

Frank shook his head.

He took a sip of coffee. "One thing keeps bugging me," he said. "Why Gloria? Why that kid in particular? Her apartment's fifteen floors up. There's security in the building. There must be hundreds of babies living in houses at street level or in ground floor basement suites with badly latched windows – places with a lot easier access. Why go after that particular baby?"

"Maybe it was just a crime of opportunity," she answered. "Someone in the building became fixated on Gloria and Ralphie. I used to see that kind of thing when I was working in therapy. Anything can trigger it: a chance look, a way of dress, even a hairstyle."

"Maybe. Gloria told me the father died in a construction accident eight months ago."

"It was before Ralphie was even born. He wasn't interested in the baby anyway. His only interests were drinking and chasing other women."

"Could some relative of the father be hanging around?"

"Not as far as I know. I think whatever relatives he had are back east somewhere." Rebecca sat back. "It makes no sense at all. And then to find the poor thing... that way. Poor Gloria." Her voice broke again. "You'd think that would rule out any relative – if they wanted Ralphie they would have kidnapped him, not killed him."

"Speaking of Ralphie," Frank said, "I hope you don't take this the wrong way, but... did you find anything strange about him?"

She shrugged. "Not really. He had an unusual way of staring at you."

"Like an animal."

"Yeah, I guess."

The waiter brought the panini Rebecca had ordered.

"Something's missing," Frank said, once the waiter had left. "Too bad we can't get a copy of the Coroner's report."

"My ex-roommate from university is pretty high up in the Coroner's office," Rebecca said. "I might be able to convince her to give me a copy."

Frank leaned forward. "Could you do that? We don't have much to go on, but it's a start."

He grabbed a sugar packet out of a bowl on the table, shook it a few times, nervously, and put it back.

She narrowed her eyes at him. "Are you sure you're up for this?"

He took a large swig of his coffee. He needed a smoke. "Don't worry about me," he said, getting up from his chair. "I'll be in touch. Let me know if you hear anything."

☼

A few days later, Frank was wakened by a loud noise. He found himself lying cross-ways on his bed, still in his clothes. At first he was confused, and rolled over to swat his alarm. Then he realized it was something else: his phone was ringing. He staggered to his feet and reached for it.

It was Rebecca.

"My friend came through," she said. "I've got a copy of the Coroner's report, if you want to have a look."

They agreed to meet back at her office. Frank formally met Judy, Rebecca's receptionist.

"Wow, a real live detective." She smiled, as Frank shook her hand and introduced himself.

"Ex-detective," he corrected her, smiling.

Rebecca led Frank to her office and Judy brought them both coffee. When she was gone Rebecca closed the door and took a seat behind her desk. Frank sat facing her. She unlocked a drawer, pulled out a white plastic flash drive, and plugged the device into her computer. She swiveled the screen around for Frank to view.

"I've read it already," she said. "The cause of death is asphyxiation, either accidentally or on purpose. The burning of the body occurred after death."

Her face was drawn, like she was fighting to hold it together.

"The report's not due to be officially released for a few days," she continued. "I'd appreciate it if you didn't broadcast that you'd seen it."

"My lips are sealed," Frank said. "Can I borrow your mouse?"

Rebecca passed him the mouse. He flipped through the written records, scanning the comments and conclusions. He stopped at a page with photographs of the dead child. His stomach turned as he viewed the charred corpse. Even with his years of experience with death and mutilation he found the images shocking. He switched on his cop's detachment and forced himself to look.

"Huh?" he suddenly said, zooming in on a photograph. "I'll be damned..."

"What?"

"They're gone."

"What? What are gone?"

"The teeth."

"Teeth?"

"There's a clear shot here of the mouth and gums. There's no sign of any teeth."

"Well, of course...is that so surprising?"

He looked up from the screen. "When I first met Gloria at Janet's place she had Ralphie with her, and we all went to look at him. He had two top incisors coming in. I saw them myself. She said they'd just come in within the past couple of days. She was kind of proud of it, like it made him special somehow."

"But the photographs show something different."

Frank nodded.

42

"Are you sure about this?"

"As sure as I can be without being officially involved and having more access to the records. I saw the teeth myself. We've got the report right in front of us. Teeth are actually pretty unusual for a kid that age."

"So...what are you saying?"

"If I'm right, there's only one explanation."

"And that is?"

He locked eyes with her. "This isn't Gloria's baby."

"What!" Rebecca sat up straight in her chair. "You mean to say that someone killed another baby and exchanged it for Ralphie? Why would anybody want to do that?"

Frank shrugged. "Somebody who lost their own baby, a childless couple with access to babies who died... It would explain why the corpse was burned. That could have been deliberate – to cover up the exchange."

Rebecca reached out to swivel the monitor back.

Frank caught her arm. "Wait. I don't know if you had a good look at these pictures before. They're pretty graphic."

She closed her eyes for a second and swallowed. "I saw them."

She swiveled the monitor and cringed as she studied the photograph.

She shook her head slowly. "Is it possible that somehow the fire destroyed the teeth – or swelled the gums and made them invisible, or something?"

Frank absently picked up a pencil and tapped the eraser on the desktop. "I don't think the fire would have destroyed them. Anyway, that's a pretty clear picture of the inside of the mouth. It doesn't look like it suffered much damage at all. The gum thing – we'd have to talk to an expert to know for sure. It's easy enough to confirm whether or not the baby was Gloria's. Just compare the DNA."

"God, this is terrible," Rebecca said. "So my poor sister killed herself thinking her baby was dead… There's got to be some other explanation. I'll talk to my friend in the Coroner's office. Maybe she can give an opinion about whether there ever were any teeth, and she might be able to convince the Coroner to order a DNA test."

The tapping of Frank's pencil became insistent. "I know the guy in charge of the case. He's going to fight like hell to get it closed and off the radar before he can screw it up any more than he has already. He'll be in shit as it is with Gloria's suicide. He won't want to do anything to prolong it."

Frank's tapping grew louder and more intense. He looked up. Rebecca was staring at him.

"What?" he said. Her eyes moved to the pencil. "Oh." He replaced it in a cup on the desk and interlaced his fingers in front of him. "Sorry."

"Frank," she said. "I appreciate you trying to help, but maybe you're not ready for the stress involved in an investigation."

"What, because I tapped a pencil on the desk?"

"Of course not. But that's an indicator of your stress level and your underlying psychological condition."

"I told you I don't want to talk about that. I'm here about the case – that's all."

"There *is* no case, Frank. You're not on the force anymore, remember? This is just an attempt to assuage your guilt over what happened to Gloria."

Frank's hands separated and bunched into fists. "I know it's not an official case," he said, his voice rising. "Why do you people always have to read all this mumbo-jumbo into everything a person says? It's just a manner of speaking. Sometimes words are just words, like 'assuage'. Sometimes they don't have any mysterious double meaning."

Rebecca was still staring at him.

"And don't give me this analytical crap about my underlying psychological condition," he continued. "I'm fine. Let me get on with my work and maybe we can solve this thing."

"You have no work, Frank," Rebecca said, raising her own voice. "You're out on stress leave. Your priority should be getting your own life back on track – dealing with what happened and putting it behind you. I want to find the person responsible as much as you do, but I'm more concerned about you. You'll make things worse if you keep pushing. I should never have shown you the report."

Frank's lips tightened and he scowled as he pushed back his chair in a replay of his first visit. "This is a waste of time," he said. "You're more interested in busting my balls than finding some answers."

"God, you're pig-headed!" Rebecca said, her face turning red. "I'm just trying to help you. I've lost my sister and probably my nephew – I don't need another tragedy on my conscience. Your behaviour makes it clear that you're not ready, Frank. Continue on this path and you'll be cruising for another breakdown."

Frank rose from his chair with a sense of déjà-vu. "Thanks for the information. I'll let you know if I come up with anything."

"Frank," Rebecca said in exasperation. "Come on, be reasonable. Settle down, take a few deep breaths. Maybe look into the case in your spare time. Gloria and Ralphie aren't going to be any worse off if you take it slow."

"And what if Ralphie's still alive?"

She looked at the floor.

"I'll talk to you later," he said, heading for the door. He strode out of the office, past a bewildered Judy, down the hallway, and into the glaring light of day.

"Never again," he said as he stomped down the stone steps and into the cobblestone alley. "Never again."

FIVE

....

FRANK GOES IT ALONE

After his blowout with Rebecca, Frank stepped through his front door and slammed it behind him, vowing to continue his investigation alone. That night, an unfamiliar dream jammed its way into his tortured sleep. A mother, on a picnic with her three children near a river, turned away for a few seconds to settle a quarrel between the two eldest. When she turned back, her youngest, a baby about nine months old, had disappeared without a trace.

When the hammering bell of the alarm clock shocked him awake he sat up in bed, scratching his head. A nagging familiarity in the dream floated around his psyche for a couple of hours, stubbornly refusing to surface.

Finally he remembered – it had really happened. It was a case he'd been involved in when he first became a detective. In the beginning they'd accused the mother, like Stocker had Gloria. They had no evidence, and no motive, so in the end they cleared her and assumed the kid had crawled into the river and drowned; his body was never found.

For the first time in almost a year, Frank waded into his debris-strewn home office, clearing a path to his desk. He swept the pile of newspapers and dirty laundry from the computer, and cleared a spot beside it.

On a whim, he sifted through old news stories online about kidnapped children. He found the one he'd dreamed about and confirmed the details. As he continued to dig, he discovered several incidents in the following years that were eerily similar to Gloria's.

He put together a list of the cases with the greatest similarities and contacted a couple of colleagues at the squad who still respected him enough to stick their necks out and use police resources to gather more detailed information.

When he got the printed results a few days later, they made his hair stand on end. Since the case he'd dreamed about, at least five babies, ranging from three months to two years old, had gone missing in a manner similar to that of Ralphie.

In every case, either the body was never found or was mutilated to such an extent that it couldn't be positively identified. In every case, the mother was implicated or made to believe some plausible accident had taken her child.

Over all those years, not one of the investigators had considered that the cases might be linked.

☼

The first panic attack struck the next morning when Frank was still blocks away from the Vancouver Homicide Squad – the place where he'd worked for fifteen years and had once felt more comfortable than in his own home. He'd parked a few blocks away so he could approach at his own pace. As he walked, he fought for control, and won at least a temporary victory.

On the final block he willed himself across the street to the sidewalk in front of the squad building. Already he was trembling and his palms were slippery with sweat.

A half-block away he paused to confirm that none of his former colleagues were in sight. As long as he didn't run into anyone he knew, he still had the option of aborting the operation and walking away. Contact with someone from his past life would drive him across a threshold; he'd be forced to push on and enter the squad room. He wasn't sure he was ready for that.

He reached the stone steps leading up to the door, and paused one last time. Soon there would be no turning back. His muscles tightened and his throat went dry. With each step the pressure mounted, like he was descending underwater.

Just as his foot touched the top step the door swung open. He panicked, certain he'd see a familiar face. A middle-aged woman emerged – someone he'd never seen before. She stared at him, and he realized he was bathed in sweat and visibly shaking. He hurried back down to the street and into a nearby alley.

He fought the urge to run to the nearest bar. Instead, he walked a few blocks to minimize the chance of seeing anyone he knew, and slid into a booth at the back of a hole-in-the-wall coffee shop. After three cups and several aborted attempts, he stood once again outside the imposing glass doors of his old workplace.

The squad room flickered like a heat-stroke hallucination as he pushed open the doors and stepped inside for the first time in more than a year. He drove himself forward. His mind was numb but his body reacted, muscles pulling against one another as if they were fighting to escape from an invisible straitjacket.

The movement around him slowed and shapes blinked, strobe-like, in and out of existence. Colours were amplified and the range of hues collapsed until the squad room looked like a panel out of a comic book. The surrounding clatter reverberated inside his skull. The smell of paper dust and body odour made him nauseous. He glanced at the path to his old office and shuddered as memories of that night pushed up inside him like the bubbling magma inside a volcano. By sheer strength of will he calmed his trembling hands.

The activity in the room gradually ceased as, one by one, his former colleagues became aware of his presence, and the bustle faded to an uncomfortable silence.

Finally Art Crawford, a solid detective and one of Frank's ex-poker buddies, strode over and shook his hand.

"Frank – good to see you! How's it going? We've missed you."

"Hi Art," Frank said.

Jill Stamford, one of the new recruits for whom Frank had been a mentor, also shook his hand, though, Frank thought, tentatively.

"Great to see you, Frank," she said. "It's been too long. Hey, you know I made detective!"

"Congratulations," Frank said.

He studied the other faces in the room. They were a confused blend of pity, condescension, and genuine friendship. The tension expanded through his body: blood pumping harder, breath accelerating. A vein at his right temple twitched annoyingly. He wondered if coming here had been a mistake.

Near the back of the room, standing at the center of a knot of activity, stood Grant Stocker, Lead Detective – the job that should have been Frank's. Frank pushed past his former colleagues, shaking the occasional hand and nodding this way and that, until he was face to face with Stocker.

Grant Stocker was a big man with a profile like a side of beef, who seemed perpetually in danger of popping the buttons on his suit. His nose was large, red, and laced with spider veins. His fine brown hair had disappeared on top, a condition he tried to conceal by combing several long wispy strands over his baldness.

When he was presented with a difficult problem, Stocker's face would contort into a pinched bundle of wrinkled seriousness, a façade behind which, Frank was convinced, nothing was actually happening. Stocker had been a pain in Frank's ass ever since the day they both entered the Police Academy. He was ignorant, arrogant, and not very bright, but that never seemed to stand in the way of regular rewards and promotions. Something always seemed to prevent Stocker's many blunders from sticking to him, and he'd been propelled to ever higher levels of responsibility.

When Jack Sanders, the previous Lead Detective, chose to retire, Stocker had been Frank's only rival for the vacated post. The overwhelming sentiment in the squad was for Frank to get the job. Frank was intelligent, resourceful, able to think on his feet, and potentially a great leader. His breakdown had changed all that, and with Frank out of the picture, the administration had promoted Stocker to the position.

Beside Stocker stood a younger man Frank didn't recognize. He was shorter than Stocker – in fact dwarfed by Stocker's bulk. The man bore a disturbing resemblance to Frank himself – thin, with a dark complexion and straight jet-black hair. The collar of his dress shirt was too tight; it made the skin bulge out around his neck. He was glued to Stocker's side like a pet dog waiting for a command.

Stocker made an unsuccessful attempt to project compassion on seeing Frank back in the squad room.

"Hi Frank." He pumped Frank's hand in a painful grip. "It's been too long. How're you doing?"

He tilted his head at Frank's double. "This is Terry Hastings, my new assistant."

Frank nodded and shook the assistant's hand, then turned back to Stocker. "I need to talk to you in your office."

"Sorry, buddy," Stocker said, a smile on his jowly face. "Can't spare the time – got some major investigations on the burner. I can spare a minute right here and now if you want."

Frank ignored the dig. "Okay," he said, fighting to maintain his cool. "It's about this baby kidnapping case – the Hanon woman."

Stocker peered down at him like he was a child asking for his first sip of beer.

"Frank," he said. "You of all people should know that I can't discuss an active case with a civilian. You got information that bears on that investigation, make an appointment to talk to a *detective.*"

Frank lost it. "Cut the crap," he shouted, taking a step toward the Lead Detective.

Stocker stepped back like he'd been slapped. The conversations around them halted.

"You've been running with the idea that Gloria Hanon murdered her own child," Frank said. "You've got it wrong."

"And you base that belief on what?" Stocker snapped back.

"I knew her. That baby was her life – there's no way she would ever have harmed him."

"Well, that's a pretty compelling argument, Frank," Stocker said, smiling and rocking back on his heels. "But here at the squad, we put together cases based on *hard evidence.* I'm glad you hit it off with your little friend, but based on the *evidence,* the investigation's a done deal."

Frank clenched his fists and again fought for control.

"Gloria Hanon couldn't handle the stress," Stocker continued. He stared at Frank as if to say: *You should know something about that.* "She snapped and did away with the kid, then came on with the grief-stricken mother routine. If you're aware of any *facts* that would indicate otherwise, I'd love to hear them."

Frank hesitated, knowing how what he was about to say would sound.

"I don't think the baby they found in the car was the Hanon baby," he finally said.

"What!" Stocker said, incredulous.

Frank pushed on. "I think you should conduct DNA tests on Gloria Hanon and the baby from the car."

The room was eerily quiet.

"Hoooold on," Stocker stifled a laugh. "Let me get this straight. You're saying that someone snuck up fifteen floors to Gloria Hanon's apartment, broke in, kidnapped her baby in the ten minutes that she was having a shower, stole her car, replaced her baby with another baby, torched the car, and – then what – kept the Hanon baby?"

"That's exactly what I'm saying."

Stocker laughed. "Wow – that's one twisted perp you've got there Frank."

"Do the test. It's not hard. Prove me wrong."

Stocker's smile disappeared. "We found the Hanon woman's car. We found the baby inside it. I'm not going to waste the taxpayers' money on a pointless test just to please you."

"I've looked into some other cases," Frank said. "I've found several that strongly resemble the Hanon case."

Stocker stared down at him. "So what are you saying? You think this is some kind of baby-napping conspiracy?"

Frank answered. "I think that some group – and it has to be a group, because it's well organized – is systematically kidnapping children. The abductions are meticulously planned to lead investigators to conclusions other than kidnapping."

"Meticulously planned, eh Frank?" Stocker said, casting his gaze around like he was playing to an audience. "A conspiracy, you say – and who's behind it?" Again he scanned the room, laughing. "Aliens? Aliens, Frank?" Stocker widened his eyes and wiggled his fingers in front of his face. "Landing in their little ships and kidnapping all the little babies?"

A couple of Stocker's cronies laughed openly, and a few of the crowd, even some of Frank's closer former colleagues, stared uncomfortably at the floor or looked away. The pressure he'd felt earlier intensified, as if gravity had been re-jigged at a hundred times its normal level. It drove him into the floor and threatened to choke him and crush his vital organs. He fought for breath. The walls of the room began to twist and shear sideways as the ceiling moved downward.

Stocker turned to his assistant, who looked embarrassed. Stocker nodded at Frank. "You know how they found him before he took his little 'medical leave'? Curled up in a corner of his office like a little baby, crying his eyes out." Stocker made a mocking gesture rubbing his eye with the knuckle of one hand. The room was breathing, expanding inward and outward.

"Isn't that touching?" Stocker said. "Just like a little baby."

He turned and sneered at Frank. "Go home, Frank. You don't belong here. You haven't got what it takes to do this job. You're smart all, right – but you haven't got the cojones..." He grabbed at his crotch. "You should switch to a more laid-back line of work, say - selling insurance, or - I know the perfect thing - basket weaving." He laughed out loud.

Frank rushed at him and hauled back for a punch. Something caught his arm from behind before he could strike. He looked back – it was Sergeant Reid, the head of the unit.

"You don't want to do that, Frank," Reid said.

"Too bad he stopped you," Stocker said. "I was looking forward to charging you with assaulting a police officer."

"Screw you," Frank said, dropping his arm.

"Frank, why don't you come into my office and talk," Reid suggested.

"Sure, why not," Frank said, gratefully turning his back on Stocker.

"Nice talking to you, Frank," Stocker called after them as they walked away. "Keep up the good work. Keep me posted about the aliens!"

They entered Reid's office. "Close the door," Reid said, taking a seat behind his desk. "Sit down." He motioned to a chair in front of the desk and Frank sat. "What brings you back here, Frank?"

"The Hanon case. I don't think the baby they found in Gloria Hanon's car was hers. I wanted Stocker to do a DNA test to confirm that."

"And he refused?" Reid said. He pulled at one end of his bushy mustache.

"What do you think? Isn't there something you can do to force him...?"

Reid leaned forward.

"First off," he said, "you've got no business involving yourself in an ongoing police investigation. You're not on active duty. That may change, but until then..."

Frank opened his mouth, but Reid cut him off.

"Second, you know as well as I do that it's Stocker's case. I can't force him to pursue an avenue he doesn't believe will lead anywhere. If I had compelling proof that the test was warranted..."

Frank wanted to mention the teeth, but couldn't break his promise to Rebecca about the Coroner's report.

"I've got new information I can't divulge right now," he said instead. "You'll just have to take my word for it."

"I'll do what I can to convince him," Reid said, "but like I say, in the end it's his decision."

The two men studied each other. Finally Reid said, "How're you holding up, Frank?"

"I'm fine. Never been better."

"You've looked better."

Frank shrugged.

"You know," Reid said leaning back, "I've lost count of the men and women I've prepared for the squad over the years. Every one of them was subjected to a rigorous barrage of tests: strength, judgment, moral fiber, psychological fitness. You know the drill. You went through it like everybody else."

Frank stared at him but said nothing.

"Fact is," Reid continued, "None of those tests can predict with absolute certainty how someone will cope with a specific set of circumstances."

"What exactly are you getting at?"

Reid leaned forward again. "It takes a certain type of person to be a homicide detective. You've got to be able to cope with situations that would make the average Joe run away screaming.

"You're a good guy Frank, and you were good at your job – you were better than good – you were one of the best detectives I've ever had in the squad, but – maybe that's not enough. Maybe you don't have the psychological armour to handle some of the stuff that goes on here. No shame in that. That would put you in a club with ninety-nine percent of people on the planet. That should have shown up on the tests, but like I said, the tests aren't always a perfect indicator."

"So you don't think I can take the pressure?"

"All I'm saying is that you should think about it. What happened to you is the worst I've ever seen, but we have to be able to handle the worst. That's our job."

Frank slunk out the back door, his fists still clenching and unclenching, feeling like a bum tossed out of a bar. Reid had recommended it to avoid another run-in with Stocker. It was humiliating, but he jumped at the chance. An urge he'd been fighting since his decision to revisit the squad now struck him full force.

He needed a drink.

SIX

....

FRANK MEETS ANOTHER
BOTTLE

*M**acky's*, the bar he walked into, was a dump: dark, dirty, and tinged with the odour of urine and vomit.

Good, he thought. *Not much chance of meeting anybody from the squad.*

The place was almost empty. An unshaven drunk in rags hunched over a table in one corner, an empty beer glass in front of him. He was carefully sliding coins from one tiny pile to another. A pair of bikers sat near one of the smoke-streaked windows laughing, their feet stretched out on chairs in front of them.

Frank made his way to a table in the darkest corner and sat with his back to the wall. After a few minutes he still hadn't been served. He gave up and went to the bar. The bartender was talking to the lone patron sitting on a barstool.

"You know what I mean," Frank overheard the man say.

"Yeah," the bartender said. He finally noticed Frank and came over. Frank ordered a sleeve and the bartender brought it. Frank turned to head back to his table, but it had been taken over by a nodding old man. Frank sat back down on the barstool.

"How about you, Bob," the bartender said to the other patron.

"Sure," Bob said, "gimme another one – 'just like the other one...' he sang.

Bob and the bartender resumed their conversation.

Frank stared into the mirror behind the bar. He saw his image but it was like he was looking at someone else. The guy in the mirror took a long pull on his beer, felt the familiar buzz, and waited for the memory of the humiliating events in the squad room to fade.

He ordered another beer, and added a shot of scotch to the mix. They went down fast and he ordered a couple more, still crushed by the image of Stocker sneering down at him like he was some pathetic loser, still devastated by the expressions of pity on the faces of the men whose respect he'd once commanded.

Frank reached for his latest beer and knocked it over. The bartender cleaned up the mess and brought him another one. He then returned to his conversation with Bob, the other man at the bar. With nothing better to do, Frank listened in.

"Shit, it's not my fault," Bob drawled, almost sliding off the bar stool. He wrapped his hand around his beer like it would hold him in place. A patch of drool tinged the corner of his mouth.

The bartender nodded.

"He wants to drink, that's his lookout," Bob said. "I drink," he laughed, like he'd said something clever, and held up his beer. "But I can handle it. Yeah, maybe I got him started, but nobody put a gun to his head to keep goin'."

"He hit the skids pretty bad," the bartender said, polishing a glass. "I saw him passed out in the alley a couple of nights ago, lying in his own puke."

"He's a grown-up," Bob said. "'Least he is now."

Frank ordered another round. He almost knocked it over again – the glass rocked precariously sideways but he caught it before it fell. He ordered another shot of scotch.

Bob and the bartender talked about Bob's alcoholic buddy. It turned out that Bob had encouraged, even coaxed, the other man, who turned out to be his younger brother, to drink when the brother was only a teenager. With each new detail Frank felt the pressure in the room intensify. An overwhelming rage boiled up inside him.

"I don't owe him nothin'," Bob drawled.

"But he *is* your little brother," the bartender said.

"Yeah, so?" Bob said. "Don't get on your high horse with me. I'm not my brother's keeper..." Bob laughed and nudged the bartender's elbow. "Get it?" he said. "My brother's keeper."

Frank slammed his empty glass on the bar. Bob and the bartender stared over at him.

"What the fuck's your problem?" Bob said.

"You scumbag," Frank said. He scowled at Bob's reflection in the mirror behind the bar.

"You talkin' to me?" Bob said. "I'm a what?"

Frank turned to face him. "Your partner looks up to you, you're his role model, and you ruin his life."

"Partner?" Bob said. "What fuckin' partner? You some kind of mental case? Anyway, who you think you're talkin' to, asshole?"

He slid off his stool, almost collapsing, and took a step toward Frank.

"Come on, guys," the bartender said. "Settle down. Let's be friends."

"There's a special kind of Hell for scum like you," Frank said.

"And I guess you're the one that's gonna teach me a lesson," Bob said.

Frank slid off his own stool.

"Okay, you're cut off," the bartender said to Frank. "Drink up and get the hell out of here."

"You're the scumbag," Bob said. He grabbed an empty bottle, smashed it against the bar, and jabbed the glass weapon at Frank. "I'll teach you to mind your own fuckin' business."

Frank side-stepped the bottle and swept his leg behind Bob's feet. The already staggering drunk collapsed and fell backward, dropping his weapon. Frank jumped on top of him and smashed at Bob's face with his fists.

"Get him off me!" Bob screamed. The bartender jumped over the bar and tried to haul Frank off. He was joined by one of the bikers. Together they pulled Frank away and the biker held him down. Bob struggled to his feet and kicked Frank in the head.

"Get the hell out!" the bartender yelled to Bob, and he staggered out the front door. Frank still lay on the floor, held now by both bikers. The bartender picked up the phone. A few minutes later the squeal of a siren approached and a spinning red and blue light filtered through the windows. Two cops strode in, their hands on their weapons.

"What's going on here?" the larger of the two said.

"Just get him outta here!" the bartender yelled. "He's outta control!"

Frank struggled against the bikers' grips. They held him long enough for the cops to get the handcuffs on, then they took over.

"Settle down," the smaller of them said to Frank.

Frank was quiet as they marched him, one on each arm, out of the bar and toward the police cruiser. As they reached the sidewalk Frank head-butted the larger cop, broke free, and took off down the street, wrists still handcuffed behind his back.

They caught up and tackled him, driving him to the pavement face first. Both men jumped on top of him and each drove a knee into his back.

"Are you going to behave?" the larger one said into his ear.

Frank nodded. They hauled him to his feet, dragged him back to the cruiser, and shoved him roughly inside. He passed out. When he woke up they were hauling him out of the car. They propelled him through the front doors of the station and up to the booking desk.

"Let's see some ID," a cop at the desk said.

Frank swayed as he struggled to reach the wallet in his back pocket with his cuffed hands. The larger cop grabbed it for him and handed it to his colleague.

"Frank Langer," the desk cop said, reading the driver's license. "Do I know you?"

Frank leaned against the desk but said nothing.

"Morton," the desk cop crooked his finger at the one who'd handed him the wallet. The two drew aside. "This guy's a cop," Frank heard him whisper. "A detective – you remember – the Mastico thing?"

"That's the guy?" Morton said, staring over at Frank.

"I've seen his picture," the desk cop said. "I recognize the name."

Morton shook his head slowly. "Christ – no wonder he's out getting hammered."

Morton took Frank's watch and ring and handed them to the desk cop, who slid them and the wallet into a brown envelope. Morton stepped over and whispered to his partner for a few minutes. They returned and walked Frank, more gently this time, to one of the holding cells. Frank put up no resistance.

They took his belt and shoe laces.

"Why couldn't they do that for Gloria?" Frank mumbled as they removed the handcuffs, took off his jacket, and shoved him inside. He collapsed on the cot.

"Sleep it off," said Morton. He slung the jacket over his shoulder. A thin, rectangular object fell from one of the pockets and floated to the cement floor. Morton reached down and picked it up. It was a business card.

☼

When Frank woke up he couldn't remember everything that had happened the night before, but he was pretty sure he shouldn't be where he was – at home in his own bed. He rolled out and, after a failed attempt to stand, collapsed to the floor. His head throbbed; each pulse threatened to split his skull apart. The left side of his face stung with pain. He reached up and felt crusted ridges of dried blood on his cheek and forehead.

He fought the urge to be sick long enough to make it to the bathroom. After voiding everything he'd eaten the day before, he struggled from his position over the toilet, stood shakily, and staggered to the sink. He washed the vomit from the corners of his mouth, and did his best to clean up the diagonal scrapes across his face, then stumbled down the stairs to the living room. On the couch was a shape under a blanket. Several strands of long brown hair hung down past the blanket's hem.

Still half asleep and confused, he headed for the kitchen, where the automatic coffee maker had just started bubbling. He was going to light a cigarette, but changed his mind and decided to take a shower. Feeling better after the shower and a couple of Ibuprofen, he went back downstairs. In the living room, the blanket was now neatly folded and lay on the coffee table. He moved to the kitchen.

"Hi Frank," Rebecca Hanon said, as she tilted the decanter over a cup. "You look like shit. Coffee?"

"Sure, thanks," Frank said, surprised at how pleased he felt seeing her again. Fragments of what had happened the night before came back to him and he felt a rush of warmth on his cheeks. He fought off a sudden wave of nausea.

"You brought me back here?" he said.

"The cops found my card in your coat pocket," she said, pouring coffee into the cup and handing it to him. His hand shook as he reached for it. "They thought I was your therapist," she continued, "and I didn't say anything to contradict them. I heard what you did. You're lucky they figured out who you were. They didn't want to charge you with anything. I convinced them to let me take you home."

She leaned back against the kitchen counter. "One of the cops said you mumbled something about going back to your old squad room. I could have told you how that would turn out. It's probably one of your biggest psychological triggers."

"Don't start with that psych-" A sudden throb of pain expanded into his skull. He thought better of what he was going to say. "Sorry about the place," he said instead. "I've been meaning to clean it up."

"Yeah," she said, scanning around the room. "It's got that classic Downtown Eastside crack-house ambiance. I hope you won't fly off the handle if I tell you that it's standard for someone with your condition."

Frank's hands were still shaking. He pulled a kitchen chair out with his foot, flopped down on it, and sat his cup on one of the few clear patches on the table.

"I'm still working on the case," he said. He looked up at her. "I know it's not really a case – I know I'm not really a cop at the moment..."

"I'm sorry, Frank," she said, smiling. "Maybe I was a bit hard on you. I'm still upset about what happened to Gloria and her baby. Counselors can have emotional problems too, you know."

"But you should be able to cure yourselves."

"Yeah, that's right," she laughed and her face seemed to light up.

"I guess I kind of overreacted," Frank said. "I've been on edge for a while now, with the drinking, and not getting enough sleep..."

He patted the pile of debris on the table for his cigarettes. Rebecca tapped him on the shoulder. He turned. She was holding the pack.

"On the counter," she said, nodding toward it.

Frank's hands shook as he extracted one, lit it, took a puff, and exhaled a large blue cloud. Rebecca screwed up her nose.

Neither spoke for a few seconds. Finally Frank said, "I've got some new information, if you're interested."

"Of course I'm interested."

"Maybe you should sit down," he said. She poured herself a coffee and sat on a chair opposite him.

"Gloria's baby isn't the only one missing," he said.

"What?"

"You're going to think I'm paranoid, but something's going on here – something beyond one kidnapping."

He took a puff on his cigarette. "What kept bugging me was the plausibility of the case against Gloria. I never believed she was guilty, but she *looked* guilty – almost like it was planned; like it was a setup. And then there was the thing with the baby in the car not being hers.

"She didn't seem to have any enemies. My nose kept coming back to some kind of conspiracy. I got ahold of the statistics on children under the age of two that disappeared in the past fifteen years."

"And?"

"There's at least five I'd put in the same category as Gloria's. Funny thing is, they're all similar, but at the same time all different – almost like they were planned to be that way."

"What do you mean?"

He told her about the case he'd been involved in, with the mother and children on a picnic.

"In another one," he said, "the mother murdered her own baby then committed suicide."

"That sounds more like Gloria."

"Yeah, only this time it all happened at once. The baby's body was never found, but there were traces of blood around the apartment. They figured she'd disposed of the body somehow, then felt remorse and did herself in."

"Were all of the women single mothers?"

"The one at the picnic – she was married, though I don't think the husband was there. There doesn't seem to be any pattern that way. Another mother was pushing her baby daughter in a cart through a crowded fairground. She turned around for a second and the baby was gone, and again, it was never found."

Rebecca's hands tightened around her coffee cup.

"They all could have happened according to the official line," Frank continued, "but there's a thread of similarity. If you were in the business of kidnapping babies and you wanted to make sure the kidnappings went under the radar, you'd arrange them to be different enough that nobody would connect the dots."

Frank took a sip of coffee.

"There's another explanation," Rebecca said.

Frank raised an eyebrow.

"That the disappearances really aren't connected," she said, smiling. "That you *are* paranoid. But let's assume you're right and there is some kind of conspiracy – do you have any theories about why?"

"I haven't gotten that far – yet."

Frank put down his cup and ran a shaking hand through his hair.

"Frank," she said, "I appreciate what you're doing, but take it from me – it was my business for years. You need help. You seem determined to pursue this no matter what I say, but I'm worried about what it'll do to you."

Frank opened his mouth to say something, but changed his mind.

"The past few weeks have been a nightmare," she said, her voice breaking. "I want to clear my sister's name. If you're right and it's possible Ralphie is still alive, I want to find him.

"The police have already tried Gloria and found her guilty. I contacted the lead detective, Stocker. I see what you mean about him. I tried to convince him to do a DNA test and he dug in his heels. He's more pig-headed than you, and not half as intelligent."

She leaned forward. "As it stands, you're the only one who cares enough and has the skills to find out what really happened."

She looked in his eyes. "From what you've uncovered so far, you might be able to use somebody with a medical background. I'll help you with the case – the case that isn't a case – on one condition."

Frank took a drag on his cigarette. "What's that?"

"That you accept that you need help – that you're open-minded about the whole therapy thing. I can recommend some excellent therapists. You can take your pick."

He shook his head. "I told you – I've had it with shrinks."

"Come on, Frank."

He said nothing.

"If you're not willing to see an actual psychiatrist," she said, "maybe I can help you. We can work on your issues on the side, informally, a little at a time. I won't hound you. I won't try to push you anywhere you don't want to go or any faster than you want to get there."

Frank stared into his coffee cup.

She put a hand on his sleeve. "Somehow, someday, you're going to have to come to terms with what happened."

Finally he nodded.

"One other thing," she said. "If I tell you to slow down, if I think the case is getting to be too much, you'll do as I say and take a break. Deal?"

Frank hesitated and finally said, "Deal."

They shook hands.

She smiled. "Now where do we go from here?"

SEVEN

··

A STRANGE PARTNERSHIP

"Remember our agreement," Rebecca said the next day, as she
and Frank sat across from each other at the desk in her office.
Frank cringed. "I got a feeling I'm never going to forget
it."

It was after hours, and Judy had gone home. The daylight was beginning to fade outside. Frank sat studying his hands, which rested on
the wooden desktop. Rebecca sat with a notebook in her lap.

Frank reached out for a paper clip from the holder in front of him,
then checked himself. Instead he lifted his head and glanced around the
office, wishing he could be anywhere but there. His eyes came to rest
on the opera posters on her wall. One in the farthest corner depicted a
knight in armour with a winged helmet and a sword, standing solemnly
in a boat being towed by a swan.

"Who's that guy?" he asked, nodding at the poster.

She turned to look behind her. "That guy? That's Lohengrin. It's a
Wagner opera."

"He looks pretty creepy."

"As a matter of fact," she said, "there's a production of it at the Queen E Theatre sometime next month. You should go," she smiled, "broaden your horizons."

He grunted at the desktop.

She studied the image. "Actually, now that you mention it, he's got a few parallels with you."

Frank made a face. "How do you figure?"

She tilted her head toward the poster. "In the opera, that guy, Lohengrin, appears after a princess prays for a hero to rescue her from an evil king."

"Is that so," Frank laughed. "So, I'm your knight in shining armour?"

"Not exactly," she said. "I'm no princess. But you *are* battling your own personal demons to help me clear my sister's name. Anyway there's more. Lohengrin agrees to help the princess, but in return she has to promise not to ask about his past."

Frank sneered and shook his head. "The shrinks have even taken over opera."

"Yes," she laughed, opening her notebook, "and your tactic of luring me into talking about opera to get out of a session is clever, but it won't work."

She flipped through the notebook and reviewed the last few pages.

"You were talking about a case you were assigned," she said, looking up, "tracking a serial killer. If you feel like it's getting to be too much, just say so and we can pull back, or even call it quits. Okay?"

Frank nodded. He hesitated for a long time. Rebecca was opening her mouth to say something when he finally spoke.

"The guy's name was Eugene Mastico," he said, leaning back in his chair. "He'd already racked up three victims before I ever saw the case. It took a while for them to figure out that the killings were connected. The victims were all young women. In the beginning Mastico wasn't contacting anybody. I think he was waiting for the cops to figure it out. He had a long wait."

Frank slowly rubbed his hands together. "He was a detective's worst nightmare: narcissistic, sadistic, brilliant at manipulating the press. He sent us messages: by e-mail, phone, snail-mail; I think once he even sent us a fax.

"Of course, we'd try to trace them, but they'd be redirected from some anonymous server, or sent from an Internet café and nobody remembered who was there, or from a pay-phone and nobody saw who made the call. They all had the same theme: 'I'm going to keep on killing and you can't stop me'."

Frank shifted in his chair.

"Are you okay?" Rebecca said.

"Fine."

"You're doing great so far, keep going," she smiled supportively.

Frank moved his hands to the arms of the chair.

"The papers mentioned a couple of times that I was leading the investigation. Mastico homed in on that and started targeting me personally. It was the same crap we'd gotten before, but now directed at me. I guess he'd researched my background. One note went on about my university degree and my graduation with honours from the Police Academy – 'and you still can't keep up with poor little old me!' he said."

"How did you feel about all this?" Rebecca asked.

Frank scowled and opened his mouth to say something.

"Don't forget our deal," she said.

"How can I forget when you keep reminding me?"

She rolled her eyes.

"Okay," he said. "I guess part of me loved it – loved being in charge and matching wits with the guy. I guess a part of me even liked being in the limelight – being mentioned in the papers. The novelty of that wore off pretty fast.

"It was like a chess game. Trouble was, it was a game where the stakes were other people's lives – and so far, Mastico was wiping the floor with me."

Frank gripped the arms of the chair.

"I felt responsible every time they found a new victim. Hell, I *was* responsible. Mastico loved to remind me, too. He'd send us e-mails: 'Another poor little innocent angel dead – all because Langer doesn't measure up!'"

"I actually remember the case," Rebecca said, sitting up straight. "There was a lot of public pressure…"

"Are you kidding?" Frank sneered. "Mastico loved to talk to the press. He loved the attention. He started tipping off the press after a kill, so they'd be at the scene before us. Made us look like morons."

Frank's fingers started massaging the arms of the chair. "Part of me was scared shitless. I kept picturing all these new victims – all dead because of my incompetence. Part of me started believing what Mastico, and some of the press, were saying. Part of me thought maybe I wasn't up to the job, maybe somebody else should be doing it –

somebody who could catch the guy. Randall and I spent a lot of sleepless nights over it."

"Randall?"

Frank's muscles tightened. His breath caught in his throat.

"Are you okay?" Rebecca said.

Frank didn't speak for several seconds. His breathing was laboured. Finally he nodded.

"Kid named Jeff Randall," he said. "Just out of the academy. He was my partner. I guess I'd gotten a bit of a reputation. He said working with me was like a dream come true."

"How did you react to that?"

Frank's breathing got heavier. "You mean did it give me a swelled head?" He could feel the beads of sweat forming on his forehead. "Well, yeah, I guess it did." His fingers dug into the arms of the chair. "Randall came along just before the Mastico case landed on my desk, so it was basically the first one he ever worked on. He was smart, dedicated…"

"Frank, we can stop if you don't feel up to it."

Frank ignored her and stared at a building outside the window. "He'd done a lot of criminal behaviour stuff at the academy, so he made himself pretty indispensable. He'd just gotten married. They were trying for their first…"

"That was when…" he started to say. The tips of his fingers gripped the leather arms of his chair like talons, making deep impressions. He started to tremble. The light in the room faded and the walls closed in around him. He shut his eyes.

"Frank," he heard a voice.

"Frank," the voice repeated. He opened his eyes. Rebecca was staring at him.

"That's enough for now," she said. "Are you alright?"

"Yeah," he said, still shaking. "A little stressed out."

He rose unsteadily, walked away and splashed some water on his face in the bathroom, then returned.

"Go home and get some rest, Frank," Rebecca said. "You look beat."

As they walked out of her office door, she paused. "If you're feeling up to it later, why don't you let me reward you for your effort. You can take me out to dinner."

"*My* reward is taking *you* out to dinner?"

"You sound disappointed."

Frank smiled. "No, come to think of it that's a great idea."

"By the way," he said as they left the building, "you ever had your office swept for bugs?"

"Of course not, why?"

"You should. I know some people. I'll give you the number."

"I can see you've got expensive tastes," Rebecca said as they strolled down Robson Street heading for the 'Japadog' food truck. The sidewalk was crowded with people getting late off work, or early for evening shopping. The night was warm, and the lights of the shops and cafes spilled out onto the street.

Frank smiled. "Try the 'Terimayo' – teriyaki sauce, mayo, and seaweed. That's what I'm having."

She screwed up her nose.

They got their dogs and headed for the Art Gallery.

"You know, this isn't half bad," Rebecca said, taking another bite of her Terimayo.

They reached the Gallery, and sat down on the broad curving staircase opening onto Robson Square.

Frank hauled a can of Canada Dry out of one jacket pocket, two plastic cups out of the other, and poured them each a drink. He held out his plastic cup, and she 'clinked' hers against it.

"Tell me about your wife," she said.

He studied her in the dim light. He'd never been attracted to intelligent women, especially assertive ones, as Rebecca definitely was. He was surprised at the way his pulse quickened when he was near her.

"Would you call this a date?" he asked.

She looked up, startled. "What? I don't know. There's no candlelight or gypsy violins. You're a man, I'm a woman. We're having dinner." She held up the remains of her Japadog. "I guess I'd have to call that a date. Anyway, you haven't answered my question."

"Sheila?" he smiled. "It's a funny thing…Sheila was everything I always thought I wanted in a woman – beautiful, submissive, not overly bright…"

Rebecca rolled her eyes.

"I know, I know. I wasn't exactly a poster boy for women's lib. I like to think I've matured since then."

"I hope so."

"Anyway, I guess in a way it's kind of poetic justice. I think she had the same stereotypical image of me. I was the ultimate macho cop who could leap tall buildings in a single bound. She couldn't handle the emotional problems and mood-swings I went through after the breakdown. She made sort of a half-hearted attempt to understand, but in the end it was too much for her."

"That must have been tough."

"Yeah, with everything else. It was just one more straw, like they say. Fact is, her leaving was the thing that bothered me the least."

"So what bothered you the most?"

He swished the ginger ale around in his cup. "The most? Not being a cop anymore. It's who I was. I couldn't separate myself from it. The first few months I felt like nobody. Like I didn't exist."

"And now?"

"At first all I could think about was getting back there – getting my old job back, maybe even taking over the Lead Detective spot. After a while I started thinking: maybe it's not healthy to make your job your life. Being a cop's not like any other job, but it's still a job. Part of me's glad I got the chance to think about who I was outside the force."

A scraping sound of metal against metal across the square made them both turn and look. A kid on a skateboard was practicing jumps onto a metal handrail.

She turned back to him. "What made you want to be a cop in the first place?"

"What do you mean?"

"Was there some sort of 'ah-ha' moment when you realized that was the career for you?"

He shrugged. "I never really thought about it – it was just always what I was going to be. My dad was a cop – not a detective, just a beat cop. Everybody always assumed I'd be one too."

"Where are they now? Your parents."

He narrowed his eyes. "Is this a session? Are you messing with my head?"

"No," she laughed. "I'd just like to know a little more about you."

"My dad was killed on the job about twenty years ago."

"Oh God, I'm so sorry."

"He stopped a car for speeding and the driver blew him away and took off. The car was stolen. They never caught the guy. I guess that's when I finally made the decision. I couldn't just stand by and let people get away with stuff like that."

"And your mother?"

"She never really got over Dad's death. She died a few years ago. Stroke. I just went to see them both yesterday."

Rebecca stared at him.

"At the Columbarium," Frank smiled at her confusion.

"Colum what?"

"It's a sort of mausoleum where you can put the ashes of your 'loved ones'." He held up his fingers like quotation marks. "It's like a wall of little cubbyholes with urns inside.

"I'm not into any of that, but it's what my mother wanted, so that's where they are. You can put flowers and little mementos or pictures if you want. There's a glass door and they give you a key."

"Well, that's a new one on me," Rebecca smiled. "It's nice that you actually go and visit them once in a while."

78

A pigeon swooped down and pecked at the ground in front of them. Rebecca broke off a crumb from what was left of her Japadog bun and tossed it toward the bird.

"So what about before?" she asked.

"What do you mean?"

"You said your father's death clinched your decision to become a cop. Does that mean you had other things in mind before?"

Frank stared at his drink. "Yeah, I had a couple of ideas. They weren't all that serious."

"Like what?"

"You sure this isn't a session?"

"Don't get defensive, Frank. It's just a friendly conversation."

Frank made one last swirl and took a drink. He turned to her. "You promise you won't laugh."

"Of course."

"For a while I wanted to be a singer – you know, like Sinatra or Michael Buble or something."

Rebecca smiled.

"You promised," he reminded her.

"I'm just trying to picture you in a sequined suit at the Tropicana in Vegas. Look, I think that's wonderful Frank. I knew there was more to you than I could see on the surface. So you're a musician?"

"Used to play piano. Haven't touched one in years. Don't even own one anymore. I was just a kid. You know how it is. You figure it'll probably never happen, but it gives you something to dream about."

She smiled at him. "You're a funny guy, you know, Frank. You come on with this cliché macho cop persona, but you're not a typical cop at all, are you?"

"Hey, being a man doesn't mean you've gotta be ignorant – not all the time, anyway…" he laughed.

"But I'll bet not many of 'the boys' at the squad are like you."

"I'm not sure whether I should be flattered or insulted."

Rebecca smiled at him. "Be flattered."

"How come I'm doing all the talking here?" he said. "I should have a chance to dig into your past. When did you first realize you hated your dog?"

Rebecca laughed.

They talked for a while about Montreal, where she grew up, her previous failed marriage, and her parents, both dead and buried for several years.

"At least they didn't live to see what happened to Gloria," she said, her voice breaking.

"Do you mind talking about her?" he said.

She looked down at her feet. "No, it's okay."

"Were you two close?" he asked.

"I've always been a bit of a mother to her. I guess I'm a typical social worker, with the mothering instinct. She was the type of person that needed someone looking out for them. I guess I blew it on that score."

"There's nothing you could have done," Frank said. He had the impulse to take her hand, but he was afraid of how she'd react. "Sometimes stuff just happens."

For a few minutes they watched the traffic go by.

Finally Rebecca spoke. "I know I've been hard on you. It's not that I don't appreciate the help; it's just that I'm worried about you."

"I can take care of myself. Anyway, I'm not just doing it for you. Like I said, I hate to see people get away with stuff like that – and I feel like I owe it to Gloria."

"What do you plan to do next?"

"There's not much to go on, and we don't have any resources. I've used up most of my favours at the squad, and I don't think I got any new fans after that last visit."

There was a cracking sound and he opened his clenched fist to reveal a crushed plastic cup. He glanced at Rebecca sheepishly. She said nothing.

"Give me yours," he said. He stood up and held out his hand.

He tossed the cups in the garbage and returned. "We start with the usual: who knew Gloria, who had access to her apartment, who had a motive… and we hope something turns up."

EIGHT

....

GLORIA'S APARTMENT

"**Y**ou're getting to be a regular here, Frank," Judy smiled the next day as he stuck his head in the office door.

"I just come to see you," Frank teased her.

"Why, you'll turn my head with such talk," she laughed. She nodded toward the hallway. "She's expecting you."

He headed down the hall and into Rebecca's office. She had her hair in a ponytail. For a few seconds he was hypnotized by her long neck and the curve of her jaw. The hairstyle changed the character of her face completely, making it younger and more innocent. It wasn't a look Frank normally went for, but on her he found it striking.

Judy brought them coffee. When she was gone Rebecca closed the door.

"The guys came and did their thing?" Frank said, scanning around the office.

"What? The bug sweep?" She smiled. "I could have told you – we're clean as a spring rain."

"Doesn't hurt to check," he said, pulling a small notebook from his jacket pocket. He clicked his pen open, leaned back in his chair, lifted his feet, and was about to set them on her desk. At a glare from Rebecca he flashed a smile and put them back down.

"Let's look at connections," he said. "If some individual, or more likely some group, is behind all the kidnappings, there must be a common thread that joins them. We find that thread, we'll be a lot closer to understanding what's going on."

"Okay…"

"So," he said. "We list the things the mothers of the kidnapped children have in common."

"Sure."

Frank positioned his pen on the notebook.

"Marital status?" Rebecca suggested.

He waved his hand dismissively. "We already know there's no commonality in marital status."

"Don't you think we should include everything? We can eliminate things that don't apply later – but at least we know we've covered everything. I'm no detective, but…"

"Yeah, yeah, okay, you're right."

"We don't have to do it that way if you don't want…"

"Your way is fine. Let's get on with it. So, marital status. What else?"

"Race? Religion? Social position?"

"Sure." Frank scribbled in his notebook. "Then there's where they live, where they work."

"This whole business seems to revolve around babies," she said, "so it might involve hospitals, doctors, gynecologists, pediatricians. I could help look into that."

They continued and compiled a comprehensive list.

"Great," Frank said when they were finished. "Maybe you can have a look at the medically-related stuff and I'll check on everything else…"

"Sure," she answered.

Frank turned a page in his notebook. "The other thing we need to look at is motive. Why – why would somebody want to kidnap Ralphie? It usually comes down to money. Somehow somebody's getting paid."

"Like you said before," Rebecca said. "Baby smuggling."

"That's the most likely motive. There's childless couples out there that would pay a fortune for a baby, no questions asked."

"I hate to even suggest this," Rebecca said, "but how about organ harvesting. Find a baby with the right genetic makeup and sell them to somebody desperate for the organs."

"You've got a sick mind," Frank smiled. "But you're right. Let's start with the baby smuggling angle. It seems the most likely. If it doesn't pan out, then…"

"Frank," she interrupted him.

He glanced up from his notebook.

"Are we sure?" she asked.

He frowned and raised an eyebrow.

"I mean, about all the kidnappings being connected?" she said. "If they're not, we're wasting time we could be spending looking for the killer…"

"We're sure."

She stared at him.

"Okay?" he said, his thumb poised on the clicker of his pen like it was the plunger of a detonator.

She gave a tiny shrug.

☼

Some of the tasks Frank had assigned himself proved easy. The mothers' marital status, race, and current address were in the reports he'd copied earlier. There was no correlation among any of them.

Employment was harder; he no longer had a cop's ability to access police files, but he managed to fill in the blanks on all the women. It was disappointing. Other than one or two superficial similarities, none of the victimized mothers seemed to have anything in common.

He called Rebecca and they agreed to meet and compare notes at the same cafe where they'd first gotten together.

Frank got there early, and chose a table distant from any other patrons. He studied Rebecca's movements as she approached: the swing of her hips, the bobbing of her hair, once again down and flowing over her shoulders. She smiled and waved as she spotted him.

"I might have found something," she said once they'd ordered coffee. "It might or might not be important."

Frank glanced around them to make sure no one was nearby, then nodded. "Fire away."

"I made a list of the gynecologists and pediatricians for the cases you gave me," she said. "Gloria's pediatrician works for a private pediatric clinic, but she volunteers for a non-profit organization."

"Yeah?"

"Guess what the non-profit organization does?" she teased, stirring her coffee.

Frank shrugged.

"They help childless couples adopt."

Frank raised an eyebrow.

"It doesn't prove anything," she said, "but it makes you think."

"Definitely."

"The place is called 'Child Connect'. I did a little checking on them."

"Wow, you're a regular Sherlock Holmes."

"It's kind of exciting isn't it, detective work?" she smiled. "Imagine going undercover – like in some kind of spy novel."

Frank narrowed his eyes at her. "This isn't TV," he said. "When things go down in this business, people get hurt."

She shrugged. "Anyway I didn't find much. I figured I'd leave the heavy-duty detecting to you."

She passed him a slip of paper. "Here's their address and website. The pediatrician's name is Dr. Monica Gilford."

Frank glanced at the paper and put it in his wallet.

He put his hand on her sleeve. "You should be careful when you do this research."

"You're being a bit paranoid, Frank."

He leaned forward and whispered. "Look, we're talking about multiple kidnappings, and maybe even murder. We don't know who the conspirators are, or how big this thing is."

An opera aria blasted from her purse. She fished out her cell phone, stood up, and walked away to take the call. A few minutes later she returned.

"The police have released Gloria's apartment," she said. "Want to have a look?"

☼

Frank studied Rebecca's face as she unlocked the door to her dead sister's apartment. Her mind was elsewhere, and her eyes were moist with tears.

"You sure you want to do this?" he said. "I can look by myself."

"No," she said, her voice trembling. "I'm fine. I want to be here."

Stocker had formally closed the case, and the police no longer had any interest in it. The apartment was a mess, clothes thrown in heaps on the floor, cigarette butts in the ashtray. *Did she even smoke?* Frank tried to remember. Plates of half-eaten food lay scattered around. Frank felt his face flush red; it looked disturbingly like his own place.

The door knobs, door jambs, and mirrors were still stained black with fingerprint dust.

"You're the expert," Rebecca said. "What exactly are we looking for?"

"Evidence," Frank said, smiling.

"Great – I'll keep that in mind."

"We're looking for anything that would link Gloria to someone who might want to do this," he said.

He stepped into the tiny bathroom and opened the mirrored door of the medicine cabinet. The bottom shelf held the usual collection of hair and skin products and makeup. On the second were various non-prescription drugs. The third held Band-Aids, tubes of skin cream, a bottle of antiseptic. He checked the cupboard under the sink, but found nothing interesting.

They moved to the bedroom. The bed was unmade; the gaudy pink bedspread lay in a heap on the floor. The crib from which the poor child had been abducted stood against one wall. He imagined Gloria leaning over the empty crib, torn apart with grief. For a second he felt physically sick. He glanced over at Rebecca; she seemed to be holding it together.

In a corner near the bed was a small bookcase. He checked out a couple of paperbacks on the top shelf. Most were cheap romance novels. He smirked at the bodice-ripping pictures on the covers. As he replaced the last one, his hand brushed against something. He bent down and peered along the tops of the books. Sticking out of one of them was a tiny slip of paper. He pulled out the book, removed the paper, and examined it.

"Hmm…" he said. Rebecca strolled over to join him.

"See this?" He held up the slip.

"It's the label from a pill bottle," she said.

"She was using it as a bookmark. Olmerol – 500 milligrams. Interesting. I didn't see any other indication that she ever used it – any bottles in the medicine cabinet."

"That name sounds familiar," Rebecca said. "I remember – Olmerol – I remember it because it reminded me of Armor All – you know, the car cleaner? I think she was taking it for morning sickness. No wonder there's no bottles. That must be a really old label."

"It *is* a drug," Frank said, slipping the label into his wallet. "Something a gynecologist might prescribe. Just out of curiosity, there's something I want to check."

They returned to the bathroom, and he re-opened the medicine cabinet. This time, he carefully lifted each pill bottle on the second shelf.

"Hmm," he said, inspecting the shelf beneath a raised aspirin bottle.

"What?" She peered over his shoulder. "I don't see anything."

"See the diameter of the bottle I'm holding?"

Rebecca nodded.

"See the imprint of a bottle where this one was sitting? Notice anything?"

"They're a different size…"

"Someone recently moved the bottles around. It may have been Gloria. Or somebody might have removed a bottle that was incriminating."

"Incriminating how?"

"It's probably nothing – but it's worth taking note. You never know."

"Maybe the police moved them."

"Maybe. I'll try to find out, but I don't have much pull over there anymore."

They returned to the bedroom and made a more detailed inspection of the crib. Nothing. On the night table by Gloria's bed stood a larger copy of the picture Frank had seen when he visited her – Gloria, with an ecstatic grin as she held Ralphie in her arms. Rebecca picked it up and once again choked back tears. After a few seconds she put the picture down, turned her back, and walked out of the room.

"You okay?" Frank said as they exited the elevator.

"Yes," Rebecca said. "It's just sad, that's all."

As they walked through the lobby he handed her the label. "Think you could check out the drugstore this label came from and find out who prescribed it?"

"It's just a label. You really think it's worth looking into?"

Frank shrugged. "We're dealing with stolen babies. Maybe a drug for morning sickness fits in. I'm going to look into this Child Connect place. I'll call you in a couple of days."

"I could do some research on Olmerol."

"That would be great."

He walked her to her car. She unlocked the door, and was about to get in when he called, "Rebecca." She turned and looked up at him.

"Don't talk to anyone about this," he said. "Not anyone. And be careful when you do the research."

"Don't you think you're overreacting?"

Frank stared at her.

"I'll be careful," she said.

NINE

···

CHILD CONNECT

D r. Monica Gilford was an earnest, thirty-something woman
with short brown hair and glasses. She rose from her chair as
Frank entered her workspace at Child Connect, and shook his
hand as he introduced himself.

The place was cramped, with a single desk and a tiny window in
one wall, but it was spotless and meticulously laid out. The books on
the bookshelves were ordered by size, and even by colour, as were several stacks of paper on top of the filing cabinet. There was a jumble of
pens and papers directly in front of the doctor's chair, but the remainder
of the desktop was arranged with obsessive precision.

"You certainly keep a clean office," Frank said.

"Oh, that's not me, I'm afraid," she laughed, speaking with an English accent. "I'm a bit of a slob, actually. That's Catherine, Dr. Lesko,
one of the other volunteers. We share the office."

She leaned toward him like she was whispering a secret. "She's
very picky."

Frank had convinced Art Crawford, his former colleague at the
squad, to look into Child Connect. Art had come up with nothing. The

place was squeaky clean, and backed by a prominent religious organization.

It looked like a dead end, but Frank had decided to check it out in person anyway. The organization operated from a small space in Yaletown, not far from Rebecca's office. He'd shown the smiling receptionist one of his old business cards. That was enough to satisfy her that he really was a detective.

When he told Dr. Gilford about Gloria and Ralphie she flinched and caught her breath. Either she was a consummate actress or she really hadn't heard.

"Sorry," Frank said. "I thought you knew."

"That's terrible," she said. "I didn't have that much contact with them, but they seemed very nice."

She couldn't divulge any medical information about Ralphie, but said she'd seen him three times since his birth, the last time one month ago. She was unaware of anyone showing an interest in Ralphie or acting suspiciously around him.

Frank saw no reason not to believe her. It looked like he was wasting his time.

"There was one thing," she said, as he turned to leave. "It might not have anything to do with Ralphie..."

He turned back to face her.

"I think somebody might have broken into my office. Not here, at work – at the clinic. It was strange. They didn't take anything. But there were little things."

"Like?" Frank said.

"A couple of items on my desk had been moved around. Not much, but enough to notice. Also, I'd accidentally filed a few of my files out of order – including Ralphie's. I'd been meaning to straighten them out but I hadn't had time."

"And?"

"I went through them in case any had been taken. None were gone, but Ralphie's was in the right spot."

"You're sure about this?"

"Like I say, so little had changed I almost didn't believe it, but I'm pretty sure."

Rebecca studied Frank's lined and unshaven face as they sat at a sidewalk cafe near her office in Yaletown. She'd called to ask him about Child Connect, but he hadn't wanted to talk on the phone, so she'd agreed to meet him here. Frank seemed have grown some new gray hairs, though she'd seen him only a few days ago. Was it just the light?

She felt a fresh stab of guilt about involving him in her sister's case. While it might be true that at some level the familiarity of detective work was good therapy for him, it also presented stresses that could push him over the edge.

She tried to justify what they were doing with the knowledge that Frank would pursue the case whether she helped him or not, but part of her understood that she was enabling him, distracting him from what should be his focus – getting well again.

"Nothing," he said, when she asked him about Child Connect.

"So it's a dead end?" she asked.

"Not quite."

He explained the circumstances surrounding the break-in.

"So she could be imagining it," she said.

He shrugged. "It's thin, but right now it's all I've got. I'm going to look into a few of the other doctors from your list. Maybe there'll be a tie-in. How about you?"

"I did some research on Olmerol," she said. She leaned forward in her chair. "I was right. It was developed in the fifties to alleviate morning sickness, around the same time as Thalidomide – now there's a scary parallel – by a company called Kaffir Pharma."

"I've heard of them," he said.

"Olmerol was never banned like Thalidomide – it's been in use for almost sixty years."

"There were no side effects?"

"There's always side effects, but none serious enough to justify discontinuing its use. One study suggested a higher incidence of autism in children whose mothers had taken the drug, but it wasn't conclusive. Of course, Kaffir disputed the results, and only that one study showed a connection."

She took a sip of her coffee.

"How much do you know about Kaffir?" he asked. "You heard any stories about them? Any big hits on their reputation?"

"They market one or two psychiatric drugs I'm familiar with. They're your typical faceless, soulless, multinational pharmaceutical company. You could argue that they're all evil in a way, but I don't think Kaffir is any more so than the others."

"For a junior detective, you're doing great," Frank smiled. "Keep it up."

"Coming from you, that's a big compliment," she said. "What any of this has to do with Gloria's death is another question."

"We don't know much," Frank said, "but all we can do is go with what we've found so far."

He downed the last of his coffee. "I'll call you if I find anything."

He stood. His hands shook as he opened his wallet.

"You okay, Frank?" she asked. Her guilt resurfaced. "You know, you don't have to continue with this – we can quit anytime."

"I'm fine," he said, annoyed. He dropped a five on the table and walked away.

Over the next few days Frank checked out three more of the physicians on Rebecca's list. None of them remembered any special circumstances surrounding the disappearance of the child in their care.

He also asked them about any volunteer activities and any break-ins, but nothing stood out. This avenue of investigation was starting to look like a dead end. He resolved to try one more before giving up.

Dr. Joyce Hunter, the final name he chose to visit, had been the pediatrician for the family in the incident most like Gloria and Ralphie's, where the baby had gone missing and the mother had committed suicide.

Dr. Hunter was on record as working at the Pacific Coast Pediatric Clinic. The receptionist there went pale when Frank mentioned her name.

"I'm sorry," she said. "Dr. Hunter was killed in a hit and run accident two years ago."

"Sorry to hear that," Frank said.

"The car and driver that hit her were never found," she continued. "It was terrible – such a huge loss."

Frank arranged to talk to Dr. Hunter's former supervisor, Dr. Carol Raskin.

☼

"I remember it like it was yesterday," Dr. Raskin said as Frank sat across from her in her office. "It was a terrible tragedy."

He asked her about break-ins. She retrieved a folder from her filing cabinet, and opened it on her desk. "Oh yes, that's right," she said. "Joyce admitted that an unauthorized person had been in her office. Not exactly a break in – apparently, they'd somehow gotten hold of a key. She said she knew who it was. She was going to talk to them and give them a chance to explain themselves."

Frank straightened in his chair. "You're sure she said that? She knew who did it?"

"Yes," she answered. "We were quite concerned. There were no drugs in the office, but there were records for most of her patients. I wanted to call the police, but she insisted on handling it herself."

"And that was just before she was killed?"

Dr. Raskin nodded.

"She never said who it was?"

"No," Dr. Raskin shook her head. "Such a shame what happened to her."

"Did she say anything else about the break-in?"

"No more than I've told you. After her death we never pursued it further, though we did upgrade some of our security procedures."

Frank got up to leave. He could check out the hit and run, but if investigators had come up empty back then, what chance did he have two years after the fact?

"Thanks for your time," he said, turning for the door.

He opened it, then turned back. "By the way, did Dr. Hunter do any volunteer work?"

Dr. Raskin checked the file folder.

"Oh, yes," she smiled. "I remember – she volunteered once a week at the Painted Pony Farm. It's a camp for sick children."

☼

Donkeys and goats nibbled on the sparse grass behind the split-rail fence that snaked around the Painted Pony Farm, deep in the rustic sub-urb of Langley. Bunny rabbits hopped, pot-bellied pigs snorted, and chickens scratched, in the large wire cages that dotted the compound.

The volunteer angle was a thin lead, but Frank had gone this far – he figured he might as well see it through.

The rotund director of the camp, Gordon Lambert, was bubbly and outgoing. He smiled broadly as he shook Frank's hand.

"Your work must be very satisfying," Frank said, as a small pony carrying a young child plodded by, led by a camp worker.

"We're very proud of what we do here," Lambert beamed. "We give sick kids a chance to forget about their medical issues for a while and just have fun."

They strolled to Lambert's office, a well-maintained log cabin in the heart of the action.

"We were very sorry to lose Dr. Hunter," Lambert shook his head as they walked. "She was so dedicated to the children."

They entered the office and sat at a small table in one corner. Lambert offered Frank coffee and he accepted.

"Did Dr. Hunter ever mention anything about her office at work being broken into?" Frank said.

"At work?" Lambert scratched his head. "She never talked about her work. I think she came out here to get away from work – to unwind, you know? We talked about the kids, the animals, even the weather, but never her regular job."

"Was there anybody here she was close to? Anybody she might have confided in?"

Lambert shrugged. "She only came once a week. I believe she was quite friendly with one of the other volunteers, Dr. Lesko. I know I saw them together at the lunch table a few times."

Frank looked up from his notepad.

TEN

....

KAFFIR PHARMA

Rebecca stepped from the doorway of her office building to the cobblestones of Yaletown, shielding her eyes from the glare of the afternoon sun. It was a blazing, luminous day typical for late summer in Vancouver, the kind she liked the best.

She smiled at the warmth of the afternoon, unbuttoning her suit jacket as she strolled toward the Stadium Skytrain station. In the brilliant sunlight, the dark days following Gloria's death seemed to fade into the past. Rebecca's briefcase swung jauntily in her hand as she turned the corner onto Beatty Street, glad for some exercise after sitting at a desk all afternoon.

Several days had passed since Frank had last come in for an informal 'session', as stipulated in their agreement. He'd come willingly, but his mind had been elsewhere; they hadn't accomplished much. She'd given him some exercises for homework, to help him relax and improve his sleep.

Since then, she'd heard from him only once, by phone. He said the investigation was 'progressing'. Later, she'd tried to call him several times – she had news. Each time a disembodied voice had told her that the cellular customer was unavailable.

She thought about Frank and smiled again. He was nothing like any of the men she'd been involved with in the past (not that they were actually involved), and not at all the type of man she thought she'd be interested in (if she really was interested). Still, despite his many issues and personal problems, maybe even because of them, she found herself waiting for his next call.

She'd just caught sight of the Skytrain station when a muffled ringtone issued from inside her purse. She fished out her phone and answered.

"Keep walking," said a voice on the line.

She froze for a second, startled, until she recognized who it was.

She dropped her shoulders and sighed. "What the hell are you doing, Frank? Where are you? You scared the hell out of me." She scanned the block for any sign of him, but saw nothing. Following his instructions, she continued slowly along Beatty Street.

"I need to talk to you," he said. "There's a coffee shop a few blocks away, on East Hastings, called 'Uncle Mac's' – you know it?"

"Yeah, I know it," she said. "You sure you want to go there? The place is a major dump. As your pseudo-therapist I think I should advise you that you're behaving pretty strangely all of a sudden."

"Just humour me, okay?"

"Whatever you say."

Uncle Mac's was a hole-in-the-wall greasy-spoon in Gastown. Rebecca got there first and headed for a booth in the corner. She passed an old man in rags, his head resting on a table along with an uneaten, stale-looking sandwich and a half-empty glass of beer. There were only one or two other customers. She pulled a tissue from her purse and wiped down the cracked vinyl of the bench seat, then sat and waited. A few minutes later Frank arrived and slid onto the bench across from her.

Rebecca watched as the proprietor (Uncle Mac?), wearing a sleeveless undershirt, hauled a filthy rag from under his naked armpit and used it to wipe down one of the tables.

"You sure know how to sweep a girl off her feet," she said to Frank.

"I wanted a place that's out of the way," he explained.

"Congratulations, I think you found one. Is it safe to eat here?"

"I'd order something deep fried."

"I hope all this cloak and dagger stuff is really necessary. Food poisoning wouldn't be my first choice for a way to die."

They both ordered coffee.

"Okay?" she said. "Happy?"

Frank raised his hand for silence. A bored looking waitress came up behind Rebecca, plunked a cup of coffee in front of each of them, and moved on. He waited until she was well away, then nodded.

"How have you been sleeping lately, Frank?" she asked.

"Like usual."

"You've got bags under your eyes that could hold my entire wardrobe."

"I'll get over it."

"Have you been doing the exercises I gave you? Are you feeling any better?"

He shrugged. "Sure, way better."

She rolled her eyes skyward.

"You're doing a great job," he said. "You're a miracle worker. I'll be cured in no time."

She shook her head resignedly.

He glanced around them, then lowered his head and said, in a low voice, "Catherine Lesko."

"What?"

"The common link. Dr. Gilford and two of the other doctors I checked from your list knew her. Apparently she's a pediatrician here in town. She volunteered at the same places they did. I'm pretty sure that either she or somebody connected to her also broke into their offices looking for information. She may even have murdered one of them."

Rebecca stared at him, horrified, as he explained about Dr. Hunter's death.

"Lesko quit the volunteering gigs once her job, whatever that was, was done. I'm trying to track her down."

Frank fished a pack of cigarettes out of his shirt pocket. Rebecca nodded her head toward a sign on the wall with writing in large black letters: 'This is a smoke-free environment'.

Frank winced and put it back.

"You've been a busy boy," Rebecca said, smiling. "I've been busy myself. If you'd been around…" she shot him a chastising look, "I could have told you *my* news."

"Which is?"

"I managed to get some information on the women whose babies were kidnapped – best not to ask me how. All the mothers of kidnapped babies took Olmerol regularly for their morning sickness."

"What the hell?" Frank said, scratching his head.

"But thousands of other women take the drug," she continued. "They seem to have been left alone. Of course, it could still all just be coincidence…"

He rose from his seat. "Sorry," he said, holding up the cigarette pack. They walked out of the cafe. He lit up, and they stood on the sidewalk in front.

"I'm sure I don't have to remind you that those things will kill you," she said.

He gave her a withering look.

Neither spoke for a few seconds.

"So," Frank finally said, blowing out a puff of smoke, "there's something special about these women and Olmerol."

He tapped the ash from his cigarette. "So, does Lesko work for Kaffir? Maybe our buddies at Kaffir have their own medical people, like Catherine Lesko, monitoring the mothers – to keep an eye on them. But why? And why the kidnappings?"

He took another drag. "So is it Kaffir that's kidnapping babies, or somebody else? Maybe Kaffir's guarding them."

"If they're trying to protect the mothers and babies, they're failing," Rebecca said.

Frank stared at his feet, thinking.

"Shit!" He said loudly. He dropped his cigarette butt and stubbed it out on the pavement.

"What?" she said.

Frank straightened up and faced her. "Maybe Olmerol's got side effects after all."

Rebecca applied generous portions of hand sanitizer from a bottle in her purse as Frank went back in and dropped a five-dollar bill on the table. He offered to walk her to the Skytrain. Bustling crowds, heading home from work, pushed by them as they moved.

"What if I was to visit Kaffir?" she said. "Their headquarters are right here in Vancouver."

Frank froze mid-step and put his arm out to stop her. The moving crowd parted around them.

"Absolutely not," he said. "No way."

"It wouldn't be a big stretch for me to show an interest in them. I was in pre-med before I switched to Social Work. I wouldn't even necessarily have to ask about Olmerol. I could say I'm interested in one of their psychiatric drugs. Maybe I'd come across something that would help us..."

"Put that idea out of your head," Frank said, his voice rising. He lowered it again. "Didn't you hear what I told you?"

"You're blowing this way out of proportion," she shot back. "Anyway, I've been around. You should see some of the people I used to come across at work. It's possible I've seen a worse side of humanity than you..."

"No, you haven't!" Frank shouted, clenching his fists. A couple of people on the sidewalk turned and stared at them. "You haven't," he repeated, lowering his voice.

They started walking again. He didn't say anything for half a block, and nervously scanned the street around them. When they were far from any other pedestrians he finally spoke, without stopping or looking at her.

"Just keep walking and listen to me carefully," he said. "This isn't a game and I'm not joking."

"You're really creeping me out, Frank."

"Good," he said. "Think about it. We're dealing with a conspiracy to kidnap and possibly kill children. Whoever's behind it has some connection to a multi-billion-dollar corporation."

"So you *think*," she said. "For all we know, this Catherine Lesko is acting alone."

He stopped and turned to face her. "So I *know*."

He started walking again. "Right now, Kaffir has no idea you or I exist. You go sticking your nose into the head office, you're going to appear on their radar. I can guarantee you don't want that to happen. I'm sure you've dealt with all kinds at work. Maybe some of them were even dangerous..."

He stiffened, as if fighting some inner turmoil. "There's people out there that'd kill you as easy as they'd swat a fly, then they'd go for dinner and drinks like nothing happened."

Rebecca shuddered. She wasn't sure whether she was more afraid of the threat Frank was imagining, or of Frank himself.

"Well, what do you want to do?" she asked.

"I've got a couple of ideas. It's probably best if you don't know what they are."

"What about me?"

"You? You're going to do nothing."

"Gloria was my sister," she said angrily. "I'm not going to just sit on my ass."

"Yes you are."

She stopped walking and grabbed him by the elbow. "Who the hell do you think you are? Where do you get off telling me what to do?"

Frank looked into her eyes. "You're not going to listen to me anyway, are you?"

"Sorry."

He studied her face.

"Okay," he said, "if you've got to do something…"

She raised an eyebrow. He gestured with his hand and they started walking again.

"Do some more research on Kaffir and Olmerol," he said, without looking at her. "They seem to be the key to this whole business. Who were the people that developed the drug? Are they still around? Any of them leave the company suddenly? Any of them fired? Anybody holding a grudge?"

The station came into view. "You said you found a few studies," he continued. "Are there more? Any lawsuits involving Olmerol? Is Kaffir on anybody's hit list, for any reason?"

"Okay."

He studied the faces on the sidewalk. "Don't use your own computer, or any other that can be traced back to you. Use an Internet café, or a computer store, or the library. Disguise yourself. Wear a hat that covers your hair. Wear baggy clothes and sunglasses. Wear a wig – anything to make it hard for whoever runs the place to trace you."

Rebecca shook her head, incredulous. His precautions seemed way over the top.

"Never stay logged in for too long. Wipe the keyboard and any surfaces you've touched before you leave. You get the idea?"

"Sounds like something out of a spy movie," she said.

"Pretend your life depends on no one finding out," Frank said. "Maybe it does. Promise me you'll do everything I just said – and more."

Rebecca nodded.

"We need a way to contact each other," he said. "I don't trust the phone. I definitely don't trust e-mail. How about if we just meet at your office?"

"My office?"

"I'm sort of a client anyway. If I drop by regularly nobody's going to be surprised."

"I guess."

"What's your slackest day?"

"Tuesday."

"If I've got anything to tell you I'll show up at one PM on Tuesday."

"I'll make sure not to book anything."

"You may not hear from me for a while."

They reached the station and stopped outside the main doors.

"What about our sessions?" she asked.

"They'll have to take a back seat for the time being."

She frowned at him.

"Only for a while," he said. "I promise. After that, maybe we can combine the two." He smiled. "You know, information dump slash therapy session."

ELEVEN

....

A MANSION IN POINT GREY

I t was a sweltering day, and the fan in Frank's car had been busted for months. He'd almost nodded off when the strikingly beautiful Catherine Lesko finally exited the main doors of her office building and strolled through the shimmering afternoon heat toward a gray BMW. After an almost imperceptible glance around, she opened the door and got in. Frank slouched behind the wheel.

Lesko hadn't shown up again at Child Connect. After days of dead ends and wasted phone calls he'd finally located her, at a well-heeled private practice downtown. Out of the corner of his eye he watched as she started the car and drove off. He started his own and followed at a safe distance. They drove for about twenty minutes, to an upscale but undistinguished low-rise in the back streets of the West End.

She parked on the street and entered the building. Frank found a sheltered spot with a view of the front door and parked. A few minutes later, the curtains fluttered in the window of a second floor apartment. He looked up just in time to catch a glimpse of Lesko.

He sat and waited. He was probably wasting his time, but you never knew. He'd been through the drill. Experience had taught him the technique of half-daydreaming, half-sleeping, while at the same time paying fleeting attention to a surveillance target.

As he waited, he considered how long he was willing to sit there before giving up. One hour, two, three…definitely no more than three. Chances were good that she was in for the long haul and wouldn't be leaving until morning.

An hour later his eye caught a movement in the target apartment. He sat up, rubbed the knot of pain in his back, and focused his attention on the window. One of the curtains swayed slightly. He shifted his gaze to the main doors of the building.

To his surprise, a few minutes later Catherine Lesko appeared, having changed her clothes. Once again he slouched behind the wheel. She glanced around before getting into her car, but didn't notice him. Was she up to something, he thought, or just a beautiful woman being careful in a dangerous world?

Her car pulled out and again he followed. She crossed the Burrard Street Bridge and headed west. As they drove, the opulence of their surroundings steadily grew. Featureless middle-class homes transformed into spacious upper-class ones, then into mansions, as they climbed a hill with a stunning vista of English Bay. They turned onto an expansive boulevard lined with giant Catalpa trees that arched over the roadway like the vaulting ribs of some massive cathedral.

They penetrated deep into the wealthiest section of Point Grey, past gated properties surrounded by impenetrable walls and hedges. The most expensive homes, he considered, were the ones you never actually saw; they were concealed behind forbidding barriers, securely hidden from the view of the peasants below.

It got more and more difficult to maintain his view of Lesko's car and still blend in with his surroundings. It was the dinner hour; there wasn't much traffic in this part of town, and he guessed that not many folks in this neighbourhood drove a nineteen eighty-nine Ford Topaz. He was forced to hang way back, which made it tough to maintain visual contact.

It was more important not to be spotted than to keep following. He was about to give up when she slowed, and finally stopped in front of a massive wrought-iron gate set in an impressive three-meter hedge that completely obscured the interior.

He kept driving and parked on the slope of a nearby hill. In the distance, beyond the massive hedge, the slate-tiled vaults of a magnificent mansion rose like a mountain range above the treetops. Far beyond, tiny sailboats dotted the white-tipped waters of English Bay.

The gate guarding the entrance opened, and Lesko drove inside. Frank waited for half an hour. There was nothing. He couldn't stay where he was without arousing suspicion. He finally gave up and drove home.

He continued the surveillance for a couple of weeks, alternating between Lesko and another woman who visited the mansion, though only once. He convinced Art Crawford to run the second woman's license plate, and learned that her name was Madeline Lyon. Her profession was listed as 'Gynecologist'.

Both Lesko and Lyon showed a similar pattern: a quick stop at a nondescript apartment – Lyon's was in Yaletown – followed by a drive to a far more prestigious location – Lyon's regular stop was another magnificent mansion in the heart of one of the wealthiest neighbourhoods in Vancouver, the British Properties. The trips didn't happen every night, but frequently, more often than not. On a hunch he staked out the women's apartments the morning after their visits. Both showed up just after sunrise, changed clothes, and went to work.

He researched the two women, looking for any connection to Kaffir. It turned out that Catherine Lesko got her Ph.D. on a scholarship from Kaffir, and Madeline Lyon rented an office owned by a company controlled by Kaffir. He watched the comings and goings to both mansions, and noticed several other regular visitors, all of them women.

He followed a couple of them home and then to work. One was a lab technician at a research company in which Kaffir had a significant stake. The other was the first he'd come across with no clear connection to Kaffir.

She worked for Statistics Canada.

At the same time, he researched the ownership of the Point Grey mansion. It was officially owned by a numbered company out of Hong Kong. After hours of meticulous navigation through a labyrinthine maze of companies, subsidiaries, and subsidiaries of subsidiaries, multiple long-distance calls, and the conning of several government officials, he eventually settled on a reclusive financier named Arthur Dogan.

It was tough to find anything on Dogan. The man's public persona was a blank slate. It was unclear what he did and what his affiliations were. He had no known connection to organized crime or any other illegal activity. He was rarely seen in public, either at social functions or in business gatherings.

Frank couldn't find any direct connection between Dogan and Kaffir, though he did find indirect references to social connections like golf games with Kaffir board members.

Frank thought again about the unusual behaviour of Catherine Lesko and Madeline Lyon.

Why? he thought. *If the women are going to live there, why not just live there?*

The next afternoon Frank followed Catherine Lesko again to the mansion in Point Grey. Once she entered, he drove along the massive hedge, hunting for a weakness. He found what he was looking for – a scalable section conveniently distant from the front gate and the gatehouse. Satisfied, he back-tracked, found a nearby coffee shop and sat for a couple of hours, waiting for nightfall.

What he was planning was insane; it could land him in jail, or worse. He'd thought about it a lot and couldn't come up with an alternative. If he was still a cop he'd have the authority and resources to gather more information about what went on inside the mansion. Alone he was basically powerless to find out much more than he already knew.

He'd considered trying to gain access legally, maybe disguised as a tradesman or a delivery person, but the stakes were too high. He still didn't know much about the people on the other side of that hedge, but what he did know scared him. If they saw through his disguise…

He nervously downed cups of coffee until it was dark, then drove his car to a side-street not far from the spot he'd chosen earlier, parked, and started walking.

The hedge turned out to be harder to climb than he was expecting. He had trouble even finding the right spot again in the dark. The branches were thin, and bent back when he applied his weight. They also had spines – a detail he hadn't noticed before. His hands were red and bleeding as he dragged his way upwards.

He was about half-way to the top when he heard the grating sound of the front gate opening in the distance. Twin beams of light tracked through the trees as a vehicle steered out of the driveway and onto the road.

Frank was clinging to the hedge in full view of the roadway, too far up to jump to the ground. He climbed down as quickly as he dared, scraping his knuckles and stabbing his fingers on the spines. He'd just reached jumping height when the car turned the corner and two blinding beams of light played over him.

He froze, hoping the driver might not see him, but his hopes were crushed when the car pulled over and skidded to a stop. He jumped to the ground and landed heavily, twisting his ankle. Cursing, he limped toward his car, followed by the pounding of running feet. He dove into some thick brush, hoping he could lose his pursuer in the dark. Hammering footfalls flew by him and continued into the distance. Somehow, he stumbled onto a path in the darkness and headed for his car.

As he reached it, the footsteps once again got louder. He stopped for a second and stared behind him, but could see no one. He fumbled the keys out of his pocket and bent down to find the door lock. He'd just inserted the key when there was an explosion at the back of his skull and everything went black.

☼

He awoke in total darkness. He tried to move but both his hands and feet were tied. Something rigid and uneven dug painfully into his back. The space reeked of dust and motor oil. When he tried to lift his head, it hit something metal and hard. He gathered that he was in the trunk of a car – probably his own.

The blackness pressed down, choking him, like he was being crushed at the bottom of the sea. His breath came in accelerating gasps. His gut twisted with a sick foreboding and his heart hammered in his chest. It was coming…

Drawing on every iota of his will, he fought for control, fought to wrench his psyche out of its deadly trajectory. To his surprise, he had some success; the panic attack subsided – at least for now. He tried to free his hands, but they were bound too tightly. He heard footsteps around the vehicle.

A few minutes later the trunk opened. On a hunch he faked unconsciousness. A pair of hands lifted him easily out of the trunk and dropped him heavily on the ground.

Frank continued his charade. The act must have been convincing; his attacker leaned down and listened for a heartbeat. Satisfied that

Frank was still alive, the man carried him to the front of the car, shoved him roughly into the driver's seat, wedged his body into a sitting position, and started to untie his feet and hands.

Through the slits of barely open eyes Frank peered out the windshield far into the distance and saw the lights of dozens of ships floating in English Bay. As he tracked back toward the space in front of him, the lights abruptly disappeared.

Suddenly he knew where he was. Not far from where his car had been parked, towards the university, was a series of cliffs overlooking the bay, and a curving road that presented an ideal location for a faked 'accident'. Whoever was working so diligently to untie him was setting him up to die.

The kidnapper finished removing the ropes, leaned over and released the hand brake, then started to push the car, with the driver's side door open and one hand on the steering wheel. The car rolled slowly forward, the tires whispering over the long grass.

Frank came up with a plan and mentally rehearsed what he had to do. He would only have one chance to catch his attacker off guard. Satisfied, he sprang into action. He swiveled to face the open door, leaned back with his hands braced on the seat behind him, and kicked his assailant's torso with both feet. The man grunted and staggered backwards. He lost his grip on the steering wheel, but grabbed the door handle with his left hand and swung out, running alongside.

The car gained momentum as it rolled down an increasingly steep slope. The attacker was off-balance. He hung onto the now flapping door as he stumbled on the uneven ground trying to pull himself in.

They hit a bump and the door flew in almost shut. Frank hauled back again and hammered both feet against it with all his strength. The door exploded outward, taking the attacker with it, then sprang back on its hinges and slammed him against the car. He went down. Frank heard a scream and a sickening wet sound as the back tires rolled over something soft.

The car continued to accelerate and broke through the split-rail fence guarding the cliffs. The edge was seconds away. Frank lunged for the steering wheel. Saying a silent prayer, he hauled the wheel as hard as he could to the right. The car performed a sideways drift that slammed the still-open driver's door shut. A shower of gravel trickled over the cliff face.

Still coasting, the car didn't have enough speed to make it up the hill. Frank hauled on the wheel with one hand and frantically twisted the key with the other. The engine started and he stomped on the gas. The vehicle tore through the fence again and up the steep embankment, spraying a cloud of dirt and grass behind it. It finally came to rest on a level area not far from the road.

Frank sat shaking for several minutes. Finally, he got out and stumbled over to the motionless body of his attacker. The man lay on his back, a deep depression across his chest where the car had crushed him, a bloom of darkness spreading over his shirt. His staring dead eyes and pockmarked face were unfamiliar.

Frank rifled through the dead man's clothes looking for identification. In an inside jacket pocket, he found a wallet. It was too dark and too dangerous to check it now. If anyone had seen or heard anything

116

the cops could be there any minute. He shoved the wallet into his own coat pocket.

What would happen if the police connected him with the death? Many of his former colleagues still considered him mentally unstable. Would they believe his claim that the killing was in self-defense? What if Grant Stocker was in charge of the investigation? Was the Lead Detective's childish grudge against Frank so all-consuming that he'd try to pin a murder on him?

Then there was the body. He ventured to the brink over which he'd almost plunged, took a chance and flicked on his lighter. In the dim light the ground fell almost straight away, the steep slope collapsing into a thick clump of woods at the bottom.

The body was only a few meters from the edge. Fighting to control his shaking hands and the reflex of his gut, he rolled it to the edge and over, cringing at each bump it made on the way down. He couldn't tell whether it landed out of sight. Again, he risked flicking on his lighter and searched the ground for any evidence of the horror that had taken place. Other than the tire tracks there was nothing.

Exhausted and still shaking, he stumbled back to his car, the staring eyes of his assailant etched into his brain.

He fishtailed along Point Grey Road, barely conscious of where he was and what he was doing. He'd gone a few blocks when the crushing weight of terror struck suddenly, like a lightning bolt splitting his skull. The shaking returned, so violent this time that he couldn't handle the car. He spotted the parking lot for the beach at Spanish Banks. It was almost empty.

He skidded into the driveway and screeched to a stop in one of the parking spaces. The interior of the car was contracting, threatening to crush him. He threw the door open and staggered outside. The reality of what he'd done finally hit home. He doubled over and spilled his guts on the pavement, then straightened up and headed for the beach. The ocean pounded in the distance; the hiss of the surf drilled into his brain.

He stumbled across the sand, tripping over logs, falling and rising again, frantic to escape the terror that dogged his every move. As he climbed over a giant log he slipped on its spray-soaked surface, fell, hit his head, collapsed, and knew no more.

Sometime later a screeching sound woke him. He opened his eyes. It was almost light. A seagull was perched on the log beside him, cocking its head and staring down at him. He lay on his back in the sand, hidden behind the massive log.

It took a few seconds to remember where he was. He felt the pair of painful lumps on his head and checked his hand for blood. There was none. There were noises in the parking lot. He rose to his knees and peeked over the log. A homeless guy was hovering around his car, the only one in the lot. The man's shopping cart stood nearby. He leaned down and peered into the passenger's window.

Frank staggered to his feet and yelled, "Hey!"

The bearded man jumped back. He spotted Frank, grabbed his cart, and took off. Frank staggered to his car. The shaking had finally stopped. He fell into the driver's seat and limped home.

TWELVE

··

LAWRENCE RETIGO

F rank slept through most of the day. He neglected to set the alarm, but was so exhausted that for first time in almost a year he wasn't plagued by nightmares. Once or twice he was vaguely aware of the ring of his cell phone, but went back to sleep without answering it.

When he woke he felt like he'd been in a train wreck. His body ached with a brutal combination of strained muscles, scrapes, scratches, and bruises. His left ankle was stiff and swollen, and throbbed painfully. Slowly he remembered what had happened the night before, and once again had to stamp down a panic attack.

He'd killed a man. It had been in self-defense, but the man was no less dead. Though he'd been a police detective for many years, it was only the second time Frank had ever taken the life of another human being. He was still having trouble dealing with the first time.

He stumbled out of bed, showered, and dressed. Putting on his pants he felt for his wallet, and remembered the one he'd taken from his attacker. He grabbed his jacket, removed the wallet, and looked inside. It held a few hundred dollars in cash, one platinum VISA card, and a driver's license with his attacker's picture. The name on the cards meant nothing to him.

Stuck behind the cash was a slip of paper. He pulled it out. It was a photograph, the size of a passport photo. It wasn't his assailant. The man in the picture looked in his early thirties, thin, with longish ginger hair and a goatee. Frank turned it over. On the back were hand-written two names: 'Lawrence Retigo, Apartment 401 – 754 Newbury Place'. Lower down, almost as an afterthought, was written: 'Ricky Augustus, Mountain View Psychiatric Clinic'. Neither of the names meant anything to him. He placed the picture in his own wallet.

He turned on the TV, and was relieved to find nothing about the killing on the news. If the body had been found it might make it into the afternoon paper, which would be out any time. Nervous at home, he went for a walk, detouring to a coffee shop to grab a cup while he waited. He saw the paper delivered to the convenience store across the street and rushed out to buy one, dreading, against all logic, that he'd see his picture splashed across the front page.

Back at the coffee shop he rifled through the paper, searching for news of the death. Nothing. He was surprised and puzzled, but breathed a sigh of relief.

He scanned through a second time to double check. Again there was nothing, but a name in a small piece near the back caught his eye and floated unanchored in his memory for a few seconds. At first he wasn't sure what he'd seen. He had to re-read several articles before he located the name that had drawn his attention: 'Lawrence Retigo'. He pulled out his wallet and checked the back of the photograph from his assailant. The names matched.

He read the article:

Local Reporter Dead

A man killed in a tragic car accident last Tuesday has now been identified. Lawrence Retigo, a reporter for the community newspaper 'CityLine' died when his car crashed through a guard-rail on Highway One and rolled several times down an embankment before bursting into flames. Retigo's dental records had to be used for identification. The cause of the accident is still under investigation, but no foul play is suspected at this time. Speed and alcohol are believed to be involved.

Mr. Retigo was well-known in journalistic circles and had been a fixture at CityLine for more than five years, primarily covering local events and human-interest stories. His editor, Harold Rawlings, said of Retigo: 'He was an able journalist who was well-liked by his peers – he will be sorely missed'.

It occurred to Frank that there was something familiar about Retigo's address. He racked his brain for an answer and when one finally came, the hair at the back of his neck stood on end.

☼

Frank was stretching his goodwill with Art Crawford to the limit, but he convinced his friend to check out the VISA card and driver's license Frank had removed from his attacker's body.

He spent a gut-wrenching morning the next day waiting for the result, knowing he risked being implicated in a murder.

"Nothing," Art said when he finally contacted Frank. "As far as I can make out, both the credit card and driver's license are bogus."

"As for the other thing," Art said, "yeah, a body was found out near the university. They're investigating. What the hell are you mixed up in, Frank?"

"Don't worry about it," Frank said. "Thanks, Art. I owe you big time."

He searched the web for a picture of Retigo and eventually found one. It confirmed that Retigo was the man in the photograph from his assailant's wallet.

But who was the other name – Ricky Augustus?

☼

The next day, Frank tensed as Rebecca got up from her desk to study the bruises and scrapes on his face.

"What happened to you?" she asked. "Not another bar fight."

When he'd answered the phone that afternoon, she said she'd been calling him for a day and a half, worried that something had happened. He'd chewed her out for breaking their agreement and using the phone.

Now he cursed himself for agreeing to come to see her.

He smiled. "My bar fighting days are over – I hope."

"Come on Frank, what's going on?"

"I think I had a run in with somebody from Kaffir."

He told her about following Catherine Lesko, staking out the mansion and about the man attacking him. He didn't mention that he'd tried to break in, that his attacker had tried to stage his death, the man's wallet, the photograph, Lawrence Retigo, or most importantly, that he'd killed somebody.

"So, someone caught you sneaking around outside the mansion and attacked you," Rebecca said. "You sure you didn't just get mugged?"

"In Point Grey? Anyway, I think I'd know the difference."

"Did he say anything?"

Frank shook his head.

"What happened to the guy?"

Shit, he thought. *I've opened a can of worms now.*

"He took off," he lied.

Rebecca stared at him.

"You don't believe me," he said.

"It just seems far-fetched. What you'd expect them to do is call the police. What are you doing creeping around somebody else's property anyway – especially in that neighbourhood. You're going to wind up in jail again. The cops might not be so sympathetic next time."

He realized that if he said any more he'd be forced to tell her everything. His first thought had been that by telling her he'd impress on her the level of danger facing them. He hadn't thought about how she'd react.

"Anyway, how does it involve Kaffir?" she said. "Some billionaire's security guy works you over. Pretty heavy-handed, but I don't see the tie-in with Kaffir."

"You're right," Frank said. He decided not to mention the relationships he'd found between the women he'd been following, Kaffir and Arthur Dogan. "There's nothing to say Kaffir had anything to do with it. I'm over-reacting."

Again she eyed him strangely. "Aren't you going to the police?"

"So they can arrest me for loitering?"

"There's something you're not telling me."

Frank waved a hand dismissively. "Forget it. It's nothing. I shouldn't have mentioned it. You're right; it was probably just some gung-ho security guy."

She stared at him for a few seconds, unconvinced.

Finally she said, "You look terrible, Frank. Maybe it's time to take a breather."

His fingers dug into the arms of the chair.

"Remember our deal," she said.

He calmed himself. "I hope you're not going to invoke 'the deal' every time we hit the slightest snag…"

"The slightest snag? Have you looked at yourself in the mirror?"

"Look, everything's fine. I just don't want to talk to the cops. They figure I've lost it as it is. They'd just think I was delusional." As the words escaped his lips, a thought occurred to him: Rebecca might think he was delusional too. He put the thought aside.

He realized that just by being here he was putting Rebecca in danger.

THIRTEEN

....

THE BAD SIDE OF TOWN

C ityLine News occupied the bottom floor of a crumbling brick building at an address perilously close to the Downtown Eastside, the poorest and most infamous neighbourhood in Vancouver, where the hollow-eyed, skeletal frames of junkies shuffled along the sidewalks, and discarded condoms and syringes littered the alleyways. CityLine had the look of a business that was barely staying afloat.

Frank pushed open the graffiti-plastered front door, walked down a short hallway, and ended up in a dingy reception area.

"I've got an appointment with Harold Rawlings," he said to the black-clad and heavily pierced girl behind the desk.

"Just a sec," she said, chewing on her gum. She pressed a button on an antiquated intercom.

"Mister Rawlings, a Mister..." she let go of the button and looked up at Frank.

"Detective," Frank corrected her. "Detective Frank Langer. I called earlier."

"Oh, yeah," she said. "About Larry."

She pressed a button again. "A Detective Langer to see you."

"Send him in," crackled a voice at the other end.

The girl nodded towards a hallway on Frank's right. "First door on the left."

Rawlings' office was a disaster, his desktop obscured by stacks of paper, the drawers of the filing cabinets blocked half open by bulging folders stuffed into them.

Rawlings looked in his fifties. His gray hair was mostly gone on top. He wore what was left of a suit – that is, the pants, a dress shirt, and a tie loosened so it hung ludicrously below his unbuttoned shirt collar.

They shook hands, and Rawlings directed Frank to have a seat.

"You know, I talked to the cops already," Rawlings said, taking a seat himself behind his desk.

Frank tensed. "Yeah, I'm aware of that." He winged it. "Some new information has come up that might have a bearing on the case." He leaned forward. "There are indications that Lawrence Retigo's death may not have been an accident."

Rawlings sat up straight in his chair and his eyes opened wide. "What the hell would make you think that?"

"I'm not at liberty to reveal anything at this point," Frank said. "I'd just like to know if Retigo was working on anything that might have gotten him killed."

Rawlings threw back his head and laughed. "Lawrence Retigo?" He wiped his eyes on his sleeve and shook his head. "Sorry, I don't mean to be insensitive. Not to speak ill of the dead, but Larry wasn't exactly our star reporter. He covered stories like the woman with a potato chip shaped like Elvis's profile, or the guy who could eat a hundred hot-dogs in one sitting."

"He was never given any bigger assignments?"

Rawlings shook his head. "He was always a bit of an oddball. But he really started to go strange a couple of months ago – even for him. Losing it, you know? I was actually on the verge of letting him go. I kept him on mostly out of sympathy, hoping maybe he'd get his act together. Well, now it's out of my hands."

"Losing it how?"

"He jumped at the slightest sound. Kept the blinds beside his desk shut tight all the time. More than once I saw him peeking through the slats, like he was looking for somebody. Sometimes he'd take off in the middle of the day and not say where he was going."

"There wasn't anything he was working on that stands out – that could have made him a target?"

Rawlings shrugged. "Lately he was always hunkered down working at something, even when I hadn't assigned him any stories. Larry always took his job pretty seriously. You'd think he was covering the moon landing instead of a cat stuck in a tree. But lately he got real serious – way worse than before. I asked him a couple of times what was going on, but he wouldn't say.

"Anyway, you never know when some harebrained idea might turn out to be something. I didn't see any harm in it – maybe I was wrong."

"Anybody around the office he might have confided in?"

"He wasn't tight with anybody here, especially lately. Everybody avoided him like the plague. He was too out there…"

"What about friends, or girlfriends?"

"I think he had a sort of on-again, off-again relationship with some girl named Grace. I don't think it was all that serious. I never met her, but I might still have her name and address somewhere. He gave her as his next of kin – how pathetic is that? I can find it for you if you want."

"I'd appreciate that."

Rawlings fought to pry open one of the drawers of the filing cabinet, hauling out sheaves of paper in the process and tossing them on top of the already large stack on his desk. Frank smiled, trying to imagine the man's filing system.

With surprising speed, Rawlings snapped out a sheet of paper and copied something from it to a post-it note. He handed the note to Frank. "I don't know how current this is – she might not still be there. Anyway, that's all I've got."

"Great," Frank said. He rose from his chair, stuffed the note into his wallet, and turned to leave.

"That's it?" Rawlings said.

Frank nodded. "For now."

"By the way," Rawlings said as Frank reached the door. "Aren't you guys supposed to show your badges before you interview somebody?"

Frank's throat tightened as he looked Rawlings in the eye. "You want to see my badge?" he asked. He made as if to reach into his jacket pocket. There were a few seconds of strained silence.

"N...No," Rawlings finally spoke. "I guess that won't be necessary."

☼

Detective Frank Langer's approach to an investigation was a lot like that of an artist to his work of art. Like a painter facing an empty canvas, Frank started with nothing, with zero knowledge about the new case. As the painter added brush-strokes until the finished work matched the image in his imagination, Frank pieced together bits of information until they coalesced into something real.

But while an artist imposed his own vision on the medium in which he worked, it was Frank's job to allow the information he'd gathered to drive the investigation, to impose some form upon his mind. He maintained a holistic, unbiased impression that transformed itself like a Rubik's cube as important pieces of the puzzle surfaced.

And while the artist typically defined the largest areas of a piece at the beginning, gradually refining the image into greater detail, in Frank's work tiny details that weren't in themselves important, but lent colour to the investigation, drifted in continuously, while profound revelations that completely altered the direction of the case could come at any time.

Frank's gut told him that one of those revelations had fallen in his lap when he'd taken his assailant's wallet. He opened his notebook and re-read Retigo's address on Newbury Place, in a rundown section of the West End. He didn't really need to check the address. As it happened, he'd parked next to Retigo's building several times before.

Lawrence Retigo lived across the street from Catherine Lesko.

☼

On the phone Retigo's ex-girlfriend, Grace Hatcher, had sounded nervous and suspicious, but when Frank told her that some questions had been raised about Retigo's death, she reluctantly agreed to meet with him. She insisted on someplace public. They settled on a Blenz on Robson Street.

Frank got there early and staked out a quiet table in the corner. The place wasn't busy; they weren't likely to be disturbed.

"I'm a little overweight," she'd admitted as she gave a description so he'd recognize her.

That's an understatement, he thought when she walked in and introduced herself. Her appearance was deeply at odds with her name. She wasn't a very attractive girl – obese, with frizzy black hair like steel wool and freckles that would look cute on some girls but for some reason didn't on her.

She wore a tank top and skin-tight Capri pants that emphasized her bulges in all the wrong places. Conspicuous on her right wrist was a charm bracelet with a jumbled mass of figures that jingled whenever she moved her arm.

After his experience with Rawlings, Frank didn't want to take any chances. He brought the fake but realistic-looking police badge he'd gotten as a gag gift at one of the parties at the squad. He was glad he did; she asked to see his badge first thing and his quick flash of the fake was enough to convince her.

Frank ordered her a coffee and a blueberry muffin and they sat down to chat.

"You look kind of beaten up for a cop," she said as she dumped three packets of sugar into her coffee.

Frank tensed. He decided to take the offensive. "We're not here to talk about me. We can have this conversation down at the station if you want."

A panicked expression swept across her face.

She's got something to hide, Frank thought. *Good.*

"Relax," he said. "I don't care what you're into. I just want to know about Lawrence Retigo."

She sat back in her chair.

"Larry and I were never that close," she said, her hands wrapped around her coffee cup. "He was just somebody to hang out with."

"How often did you see him?"

"We spent a lot of time together when we first met." She smiled. "He was fun then, always laughing and making jokes. We had some laughs."

"There was nothing strange about him?"

"Strange how?"

"You tell me."

"Well, I was kind of creeped-out by some of his 'preferences' in bed. I won't go into detail – let's just say there was lots of rope and plastic sheeting involved. I never dreamed I'd be going to Home Depot for marital aids."

Her bracelet jingled as she brushed a strand of hair behind her ear. "I could handle that, but a few months ago things changed."

"Changed?" Frank said.

She took a big bite out of her muffin. "He turned into some kind of paranoid dick-wad. Said he was onto some big story that would make us both rich, but he'd never tell me what it was. I started seeing him less and less, and when I did he wasn't the same guy from before. It was like he wasn't there – like he was always someplace else.

"He'd jump at the slightest noise. He'd stare at people on the street. He kept saying we were being tailed. He'd go through these weird maneuvers in and out of back doors and down alleyways, so nobody could follow."

"Did you ever see anybody?"

She shook her head. "It was like something horrible was chasing him, but if it was there I never saw it. I kept asking what was going on but he said if I knew, my life would be in danger. I told him he should give up on the story – that it was affecting his mind, but he said it was too late – he was in too deep. One of my girlfriends told me she thought he was crazy. I started thinking maybe she was right."

"He ever talk about a woman who lived on his street?"

"Woman?"

"A woman living in the apartment building across the street from him."

She scrunched up her nose. "He never talked 'threesome' if that's what you're implying."

Frank changed the subject. "When did you see him last?"

"I never saw him for ages, then finally we met two or three weeks ago, but he hardly talked to me. He got freaked out about something and said he had to leave – he'd forgotten something he had to do. Good riddance, I thought by that time."

"And that was the last time he contacted you?"

"He called me on my cell phone about a week and a half ago. I had it turned off, but he left a message."

"You still got it?"

She scowled at him. "Don't you need a warrant or something for that?"

"You've been watching too much TV. We can always go downtown…"

She stiffened. "Okay…" She fished through her suitcase-sized purse and hauled out a pink flip-phone.

"There's nothing bad in it anyway," she said.

She punched a few of the keys, then handed the phone to Frank. He held it with his chin as he listened to the message and made notes. He handed the phone back to her.

"By the way," he said, "you got keys to Larry's apartment?"

"Yeah."

"I need to take a look around."

"Can't you get it from the manager or something?"

Frank swallowed. He could feel the sweat rising under his shirt. "I talked to him already," he said. "Larry had a special lock installed. We don't want to have to break down the door."

She looked like she was about to complain again, but then said. "I guess. He's dead now, what's it matter?"

She dug through the voluminous purse for the keys and gave them to Frank, then stood up and slung the purse over her shoulder. "I gotta get ready for work."

"I'll get the keys back to you in a few days," he said as she turned to go.

She headed for the door.

"Hey," he called after her.

She turned back to face him.

"Do me a favour," he said.

"What?"

"Don't erase that phone message till I see you again."

FOURTEEN

··

A SECRET REVEALED

R ebecca would say he was paranoid, but a little voice in Frank's
head told him that, based on what he'd uncovered so far, whoever he was dealing with had to be very rich, very intelligent,
very methodical, and probably very dangerous.

He shuddered as he thought about the call he'd gotten from Art
Crawford that morning. The investigation of the body at the university
had suddenly been curtailed and the death ruled accidental. No medical
examiner in their right mind would come to that conclusion.

He approached Retigo's apartment complex warily, strolling along
on the other side of the street, scanning the surrounding buildings.
When he was close enough, he stole a glance at Catherine Lesko's window. The curtains were almost completely drawn and there was no sign
of movement through the tiny gap that remained. He was about to look
away when the curtains swayed slightly. His stress level ratcheted up a
notch.

On life's cruel wheel I have been broken
Still I wield the key of my final love token

The lines kept replaying in Frank's head. They were the last thing Retigo had said to Grace in his final phone message, after several minutes of raving about Satan and his disciples. Looking back, there had been a distinctive tone to those lines – like Retigo had surfaced in a momentary flash of reason from the cataclysm of his unraveling mind.

Retigo had stopped mid-sentence – like he was waking from a dream. Frank's gut told him that there was a purpose to the fragment; that it really meant something.

He crossed the street and strode to the entrance like he belonged there. The building wasn't much – unattractive seventies-era with a cheap-looking brick façade. He fiddled with Retigo's keys and found the one for the outside door. There was threadbare carpeting in the lobby, and peeling beige paint on the walls.

He took the stairs up, thinking he'd be less likely to run into anybody. On the second floor, he opened the fire door a crack and peered in both directions down the hallway. It was empty.

He pushed the door open and cringed as it squeaked loudly. The place reeked of mold and the grease of people's cooking. The elevator was beside him. For now, it was silent. At Retigo's door he gave one last glance in each direction. He was alone in the corridor.

Frank smiled. He'd been right about the locks. There were three massive deadbolts - definitely not standard issue. His hands shook as he worked out which key was which. He unlocked the door and pushed it open carefully, remembering the fire door, but it didn't make a sound. He slipped inside and gently closed it behind him. The apartment was old and tired, like the rest of the building, with aging shag carpeting and dated fixtures. A steel security bar leaned against the wall beside the door.

The living room, dining room, and kitchen were open concept – there were no walls. Interior design wasn't Retigo's strong suit; a single couch that looked like it had been hauled out of a dumpster was the sole piece of furniture in the living room. A tiny CRT TV sat on a cardboard box next to it. Bedsheets were draped over the curtain rods to cover the windows. The bottoms of the sheets had been thumb-tacked to the wall. Retigo had been on the edge.

A dull light still filtered into the room. A few curl-edged posters dotted the walls, most depicting big news stories: 9/11, the Berlin wall coming down, the first moon landing. Stories that Retigo probably wished he had covered.

A fifties-era chrome table stood in the dining room, with a single chair; Retigo didn't get much company. On the table was one of the things Frank was most interested in examining – Retigo's aging laptop. He would come back to that after he'd had a look around.

Down a short hallway was the single bathroom and single bedroom. The bedroom floor was covered with clothes. In the middle of the pile was an overturned Coke bottle. Frank kicked at one of the socks lying beside the bottle; it was as solid as cardboard – the spilled Coke had soaked into everything and hardened. He checked under the bed and in the closet but found nothing of interest.

Back in the living area he had a quick look in the kitchen. The fridge was almost empty, and what little was there was junk – Coke, rotting cheap salami, cakes that probably didn't need to be in the fridge, since they contained no real food value and would never go bad. All in all, the place bore a disturbing similarity to Frank's own.

He came back to the laptop. A paper plate with a moldy half-eaten slice of pizza lay beside it. He sat down and pushed the power button. The inane 'Windows' musical intro blasted forth as it started up.

"Shit," he whispered as he tried to cover the speakers with his hands. As soon as it was booted he muted the sound system.

He spent half an hour scouring the files. There were notes from bland stories about flower shows and Miss Whatever pageants, but nothing about the story Retigo had thought was so important.

Disappointed, Frank did one last sweep of the apartment. Nothing. The absence of material itself was disturbing. Retigo had been working on a story 'that would make us both rich'. How could it be that there wasn't a shred of evidence the story ever existed. Either Retigo was so paranoid he didn't dare keep any information here, or someone had beaten Frank to it and cleaned it out. After all, Catherine Lesko was just across the street.

He finally gave up and got ready to leave. He considered taking the computer, but in the end decided against it. He'd found everything he was likely to find. He'd already committed a B & E; no point in adding theft to the mix.

He tip-toed to the door and peered through the peep-hole. The hallway in front of him was clear. He was about to turn the handle when he heard the elevator door open in the distance. Soon the distorted fisheye image of someone approaching appeared in the peep-hole. As he continued to watch his spine stiffened. It was Catherine Lesko.

On reaching his position she stopped, stood in front of the door, and sniffed at the air.

Shit, shit, shit! He thought.

She stepped toward the door and his heart was in his throat as she placed her hands against it and bent her head to look through the peephole from the other side. He didn't dare move away – she would see the shadow of his movement.

His heart thumping, he leaned sideways and angled his head away. He held his breath and froze, listening as she shifted positions inches away on the other side of the door, watching the faint shadow of her movement in the glass bulb of the peep-hole.

After a minute of tense silence, he heard her fishing through her purse, and heard the jingling of a set of keys. He panicked, trying to decide whether to run and hide or stay and be caught.

He was about to turn and hunt for a hiding place when a chime issued from Lesko's purse – her cell phone. Frank took a chance, straightened up, and peered through the peep-hole. Lesko was standing with her back to the door whispering, with the phone against her ear.

She stood for a few seconds and he heard a muffled jingle as she slid the keys back in her purse. He waited with his heart hammering in his chest. She turned and strolled toward the elevator, still talking on the phone. Frank exhaled deeply as her voice was extinguished by the faint thunk of the elevator door.

Still shaking, he rushed from the room. He carefully opened the squeaking door to the stairwell and waited on the landing, allowing time for Lesko to leave the building, before heading down and back outside.

As he walked out the front door, he snuck another glance at Catherine Lesko's window. Once again the curtains fluttered.

He licked his parched lips. Suddenly he had the overpowering urge for a drink. He clenched his fists and steeled himself against the onslaught. After several minutes he won the battle, at least for now. He willed himself to relax and headed for his car.

His image of Retigo was coming into focus. A loner, a paranoid loser, drawn into something way over his head, crippled with terror, whether of something real or from his disturbed imagination. Suicidal? For some reason Frank didn't think so.

Analyzing his new understanding of how Retigo ticked, Frank decided it wasn't all that surprising he'd found no evidence in the reporter's apartment.

It was possible, even likely, that Catherine Lesko, or one or more of her cohorts, had swept the apartment, and the computer, clean of anything that could link them to Retigo. But Frank guessed that they wouldn't have found much. Anyone with Retigo's depth of paranoia wouldn't leave evidence lying around; he would devise a hiding place as convoluted as the escape patterns he followed to elude his invisible pursuers.

And only one connection remained, however thin, between Lawrence Retigo and objective reality.

"Did Larry give you many presents?" Frank asked Grace Hatcher the next day. He'd convinced her to meet him once more, using the excuse of giving back Retigo's keys, and claiming that there were some loose ends that needed tying up.

They sat on the patio of a sidewalk café on Denman Street. The sun was out. Traffic was light, and strollers already crowded the beach to the west.

"Presents?" she laughed, "like as in 'things for free'? Larry's idea of generous was springing for a large fries at McDonald's."

She fidgeted with her cell phone, and declined his offer to buy her another coffee and muffin.

"I gotta get to work," she said.

She pushed back her chair. Frank put a hand on her sleeve. "Look, just bear with me this one last time and I won't bug you again."

She rolled her eyes and stuffed the phone in her purse. He bought her a coffee. At first she sat on the edge of her chair, ready to bolt. Resigned, she sat back and reached for her cup.

"He did give me a little wooden jewelry box the last time I saw him," she answered him. "I thought it was weird because it was so out of character."

"Anything else?"

"I don't know – a picture of us together…"

"He talks about a 'love token'."

Grace gave him a puzzled look.

"At the end of his phone message," Frank said. "He says: 'I wield the key of my final love token'. Is there anything he gave you that might fit that description?"

"Love token?" she repeated, scrunching up her nose. "I don't know… I figured he was just out of it."

142

She hauled her purse up on the table and started to rummage though it – for a smoke, Frank assumed. Her ungainly charm bracelet jingled as she plunged her right hand in and sorted through the numerous pouches.

Frank watched the rhythmic motion of the charms as her hand moved in and out of the purse – a jeweled heart, a golden star, a miniature house; then, a key – a tiny silver key. He focused in on the charm. It seemed out of place somehow, plated more crudely than the other charms. In fact, it looked for all the world like a real key, with a simple tooth-structure, but…

The hand with the bracelet finally located a pack of Export Menthols, and removed one.

"You mind?" she said, nodding at the cigarette.

"Sure," Frank said. "I'll join you."

They walked an acceptable distance away from the tables.

"Did Larry give you that bracelet?" Frank said as he lit her cigarette.

"What?"

She paused, blowing out a puff of smoke.

"The bracelet?" she took another drag on the cigarette. "Well…yeah, I guess he did. I forgot about that. I guess it slipped my mind because he gave it to me the same time as the jewelry box." She laughed. "Two presents at once – talk about out of character."

She slid the strap of her gigantic purse off her shoulder and set the bag on the ground. As she bent down, her head tilted and her hair fell back, exposing the bare skin of her neck where it met her shoulder. Frank stared, stiffening and clenching his fists at his sides. He couldn't breathe. Beads of sweat formed on his forehead.

She straightened and stared at him. "What's with you?"

"What?"

"You're shaking."

"It's nothing. It'll pass."

She eyed him suspiciously. "Well, just give me the keys – I gotta get going."

Frank fought to calm himself. "I need to see that jewelry box."

Her eyes widened. "No fuckin' way. What's your problem? I don't think you're a real cop..."

He reached out, grabbed her hand and squeezed. "You know why we're suddenly so interested in Larry?"

She winced in pain and tried to pull away, but he squeezed harder and held her in place. "New evidence has come along suggesting that your boyfriend was murdered."

Her eyes went wide. She scanned the street for an escape route.

"Larry was worried your life might be in danger," He twisted her arm and she turned back to face him. "Maybe he was right. Let us investigate and maybe it'll all go away."

"What do you want with it?" she said weakly.

"I just want to look at it, that's all."

☼

Frank sat on the threadbare Ikea sofa in Grace Hatcher's living room as she disappeared into the bedroom. She'd made him leave the front door open, and he promised to go as soon as he'd seen the box.

She returned in a few minutes and handed it to Frank.

144

"I took the jewelry out," she said.

"No problem," he said.

He stood up and turned the box over in his hands. It was rectangular, about ten by fifteen centimeters, inlaid with angular patterns of light and dark wood. It was nothing special, but definitely not junk. Frank traced his finger around the herringbone pattern that decorated the bottom. About halfway along one side he found a hole, difficult to see because it blended so well with the surrounding pattern.

"Ever notice this?" he said, pointing at the hole.

Grace bent down to inspect the box.

"No," she said. "I guess I never looked at it that close. What is it?"

"Larry never said anything about the box having a compartment?"

"Not that I remember," she stared at the tiny hole in the base. "He was pretty out of it. I remember him saying something about always keeping it with me – 'Never let it go', I think he said. I thought he was just being poetic."

"Have a look at your bracelet."

She held the bracelet up and sorted through the charms.

"A key…" she said.

"Let's see it for a minute."

She stared at him. He stared back and made a 'come hither' motion with his hand.

She undid the clasp and handed him the bracelet. He fiddled with it, trying to separate the tiny key from the other charms. He finally succeeded, grasped the key with his fingers, and inserted it into the hole in the box. It fit perfectly. He turned it gently. With a faint click a tiny wooden drawer popped out of the side. Grace gasped.

In the drawer were two items: a folded slip of paper and a flash drive.

He read the slip of paper. It contained only a few hand-written lines:

Grace,

If you read this message I'm probably dead. Under no circumstances are you to look at the documents on the flash drive. Reading them will put your life in danger. Give the drive to the police.

Larry

"What's it say?" she asked.

"I'm taking these," Frank said, holding up the paper and drive.

"Those are mine," she shouted, stepping toward him. "Larry gave them to me. You got no warrant or anything – you got no right..."

He held out the slip and let her read it. Her eyes bugged out of her head.

"But what is it?" she said. "You can't just take it..."

Frank shoved the slip and the flash drive in his shirt pocket, handed her the box and the bracelet, and headed for the door.

She chased him into the hallway, shouting. "Those are mine! Hey, I want to see your badge again, asshole! You're not a real cop!"

He ignored her and kept on walking.

"Well, screw you," she yelled after him. "Good riddance to both you bastards!"

FIFTEEN

....

REBECCA VISITS KAFFIR

Rebecca felt a stab of guilt the evening after her meeting with Frank, as she dialed his sister Janet's number. She was breaking her trust with him, and she'd sound like a fool, but she had to know. Either he'd been holding something back or outright lying to her. If that was the case, could she believe anything he said?

"I'm sorry, I don't have much time," Janet said. "We're meeting some people for dinner."

"I'm sorry for calling you out of the blue," Rebecca said. "Frank's been helping me look into Gloria's death. I'm a little concerned about whether he can handle it – psychologically. You probably know him better than anyone – what do you think?"

"He *was* a detective…" she answered. "A very good one too, from what I've heard. Has he done something you're worried about?"

"He seems fixated on this conspiracy angle, but he won't tell me anything about it."

"Oh," Janet said.

"What? Does that sound familiar?"

"Well... Frank did go on for a while about the force conspiring to get rid of him," she said. "But that was when he was still in the psych ward."

"Psych ward?"

"He was there for more than a month. He wasn't thinking straight. Dr. Sampson said the whole conspiracy thing was part of his... pathology."

Rebecca's chest tightened as she spoke. "I know this must seem like a stupid question, but remember the night when Frank first met Gloria over at your place?"

"Sure."

"He went in to look at Ralphie that night. He told me Ralphie had a couple of teeth coming in. Do you remember seeing them?"

"Teeth?" Janet said. "That's unusual for a baby that age, isn't it? No, I was outside the room when he was looking at Ralphie. But if Frank says he saw teeth..."

A jolt went up Rebecca's spine. "So - you never saw any teeth?"

"Well, no, but I never really looked that closely – there could have been..."

"You're sure about that? You didn't see any teeth?"

"No, I'm sorry."

"Thanks." Rebecca felt like a chain was tightening around her stomach. "I also wanted to ask you about his experience a year ago – the one he has nightmares about..."

The line was silent. "I'm sorry," Janet finally said. "If Frank doesn't want to talk about that I don't think it's my place..."

"I understand," Rebecca said, with a renewed sense of betrayal. "Thanks. Sorry for bothering you. I'd appreciate it if you didn't mention to Frank…"

"Of course," Janet said.

Rebecca hung up the phone. She'd always feared that Frank's theories were a house of cards. A stiff wind was shaking that house to its foundations.

☼

A few days later, Rebecca was apprehensive as she climbed the concrete staircase that swept like a terraced hillside around the man-made mountain that was the Kaffir Pharma building. People on either side of her rushed up and down like worker ants, entering and exiting the glass entranceway that wrapped the entire ground floor of the structure.

She hesitated at the top of the stairs, still unsure about her plan. She'd been shocked when her request to interview the VP of Research was immediately granted. With no credentials as a journalist, and no background in pharmaceuticals, she'd expected to be brushed off instantly. She should have been happy at her success, but for some reason it made her nervous.

Stalling, she studied the statistics on a plaque on the wall beside her. It celebrated the construction of the edifice that loomed above her head, one of the most important landmarks in the city.

A million metric tons of concrete. Thirty thousand kilometers of rebar. Twenty-five thousand square meters of glass. Ten thousand kilometers of copper wire and piping. Half a billion dollars, a million person-hours.

A thousand careers won and lost in the construction of this single edifice, all in pursuit of a vision pouring inexorably from the corporation she was about to risk gaining as an enemy.

She considered what Frank had said about the power behind the organization and shuddered. Then again, Frank said a lot of things.

She'd been caught up in Frank's version of reality, uncertain whether his theories were part of a delusion or statements of fact. His warning about Kaffir only made sense if his theories about a conspiracy were correct. Even then, the relationship between Catherine Lesko and Kaffir seemed tenuous at best. Maybe Lesko was psychotic, acting alone, following some deranged agenda.

Rebecca needed some kind of anchor – something to prove or disprove what Frank was saying. He'd be furious if he found out. Just the same, she pushed through the entrance doors and walked up to the semicircular marble reception desk.

She told the receptionist about her appointment, and after a few minutes' wait was escorted, through several layers of card-controlled security, to a foyer on the tenth floor. Her original escort waited discretely until a new one, wearing a white lab coat and different coloured security badge, took charge.

Her new escort led her through a secured door on their right and they stepped into a gigantic laboratory. Rebecca glanced around her. As she expected, it was spotlessly clean, tinged with a chemical, antiseptic smell.

Technicians in white coats sat on stools marching into the distance. They hunched over long white workbenches, fiddling with glassware formed into bizarre geometric shapes like ice sculptures, dropping test-tubes into machines for processing, dipping long glass pipettes into lattice-works of samples, examining computer screens or printouts, typing at their computers. The sounds of clinking glass mingled with the whir of centrifuges and the occasional chime from one of the machines.

Her escort led her to a single office in the far west corner of the expanse. Its walls were made entirely of glass – appropriate for the setting, she thought. Sitting behind the desk inside was a woman, also in a white lab coat.

A plain black and white name-plate beside the door read:

Dr. Carla De Leon
Vice President – Research

As they entered Rebecca glanced around the office, then studied the desk in front of her. Something about it was unusual. At first she couldn't recognize what it was.

Finally it dawned on her. Every object on it had been meticulously positioned. The pens and pencils were placed at exactly the same distance from each other, and though she had no way of measuring, her eye told her they were also lined up exactly in parallel with the edge of the desk itself. Others in a pen-holder were arranged by size and colour. She glanced around the room and noticed that the entire office was laid out with equal care.

The woman behind the desk looked up and noticed them at the door. She smiled and motioned with one hand and they entered. The escort introduced Rebecca and begged off.

Rebecca's research indicated that Carla De Leon had been with the Olmerol project for almost thirty years. In fact, she'd spent virtually her entire career studying the drug.

Dr. De Leon's age was listed as fifty-seven, but if Rebecca hadn't known she would have found it difficult to guess. The difficulty had nothing to do with cosmetics, either surgical or the drugstore kind. Dr. De Leon wasn't wearing any makeup, and had the aura of a woman who simply didn't think such things were important.

She had long chestnut hair parted on one side, which gave her a little-girl look incongruous with her age and prestigious position. Her hair didn't show any gray, and, in keeping with Rebecca's impression regarding makeup, didn't look like it had been coloured.

Dr. De Leon smiled as she stood and held out her hand.

Rebecca shook it. "Thanks for seeing me, Dr. De Leon. I know how busy you must be. Mr. Davis explained why I'm here?"

"Please call me Carla," De Leon said. She gestured toward a chair across from her and Rebecca sat down.

"Yes," she said once Rebecca was seated, "Mr. Davis explained your interest, but I should warn you – I'm a scientist, not a PR person."

Rebecca pulled a pocket recorder from her purse and set it on the desktop. "I'm writing a freelance article on drugs from the fifties. I'm planning to title it something like: 'Successes and Disasters'."

"And in which of those categories would you put Olmerol?" Carla asked, smiling.

Rebecca felt a flush of warmth on her cheeks. "Well, a success, of course," she said. "The idea is to compare disasters like Thalidomide with long-term successes like Olmerol. I'm most interested in what studies have been done on Olmerol, what side effects have been found, and Kaffir's strategy for dealing with them."

Carla casually laced her fingers together on the desk in front of her. "How did you come up with the idea?" she said.

"Idea?"

"The successes and disasters idea. I believe your background is in social work – not pharmaceuticals or obstetrics."

Rebecca hadn't expected the question. She sensed her host's eyes fixed on her as she fought for a plausible explanation. After Frank's warning, the last thing she wanted to do was mention Gloria. She glanced at her host and saw the tiniest hint of a smile on her face. She had the disturbing impression that De Leon already knew about her sister.

Rebecca laughed to cover her nervousness. "I'm branching out, trying something new. There's been a rash of pregnancies among my friends, and a couple of them mentioned taking Olmerol. I knew Olmerol and Thalidomide had been developed around the same time, and were prescribed for the same issues." She shrugged her shoulders. "It seemed like an interesting story. I was pre-med before I took up social work, so I have some background..."

Carla unlaced her fingers. "Which friends?" she asked.

"What?"

"Which friends were taking Olmerol?"

Rebecca's stomach tightened. Her host was looking at her expectantly. She was going to have to answer. She glanced down. Her nails
dug into the leather arms of her chair.

She willed herself to relax. "I don't think I'd be comfortable…"

"You don't have to answer," Carla's smile broadened. "I'm sorry,
I've put you on the spot. I just thought, as a friendly gesture, I could
arrange for some kind of discount."

"Oh," Rebecca said. She was relieved, though she wasn't sure she
bought Carla's explanation. "Thanks for the offer, but I think they're
past that phase."

"Are you working for anyone in particular?" Carla said.

Rebecca *had* anticipated this question, and several others Carla
asked regarding her background as a journalist, saying that this was her
first foray into journalism, and that she was simply hoping to shop the
article around. If Carla or anybody else at Kaffir were to dig into her
life, as they obviously had, the facts would fit.

"I'm sorry," Carla said, "you're supposed to be the one doing the
interviewing."

Rebecca relaxed a little. "I was expecting to find you in a more corporate setting," she said.

The tiny office was sparsely decorated. There were no pictures on
Carla's desk, and the one or two that hung on the wall were generic
Kaffir Pharma promo photographs, showing scientists and administra-
tors hard at work. Judging from the rest of the office, Rebecca guessed
that Carla had simply told the company to come up with something.

"I actually have another office on the floor above," Carla said, but I prefer to be down here, in the trenches. Research is my first love, and I still feel more comfortable here."

It took no more than a few minutes for Rebecca to grasp that Carla De Leon had a brilliant mind, and as she continued to interview the VP of Research, it became clear that Carla had a profound knowledge of Olmerol, though it must be a relatively minor drug in the company's inventory. She briefly described its history and development, the refinements they'd made over the years, and the hurdles they'd overcome.

Carla showed no hostility, or even resistance, toward studies suggesting that Olmerol might have negative side effects. She projected a simple desire to get at the truth, and possibly make improvements to the drug. She cheerfully provided Rebecca with references to more than a dozen studies on Olmerol.

After Frank's lecture about the threat of the organization, Rebecca had built up an image of its employees as an army of black-suited murdering psychopaths. That image couldn't have been farther from that of Carla De Leon. She was friendly, soft-spoken, even self-effacing, and dedicated to her work. In fact, her host's highly organized, no-nonsense persona was a welcome break from Frank's chaotic, conspiracy-obsessed world.

Buying into Frank's theories, Rebecca had been hoping to somehow maneuver the VP of Research into giving away incriminating information about the drug's side effects.

As she packed up the recorder and got up to leave, she had the unsettling feeling that if anything the opposite had occurred, that she was the one who'd said more than she intended.

She was turning for the door when Carla spoke. "We must go for coffee some time."

A jolt went up Rebecca's spine. It took a second for her to recover.

"Coffee?" was all she could think to say.

Carla quickly checked the smart phone on her desk. "I'm free on Tuesday at two PM."

Rebecca wondered what she'd gotten herself into. What was Carla playing at?

A badged escort appeared to take her back downstairs.

"The Boathouse on Kits Beach," Carla said.

Rebecca felt a knot in her stomach. The escort stood aside to clear the way for her. She considered her impression of Carla, a brilliant, thoughtful, unpretentious, not to mention powerful, woman. A woman she couldn't help but admire.

"I'm sorry," Carla said, "I've put you on the spot again. It's just that it's rare for me to find someone outside work, especially another woman, to talk to. I feel as though we have a connection. It would mean a lot…"

Rebecca was touched. Carla's eyes reflected a profound loneliness. Suddenly Rebecca felt a tinge of pity for her. In any case, she had to admit that as a fact-finding mission today's meeting had been a failure. Maybe she could do better next time.

"Alright?" Carla asked.

Rebecca smiled. "I look forward to it."

The escort led her out the door.

SIXTEEN

....

RETIGO'S JOURNAL

B ack at home after the blowout with Grace Hatcher, Frank plugged the flash drive into his computer. On it were two WORD documents – one very small, the other much larger.

He loaded the smaller document, *readthisfirst.doc*:

Lawrence Retigo – Reporter, CityLine News – May 10th

I think I've stumbled onto something big. I don't completely under-stand it yet, but whatever it is I think it's going to be the scoop of a lifetime.

It started with the woman in the swanky new apartment building across the street. I'd seen her around and thought she had a hot body, but I never had the nerve to talk to her.

I figured a woman that gorgeous would attract a lot of low-life scumbags, so I decided I'd look out for her. From watching the lights in the windows, I worked out what unit she was in. I snuck into her lobby behind the mailman, and found out her name is Catherine Lesko.

One night I was in front of my building locking my car when her apartment lights came on. Her bedroom curtains weren't completely closed. I could see her moving around inside. I moved behind a tree. While I watched she got undressed, walked away naked, I guess to the shower, then came back and got changed. Wow! After a while she left and drove off somewhere.

I know how it sounds, but it's not like that. A woman that hot needs protection. It was my duty as a good neighbour to keep an eye on her.

I went again a couple of nights later, but some asshole jogger spotted and threatened to call the cops. I took off before he got a good look at me.

At least three or four nights a week she'd get home, shower, change, and go out again – like clockwork. I got to wondering where she was going at night.

Finally, I had to know – my reporter's instinct, I guess. I followed her to a massive property in Point Grey. I couldn't see much – it was dark and the place was surrounded by a three-meter hedge. I did it a few times. She always went to the same place.

One night I decided I had to know what was going on. I waited until she went in, found a spot away from the gate, and climbed the hedge.

The place was gigantic, three stories tall, with stone walls, like a castle. I didn't know they even had places like that in Vancouver.

Massive plate-glass windows were set into the ground floor walls, but they had venetian blinds that were swiveled almost shut. For the first of many times I thought about getting the hell out of there and not coming back. I couldn't see anything anyway.

Then I spotted a good solid tree that overlooked one of the windows. It was easy to climb and had lots of leaves to hide behind. When I got to the right angle I could see through the partly-open slats. I was looking down into a huge mansion-sized living room, with lots of couches and coffee tables.

That was the first time I saw them. Women, of all ages, walking around – like they lived there. Some, dressed in work or business clothes, drifted in and out. Others, like my neighbour, Catherine Lesko, were in formal evening dress, sitting around on the couches talking. Through a door on the south wall was some kind of boardroom. Inside, people sat around a massive table.

All this time I never saw any men. After about twenty minutes an older guy, tall, thin and distinguished-looking with long gray hair, walked out of the boardroom. He checked out the women lounging on the couches, and finally strolled over to Catherine Lesko.

She was in the middle of talking but he didn't care. She noticed him and looked up. He lifted her hand like he was going to kiss it, but he didn't, he just lifted, and she stood up.

He led her around to the back of one of the couches and draped her over it, face first. She didn't object. She was wearing a long evening gown. He hoisted up her dress, pulled down her panties and fucked her right then and there!

His face was all contorted like he was screaming. His hands were wrapped around her breasts. Her mouth was open like she was gasping for breath. The other women just sat there talking like it happened every day!

I've got to admit it was a turn-on. It was tough maintaining my reporter's objectivity with the bulge I had in my pants. In a few minutes he finished the job. He zipped himself up and walked away like nothing happened. I freaked, and took off out of there. I found a tree near the hedge and used it to climb over. I could hardly walk on the way back to my car.

I know what I did was illegal, but hey – it's my duty as a reporter to uncover the truth. And something outrageous is going on in that place.

Frank loaded the second document, titled *cult.doc*. It looked like some kind of journal or diary, with dated entries. He started reading:

Lawrence Retigo – Reporter, CityLine News – May 19th

I knew it was dangerous to go back to the mansion in Point Grey. I had no idea who these guys were, but even from what little I'd seen it was clear they weren't like other people. Something told me I'd be up shit creek if they ever caught me there. I was lucky the first time, and I was probably crazy to go back, but I couldn't help myself. Anyway, I was hoping I could get some pictures. Otherwise, nobody would believe me.

I followed Catherine Lesko again and climbed the tree by the window. A waste of time – nothing happened, just a few women sitting around talking. After about half an hour, I heard footsteps. I was up this tree and not that well hidden. All anybody would have to do is look up…

A guy walked around the corner of the building and headed straight for me. He had a rifle slung over his shoulder. My heart was pounding so hard I thought my chest would burst, but he didn't look up, just kept walking and disappeared around the far corner.

My balls were in my throat. As soon as I was sure he was out of sight I climbed down and took off out of there.

Lawrence Retigo – Reporter, CityLine News – June 2nd

The other night scared me so much I didn't even think of going back for more than a week, but after a while the urge took over. Even then it took a few days to get up the nerve. I don't know what's driving me – it's some kind of compulsion.

It seemed like most of the time Catherine Lesko only went to her apartment to get changed – like the place she really lived was the mansion. I didn't get it.

I snuck in again and climbed the tree, keeping an eye open for the security guy. I was hoping I'd see another fucking session like the one before (to record it on my cell phone – as evidence), but for a long time it was pretty boring. I was about to take off when something happened – something so outrageous I'll never forget it.

It was the usual scene – a few women lounging around on the couches and chairs, talking. There are always lots of women in this place, but I've never seen more than a handful of men. The old guy walked in, the same guy from before.

He inspected the women like he'd done the first time. I knew what he wanted. He picked one – not my neighbour this time, but one just as hot. He took her hand, lifted her up like before, and started leading her away. I was pissed – it looked like he was going to take her to some other room where I couldn't see.

But then something happened. This other younger guy showed up. Early twenties, tall, dark and muscular, with close-cropped black hair.

The Arx

It looked like Junior had decided he wanted the same woman Grandpa was after. There were two or three others there that were just as gorgeous, and from what I'd seen these guys could take their pick. I think he was just being an asshole – trying to throw his weight around, trying to challenge Grandpa's authority.

The old guy said something to him. Of course I couldn't hear, but from the body language I think it was something like – 'go find your own woman, sonny – this one's taken'. But Junior didn't want a different one – he wasn't going anywhere.

Grandpa let go of the woman's hand and faced the young guy. The other women rushed into a corner, and the one they were fighting over ran and joined them. Grandpa and Junior circled each other like wild animals, then started going at it.

Grandpa moved around the floor like a dancer, maneuvering his body into position and striking with unbelievable speed – step to the left, drive a fist into the side of Junior's head; step around behind, deliver a kick to the kidney – all with the precision of a surgeon.

They both fought like that. They were like Ultimate Fighters with Ph.D's, analyzing each other's strategy and staying one step ahead – but it happened so fast I could hardly follow. It was more like a chess match than a cage match.

Junior was good, but Grandpa was a master. He didn't even break a sweat. He systematically took Junior apart like he was dismantling a fine mechanical watch. He'd avoid the punches and kicks, or at least block them or move to minimize their impact, wait until Junior had committed himself, then strike so fast it was a blur.

Junior started to look worried. The cocky expression on his face when he first came in was dissolving fast. But then Grandpa made a mistake. He was a bit slow getting out of the way of one of Junior's punches, and it caught him squarely on the jaw. He staggered backwards for a split second. Junior moved in for the kill. He pulled a knife and made a sweeping cut across Grandpa's chest. A diagonal line of blood soaked into the old guy's shirt.

The old guy looked like he was finished. He was stunned, but he snapped out of it and caught Junior with a punch to the head. Then he drew his own knife. A sneering smile swept over his face.

Junior still thought he had the upper hand. He raised his weapon for some kind of death blow, but Grandpa reached up under his guard and drove his knife up into Junior's chest from below. The young guy's eyes bulged out of his head and the knife fell from his hand. Blood gushed from his chest big time. He looked down like he couldn't believe what he was seeing.

I'll never get the image of what happened next out of mind. Grandpa lifted the poor bastard right off the ground, still impaled on the knife! The old guy had this evil smile on his face. He looked Junior in the eye and shook him like a dog shaking a dead rat.

Junior hung up there for at least thirty seconds at the end of the old guy's arm, the life draining out of him. He was a big man, too.

Finally, Grandpa dumped Junior on the floor in a bloody heap and walked away. The women were still standing there watching. They didn't even seem fazed by the whole thing. A couple of them left the room, came back with a plastic sheet, and wrapped the dead guy up. Two of them carted him away, while a couple more got buckets and mops and cleaned up the mess. None of them seemed upset – you'd think somebody had spilled a bowl of spaghetti on the floor or something.

I heard a noise to my right. A group of women in work clothes had opened a door and were carrying the wrapped-up body outside. There were several others with shovels. I almost shit myself when they turned in my direction, but then they veered away to an area under a tree near the driveway. I had to wait there, shaking in my own tree, while they dug a hole in some loose soil and buried the body.

I looked down and cursed when I realized I'd been so freaked out I'd forgotten to use my cell phone camera. I waited until long after they'd done their thing and gone back inside. When the shaking finally stopped I climbed down and took off like my life depended on it – which it probably did.

Lawrence Retigo – Reporter – June 17th

I swore never to go back. I was fine for a couple of weeks, but it's like something goes off in my head that I can't control. Maybe it's my natural instinct to get the story. I didn't even care about the sex anymore. I had to know who these guys were and what they were up to. Whoever they are, they're out there. One thing I'm sure of – if they ever found out about me, I'd be dead.

At first I thought Grandpa was the top of the heap, but the other night I found out different. I was in my usual position in the tree. A bunch of the women were there, including Catherine Lesko. Grandpa was there, but I guess he wasn't horny or he had something else on his mind. No hanky-panky that night.

I was about to climb down when everybody in the room stopped what they were doing and looked toward the door on the west side. A couple of seconds later someone came through it. They wore a robe with a hood, so I couldn't see the face very well, but it was definitely a woman.

Everybody, including Grandpa, bowed their head when she came in. She talked to Grandpa for a few minutes, then left through the other door. I never saw her face, and I never saw her again.

I tried to research who owns the place, but lately I'm so stressed out and preoccupied I can't concentrate. I'm sure nobody at the mansion ever saw me, but they're not normal people. I'm shitting my pants worrying they might know something.

Frank continued to read through the file. Retigo never mentioned another death match, though he said there were skirmishes – always between men. The women didn't fight. Nobody shed any tears over the losers.

As the journal progressed, it got more and more disjointed and irrational. Retigo seemed to be losing it, raving about Satanist cults and evil conspiracies. If it was a religion, it didn't sound like one Frank had ever heard of.

He reached the final few entries:

Lawrence Retigo – June 23rd

Shouldn't have gotten wasted before I left. I was in the tree with my cell phone out. Put it back in my pocket, but when I got home it was gone. Must have fallen out when I climbed down or when I scaled the hedge. I searched the path to my car and even climbed back over and searched the grounds. Nothing!

June 25th

Passed Catherine Lesko on the street. She looked at me and sort of smiled. She knows. Somebody broke into my apartment. They didn't take anything. No sign the door's been tampered with. Stuff's been moved. Like this crooked picture I hadn't gotten around to straightening. Somehow it straightened itself. Why the fuck would somebody break in and straighten a picture?

Got to get out of here – move to another city – another country – another planet! How far do I have to go? Whoever these guys are, they've got money up the ying-yang and they kill without remorse. How do you hide from somebody like that?

The final entry was dated just two weeks before Retigo died:

June 27th

They're messing with my mind. Everywhere I go, they follow me. They don't do anything, just look at me and smile. No matter how careful I am they find me.

At night, I see them lurking in the shadows on the street below, and hear them creeping down the hallway outside my front door. I draped blankets over my windows, but still they see inside.

All thought of the story has been forgotten. All that remains is survival – survival and paralyzing fear. They are instruments of the devil.

They know nothing of compassion, empathy, or love. They have stolen my livelihood, my life, my soul.

They were inside my apartment again. I know they're going to kill me, but they don't – they're playing this bullshit game. Why don't they do something? Kill me! End the madness!

The document ended. Frank wasn't sure what to think. Retigo had been on the edge, either headed for a breakdown or already in the throes of one, when he was killed. Was the journal the ravings of a delusional madman? How much, if any, of it was true?

Dogan's mansion existed, and he knew Catherine Lesko went there regularly – that much was certain. He thought about the sprawling property surrounding the place.

You could do just about anything in there and nobody would know, he thought.

SEVENTEEN

....

FRANK MEETS RICKY AUGUSTUS

T he Mountain View Psychiatric Hospital was situated on a cul-de-sac terminating a long drive so deep in the suburbs that there were swaths of wild countryside surrounding it. Frank pressed the green access button that unlocked the front door of the aging wood-frame structure and strolled inside.

A white-haired old man in a wheelchair slept with his chin on his chest in a corner. Another man stood by a window, clenching and un-clenching his hands over his head like he was grasping at non-existent insects. A middle-aged woman shuffled up to Frank, grabbed his sleeve, and said something urgently in what sounded like Polish. Frank shuddered, recalling his own time in the psych ward. He smiled at her and made his way to the reception desk.

He'd spent a day trying to come up with a plausible explanation for wanting to see Ricky Augustus, with no idea who the man was: a pa-tient, a worker, a nurse, even a doctor. In the end he was forced to in-volve Rebecca, who, through her connections, was able to determine that Ricky must be a patient.

169

Frank stated his appointment with Susan Carstairs, the head nurse for the afternoon shift. The receptionist paged her. Several minutes later Carstairs, blond and wearing a white lab coat, walked in. They shook hands and walked to her office.

"You'd like to volunteer as a companion for a patient," she said.

"That's right."

"The information you provided says you're on stress leave," Nurse Carstairs said. "Are you sure you're up to dealing with someone who's mentally ill?"

"I was in a high-stress job," Frank said, trying his best to come across as well-balanced. "I'm not quite ready to go back to that work, but I'm fine. Volunteering would be good therapy for me. And the structure will help ease my way back into a work environment."

Carstairs bought his story and took him on a tour of the facility. They passed through a hallway somewhat bizarrely decorated with paintings depicting the English countryside. Thatched cottages nestled behind crooked fences along streams and rustic country roads. Hunters clad in crimson jackets and black helmets galloped on horseback in search of elusive foxes.

The hallway funneled into a bright and airy rec-room in the south-west corner of the building. Floor-to-ceiling windows provided lots of sunlight, though the bars behind them reminded Frank where he was. Shabby tables and rickety chairs dotted the room. At a few, patients sat thumbing through magazines or playing cards.

The nurse began to introduce Frank to the patients he might want to occasionally come and spend time with. Half an hour later they'd met almost all of them and he still hadn't spotted Ricky.

In a far corner, facing the wall, was an electric wheelchair. Finally they headed for it. A balding blond head, leaning to one side, projected only slightly above the push handles. A freckled, withered hand rested on the right arm just behind the motor control. As they arrived, Frank noticed the name scrawled on a worn strip of masking tape on the back: 'R. Augustus'.

He took a step back. *This was Ricky Augustus?*

"Ricky?" said the nurse.

Ricky didn't move.

"Ricky?" she repeated more loudly. The fingers moved slowly, like a pale spider, crawling the hand forward toward the control. After an impossibly long delay, it reached the knob and the chair jolted to life, slowly swinging around to face them.

Rebecca's information had indicated that Ricky was in his early twenties, but the ravages of his condition made him appear much older. He was pale to the point of transparency. He reminded Frank of pictures he'd seen of translucent sea life at the perpetually sunless bottom of the ocean.

His wispy blond hair had almost all fallen out – only a sparse ring sprouted around his otherwise bald head. He slouched heavily to his right side, and his head tilted in the same direction. His condition seemed to have affected his facial muscles. His mouth drooped on the right side, and the eye on that side didn't open completely. There were a variety of bags hanging from metal hooks, and tubes connected to various parts of Ricky's body. Some seemed to be going in, others coming out.

"Ricky," said the nurse. "This is Frank."

Ricky didn't respond. He just stared stupidly at them.

"Hello, Ricky," Frank said, smiling. He reached out and attempted to shake Ricky's hand, which he realized didn't function well enough to perform that operation. He finally just lifted the lifeless fingers and did all the shaking himself.

☼

Back in Nurse Carstairs' office, Frank expressed an interest in Ricky. "He was literally left on their doorstep," the nurse said, referring to the hospital that had transferred Ricky Augustus to Mountain View.

"He was called Augustus because he came to us in the month of August," she continued. "Why he was called Ricky, I have no idea. It was all before my time."

"What's wrong with him?"

"As far as we can tell he's the victim of a genetic anomaly. We don't know the cause. We've never been able to study his lineage because we have no idea where he came from or who his parents were, and nobody's ever come by to talk to him or see how he is.

"It's sad, really. He's almost catatonic. It's difficult to know because of all his other disabilities, but the most widely held opinion is that he's severely intellectually disabled. He has extreme difficulty with even the simplest speech, and he only seems to have a dim grasp of what's being said to him. He's been here so long now – I'm afraid he's fallen through the cracks to a certain extent.

"Wouldn't you rather take on a patient you can at least talk to? Your conversations with Ricky will be one-sided. He has very limited communication skills."

172

"I like a challenge," Frank smiled.

They filled out the papers and headed back down the hallway toward the rec-room.

Again they approached Ricky's wheelchair in the corner.

"Ricky," said the nurse. "Frank would like to spend some time with you. Would that be okay?"

Ricky didn't respond.

Nurse Carstairs brought over a folding chair and set it in front of the crippled man.

"Would you like me to stay?" she said to Frank.

"No," he said. "We'll be fine. Will you be around?"

"I'll be passing in and out of here periodically."

"I'll keep an eye out and if I need anything I'll let you know."

"Don't spend too long. Ricky tires quickly. He can sometimes get overly excited for no apparent reason, but he's usually pretty docile."

"Are you alright, Ricky?" she said in a loud voice to Ricky. He grunted softly and nodded his head almost imperceptibly. She patted him on the shoulder and walked away.

Frank smiled at Ricky. "I thought you might like to have a little company once in a while."

Ricky's head was lowered, staring at a point somewhere around Frank's chest. A trickle of spittle appeared at the corner of his mouth, and ran down his chin. He gave no indication that he understood anything Frank had said.

It seemed incomprehensible that anyone would want to put a contract out on Ricky Augustus. Crippled, severely ill, and unable to speak, it was hard to imagine how Ricky could pose a threat to anyone. Frank decided that his visit here had been a waste of time. He considered that maybe the photograph he'd found on his attacker wasn't a hit list after all. Or maybe somehow Ricky wasn't the actual target.

He tried a few more pleasantries but Ricky showed no response. After about fifteen minutes, Frank spotted nurse Carstairs coming through the door and motioned to her.

"Well, I've got to get going, Ricky," he said, to the crippled man. "It was nice meeting you. I'll try to get back and see you again."

Ricky didn't move.

"You were right," Frank said as the nurse arrived. "It was a pretty one-sided conversation."

"It's hard to know whether he understands what people are saying," she said, "but any sort of human contact is probably good for him."

"I'll be back," Frank said. "Like you say, I can keep him company if nothing else."

Frank rose to leave. As he stood, Ricky finally lifted his head. Frank tensed as he peered momentarily into Ricky's eyes. Somewhere behind the vacant stare of the quadriplegic he caught a glimpse of the same strange, animal-like expression he'd seen in the eyes of Gloria's baby the night they met.

He believed he saw something else in those eyes. Whatever medical problems Ricky Augustus might have, Frank was pretty sure a low IQ wasn't one of them.

EIGHTEEN

....

DIGGING INTO KAFFIR

T he next day was Tuesday, Frank's prearranged meeting time with Rebecca. He hadn't contacted her since their last one, and he was relieved that this time she'd stuck to their agreement and hadn't called him.

"Every time I see you, you look worse," she said as he strolled through the door of her office, his clothes rumpled and stubble shadowing his face.

"I'm fine," he said. "Didn't get a chance to shave this morning."

He flopped down at her desk, facing her. She narrowed her eyes and stared at him.

"What?" he said.

"We're definitely having a session later."

He made a face.

"Remember…"

"Our agreement," he completed her sentence. "It's carved into my brain. Fine, but first, any luck with Kaffir?"

She stiffened. "What do you mean?"

"You were going to look into the company, right?"

"Oh, that." She leaned back in her chair. "I felt pretty silly wearing sunglasses and a floppy hat everywhere I went, but I followed your instructions."

He smiled at the image. "I'm surprised, but pleased. So?"

"It's frustrating. There might be something fishy going on, but it could also all be explained away."

"Fishy how?"

"Several of the original developers of Olmerol have died or disappeared."

Frank raised an eyebrow.

"On the surface there's nothing suspicious about that," she continued. "The deaths were accidental, and maybe the ones who disappeared just chose not to leave any way to get in touch with them."

"Sound's fishy alright," Frank said.

"It gets even fishier. The pattern of deaths and disappearances doesn't seem to extend to newly hired workers."

Frank's eyebrows came together. "So… somebody's doing away with people they don't like and replacing them with people they do."

"You could interpret it that way. Like I said, there's nothing concrete to say anybody did anything to these people. It could all just be coincidence. The independent studies showed the same pattern – a couple of researchers died unexpectedly before their conclusions could be released. A couple of others disappeared or gave up on their research. But again, there was nothing to indicate there was anything evil going on."

"What about the studies themselves?" he asked.

"Nothing stood out in the ones that were completed," she answered, "but they all had a thread of similarity, as if they were written by, or at least influenced by, the same person. They detailed minor side effects, like trouble sleeping or dry mouth."

"And nobody ever thought to investigate whether there's a link between all these events?"

She shrugged and crossed her legs. "I did have one interesting experience when I looked into one of the researchers who died accidentally. He was on a hiking trip with a group of friends when he disappeared. The friends lost sight of him and his body was found later at the bottom of a cliff. His father was suspicious at first, but eventually bought into the idea that his son's death was an accident."

"So what's so strange about that?"

"The son had been doing a lot of his work at home, and his father kept his room exactly the way he left it. I convinced him to let me have a look."

Frank tensed. "You met him? You went to the house?"

Rebecca nodded.

"Don't ever do that again."

"Come on, Frank," she said, smiling. "You're being paranoid."

"Promise me you'll never do that again." Frank's fingers dug into the arms of his chair.

One look in his eyes and her smile disappeared.

"Okay, okay. I promise," she said. "Relax."

"Anyway," she continued, ignoring his stare. "I had a look through the son's room. Somehow the computer with all his notes had gotten lost or stolen. But – there were books on the bookshelf. The father confirmed that his son had gotten them specifically as part of the Olmerol study.

"The books tell their own story. There was one on Thalidomide – I guess that's not so strange in itself, but combined with the others... There were a couple on autism and two or three on autistic savants. And there were a number on human brain topology, and a couple on animal behaviour."

"Animal behaviour?"

"I was thinking of Ralphie. There was something almost feral about the way he looked..."

"So was the study ever released?"

"Not under the name of the researcher that died. Another researcher, claiming to use the data collected by the deceased one, finally released it. The conclusions were like all the others, minor side effects but nothing to cause concern."

Frank was still staring at her.

She flipped the notebook shut.

"Your turn," she said.

"What?"

"To talk. Who's this Ricky Augustus character?"

"Dead end," he said.

"Frank," she scowled at him, "what the hell's going on?"

"Don't worry," he said. "When I'm ready, you'll be the first to know."

It was her turn to stare.

"Well, if you've got nothing more to say…" she finally smiled and shot him an evil glance. "You said it yourself. Info dump-slash-therapy session."

Frank made another face but said nothing. Rebecca grabbed a notebook from her desk and they moved to a corner demarcated by an oriental rug, the area Frank had dubbed the 'Interrogation Room'. They sat on opposite sides of a small coffee table. On the table sat a round crystal bowl filled with candies.

"Take your time," she said, opening the notebook on her lap. "If it gets to be too much, we can stop."

He took a deep breath and leaned back in his chair.

"Just continue on from last time," she said, flipping over a page and skimming her notes. "The serial killer, Eugene Mastico, was taunting you."

Frank blinked his eyes, exhaled, stared into space for a few seconds, then started talking. "Mastico liked to dismember his victims. And he loved the spotlight. He knew that the more gruesome the crime the more punch it would have in the media.

"A lot of times he'd send out his version of a press release – just for fun, I guess. He'd include details about what horrific thing he planned to do to his next victim. A few days later, the victim would turn up, just like he said."

Rebecca shook her head slowly. Frank swallowed hard.

"You okay?" she said.

He nodded, and pushed on. "Mastico started bringing me into his fantasies. He'd threaten to kill people if I didn't follow his instructions. It was all about power and control."

Frank felt beads of sweat rising on his forehead.

"One night he phoned me on my personal cell and claimed he'd taken a young woman hostage. He said he'd torture and execute her unless I met with him. I had to come alone. I didn't tell any of the brass about it. I knew they'd forbid me to go. I was desperate."

He closed his eyes. "I drove to the meeting spot – an abandoned parking lot on the Downtown Eastside. Nobody was there. I walked around for a while. At first I thought I got the directions wrong. I remember there was a full moon. It had rained earlier and I could see the reflection in the puddles on the ground – a blood-red moon…"

The light in the room started to dim.

"And you were alone?" Rebecca said. Her voice seemed to fade into the distance.

Frank gripped the arms of his chair.

"Do you want to keep going?" she asked.

"I got knocked on the head," he said, now breathing heavily. "I think I was out for about fifteen minutes. I woke up and got to my feet. The guy, Mastico, was standing behind a pile of trash. He stepped out and started walking toward me. There was something swinging in his hand. I went for my gun, but for some reason I froze."

Frank stared at the crystal bowl on the coffee table. It seemed to glow, first white, then blood red, like the moon in the water. The table beneath it flexed upward, like the expanding surface of an inflating balloon. It contracted again. The table was breathing, the glowing red bowl rising and falling with each breath. The pressure in the room intensified, constricting his throat, cutting off his air supply.

He reached out both hands, shaking violently now, toward the glowing bowl.

"What are you doing, Frank?" Rebecca said. "Then what happened?" Her voice seemed to come from far away.

"W...What?" Frank said, still fixated on the bowl.

"What happened next?" she said.

He broke out of his trance, dropped his hands, and gaped up at her.

"You went for your gun," she said, "and then what happened?"

He paused, still only half there. "Nothing," he finally said.

"Nothing? What are you talking about?"

"That was it."

"That's impossible, Frank. What happened to Mastico?"

"He left."

"That's all? He left? Then what did you do?"

"What?" Frank said again, still shaking. "I went home."

Rebecca shook her head. "I think maybe that's enough, Frank."

NINETEEN

....

PARANOIA

Frank spent the following week holed up at his home in Burnaby. His anxiety level, under control at first with his mind occupied by other things, was now on the rise again after the incident at the Dogan mansion, and the paranoid ravings of Retigo's journal. He was also struggling to make sense of the information he'd collected so far, with little success.

He was reluctant to show up for his meeting with Rebecca the following Tuesday - every contact potentially placed her in greater danger. But she'd said she had important news; he didn't want to risk talking on the phone.

Again, he sat across from her in her office.

"We finally caught a break," she said, beaming. "My friend in the coroner's office called. She convinced him to perform the DNA test."

"What!" Frank said, straightening up in his chair.

"It's actually a pretty unusual move," she said. "They don't normally take that step unless they're directed to by the courts or a request from the police, but I guess my friend's got enough pull. They still have tissue samples taken from Gloria when she was arrested, and a tissue sample was taken from the baby."

"When?" he asked. It seemed too good to be true.

"It should take a few days," she said. "Isn't that great?"

Frank felt like a massive weight had been lifted from his shoulders. For weeks Rebecca had gone along with his theories about the kidnappings, but there had always been an undercurrent of doubt – about the case, and even, he suspected, about his grip on reality.

"If it confirms what you've been saying," Rebecca continued, "the police will have no choice. I don't think even Grant Stocker could get out of re-opening the case."

Frank patted his breast pocket for his cigarettes. Nothing.

"There's something else," she said. "Have you seen today's paper?"

"I won the lottery?"

"No such luck." She slid a folded section over to him. "Here, in the business section. Kaffir have announced plans to release a new version of Olmerol."

"A new version?" Frank tensed as he picked up the paper.

"According to the article," Rebecca said, "the new formula reduces some minor side effects like trouble sleeping, and it's longer lasting, so it can be taken less frequently."

"When is all this is supposed to happen?" he asked.

"September sixteenth, two weeks from now."

Frank read the article. "You can bet they're not telling everything," he said, setting the paper down. "I wonder what else they've messed with."

He looked up. She was staring at him.

"What?" he said.

"You've been holding out on me – trying to protect me according to some ridiculous cop-male code of honour. I have a right to know what's going on. Gloria was my sister."

Frank was torn. At least if she knew more, she'd be frightened enough to look out for herself. He thought back on what he'd uncovered in the past few days, and studied the desk top. "I'm working a few angles," he said. "Nothing concrete."

"Really?" she said. Behind the sarcasm, her voice betrayed a naive confusion that tore at his heart.

He hated lying to her, but the deeper he dug, the more bizarre and pervasive the conspiracy appeared. She might not believe him. It seemed so far-fetched he wasn't sure he believed it himself. If half of what Retigo said in his journal was true, even the little Frank knew right now was enough to get him killed. Telling Rebecca would make her a target as well.

"It's complicated," he said. "There's things I'm still trying to work out."

"You've been saying that for weeks now."

"Trust me," he said, smiling. "All will be revealed."

She rolled her eyes.

"There is *one* thing you could do," he said, changing the subject.

"Yeah?"

He leaned forward. "Something's been bugging me. Kaffir Pharma's a pretty prestigious operation, right?"

"What do you mean?"

"It would attract some really top-notch, brilliant types."

184

"Probably."

"Well, if *we've* figured out there's a pattern to these deaths and disappearances, doesn't it make sense that one of these geniuses might have thought of it too?"

"I guess."

"You said several of the original researchers on the Olmerol project died."

"Yes, and several others disappeared."

"The ones that died – do you know much about the deaths? How they died, whether their bodies were found, whether there was an inquest?"

"I didn't go into minute detail but, yeah, I made some notes on their deaths."

"Were there any deaths where the body was never found or wasn't positively identified?"

"One guy – they were all men, by the way – died in a hunting accident. Another was in a car crash. I think both their bodies were identified. One died on a camping trip. He fell out of a canoe or something and was presumed drowned. I don't think his body was ever found. What's this all about?"

"You got any information on the canoe guy?"

"A little. I'd have to look through my notes."

All through the meeting Rebecca had seemed hurried and nervous. Several times she glanced at her watch when she thought he wasn't looking.

"Going somewhere?" he said.

She turned red, and for a few seconds looked stunned.

"Oh… yes," she finally admitted. "I'm just meeting a friend for coffee."

Frank stared at her. Was she acting suspiciously or was he being paranoid? Finally he shrugged. "Anyway, can you look into the canoe guy? It could be important."

"Come and see me tomorrow," she said. "Now I really have to go…"

☼

Frank felt like a jerk as he pulled out into traffic and followed Rebecca's aging white Mercedes at a respectable distance. He figured he was overreacting, but he had to know.

He promised himself he'd just check out her story. If she was going for coffee like she said, he'd leave it at that.

He relaxed when she pulled into the parking lot of the Boathouse Restaurant in Kits. He drove as close to the doors as he dared. Rebecca met and hugged a distinguished-looking middle-aged woman. Frank studied the woman's face before they walked through the front doors, but it wasn't familiar. Rebecca didn't spot him.

"Get a grip," he scolded himself as he drove away.

TWENTY

....

TWO WOMEN MEET

Despite her apprehension, Rebecca was flattered that the VP of Research for one of the largest pharmaceutical corporations in the world would take time from her busy schedule to have coffee with her.

As to the question of why, she pushed that to the back of her mind, accepting Carla's explanation that she just needed someone to talk to.

Rebecca's phone call to Janet had shaken her belief in Frank's theories about 'the case'. Not only had Frank said nothing to convince her that Kaffir was kidnapping children, there was no proof that, other than Ralphie, the children were victims of kidnapping in the first place, and the deaths and disappearances at Kaffir could be coincidence. The results of the DNA test might change her mind, but for now... Even if Kaffir *was* involved in something shady, Rebecca couldn't believe that Carla De Leon could be part of it.

Just the same, she lectured herself on the need to avoid saying too much or revealing anything about her original 'mission'. She was dying to ask Carla about the new formulation for Olmerol, but in the end decided to leave it alone.

Rebecca arrived at the Boathouse, a casual eatery right on the beach, exactly on time. As she reached the door she noticed Carla approaching. She waved and waited for her new friend. She was expecting to shake hands, but Carla leaned in and gave her a polite hug. Inside, they each ordered a latte and Rebecca grabbed a biscotti.

They got a table on the patio. Rebecca smiled at the expanse of Kits Beach below. Beyond it, the sparkling waters of English Bay were dotted with kayaks, sailboats and, in the distance, the rust-coloured hulls of several gigantic freighters.

Rebecca's initial nervousness melted away as Carla explained her research and implications it held for pregnant women. As the conversation got more personal, Rebecca was surprised at the depth of the bond they shared. Their life experiences were extraordinarily similar, and Carla seemed to understand – like few others, male or female, Rebecca had ever met – the forces that had shaped her.

Inevitably they got to talking about their relationships. Carla was once married, now divorced. Rebecca asked her about her husband.

Carla explained how her ex-husband, James, eventually came to resent her success and her race up the corporate ladder at Kaffir.

"He couldn't compete with you," Rebecca guessed.

Carla nodded. "In some ways, being what most people would call 'gifted' has been a curse. James was intelligent, but I think he realized early on that I was out of his league." She gazed wistfully at the crowded beach below.

"I was head of research for Olmerol when I was still in my twenties."

Carla took a sip of coffee. "It didn't help that I was a workaholic. He got downright nasty. Then he started fooling around. I decided that marriage wasn't for me. I'm too driven – you could even call it selfish – to share my world with someone else.

"James remarried a long time ago, and I think he's much happier now. We're not close, but I see him from time to time. We're not enemies, we've both just moved on."

Rebecca was touched by the sad story.

"But enough about me," said Carla. "What about you?"

Rebecca was reluctant to open up about her personal life, afraid that she'd inadvertently blurt out something she'd regret. But Carla had been so candid about her own marriage...

"I was married once," she finally said.

"Recently?" Carla asked.

"About five years ago," Rebecca answered. "Bob was everything I thought I wanted in a man – intelligent, thoughtful, charming, funny. He was a lawyer, but not the slimy corporate type. He was the sort of rumpled, hip, intellectual, free-thinking TV drama type, fighting for the common man against ignorance and injustice."

Rebecca glanced over at Carla. Her friend smiled in encouragement.

"He seemed too good to be true," Rebecca continued, "and in the end, he was. Everything was great until we got married and moved in together. It was gradual, but over time he got more and more controlling."

Rebecca picked up her biscotti. "First it would be my hair, or my makeup – and it was never just that he personally didn't like them. They were unattractive or in bad taste by definition – like his personal opinion was the gold-plated reference for the rest of humanity."

She held the biscotti between her two hands. "Then he started criticizing the way I dressed. I looked 'frumpy' or 'cheesy' or 'slutty' – and again, it wasn't just his opinion, it was some universally accepted truth. He started going with me when I bought my clothes..."

Carla shook her head.

"He even tried to order for me at dinner, like I wasn't capable of deciding what I wanted."

"I'm finding it hard to picture you in that situation," Carla said, smiling.

"I was ready to leave anyway, but any doubts I had were blown away when he got abusive. First it was minor things like grabbing me by the arm. It escalated from there. The final straw was when he backhanded my face after I refused to obey one of his commands."

Rebecca jumped as the biscotti she was holding broke in half. She felt warmth rushing to her cheeks. She laid the pieces down on her plate.

"Sorry," she said.

"I understand," Carla said.

"I walked out and never went back," Rebecca continued. "From that time on I swore I would never take crap from another man. The second I see it I'm gone, and..."

It occurred to her that she was doing exactly what she'd sworn not to do – opening up about her life. She needed to shut this line of conversation down.

"Are you alright?" Carla asked.

"I'm fine," Rebecca said. She smoothed down her skirt and took a sip of coffee. "I'm talking too much."

"Not at all," Carla said. "It's fascinating. And you've seen a lot of bad behaviour since your breakup?"

Rebecca cringed. She had to answer. "I haven't dated much since then. Maybe I've set my standards too high."

"I don't think wanting to be treated with respect is setting your standards too high. Are you seeing anyone right now?"

Again Rebecca felt herself blush. "Not really."

"Not really?"

"It's complicated... he's sort of a client."

Rebecca clenched her fists. *What am I saying?* she scolded herself.

"A client?" Carla said. "Isn't that dangerous?"

"Well, it's really more of a business relationship."

"That does sound complicated."

Rebecca tried to steer the conversation somewhere else. "I can't really talk about it. It has to do with my..."

Carla eyed her in a way that made her nervous. It occurred to her what she was about to say and who she was about to say it to.

Rebecca remembered Frank's warning: *If you go sticking your nose into the head office at Kaffir, you're going to appear on their radar. I can guarantee that you don't want that to happen.*

"It's nothing," she said. "It's really more of a friendship. I shouldn't say anymore – it's a confidentiality thing."

"Of course," Carla said, smiling and taking a sip of coffee. "I understand completely."

TWENTY ONE

....

A DEAD SCIENTIST

"**R**ichard Carson," Rebecca said when Frank showed up at her office the next day as planned. She spread several pages of notes on the desk in front of her. "He was a senior guy in the company – was there even before Carla..." She stopped short.

"Carla?" Frank raised an eyebrow.

She stared down at her notes. "Oh, Carla De Leon, the VP of Research at Kaffir."

"You're on a first-name basis?"

Rebecca blushed. "Hey, I've gone over these notes so many times I feel like I know the people."

Frank continued to eye her strangely. He finally shrugged. "So – Richard Carson."

"Like I said before, he drowned in a canoeing accident on a vacation sixteen years ago. The body was never found. I've got a picture."

She handed Frank a photocopy of a newspaper clipping titled: 'Researcher Dies in Boating Accident'. Frank read the article:

The Arx

Doctor Richard Carson, 52, is missing and presumed dead after a tragic boating accident on Lake Nipissing in northern Ontario. Carson was the lone occupant of a canoe that capsized. According to his companions, Carson was out of their sight for about twenty minutes as he paddled ahead and up an arm of the lake, exploring.

When they caught up, they found Carson's overturned canoe. Rescuers combed the area for several days, but the body was never found. Carson was a senior researcher for Kaffir Pharma, a multinational pharmaceutical company based in Vancouver. He was single, and was predeceased by both his parents.

Frank finished reading and looked up. "What did the cops think about it?"

"They found a small patch of blood on the gunwale of the canoe, but not enough to suggest foul play. Their theory was that Carson had some kind of medical event – a heart attack or stroke. He collapsed, banged his head, and went overboard.

"They spent about a week searching for the body. That section of the lake is really murky and full of debris. There's a lot of tricky currents that might have carried the body away. They sent divers down but they never found anything. The official verdict was accidental death."

Borrowing Rebecca's computer, Frank tracked down the location of the incident. It was the middle of nowhere, many miles from the nearest town.

He studied the photograph in the article. Richard Carson was undistinguished: middle-aged and pudgy, with a graying crew-cut and glasses.

Frank imagined what it would take to stage a death like that, deep in the wilderness. Carson would have had to plant food, clothing, and survival gear ahead of time, and would have had to navigate through the bush alone for several days. Was the man in the picture, an intellectual, a city dweller with a desk job, capable of such a feat?

Maybe, if he was desperate enough.

He held up the article and looked at Rebecca. "Okay if I keep this?"

TWENTY TWO

....

THE PARTNERSHIP ENDS

Frank made his way from Rebecca's building to the parkade where he'd left his car. After the meeting about Carson, she'd insisted that he stay for another session. They'd gotten nowhere. He always came away from the sessions drained and confused, like he'd just wakened from a bad dream.

He hadn't come to any conclusions about whether the sessions were actually doing any good. Many days had passed since he'd had a drink. He still had trouble sleeping, and still set the alarm as always, but several nights lately he'd woken up without the usual remnants of his recurring nightmare.

That had to be a good sign, but in the deepest part of his psyche he knew he was still damaged goods, still far from being the man he once was. There was always an obstacle in the sessions, an unassailable wall that thrust up out of the earth whenever he got too close to his demons.

He distracted himself by focusing on the case. Knowing what he'd learned so far about the conspiracy surrounding Olmerol, he suspected that Richard Carson had faked his own death.

Why? Either Carson was part of whatever was going on and for some reason wanted out, or he somehow found out about it and was smart enough to kill himself off in the eyes of the world before the conspirators did the job for real.

Whatever the reason, Frank's gut told him that Richard Carson held the key to what he was looking for. Maybe Carson could provide convincing evidence of what was happening, and prove that Frank wasn't crazy.

The problem was: how could he hope to find someone who had obviously gone to a lot of trouble to disappear? Frank shook his head as he walked. The answer was simple – he couldn't. He couldn't hope to find Carson, at least not without more information.

He was jolted awake as someone shoved him to one side. He looked up. A girl in jeans and a black leather jacket had pushed past him. As he watched she turned her head back and smiled. Frank shuddered, remembering the final entries in Retigo's journal.

A few minutes later, as he reached for the door into the parkade, a hand appeared and opened it for him. Frank looked over. A middle-aged man in a business suit had appeared at his side out of nowhere. The man swept his hand forward motioning for Frank to go ahead, and smiled.

Frank watched the man head for a nearby car, then trudged up the narrow walk that ran beside the spiral driveway leading to the third level, where he'd parked. Lately he never took the elevator; he imagined the door sliding open and an assassin waiting with a shotgun in his hands.

He laughed at his own paranoia. Anyway, he thought, that's not how these guys operated. They were a lot more subtle. They'd use a method that didn't arouse any suspicion. Of course, they could always make it look like a robbery...

As he turned a corner a sliver of shadow moved on the periphery of his vision. His muscles tensed. He listened closely and was sure he heard footsteps following him. He walked faster, finally reaching the third level. The footsteps grew louder. He scanned for any other customers in the dim light of the parkade. There was no one.

Finally he spotted his car and felt a wave of relief. He rushed toward it, glancing around him. He heard the footsteps again, closer now, still approaching, faster. He fumbled nervously with his key, slid it into the lock, and opened the door. His heart stopped when a man appeared from behind a concrete pillar beside him.

For a second their eyes met. Frank's heart was pounding in his chest. He had no gun, no weapon of any kind. He was a sitting duck. The man smiled and continued walking, heading for a sports car on the other side of the level. The man clicked his key fob and the car beeped in response. He opened the door and stepped forward like he was going to get in, then turned, smiled again, and nodded at Frank.

A jolt arced down Frank's spine.

The man got into his car and drove away.

I'm losing it, Frank thought.

He flopped down in the driver's seat, still shaking. On the way home, he told himself he was being irrational. He'd never actually seen anyone following him, and he was trained to notice these things.

Nothing had happened since he was attacked outside the Dogan mansion, and he was convinced that his attacker had acted alone and on the spur of the moment. No matter how many logical arguments he set down and confirmed, he could feel the paranoia welling up inside him.

His fear was illogical, animal, primordial. It threatened to cripple him. He thought about Rebecca's comment that he wasn't ready for this case, and considered that maybe she'd been right after all.

When he got to his house he examined it, inside and out, in neurotic detail. He found nothing. He checked the locks on all the doors and carefully drew the curtains to leave no gaps, recalling the bedsheets tacked up around the windows of Lawrence Retigo's apartment. He stumbled upstairs, determined to get some rest, but instead lay staring at the ceiling.

He got up, parted the bedroom curtains, and peered down at the street. A sports car identical to the one from the parkade was driving by, slowly, under the glow of the street lamp. He couldn't see the driver's face.

He watched for another hour, but saw nothing, and went back to bed. Finally, exhausted, he drifted off, tormented by a brand new set of nightmares.

☼

He woke the next day after only a few hours' sleep and reached out a shaking hand for his cigarettes. They weren't there. He panicked, and remembered he'd left them downstairs. He spent the day scouring the block through the slit of a pulled-back curtain, chain-smoking, and try-ing to calm his shaking hands.

His thoughts kept drifting back to the car he'd seen the night before. If they knew about him, how soon before they found out about Re-becca? By dusk he'd decided he needed to check on her.

The sky began to open just as he rushed out of his front door. He held his jacket collar together and sprinted to his car, scanning to the left and right. Again the image of Lawrence Retigo crowded into his mind. He was re-living Retigo's nightmare.

Despite the earlier incident, he drove to a parkade downtown, cir-cled to a level almost empty of cars, and parked in a darkened corner. He saw no-one as he locked the car and descended to the street.

By now it was early evening; most people were at home having din-ner. The Granville Skytrain platform was almost empty. He stood as far away from the others as possible. When the train arrived, he waited until the doors started to close before squeezing in, and was the only person who entered his car.

He rode the train for two stops to Waterfront station, checked that no one else was making a move, and stepped off just as it was about to leave. Only one or two others exited the other cars; he watched them carefully as he headed for the least crowded exit.

A woman who'd just gotten off stood texting on her phone. She looked up, and for a second made eye contact and looked back down. Frank's hands started to shake. She didn't follow as he climbed the stairs.

He stumbled around Gastown, glancing over his shoulder, peering into the eyes of everyone he passed, wondering if the guy in the jeans and checkered shirt, or the guy in the pin-striped suit, or even the over-weight, middle-aged woman in the print dress, would be the one as-signed to take him out.

He spotted a run-down hotel on the next block, slipped up a back alley, and made his way to the hotel's delivery entrance, watching for signs of a tail.

In a dark corner of the hotel's lobby he found a pay phone. He didn't want to go to Rebecca in person – they might be following. He didn't want to use his cell phone; its signal could be intercepted. He stepped up to the booth with his back to the wall and a clear view of the lobby. Once in place, he called Rebecca. She was still at her office.

"You okay, Frank?" she asked. Her voice sounded dead, with-drawn. Something was wrong. "I thought you didn't want us to contact each other by phone. You're puffing like you've run a marathon."

"I wanted to check that you were okay."

"I hope you're sitting down." Her voice was trembling.

"What?"

"My friend from the coroner's office called less than an hour ago. The DNA was a perfect match. The dead baby was Ralphie."

"What!" he shouted into the mouthpiece. His knees almost buckled. His knuckles were white around the phone.

"There's no doubt," she said, in a voice that said the foundation of her world had been kicked out from under her.

He scanned the lobby. Nothing. He switched the phone to his left hand. "After all this it turns out Gloria killed her own child?" he said, lowering his voice. "I don't believe it."

200

"Oh God…" Her voice broke. She started to cry. He felt a sudden urge to go to her, to hold her in his arms, to comfort her.

"I'm sorry," he said. For a few seconds he was at a loss for words, stunned by her revelation. Finally he said: "Look, it's still possible that Gloria's innocent. Maybe Ralphie was kidnapped by somebody else…" He spoke the words but he didn't really believe them.

He heard Rebecca grab a tissue and blow her nose. She pulled herself together. "Stocker's livid. He says the Coroner's got no business overstepping his authority."

"Big surprise," Frank said. "But it doesn't change anything. There's still the conspiracy…"

"Come on, Frank. What conspiracy? Gloria was in over her head with Ralphie and had a breakdown."

"You believe that?"

"DNA doesn't lie. The whole conspiracy theory was based on the idea that the dead baby wasn't Ralphie. The other cases could be made to fit, but they could also be coincidence."

Her voice lowered, like she was talking to herself. "Why didn't I see the signs?"

"It's gotta be some kind of mistake," Frank said. "What about the teeth?"

"I don't know. My friend didn't say anything about that. Maybe it was the gums swelling or something, like you said. Or maybe you were mistaken."

"I wasn't mistaken."

"It's my fault. I let myself get caught up in it. I knew what a fragile mental state you were in. I should never have gone along."

He held the phone with his chin and hauled out his cigarettes and lighter.

"The DNA's a match," she said. "That's all we need to know. It's over."

"I don't care what the DNA says," he said. "Something's wrong here. Maybe they've got people in the Coroner's office. Of course! Who actually did the DNA test? We'll have to look into that."

"Who's they? Listen to yourself Frank. This has gone far enough. It's horrible to have to accept what Gloria did to her child, but we have no choice. Facts are facts."

"It's not over."

"How dare you!" she snapped. "You'd prolong this nightmare by hanging on after it's clear to anybody in their right mind…"

"There's more to it," he said.

He felt like he'd been hit in the gut with a sledge-hammer. He needed Rebecca. She'd proved to be a first-rate researcher. He'd never have made it this far in the investigation without her help.

More than that, he needed her psychological support. Whether it was the little packets of therapy she'd been providing or the mere act of getting him out of the house, interacting with other human beings, and doing something approaching a job, Frank wasn't sure, but there had been stretches lately where he'd actually felt something close to his old self again.

He'd tried to deny that the case was too much for him, but inside he knew he needed someone to lean on, to share the burden.

"Frank?" she said.

But there was another reason why he needed her. An idea was suddenly dredged up from his subconscious, an idea he hadn't dared admit even to himself. He thought about her constantly, and when they were apart he couldn't wait to see her again. He'd developed an almost physical need to be near her.

"Frank," she said. "What do you mean?"

"What?"

"What do you mean, 'there's more to it'?"

The previous day, just as a mental exercise, he'd tried to imagine his life without her and found, to his shock, that he couldn't. Rebecca had become as essential to his world as the exhaling of his breath or the pumping of his heart.

"Forget it," he said. "It's nothing."

Now, at this moment, as he stood with the cigarette pack in his shaking hand, for the first time since they'd met, he came to a stunning realization of how he felt about her.

He almost dropped the phone.

"Remember when we first started looking into this case?" she said. "The case that wasn't a case – after I took you home from your little vacation at the police lockup?"

Frank said nothing. He knew what was coming.

"I made one stipulation – remember? You promised that if I thought it was getting to be too much for you – that you needed to take a break – you'd listen to me and do it. Remember?"

"This is different…"

"Remember?"

"Don't talk to me like I'm three years old, of course I remember."

"I'm telling you now, Frank. It's over. Gloria's dead. Ralphie's dead. My poor little sister killed her baby and then took her own life." Her voice broke again. "There's nothing you or I can do about it. Step away."

"I can't do that."

He considered revealing the information he'd uncovered about the case. It would be enough to convince her. As quickly as the idea arose, he discarded it. He couldn't risk the life of the woman he now realized he loved, even if it meant losing her.

"I'm not going to help you anymore Frank," she said. "I've just been enabling you. You're cruising for another breakdown – after we'd gotten so close. All the work we've done…"

"Fine," he said, tugging a cigarette out of the pack. "I'm better off on my own anyway."

"What about our agreement?"

"Fuck the agreement."

"Please, Frank," she pleaded. Her voice was trembling. "You know I only want to help you. I couldn't stand it if anything…"

He'd already compromised her safety merely by their association. He realized that his only option was to break off all contact until it was over.

"Forget about it. I'll see you later," he said, lighting the cigarette.

"Frank…"

He hung up the phone.

Then he went home and trashed his house.

TWENTY THREE

....

BACK AT THE SQUAD

When he opened his eyes the next morning, Frank was lying on the kitchen floor. He had to pry his right cheek off the linoleum; his face was glued to it by something sticky. He examined the substance and realized it was blood – his own. His cheek was covered with it. He cringed as he recalled fragments of what had happened last night.

Smashed dishes and cutlery littered the floor. Shards of glass lined the space under a pair of French doors that had contained glass panels yesterday but no longer. He vaguely remembered crashing through them, and inspected the rest of his body for cuts. Miraculously, there were only a few minor ones.

He staggered upstairs and into the shower. Having washed the blood, glass shards, and general filth away, he examined the wound on his face. It had bled a lot, but wasn't too serious. It probably needed stitches, but he rifled through a drawer in the bathroom and found a Band-Aid that more or less covered it. He hadn't even been drunk; this was something deeper, like the irresistible force of reality colliding with the immovable object of his convictions.

A confused jumble of questions and contradictions fought for dominance in his brain. Gradually he remembered his conversation with Rebecca, and once again his gut clenched. Somehow the baby he'd been convinced was a substitute had proved to be Ralphie after all.

He was also trying to deal with the stunning realization of how he felt about her. She now believed he was obsessed with a case that had never really existed. By extension, he must be mentally unbalanced. She had accepted the idea that her sister was guilty, and would no longer help him.

He gulped down a handful of ibuprofen, stumbled over to his bed, set the alarm out of habit, flopped down and passed out.

Several hours later he woke up. He checked the alarm. It had gone off but he'd slept through it. He lay with his eyes still closed.

He clenched his fists and steeled himself. He didn't care what evidence Rebecca had, or thought she had; he didn't even care if she was right about Ralphie. Something was going on; something big, something dangerous.

But somewhere in his subconscious, a tiny voice whispered. No matter how hard he fought to stifle it, the voice kept repeating: what if she and the others were right about him?

☼

It had taken the entire morning, but Frank finally stamped down the anxieties that had been ripping through his brain like a cyclone, and convinced himself that he was confident, even relaxed, as he once again approached the building that housed the Vancouver Homicide Squad.

He climbed the stairs with a deliberate spring in his step. As ridiculous as it felt, he was following Rebecca's suggestion to visualize himself handling any impending confrontations forcefully and confidently.

The exercise seemed to be working until he pushed open the glass doors and a wave of terror washed over him. He reached out to steady himself, like a bad swimmer grasping for the comfort of the pool's edge, but grasped nothing but air. As Rebecca had suggested he stopped, closed his eyes for a second, took a deep breath, and tried to relax.

He pushed forward, deeper into the squad-room. Once again, the activity ceased as his former colleagues became aware of his presence, and again he ran the uncomfortable gauntlet greeting them. As before, the pressure built, both inside and out, now amplified a hundred times. He visualized and fought for control; it seemed to come less easily this time.

He spotted Stocker behind the glass wall of his office and headed directly for it. The office was crowded with Frank's former colleagues. Stocker was telling a funny story – *about me?* – Frank thought, and scolded himself for being so paranoid. The office door was open and he just walked in.

In contrast to the self-conscious rumblings that had accompanied his previous visit and the unveiling of his theories about the Hanon case, there was an eerie silence this time, as Frank told Stocker and the others about Lawrence Retigo, Arthur Dogan, Catherine Lesko, Kaffir Pharma, and Olmerol.

Everyone in the room, even men and women Frank had worked with for years, shuffled their feet and stared at the floor, looked at their watches, or groomed their fingernails. After he finished talking, the silence seemed to go on forever.

"Let me get this straight," Stocker finally said, hooking his thumbs into his belt, which looked like it was about to burst open. "This pervert nut-bar Retigo peddles a story about how he stalked his poor, innocent neighbour to the home of one of our most distinguished citizens, a person he has no business getting within a hundred barge-poles of, trespassed on the man's private property, and spied on him.

"Then he concocts some outrageous fairy-tale about Satan worship, wild orgies, and bodies buried in shallow graves on the front lawn." Stocker shook his head slowly. "And you believe him."

"I followed the girl myself," Frank said. "I know at least part of what Retigo said is true."

"What? You've been following this poor girl too? I think you better shut up now Frank. Pretty soon, I'm going to have to arrest you for something."

"I've got a copy of Retigo's journal," Frank said, waving a flash drive. "And I found a hit list with his name on it. I don't believe his death was an accident."

Stocker sneered at him. "From what you've told me, all it proves is that Lawrence Retigo was a delusional sexual deviant who slid too far into the deep end and couldn't handle it anymore."

Frank cast around the room for any kind of support. Almost every one of the detectives around him avoided eye contact. One of the few exceptions, to Frank's surprise, was Stocker's assistant, Terry Hastings. He looked nervous, even frightened.

He believes me, Frank thought.

"It might be worth checking out," Hastings said. "Maybe we should-"

Stocker stared him down. Hastings' eyes moved to the floor.

"So, this is the 'evidence'," Stocker laughed, curling the fingers of each hand like quotations in front of him, "that convinced the Coroner to squander the taxpayers' money on a DNA test." He shook his head. "There really is one born every minute. You need help, Frank. I thought before that you might be getting better, but you're really out there. Look at yourself." He pointed at Frank's face, still unshaven, bruised, scratched, and patched with the Band-Aid. "Get lost, Frank," he said. "Go see somebody – somebody professional. Whatever you've done so far isn't working. I'm telling you this man to man."

"This isn't a joke," Frank said. He stared at Terry Hastings.

"Get out of here, Frank," Stocker said, "before I have you thrown out."

Frank took a step toward him. A couple of the detectives rushed over. They gripped Frank's arms from behind.

"I know it sounds crazy but it's the truth!" Frank yelled, struggling against their grips. They started to haul him away. "Tom – Jill – Terry – I'm telling you. People are going to die!"

The men started to drag him out of the office. Frank tossed the flash drive on the desk beside him. Terry Hastings moved toward it.

"Leave that where it is!" Stocker bellowed.

He turned to Frank, his face red and jowls shaking. "Don't come back here. Leave us alone. We've got police work to do."

It took three detectives, all of whom had once worked closely with him, to haul Frank through the main doors and pitch him half-way down the front stairs.

The pressure that had been building inside him exploded. He stumbled down the steps and people on the sidewalk stared as he fell and lay on the pavement.

An overwhelming urge boiled up inside him, an urge he hadn't felt for weeks – the urge for a drink.

TWENTY FOUR

....

REBECCA LOOKS FOR A SHOULDER

"I felt like I had to talk to someone." Rebecca choked back tears as she sat on the patio of Carla De Leon's penthouse apartment in Kerrisdale. She stared blankly at the view of Kitsilano to the north, and, farther in the distance, English Bay and the North Shore Mountains.

Carla brought her a glass of red wine and sat opposite her.

"Drink up," she said. "It will help you relax. I'm so glad you came to me. I'm happy that you consider me someone you can open up to."

Rebecca wrapped her hands around her wine glass.

"Man trouble?" Carla asked, smiling.

Rebecca nodded. She took a sip of wine and composed herself.

"The one I told you about," she finally said. "We had a big fight. I told him I wouldn't be seeing him anymore."

"What was the fight about?"

"It was about my…" Rebecca caught herself. A part of her felt like she was still infected with Frank's paranoia. Still, she resolved not to say too much.

"My friend has some psychological issues," she said. "He had a breakdown a year ago and he never really recovered. He refuses to go for treatment. I've been trying to help him, you know, just informally."

She looked up at Carla. The older woman nodded and rested a hand on hers. Rebecca continued. "He's gotten involved in something that I can see is going to end in another breakdown." Her voice trembled as she spoke. "I've tried to talk him out of it but he won't listen…"

"My dear," Carla said, patting her hand. "That's terrible. I'm so sorry."

"I feel so helpless," Rebecca sobbed. "It's like watching a car accident happen in front of you and not being able to stop it."

"But what is it your friend got involved in?" Carla asked.

Rebecca tensed. Though she hadn't known Carla for long, in that short time she felt they'd formed a special bond. Carla had always been so brutally honest, sharing her innermost secrets and fears.

Still, for all their closeness, Rebecca didn't feel ready to open up about Gloria and 'the case'. She was caught between her betrayal of Frank by seeing Carla, and her betrayal of Carla by continuing her original ruse and not telling her friend the truth.

"I'd rather not say," she said.

"You'll feel better if you get it off your chest," Carla said, squeezing her hand.

For a fleeting moment Rebecca considered telling her everything. In the end, she decided against it.

"I'm sorry," she said. "I wouldn't be comfortable saying any more about it."

A flash of what could have been anger swept across Carla's face. She let go of Rebecca's hand. As quickly as it had appeared, the expression was gone.

"It's hard for me to advise you when I don't know the circumstances," Carla said, smiling. "I suppose all you can do is be supportive of your friend and continue to try to steer him away from the path you say he's on. On the other hand, if you don't contact him for a while maybe he'll lose interest."

Carla stood and motioned for Rebecca to stand as well. The older woman extended her arms and they hugged warmly.

"I'm so lucky to have a friend like you," Rebecca said, her voice breaking.

"I wish you would put more trust in me, dear," Carla said, patting her shoulder. "Someday I hope you'll feel comfortable enough to tell me everything. You know I'll always be here for you."

TWENTY FIVE

....

STOCKER HAS A FRIEND

There was a spring in Lead Detective Grant Stocker's step as he strolled down the polished hallway of the Police Board building. Today was a pivotal day; the forces of the universe were finally converging in his favour.

For years he'd stood in the shadow of Frank Langer, from the academy to their assignment to the same office of the Homicide Squad. During that time, he'd constantly been measured against Frank, and had always come up wanting.

After Frank's spectacular meltdown and his own appointment to Lead Detective, Stocker thought his ship had finally come in. But his detectives still didn't respect him. A few hangers-on poured flattery in his ears in the hope of currying some future favour, but he knew about the sneers and jokes behind his back.

When Frank had come back the first time, Stocker thought he'd handled it well. Frank was so humiliated he almost felt sorry for him. He'd toyed with the idea of acting then, but instinctively knew the time wasn't right. After Frank's latest outburst, his unbelievably outlandish story, and behaviour that could easily be massaged into a charge of assault, he was sure that his request would fall on sympathetic ears.

It's like Darwin said, Stocker thought, as he approached the front desk, *'survival of the fittest'.*

Everybody talked about Frank: what a great detective he was, how intelligent and insightful he was, what a great leader he was. Stocker was sick of it. No one said those things about him.

He had to admit that Frank had his good points, but he also had a fatal flaw. It had been incredibly lucky for Stocker that the Mastico affair had exposed that flaw to the world.

He may not be as smart as Frank, but Stocker knew how to work the system. More importantly, he had something Frank would never have – the killer instinct. Now he was in the catbird seat. *Carpe Diem,* he said to himself, *Seize the Day.* He was going to make sure that Frank Langer's career as a detective was over for good – that his nemesis would never set foot in another squad room.

He met with Harold Chase, the Deputy Chief Constable, in Chase's office. Stocker had a tendency to dwell on his own misfortunes, but he had to admit he'd benefited from the occasional stroke of good luck in the course of his career. One of the most important had been his relationship with Chase.

They'd hooked up while Stocker was still at the academy, where Chase was on the board of directors. It had been one of those rare, magical moments when disaster had been transformed into triumph. Stocker was in big trouble; he'd been accused of cheating on an exam. In fact, he *had* cheated, but he'd proclaimed his innocence to the stars. The brass were preparing to expel him; he'd been allowed to meet with Chase in a last-ditch attempt to plead his case.

He was pretty sure Chase hadn't believed him any more than the others, but for some reason the director seemed to show an interest in him. When he arrived at Chase's office, the man who held his career in his hands told him to close the door.

"Cadet Stocker," Chase said, scowling gravely at Stocker the recruit, "these are serious charges. The board would be well within its rights to have you expelled immediately."

"But I didn't..." Stocker began.

"Come on," Chase said. "There are cameras in the examination room."

Stocker hung his head. It was over.

"On the other hand," Chase said. Stocker looked up. "One could argue that you showed initiative."

Stocker couldn't believe what he was hearing.

Chase leaned forward and looked Cadet Stocker in the eye. "I have the power to allow you to stay," he said.

Stocker was ecstatic; maybe he'd survive this after all.

"I might have a use for someone with your 'moral flexibility'," Chase smiled and continued. "I can help with your career, but I might occasionally ask you to do things for me in return – things that some might not consider above board..."

"Anything," Stocker said. It was his only hope.

"And of course," Chase said, "no one would need to know about this relationship."

Stocker nodded anxiously.

Chase scanned him up and down, the hint of smile curling around his lips.

"Congratulations, cadet," he finally said. "I'll be in touch. Meanwhile, try not to do anything stupid. There's a limit to my power to fix things."

Chase had proved to be a valuable ally. Stocker was smart enough to call on his influence sparingly, only when he screwed up badly, which, unfortunately, had happened fairly often. Still, he was confident that Chase had gotten his share out of the deal. Stocker had done some pretty unsavory, illegal, even frightening, things for his boss, no questions asked.

As Stocker's career had progressed, Chase's had moved steadily upward as well. Stocker's mentor had made it all the way to Deputy Chief Constable.

And someday, Stocker thought, *who knows?*

Now he wanted to ask Chase for one more favour. This time it shouldn't be a problem. Frank Langer was on his way out anyway; all Stocker wanted was to give him an extra little push.

"He was a good detective," Chase said, organizing some papers in front of him. "Outstanding, in fact, from what I hear."

Stocker smiled to himself once again at Chase's obsession with neatness and order.

"It's a shame," Stocker said, shaking his head. "It breaks my heart to see what's happened to him. He was a valued member of the team, but the Mastico thing did something to his mind. He needs help, and I hope he gets it, but my concern is for the department and the men under me. He's come in twice now raving about kidnapped babies and con- spiracies. He's disrupted the unit. Morale has taken a hit."

"Kidnapped babies?" Chase lifted his head.

Stocker laughed. "Yeah, real space-case stuff – a conspiracy to kid- nap babies and replace them with other babies."

Stocker had Chase's attention – he got ready for his killing blow. "Now he's gotten the idea that Arthur Dogan's involved. Who knows where these delusions come from? He was raving about orgies and mur- ders at Mr. Dogan's mansion."

Chase twitched, and, to Stocker's surprise, for a brief moment looked like he would collapse. "Where did all this happen?" he asked. "Who else heard all this?"

"The first time, right in the squad room," Stocker said. "Pretty well everybody heard. But that was just the dead baby stuff. The stuff about Mr. Dogan he said in my office a few days ago. There was just me and a few other guys. Nobody took him seriously. Frank came after me. A couple of the men had to escort him out of the building."

Stocker smiled. As it happened, he was familiar with Arthur Dogan, and knew of the chummy connection between Dogan and Chase. Frank's fate was sealed.

"And you want to get a restraining order against Frank Langer," Chase said.

Stocker nodded. "And, I hate to say it about a former fellow detec- tive, but I don't believe Frank Langer is fit to be a police officer. In my opinion he should be relieved of his duties permanently, possibly even declared mentally incompetent."

Chase put down the papers in his hands and looked at Stocker.

"Detective Stocker," he said. "I'm afraid I have to recommend that you not pursue this matter any further. At the moment Mr. Langer's behaviour is merely an irritant. If we were to take any kind of legal action there might be significant publicity. It could even make the papers. The Mastico case was high profile. It would look like we were hanging Frank Langer out to dry."

Stocker was speechless. He hadn't expected this. He'd been so sure, especially with the Dogan connection. Everywhere he turned, people were out to get him.

"I disagree, sir," he said, feeling the warmth rise to his cheeks. "Frank is a danger to the morale of the department. He's mentally unstable…"

"Leave it, Detective," Chase said. "A word of friendly advice: forget about it. I'll look into whether we can offer ex-Detective Langer any additional help."

"With all due respect, sir," Stocker said. "I think you're making a big mistake."

Stocker stood with his fists clenched at his sides.

"I don't get it…" he blurted.

"Do we have an understanding, Detective?" Chase said, rising up and straightening the cufflink on his left sleeve.

Stocker was shaking, about to explode. He nodded and stared at the floor to hide his rage. After all the laws he'd bent, broken, torn up, doused with gasoline, lit on fire, and thrown in the trash heap… Somewhere deep within his brain he understood that the optics of the force appearing to deflect blame from itself by continuing to punish Frank for the Mastico affair were bad, though as far as he was concerned Frank deserved everything he got.

"Thank you for bringing the matter to my attention, Detective," Chase said.

Stocker fumed as he stomped down the front steps of the Police Board building.

What the hell's his game? He thought.

Maybe it was time to go above his mentor's head. There were people higher up who would listen to his story.

TWENTY SIX

....

AN EPIPHANY

The days following Frank's humiliating ejection from the squad were a blur. His life descended into a downward spiral as he haunted an endless string of no-name dives downtown, on a quest to maintain a comforting level of medication in his brain.

Sometimes he'd wake up as he was being shaken before being kicked out of a bar. Sometimes he'd be lying in a trash-filled alley in the dark, sometimes in a cut-rate hotel room or a shelter.

Sometimes he'd sober up long enough to remember the horror that his life had become. He'd think about Gloria, or Grant Stocker, or Lawrence Retigo and Ricky Augustus. He'd stagger back to the next bar and repeat the exercise.

It was like all his progress with Rebecca had unraveled, like it had never happened. The recurring nightmares, which had diminished in the past few weeks, returned without warning to torture him, now riddled with images of Gloria, Ralphie, and Lawrence Retigo. He couldn't sleep, and that drove him to drink even more. The case was forgotten, but not Rebecca. No matter how wasted he got, he couldn't blot her out of his memory.

He woke one night to the sound of trickling water. He lay on the ground in another nameless alley. Something hard dug into his back. His head throbbed and his body ached. He rolled over and looked. An old drunk, leaning on his shopping cart, was pissing on the wall about three meters away. Frank struggled to his knees. His clothes were filthy. He'd been lying on a pile of garbage.

The drunk noticed him, quickly shook off the remainder of his load, grabbed his cart, and hurried away. Frank staggered to his feet. He had no idea where he was, but judging from the spent condoms, discarded needles, and the stench of dried vomit he guessed it was probably somewhere on the Downtown Eastside. An empty bottle of Alberta vodka lay on the ground where he'd been passed out.

He checked his pockets. They were empty. His wallet and keys were gone. So were his shoes. He felt something crinkly in his right sock. He took the sock off and found three folded-up twenty-dollar bills.

He tried to walk, but only made it a few meters before collapsing again into another pile of garbage. He struggled again to his feet and fought to stay upright, teetering like a rotting tree in a windstorm. Again he collapsed and everything went dark.

☼

Frank woke screaming from another nightmare and sat up, his trembling hands covering his face. He shook his head to clear it, and the sledgehammer clobbering the inside of his skull doubled in intensity. The pain was so bad he almost passed out. He closed his eyes and leaned back against the wall behind him. It was then that he realized that someone was pounding on it.

"Shut the fuck up!" a male voice yelled.

It took some time to understand where he was. Finally, a vague memory surfaced: staggering to a broken-down hotel, checking in using the cash from his sock, and passing out on the bed where he now sat.

It was morning. The light from outside filtered through the smoke-stained blinds on the windows. He stared up at the cracks in the ceiling, and cringed at the stained and torn-up couch in one corner of the room. He jumped when a cockroach scuttled across the crumbling bathroom tiles and into a crack under the sink.

His head was still pounding and he felt like puking. The stench of urine and vomit was overpowering. He swung his feet to the floor, checking for more roaches, and staggered to the bathroom.

He knelt with his head poised over the toilet just in time. The bile spewed from his gut. Even after all the pain of the past year, it was the first time in his life that he honestly wished he was dead.

He laughed bitterly as he thought about his blowout with Rebecca. How he'd slammed the phone down, vowing to pursue the case with or without her. Instead, here he was, pursuing oblivion – self-medicating big-time and puking his guts out alone in a no-name hotel.

Staggering to his feet and out of the bathroom, he checked the couch for bedbugs and bodily fluids, gave up, and flopped down for a cigarette. Scanning once again around the decaying room, he thought back on how he'd arrived at this point.

Why had it been so important for him to go on with the case, risking his own life and the lives of people close to him, and cruising for another breakdown? Was it guilt over Gloria's death? He'd barely known her. Anyway, could he have prevented her suicide, even if he'd done all that he'd promised? Probably not.

He wasn't a cop anymore, but crime investigation had once been his life's work. It was almost like fate had contrived to place him, of all people, at a certain location, at a certain time, to witness the events that had set all this in motion.

His path had become inextricably linked with Gloria's death and the events that followed. He fought against an impulse and cursed himself for giving in as, for the first time in days, his thoughts drifted yet again back to 'the case'.

His investigation so far, and his own intuition, told him that he'd stumbled onto something far more dangerous than anything he'd dealt with before. But was the information real, or was it his imagination? Could it all be explained away as coincidence? Was he finding patterns where none really existed? Was Retigo's journal just the ravings of a lunatic?

He needed to prove to Rebecca, his old colleagues, and especially himself, that he still had what it takes, and he needed to find justice for Gloria and Ralphie.

He mentally shifted the bits of information he'd compiled since Gloria's death around in his mind like the pieces of an ever-changing jigsaw puzzle: a murdering cult patronized by the rich and powerful, a multi-billion-dollar corporation conspiring to kidnap and murder innocent children, a drug-induced deformity, a baby with the facial expression of an adult and the aura of a wild animal, a slip of paper that appeared to be a hit list but contained only two names.

Something connected the pieces. Some angle of approach, some intellectual prism, would reveal the relationships among the diverse facts he'd uncovered. He lay back, eyes closed, an arm resting on his forehead.

He opened his eyes and lowered his arm, as it occurred to him that at one point he'd been close enough to reach out and touch the nexus that connected all the facts.

He sat up and blinked. Like the keystone supporting an ancient archway, the new information, or rather the new way of looking at old information, instantly imposed form onto fragments that had seemed random and unconnected, and provided the strength to hold them together. A portrait of the case had finally morphed into existence.

The form coalesced in his mind and suddenly he was wide awake. He got up and put out a hand to steady himself as he stumbled to the bathroom. The ancient plumbing creaked and knocked as he splashed cold water on his face. To his relief, he found a bottle of aspirin on a shelf in the medicine cabinet. He chugged three glasses of brownish water and used the last one to wash several pills down.

In an instant, a weight fell from his shoulders as a realization swept over him like an icy breaker on Kits beach.

He wasn't crazy.

He took off out the door.

Pedestrians stared and veered widely around him as Frank made his way to the Granville Skytrain station. The other passengers in his railcar held their noses and moved away as it sped toward the stop in

Yaletown where he'd left his car. He prayed that the vehicle would still be there.

He made it to the spot where he'd parked, what seemed like a lifetime ago, and breathed a sigh of relief. Though several parking tickets fluttered beneath the wipers, the car was undisturbed. He found the spare key he'd hidden in a magnetic holder in the wheel-well.

He didn't want to go home. The image of the car from the parkade creeping by his bedroom window still made him nervous. Here, in the decrepit underbelly of the city, he was a lot harder to find. Anyway, he was anxious to test out his new theory. Instead he drove back to his hotel. He hauled his gym bag, unused for more than a year, out of the trunk. After stripping off his filthy clothes, he showered, then slept for a couple of hours.

He awoke feeling a little better and changed into the clothes from the bag. Patrons who were probably used to the outlandish sights of the Downtown Eastside still stared as he walked into the Laundromat wearing shorts, a tee-shirt that said 'Vancouver Sun Run', and gym shoes, and used some of what was left of his cash to run the washer and dryer. The rest paid for a cheap Bic razor.

Dressed in his newly-laundered clothes and the gym shoes, he hit the nearest branch of his bank, convinced them who he was, canceled all his credit cards and arranged for a new one, and withdrew enough cash to last him a few days.

Finally ready, he headed for Mountain View Hospital.

☼

Frank wasn't sure what he was going to do when he met Ricky Augustus again. Two things nagged at him and convinced him that the quadriplegic was the key to the mystery. The first was Ricky's eyes, hauntingly similar to those of Gloria's kidnapped baby. The second was the simple fact that Ricky's name was one of two on a list Frank was still convinced was a 'hit' list. Why would anybody go to the trouble to kill a mentally challenged, speechless cripple?

The nurse had said they had no idea what had caused Ricky's deformities. If whatever was behind the conspiracy he'd uncovered related to the side effects of a drug taken during pregnancy, maybe Ricky was living proof of that fact. Maybe his mere existence posed a danger to Kaffir Pharma and those who controlled it. If they got wind of Ricky's existence…

Then there was the supposed accidental death of Richard Carson. Was Carson really dead? Like so many aspects of the case, his death could be explained away, but Frank's gut told him something more was going on.

"Hi Frank," Nurse Carstairs greeted him as he walked through the doors of the Mountain View Centre. "Good to see you back here."

"No offense," she continued, "but you look like you've been through the wringer. Maybe you should come back after you've gotten some rest."

"I've had a rough couple of days," Frank said, "but I'm fine. Actually, I think a little time with Ricky would pick up my spirits."

She smiled. "I'm glad someone is finally taking an interest in Ricky."

"That reminds me," Frank said. "The first time I came here you said that nobody had ever visited Ricky. I was just wondering – is that literally true? No one has ever visited Ricky Augustus other than me?"

Her brow wrinkled in thought.

"I can't remember anyone ever visiting him. I can check the records for you."

"I'd appreciate that."

She disappeared into a back room and returned several minutes later with a thin file folder.

"I was almost right," she said, peering down at the open folder. "Apparently Ricky did have one other visitor, a couple of years ago. It was before I started here; a man."

"One visitor? Did he leave a name or address?"

She shook her head. "No address. He was required to leave a name, but I'm not authorized to release that information. I guess it's okay to tell you that it doesn't really look like a real name anyway."

"John Smith, or something like that," Frank said.

The nurse nodded.

"Can you tell me anything about him?"

She thumbed through the papers in the folder.

"According to this, he was a distant relative of Ricky's. Ricky had so few prospects, and no one had ever come to see him, so I guess they gave the guy the benefit of the doubt."

As before, Nurse Carstairs led him to Ricky, who occupied the exact same space he had during Frank's first visit. Frank asked her to bring him a chair and he sat down in front of the quadriplegic, who this time faced the room with his back to the wall. As before, Frank told her that her presence wasn't required, and she went off to perform her other duties.

Frank glanced around to make sure no one else was within hearing distance. Satisfied, he moved his chair right in front of Ricky and leaned forward, his lips close to Ricky's ear.

"I found a list with your name on it," he said. "I think it's a hit list. I think your life may be in danger."

Ricky's expression seemed to alter slightly, though so subtly it was almost imperceptible. Frank waited for more of a response. Almost a minute passed. Frank was about to conclude that his theory had been wrong, when Ricky's fingers slowly crawled up onto the stick of his electric wheelchair and he swiveled around, first to one side of Frank, then to the other.

At first Frank thought his host was trying to get away. Then he realized Ricky was checking that the nurse was nowhere to be seen. His suspicions were confirmed when Ricky quickly swiveled back to face him.

Ricky stared into his eyes. It was unnerving. He had the impression that the crippled man was measuring him somehow, trying to come to some decision. After another minute or so of uneasy silence, Ricky spun his wheelchair to the right and Frank caught a slight movement of Ricky's head in that direction.

He was confused at first, but finally guessed that Ricky was motioning for him to move as well. He shifted his chair around so that he was once again facing the quadriplegic. Ricky continued to angle his chair away from the room, and Frank understood – Ricky wanted to be facing away from the rest of the 'inmates'. Frank moved aside to allow

Ricky to turn, then re-positioned his chair. Now their faces were both out of view of others in the room – Ricky because his back was to them – Frank because Ricky blocked their view.

Ricky's wheelchair crawled forward so that their faces were centimeters apart. To Frank's shock, Ricky's lips started to move. There was almost no sound, only eerie puffs of air coming from Ricky's mouth – puffs that were nevertheless being shaped into something intelligible by Ricky's lips. Frank tried to read those lips and strained to hear what Ricky was saying.

Ricky had to repeat himself several times before Frank nodded that he understood, and he smiled.

TWENTY SEVEN

....

CONFESSION

The golden expanse of Kits Beach stretched out below them in the afternoon sun as Rebecca and Carla sat on the patio of the Boathouse restaurant. Toddlers plopped plastic buckets onto sand castles under their mothers' watchful eyes. Shirtless teenage boys yelled as they tossed a football around. A wet and shaggy black Lab, a chunk of driftwood clamped in its teeth, waded on shore and drenched its owner shaking off the salty water.

Rebecca and Carla had just finished a light lunch. Rebecca sat bolt upright in her chair, hands gripping her coffee cup. She'd made up her mind to tell Carla the truth. She'd be admitting to betraying a woman who had become, after only a few meetings, one of the best friends she ever had. But it had to be done, and the sooner the better.

She was about to open her mouth when Carla spoke, "Something's bothering you."

Rebecca felt herself blush. "I have a confession to make," she said.

Carla smiled at her, "Oooh, sounds serious."

"To tell the truth," Rebecca said, feeling the warmth rising to her cheeks, "I'm ashamed to admit it. I hope it won't ruin our friendship.

Before I say anything, I just want you to know that I was desperate to get to the bottom of what happened to my sister."

"Your sister?" Carla said.

Rebecca stared into her cup, unsure how to begin.

Carla touched her hand. "I can't imagine anything you could say that would destroy our friendship. Go ahead, tell me."

Rebecca lifted her head and looked at her friend. "Well, the fact is that when I came to see you that first time, I wasn't honest with you. I wasn't working on an article at all."

"Really?"

"It seems silly now. A friend of mine was helping me investigate what happened to my sister Gloria."

Rebecca explained the circumstances of Ralphie's disappearance and Gloria's suicide, the theory about the baby not being Ralphie, and the DNA test. Carla shook her head slowly as she listened.

"This is the friend you spoke about before," Carla said.

Rebecca nodded. "Like I said, he's got some psychological issues. I should have known better than to buy into his story."

Carla's eyebrows knotted together. "So, if you weren't writing an article, what were you doing?"

A gust of wind licked over the patio. Rebecca pulled a wayward strand of hair behind her ear.

"My friend had this idea... it's embarrassing to even say it now – this idea that the kidnapping of Gloria's baby had something to do with Kaffir and Olmerol."

Carla laughed. "Your friend has a vivid imagination." Her expression turned serious. "So our friendship has just been a ruse to allow you to spy on me?"

"That's how it started out," Rebecca said, "but that was before I got to know you. I really do consider you my friend. I've come to value our time together.

"I hope you understand the context for all this. My sister's child was kidnapped and killed. Then she committed suicide. I refused to believe that she could harm her own baby. I was desperate to prove her innocent. I was grasping at straws."

"I'm so sorry about your sister," Carla said. "But – your little investigation is over?"

"Yes. The whole issue is closed as far as I'm concerned. I told my friend to get help."

"And do you think he'll do as you say?"

Rebecca looked out to sea, not wanting to face her friend. "He's kind of fixated, but eventually he'll come to his senses."

Carla touched Rebecca's sleeve.

"So who is this friend?" she asked. The usual childlike quality in her voice was cut with a hardness she'd never hear before. Or was Rebecca's guilt distorting her perception?

"I don't think it would be appropriate for me to tell you," Rebecca said. "I'm sorry. I hope you understand."

"But I'm afraid I don't understand."

"Technically he wasn't my client, but it would still be unethical for me to talk about it. I'm sorry the whole thing ever happened. I'm guilty of some bad judgment. Can we just forget about it and go on from here?"

Carla leaned toward her. "I know how it feels to lose someone you love. I know what it can do to you. That's why I'm willing to overlook your offensive behaviour and forget it ever happened."

Carla took Rebecca's hand as if to comfort her, but, to Rebecca's surprise, squeezed it so hard she winced with pain.

"But I need to know who your friend is, so I can protect myself. You admit he's not your client. There's no duty of confidentiality."

"You're hurting me," Rebecca said.

The woman sitting across from her was a different person from the one she'd shared her secrets with days before. Rebecca had no compelling reason not to tell Carla about Frank, but a voice deep inside her said no. Again she refused.

Carla let go of her hand. Her face remained hard for a second, but then almost instantaneously resumed its usual friendly expression.

"Should I be concerned?" Carla said. "If some mentally unstable person is stalking me..."

Rebecca shook her head. "He's not like that. He's just misguided."

Carla sat back in her chair. "I hope you'll at least keep me informed if your friend indicates that he has any designs on me."

"He's harmless, believe me," Rebecca said, praying that she was right. "But if I ever feel that you're threatened in any way, of course I'll let you know."

Rebecca felt ashamed. She didn't really know why she was refusing Carla's reasonable request, but she didn't change her mind.

TWENTY EIGHT

....

THE ARX

"Find somewhere private we can talk." Those were the words Ricky had spoken to Frank in his ghost-like whisper.

Frank found Nurse Carstairs and brought her over.

He nodded at Ricky. "Is it possible to take him somewhere outside?"

"Ricky doesn't cope well with change," she said. "Are you sure he wants to go? Did you talk to him?"

Frank tensed. "Talk to him?"

The nurse laughed. "Well I know he's not going to answer, but sometimes you can tell by his facial expression what he wants."

Nurse Carstairs leaned down in front of Ricky. "Would you like to go out for a walk with Frank?" she said loudly, like she was talking to a child. Ricky was motionless for several seconds, but finally gave a barely perceptible nod.

"Well," she said, surprised, "he doesn't seem to mind the idea. It's a nice day. There's a little garden out behind the building. Why don't you take him there for now and see how it goes. Let's limit it to a half-hour or so. Maybe next time, if there is a next time, you can take him longer. It might be good for Ricky to get a little outside stimulation."

She explained how to get to the garden. Frank walked along the dark hallway and down a zig-zagging ramp, followed by Ricky whirring along in his electric wheelchair. A small wooden gazebo stood in the center of a garden filled with ornamental shrubs and rose bushes. They moved up a brick pathway to the gazebo, and Frank sat on one of the steps.

He did a quick scan of the garden. There was no one around.

"We're alone," he said. Ricky nodded faintly.

Frank moved his head to within a few centimeters of Ricky's so that he could hear the faint whisper of the quadriplegic's voice.

"So, you can speak," Frank said.

"Apparently," Ricky whispered, with the hint of what, for him, was a smile.

"But all the nursing staff think you can't. They think you're mentally disabled."

Ricky gave a barely perceptible shrug.

"So you've never spoken to anyone in all the years you've been at the hospital?"

Ricky shook his head.

"Why?"

"D…Dangerous – g…give myself away."

"Well, why now? Why talk to me?"

Ricky swallowed feebly, as if gathering the strength to speak.

"You f…found me. Others w…will. When the Arx find me, d…death is assured…"

"The Arx?"

"W…What people you seek c…call themselves."

"How do you know I'm looking for anybody?"

"Know a…about me. No other ex…explanation."

"Tell me about the Arx. Who are they?"

"They are a r…race who live among you, but are n…not of you."

"What do you mean, 'not *of* you'?"

"They are like another s…species."

"That's impossible," Frank said. His knuckles were white on the wooden post of the gazebo.

At that moment a small group of people appeared on the walkway and headed slowly toward them.

"Somebody's coming," Frank said.

Ricky's hand moved to the control of his wheelchair.

"Wait," Frank said. "They said at the front you had a visitor, a couple of years ago."

Ricky was silent.

"They're still a long way from us," Frank said, checking the strollers. "We've got a few minutes."

"Man," Ricky finally spoke. "Tried to t…talk to me – was afraid. Y…Younger then."

Frank glanced down the walk. The group was admiring some of the flowers along the walkway.

"It's okay," he said. "We've still got time. What did he say to you?"

"Said he knew M…Mother. Didn't b…believe him. He laughed. Said I had n…nothing to fear – he'd been d…dead for years."

"What did he mean by that?"

Ricky shrugged.

Frank pushed on. "Why are the Arx after you?"

"Would s…spare no effort to destroy me – m…might reveal their existence."

"Well, you're still alive, so the guy I tangled with must have been the only one who knew about you. The names he had were yours and a reporter. You ever heard of a guy named Lawrence Retigo?"

Ricky shook his head.

"Maybe the guy wanted to use you as some kind of bargaining chip. He's dead, so you may be safe – at least for now."

"If one l…learned of my existence others will f…follow. No consequence. Not afraid to d…die. You s…should be afraid. They know about me – will s…soon know about you."

"I think they already know about me."

"T…Then your death is a…assured."

Frank looked into Ricky's eyes. Ricky was absolutely convinced that what he was saying was the truth.

Voices approached. The group was almost upon them.

"We can wait till they leave," Frank said. "Maybe they won't be long."

"T…Tired," Ricky said. "Very tired."

Ricky was clearly not going to say anymore. They retraced their steps back up the path and hallway to the recreation area.

"Tomorrow," Frank whispered to Ricky. "I'll be here."

TWENTY NINE

....

CATCH AND RELEASE

It was dark by the time Frank approached his house after the trip to Mountain View, and he was exhausted. At first he'd been uneasy about going home, but after a careful drive around the neighbourhood and half an hour on a nearby hill watching, he'd seen nothing. He was relieved as he unlocked the door and walked inside, the familiarity offering a brief respite from the horror that his life had become.

He'd decided to get a change of clothes, proper shoes, and most importantly, a gun locked in the night table by his bed. He was still feeling the ravages of his recent binge, and Ricky's statement about both his own and Frank's impending death had rattled his nerves.

He scoured the front and back yards, double-checked that all the doors were locked and the curtains drawn, and staggered upstairs. He wanted to sleep, even if only for an hour or so, but first he retrieved a key from its hiding place in the closet, and reached to unlock the night table drawer. It was already open a crack. His body tensed; the lock had been broken. He pulled out the drawer. The gun that he kept there was gone. He looked around. Nothing else had been touched.

He ran downstairs and was reaching for the front door when there was a metallic scraping sound on the other side. Through the peep-hole he saw a man in a black suit tinkering with the lock. Frank crouched as he made his way to the kitchen, which had a view of the back patio. Another man stood at the back door, waiting.

Frank had taken a single step to run back upstairs when the front door opened and a voice yelled: "Stop right there!"

Frank spun around to see the man from the peep-hole holding a gun.

The man came inside and closed and locked the door. Keeping his gun trained on Frank, he crossed the room and opened the back door for his partner. The back-door guy immediately headed for the hall closet, like he'd been there before. He returned with Frank's own fluorescent orange extension cord, the one he used with his electric lawnmower. Neither man said another word.

The one with the gun held it on Frank while his partner climbed onto a chair and strung the cord around the safety hook for the living room fan, which was sturdy enough to hold a man's weight. Satisfied, he tied one end of the cord to a nearby stair banister and formed the free end into a loop large enough for a head to fit through. Frank swallowed. Their plan was clear; he was to join Lawrence Retigo and unnamed and unnumbered others.

The one who'd fastened the cord took Frank's arm and motioned for him to climb up. Frank mounted the chair and stood facing the orange noose.

Frank's executioner climbed onto another chair and grabbed the noose. His partner continued to hold the gun. Frank scoured his panicked brain for a way out, but came up with nothing. He started to shake

240

and felt weak in the knees. The man with the noose reached out to slip it around Frank's neck.

His executioner paused and turned to listen. In the distance, the wail of police sirens approached the house. Frank's two captors eyed each other. Seconds later headlights tracked across the living room curtains, and two cars skidded into Frank's driveway, sirens blaring, red and blue lights flashing. The man holding the noose climbed down to peek through the drawn curtains. His partner lowered his gun and took a step toward the front door. Frank saw his only chance. He leapt off the chair and dove for the stairs, taking them two at a time.

He glanced back. The man with the gun raised it and fired. The bullet whizzed by Frank's head and tore into the wall beside him. He reached the landing and dove to his right as another shot blasted a hole in the hall closet. Footsteps started up the stairs but suddenly headed back down, and Frank heard the back door slam.

Through the bedroom window he saw his would-be executioners tear through the back gate, down the street, and into an alley. He checked the window on the other side. Two police cars, with lights flashing, blocked his driveway.

A fist pounded on the front door.

"Police!" a voice yelled.

Frank was confused. The men setting him up to die must either be Ricky's 'Arx' or thugs hired by them, but who were *these* guys? Were they really cops? They had the cars, but who knew what the Arx were capable of? And what were they doing here?

The pounding was replaced by a series of explosive thuds as Frank flew down the stairs, planning to follow his attackers out the back. As he hit the bottom step the front door crashed open and he was face to face with two policemen holding a steel battering ram.

"Going somewhere?" said a cop just behind them, his gun drawn.

Frank raised his hands.

They were soon joined by two other cops from the back.

"Frank Langer?" the one with the gun said.

Frank nodded.

"You're wanted for questioning in the death of Detective Grant Stocker."

"What!" Frank said. He stood with his mouth open.

Two of the men grabbed him, one on each arm. They took a cursory glance at the draped extension cord, then led him to an unmarked police cruiser, cuffed his hands, and shoved him into the back.

Frank was relieved. It looked like they really were cops. One of them sat in the driver's seat; the other went over and spoke to a pair at the front door. He returned and sat in the passenger's seat.

"Grant Stocker's dead?" Frank said as they drove away.

"Shut up," the passenger cop said.

Frank's brain was still reeling with the shock of the news. In the rear-view mirror he spotted a black Lexus with tinted windows not far behind them. Several blocks later he checked again and it was still there. He mentioned it to the cops in the front.

"Shut up," the one in the passenger seat said again, but he glanced behind him and confirmed that Frank was right. They continued on the highway into town, their shadow constantly in view.

The Lexus stayed behind them until they reached the station, then turned a corner too far away to get the license plate. The police parked their car, and roughly shoved Frank toward the station door.

☼

For a long time Frank sat alone in a holding cell, struggling to piece together what was happening.

Stocker dead? He ran the thought by again, still trying to comprehend it. One thing he did understand. In the eyes of the world, he had ample motive for killing his former colleague. Frank's relationship with Stocker was well known, and his humiliation at the last visit had been witnessed by half the detectives in the squad room. He tried to sleep, but the events of the past few days hurtled through his mind like speeding freight trains.

The place was eerily quiet; as far as he could tell he was the only prisoner. Once in a while a male voice would drift in from his right. Frank recognized it as Sergeant Fisk, the officer who had supervised his incarceration. Frank couldn't hear what was being said. Finally, exhausted, he passed out on the cot in his cell.

Several hours later he was awakened by Fisk's voice, rising in volume and echoing loudly down the hallway.

"But this is a murder investigation!" Fisk shouted. "Stocker was shot with the guy's gun!"

Frank's ears perked up at the conversation. He heard Fisk tapping his foot angrily as he apparently listened to a voice on the other end of the phone line.

"You're damned right you'll take responsibility," Fisk barked. "And I want the order in writing. I'm not going to take the rap when the shit hits the fan."

Behind it all Frank could see the workings of the Arx. He wasn't sure why they'd wanted Stocker dead. They would understand the on-slaught of publicity that would be unleashed with the murder of a senior police detective. They must have had a damn good reason.

Given that, it was an excellent plan. Kill Stocker, pin the blame on Frank, who had ample motive and was known to be on the edge already, then arrange for Frank to commit suicide at home, out of remorse, by hanging himself with his own extension cord.

It was ironic that what had probably saved his life was his several days of binge drinking. He hadn't been at home, or anywhere the Arx could find him, when Stocker was killed.

He shuddered as he pieced together the meaning of Fisk's phone conversation. Someone – someone with a lot of clout – was pushing hard for him to be released. A move like that would be highly unusual and hard to explain. Whoever was behind it must be desperate enough to risk their reputation and career.

He lifted his head and stared at the camera installed on the ceiling, then walked to the front of the cell. He could just make out the forms of the guards stationed at either end of the hallway.

Suddenly he understood. His adversaries were unable to touch him here at the station, where he might divulge their secrets and eventually find someone to believe him. They needed him outside, out in the world where he could become the victim of an unfortunate 'accident' or con-venient suicide.

Right now, he was actually much safer in jail. Problem was, it didn't sound like he was going to stay there for much longer.

A couple of hours later, as he'd expected and dreaded, a grumbling Sergeant Fisk ordered him released, and the bewildered desk cop handed over his personal belongings and told him he was free to go.

THIRTY

··

ON THE RUN

Frank staggered from the front door of the police station, blinking and shading his eyes against the morning sun. He stood for a moment, staring at the empty street. He guessed that the number of minutes he had left on earth could be counted on the fingers of one hand.

He'd tried to convince the police that he would be killed if they forced him to leave.

"You should be jumping for joy," one of the cops had said. "Walking away from a jam like that? Somebody up there's looking out for you, big time."

Frank reminded them about the Lexus. To humour him, they followed him outside and checked, but it was nowhere in sight. They patted him on the shoulder and told him he was imagining things. They even tried to call Rebecca but there was no answer.

It occurred to Frank that if they decided he was delusional, they might call for outside psychiatric help. That help might, in fact almost certainly would, turn out to be someone connected with the Arx.

246

Avoiding that possibility was more important than staying inside, so he finally just stumbled down the stairs and hit the sidewalk running.

He glanced back over his shoulder, down the street where the Lexus had disappeared. As he'd expected, it reappeared a few blocks away, and moved up fast.

Once he was out of sight of the station, the Lexus stopped. The doors opened. Two men in black suits got out and jogged after him at a distance. There wasn't much traffic. He sprinted past a few staring pedestrians.

They're waiting until there's no witnesses around, he thought. *They still want to make it look like an accident.*

The men moved closer. Frank was gasping for breath, slowing down. He checked the buildings on either side of the street. Maybe if he could dash into an open doorway... But none of the doors looked open. If he stopped to try one and found it locked he'd be trapped.

He crossed the street. The two shadows followed. The Lexus stayed on the other side, but kept up with him. His pursuers were quickly closing the gap. He looked ahead and saw nothing, not even a door to duck into.

His cigarette-scarred lungs burned and he gasped for air as he ran. He wouldn't be able to keep this up much longer. Just ahead, a wire mesh fence blocked access to a lot-sized pit where a building had been demolished. The public had been using the pit as a dump; it was full of garbage and standing water. A stink rose as Frank approached it.

Someone had pried open a gap in the fence, just enough to squeeze through. He glanced further up the street ahead. A cross-alley lay less than a block away, a perfect ambush opportunity for his pursuers. They were gaining quickly now; they would be on him in seconds. They split up, one continuing directly for him, the other moving across the street to block his escape. The Lexus raced past him and skidded to a stop next to the cross-alley.

He had only one chance. On reaching the empty lot he pulled out the mesh flap on the fence and pushed through. There was a narrow lip of earth surrounding the pit. He tried to balance along one side but slid down and ended up knee-deep in the stinking water. He slogged through the sewer-like sludge, past a rat swimming a few feet away.

He glanced back, expecting to see his pursuer to be right behind him. To his shock, the man was still outside the fence, prowling along its length like an animal pacing its cage. The man finally pulled out the mesh flap and started to squeeze through. As soon as he found himself inside he recoiled, like he was about to vomit, and fled back through the opening.

What the hell? Frank thought.

Frank reached the far edge and had only to climb up the other side. His pursuer signaled to the other, and pulled out a gun. In a panic, Frank leapt onto the far bank. He clawed his way to the top and hunted for another break in the fence at the back.

On the street, the second pursuer, also reluctant to enter the pit, steeled himself and pushed through the flap. He slid down into the stinking water, a horrified expression on his face. His partner pointed his gun at Frank.

A third man appeared, the driver from the car. Frank dove into the mud as a shot whizzed over his head.

I guess they gave up on making it look like an accident, he thought.

He found another gap in the fence and desperately shoved through it as a bullet tore a chip out of a brick beside him.

He emerged in a filthy alley, out of sight of his pursuers. He stared back behind him at the fence and the rotting garbage and his throat constricted. Darkness began to descend. The shadows of the buildings pressed in like the jaws of a vise.

"No... not now!" he gasped, clenching his fists and flattening his body against the building. He tried a breathing exercise Rebecca had shown him, and slowly hauled himself back into reality.

He took off, and ran until he thought his lungs would burst. He scanned the back doors that dotted the alley as he moved, but none looked accessible. As he approached one it swung open, and a maintenance worker emerged and walked toward a truck parked nearby. Frank rushed forward and managed to catch the door before it closed. He stumbled inside.

To his shock, he was in an upscale office building: clean, bright, modern. His feet and pants up to his knees were covered with filth and mud, as was his jacket from crawling up the bank. He was leaving foul-smelling footprints wherever he stepped. He spotted a restroom sign and rushed inside.

He stuffed his jacket and socks in the garbage, and rinsed and dried the soles of his shoes. He took off his pants, washed the bottoms in the sink, wrung them out and held them with shaking hands under the blow dryer. They didn't have to be dry as long as they didn't leave a trail of drips that could be followed.

The restroom door opened and Frank jumped back, expecting one of his black-suited pursuers. He relaxed when a middle-aged man in a

suit and tie stepped in. The man, seeing Frank standing in his under-
wear, stared at him wide-eyed.

"Spilled something on them," Frank said, laughing. The man
bought his excuse, laughed with him, and headed for a stall.

Frank got dressed and opened the restroom door a crack. The hallway was clear. With a huge lump in his throat he stepped out and crept
down it, expecting at any second to come face-to-face with the Arx.

He reached the lobby, peeked around a corner, and noticed a land-
mark outside that might save his life – a bus stop, right in front of the
main doors. He moved close enough to see down the street, praying that
a bus was coming. There was one a block away, but he couldn't be sure
if it would stop.

He stood shaking at the glass front doors, forcing a smile at the people entering and leaving the building, scanning for the black-clad figure
that would spell his doom.

The bus arrived and stopped right in front of him. Frank's plan was
to wait until the two people already at the stop had boarded, but not so
long that the bus would leave. The two, a man and a woman, climbed
on and paid.

He rushed out to jump on at the last minute. Just as he reached the
door an old woman carrying a load of packages squeezed in front of
him.

"How much?" she asked the driver.

"Two seventy-five."

"Oh…" she said. "I'm not sure if I have the correct change."

She fiddled with her purse, trying to find her change with one hand
on her packages.

Frank glanced frantically up the street. The Arx driver was rushing in and out of doorways searching, but hadn't yet spotted him. Frank ducked low behind the woman, who eyed him suspiciously.

She finally found the change and began to climb on board, juggling her packages. Frank checked down the street. The driver had emerged from a doorway and was headed towards him. Frank was in the open now. All the driver would have to do was look in his direction.

Finally, the woman moved down the aisle and the way was clear. Frank flew up the steps and crouched as he paid. The bus was crowded; he wedged himself between two tall men and hunched down. As the bus pulled away he saw the two Arx pursuers meet up with the driver and they continued down the street. He was safe – for now.

By an infinitely circuitous route that would have made Lawrence Retigo proud, Frank made his way back to the scummiest part of the Downtown Eastside. He booked a room in yet another decrepit hotel under an assumed name. He washed all of his clothes in the sink using the complementary hotel shampoo, then flopped down on the lumpy bed. He had to think.

A few hours later Frank's hands were still shaking as he hunkered down in the rearmost seat of a city bus headed for Mountain View Hospital. He'd bought a cheap replacement jacket and some socks from a thrift shop near his hotel. He didn't dare go home for clothes or his car. The irony struck him that even though the police believed him guilty of murdering a fellow officer, that wasn't his biggest problem.

As he guessed Lawrence Retigo must have done before him, he scanned the street for any sign that he was being followed. A car staying with them for too long or unexpectedly changing lanes, a glance from a driver beside them – each jacked up his pulse rate. His stomach churned and his palms were slippery with sweat. He understood what the hapless reporter must have gone through: the endless waiting, the crippling terror.

But he had to talk to Ricky again. The quadriplegic was his only link to the Arx; he had to find out more of what Ricky knew.

Since his previous visit had gone without a hitch, the staff showed no resistance when he asked again if he could take Ricky outside. Again, they headed to the gazebo and hid behind the rosebush. Ricky gulped and fought for breath as he tried to force enough air out of his lungs to produce an audible sound.

"You okay?" Frank asked. "Are you comfortable?"

Ricky nodded faintly.

"Tell me about the Arx," Frank said.

"N...Never met anyone but Mother," Ricky said. "Know only w...what she told me. Arx – new and b...better version of h...humanity. Will r...replace humans on earth."

Frank was stunned, but he pushed on. "There's some connection with Kaffir Pharma and Olmerol."

"D...Deformities – not like other deformities. B...Beneficial. H...High intelligence, especially m...mathematics and science. Eidetic m...memories."

"But a deformity like that must be pretty obvious. How come nobody's caught on?"

252

"Only affects b…brain – personality. Not v…visible to outside. Arx – m…mature earlier. Learn to behave l…like Monkeys."

"Monkeys?"

"What they c…call you, non-Arx. An a…annoyance to be r…removed whenever p…possible."

"I read a description of a fight between two Arx men," Frank said. "One of them killed the other like it was nothing."

"Arx are p…psychopaths. N…No empathy for others. W…What you call conscience, A…Arx call 'the weakness'. W…Weakness almost non-existent in Arx m…males. R…Rare in females. Arx with weakness are k…killed. Arx care about p…power, and c…continuation of species."

"The ones I heard about lived in a mansion in Point Grey. A few of the women had their own apartments."

"L…Live together. L…Large houses c…called Strongholds. Some work. O…Others rear children. Outsiders r…rarely allowed in. F…Females who i…interact with Monkey world l…live outside for c…cover. One male c…commands, with a f…few others. U…Ultimate authority is the M…Matriarch."

"Matriarch?" Frank said. A queasy sensation that had begun in his stomach moved into his throat.

"F…First of our kind. F…Founder of f…first Stronghold. Arx t…track drug distribution, medical r…records. D…Deformed babies taken – assigned to a S…Stronghold. M…Monkeys suspect n…nothing."

"I wish you'd quit calling us that," Frank said. "So, they kidnap the kids before anybody can work out that they have the deformity. Can't the Arx have their own kids?"

"Arx interbreeding p…produces Monkey children. Devastating m…mutations when Arx women t…take Olmerol."

"How do you fit in?"

"Mother said I was p…product of experiment – for Arx to p…procreate without Monkeys. M…Mother chosen to test new formulation.

"Results – as y…you see." With effort, Ricky motioned his head down at his broken, misshapen body. "Ten born. Three s…survived. All s…severely deformed. Mothers ordered to t…terminate. Others c…complied. Mother had the w…weakness. They d…didn't know. Showed c…compassion for me. Told them she t…terminated. Kept me hidden for years."

"Lived in c…closet. N…Never went outside Mother's room. Taught me, l…looked after me. My c…condition worsened. She w…worried they'd find me. P…Put me here. Arx not a…aware of my existence – until now."

Ricky took a deep breath. Speaking was obviously tiring for him.

"What happened to your mother?"

"Never s…saw her again. A…Assume she died."

"So are you like the others?"

"Mother said I was i…intelligent as others, but I have the w…weakness."

Ricky stopped and took what for him were several deep breaths.

"You okay?" Frank asked.

After a few seconds Ricky nodded.

"You said your mother snuck you out of the Stronghold. That must have been tough with somebody in your condition."

"T...Tunnel. C...Connects Stronghold to outside. Arx f...fear detection by Monkey world. R...Rarely used. Not guarded. Mother c...carried me to waiting car."

Frank's eyes widened. "Who drove the car?"

"N...Never saw f...face."

"Do you know where the place is where you grew up?"

"Never w...went outside. Original S...Stronghold - c...called Genesis."

Ricky talked for another twenty minutes in his halting, breathless voice. What Frank learned made his hair stand on end. Ricky began to tire and stopped speaking. He seemed almost in a hypnotic state. Frank waited a few minutes to allow the quadriplegic to get his breath.

"When we talked before," Frank finally said, "you said my death was assured..."

"One c...chance for you," Ricky said. "E...Expose them. Once s...secret is out, no longer any r...reason to kill you. Not like h...humanity. No pity, no compassion. Kill without s...slightest care – but only for a r...reason. No hate, no revenge.

"If you carry s...secret, death is g...guaranteed. Once e...exposed, k...killing you no longer s...serves a purpose. Not evil, not good – c...concepts alien to them. Do not take life for p...pleasure, do not spare life out of c...compassion. S...Simply do what's n...necessary."

"Why are you telling me this? Aren't these your people?"

"H...Have developed a certain a...affection for humanity. Completely u...unaware of the danger."

"You understand that if their secret is revealed it will mean the end of the Arx."

"You b…believe that?"

"Well, yeah – don't you?"

Ricky said nothing. Frank felt a lump in his throat.

"Well, if I have any say in it you're not going anywhere – at least not for a while."

"T…Tired," Ricky whispered.

Frank sat on a bench opposite Ricky's wheelchair with a clear view of the pathway. "Just a few more minutes," he said. "You said a man came to visit you. Do you remember what he looked like? Do you think you'd recognize his picture?"

"Yes," Ricky said.

Frank brought out the photocopied article with Richard Carson's picture. He unfolded it and held it in front of Ricky. Ricky squinted and stared at the picture.

"That's h…him," he said.

"You sound pretty certain."

"Like others… r…remember everything."

Frank pulled back and stared at him. "Everything?"

Ricky nodded.

"Wow. So what else can you remember about this guy? Anything that would help me find him?"

"Brown suit, w…white dress shirt, no tie. G…Glasses. 1.7 meters t…tall, 90 k…kilos, Endomorphic b…body type, approximately 28% body fat."

"Approximately?"

"Liked to e...eat fried food... hamburgers."

"Come on," Frank said. "How could you possibly know that?"

"S...Smell."

"Jesus Christ. Was he carrying anything?"

Ricky shook his head.

"Is there anything else that might help me identify this guy?"

"Paper," Ricky said, almost in a whisper. He stopped and his head dipped, like he'd fallen asleep.

"Ricky?" Frank put his hand on the quadriplegic's shoulder.

"Tired," Ricky said.

"We're almost done. Just tell me – what paper?"

"S...Shirt pocket." Ricky closed his eyes. "Words in r...red letters."

Frank's eyes went wide. "You can read what it said?"

"U...Upside down," Ricky said, his eyes still closed. "Paper u...upside down. Says: '"See R...Reverse Side of T...Ticket'."

"So it's some kind of ticket. Can you read anything else?"

"N...Numbers, vertical l...lines, 'L...Lane 13'."

"Lane 13?" Frank said. "What the hell? Anything else?"

"'Change Due – $2.57'. 'U...Undersized Vehicle'."

Frank stared at the floor. "The ferry!" he said, looking up. "It's a ferry ticket stub. Read down. Somewhere on it should say which terminals."

"'Auth Only', Ricky said, a wheeze entering his voice. "Rest c...covered up by pocket."

"Shit," Frank said to himself. "What was that about vertical lines?"

"P...Pattern, narrow and w...wide."

Frank thought for a second. "A UPC code," he said. "The numbers – can you read them?"

Ricky listed off a thirteen-digit number. Frank wrote it down.

"I suppose you remember exactly when he visited you?" he said.

"A…April 25th, 2012," said Ricky. Frank shook his head. "2:07 PM," Ricky added.

"You know," Frank said, "I may actually be able to find this guy after all."

"B…Better hurry," Ricky said.

"What do you mean?"

"Man you're l…looking for," said Ricky. "V…Very sick. T…Think he's d…dying."

THIRTY ONE

....

AN ISLAND IN THE SALISH
SEA

F rank stood in line for the cafeteria on the *Queen of Nanaimo* and watched out the window as the giant ferry lumbered away from the dock. He'd contacted BC Ferries with the number from Ricky Augustus' amazing brain, and they'd used it to trace the start and end terminals for the ticket.

A hundred islands crowded between the huge slab that was Vancouver Island and the mainland, like flagstones on a gigantic walkway. They were of every shape and size, from the heavily populated Salt Spring, just off the big Island, to tiny specks of rock that appeared on the map but hadn't even rated names.

Just inside a section of ocean known as 'Active Pass' lay one of the larger in the chain, Galiano Island, about an hour's sailing from the mainland. Its main terminal, 'Sturdies Bay', had been Carson's point of departure.

Frank believed what Ricky had said about them both being marked for death. He also believed Ricky's claim that if the Arx wanted him dead nothing could ultimately stop them. He clung to the one thread of hope Ricky had offered: that if the Arx were exposed to the world they would forget about him. That they wouldn't bother to take revenge.

He had only one option: find irrefutable evidence of the Arx's existence and of the danger they posed. Even if he could convince Ricky to tell his story and keep the crippled man alive long enough to do so, he doubted the authorities would believe it. Frank had only one slim chance: locate Richard Carson and pray that Carson could provide the proof he needed.

The labyrinthine route he'd followed to get to the ferry terminal took twice as long as he would have otherwise, but he was reasonably certain that no-one was tailing him. Anyway, if the Arx knew where he was, he would be dead by now. Just the same he continually glanced over his shoulder.

He grabbed a self-serve plastic-wrapped sandwich, filled a Styrofoam cup with coffee, and set them on the plastic tray he was carrying. He paid, found a table near a bulkhead, and sat with his back against the wall where he could watch people approaching.

After eating he wandered out on deck. He studied the crowd around him as he moved. A familiar face, a bump on the shoulder from a stranger, an unexpected glance – each ratcheted up his pulse rate.

An announcement came over the intercom that the ship's horn was about to sound. Even though he was prepared, the ear-splitting blast made him jump.

I'm losing it again, he thought.

The ferry took a sharp right and they sailed around a bend into Active Pass. The scenery was breathtaking: rugged, evergreen-blanketed cliffs plunging into the sea, separated by tiny gray scallops of gravel beach. Occasionally he spotted a home perched high on the surrounding bluffs.

Who lives in these places? he thought.

He studied one magnificent home partially hidden behind a grove of trees.

People who can never get far enough away from the world, he answered his own question.

Ten minutes later his destination was in sight.

Sturdies Bay was a small, quaint terminal that would have been dwarfed by the one Frank had just left on the mainland. He headed down the pedestrian walkway and off the ferry. There were no taxis on Galiano. He ended up renting a moped. Not knowing how long he'd need it, he put down a week's deposit. He'd never ridden one, but after a few shaky starts, he was buzzing around the island confidently.

He hit the local library and talked the bored librarian into helping him research records of home purchases on the island. He half-guessed/half-hoped that Carson had purchased something around the time he disappeared. Luckily, it was a small island; there weren't many entries. He found nothing in the records for 1999 that fit Carson's profile. He looked at rentals and had no better luck. He tried 98, then 97 – still nothing.

He got to thinking. Carson had faked his own death. He would be running scared, searching out the most remote hiding place he could find. Galiano was out of the way and not heavily populated, but it was on the main ferry routes and easy to get to. It was off the beaten path, but not by much.

He returned to the librarian's desk.

"I appreciate all your help," he said. The library was almost empty. She seemed to welcome his interruption.

"This may seem like a strange question," he said, "but hypothetically speaking, say I wanted to avoid contact with the outside world, but still wanted to be able to get supplies regularly. Say my starting point was here on Galiano – where would I go?"

"There's a ton of islands out there," she said. "Some of them aren't even big enough to build a house on. There's one right next door, just off Montague Harbour, called Parker Island. You can charter a boat. There's no real community there, but there's a few vacation homes. Is that the kind of place you're talking about?"

THIRTY TWO

....

AN EVEN SMALLER ISLAND

T he boat Frank chartered to Parker Island was for foot passengers only, but he convinced the operator to allow his moped on
board.

Earlier, he'd shown Carson's picture around to several of the dock
workers on Galiano, and finally found one who recognized him. The
man hadn't been sure of Carson's exact address, but said he lived on
the northwest tip of the island, an area with few houses. The librarian
helped Frank pinpoint the most likely house. It was little more than a
shack, but had been bought in February 1999 by a Mr. David Fox.

Carson's home was a long way from anywhere else on the island.
There were no taxis, and few roads, on Parker. Frank wobbled along
the gravel track on the moped, but within a few miles he ran out of road.
He hid the moped in some trees and hiked the final stretch.

A house hidden away on an island that's hidden away, he thought.

As he came within sight of the cabin, a gunshot blasted a chip from
a tree next to his head. He rushed behind another large tree for cover.
He poked his head out and stole a look at the cabin. The morning sun

glinted off the thin shaft of a rifle barrel protruding from a gap at the bottom of one of the windows.

There were several seconds of tense silence.

"What do you want?" a voice finally echoed from the window.

"I just want to talk to you," Frank yelled back. "I'm a friend of Ricky Augustus."

After a moment of hesitation the voice called, "You alone?"

"Yeah," Frank answered.

There was another minute or so of silence. Finally the voice yelled nervously, "Come forward. I've got my gun on you. Put your hands up and don't do anything stupid."

Frank walked forward with his hands raised. He stopped a couple of meters away from the front door, which he noticed was made from heavy-gauge steel. Behind it, he heard a shuffling sound and the scrape of metal against metal. A small panel opened at chest height, and the rifle barrel poked out of it. Another panel opened a little higher and Frank could make out the silhouette of a face behind it.

The rifle was pointed at Frank's head.

"Now who are you and what do you want?" said a low, rasping voice.

"My name is Langer, Frank Langer. I'm investigating the disappearance of several children."

The face in the shadows flinched. "So you're a cop?"

"Sort of," Frank said. For once it didn't seem appropriate to lie about his current status. "I was a cop," he said. "I had a breakdown. I'm out on stress leave."

To Frank's surprise, the man started laughing. He laughed so hard he even lowered the gun for a few seconds. The laugh quickly degenerated into a fit of coughing.

"Sorry," the voice said after fifteen seconds of hacking. "That's just too rich – seems appropriate somehow."

The voice turned serious. "Let's see some ID."

Frank lowered his right hand and reached for his only ID, the replacement credit card he'd gotten from the bank.

"Do it slow," said the man behind the door.

Frank nodded. He took a step closer, and held the card up to the opening. The rifle barrel was almost touching his chest.

A few seconds later the rifle was pulled back inside. Several heavy bolts were released and the door swung open.

The Richard Carson that stood in front of him was barely recognizable from the picture he'd studied in the photocopied newspaper article. The pudgy middle-aged scientist from the photograph had been replaced by a gaunt and skeletal wraith who stooped like he was carrying a heavy burden. What little was left of his hair had turned white, and his skin had the pale, mottled texture of someone late in the process of dying.

Carson stared into Frank's eyes, like he was trying to decide something. "How do you know about Ricky?" he finally said.

"I was staking out a mansion in Point Grey," Frank said. "I thought it had some connection with a string of child abductions. A guy tried to kill me. He had a photograph on him with a couple of names on the back. I figured it was some kind of hit list. One of the names was Ricky's."

Carson picked up his gun again and eyed Frank suspiciously. "One of them came after you? So how come you're not dead?"

Frank shrugged. "We fought and I got away."

"You got away? Bullshit. You're either some kind of genius or one lucky son of a bitch."

Frank shrugged again.

Carson's eyes widened. "Nobody followed you here?"

"I was a cop for fifteen years," Frank said. "I know when I'm being tailed."

Carson seemed to relax a little. "Ricky's still alive?" he said.

Frank nodded.

Carson twitched. "Am I on the list?"

"No, just Ricky and a reporter named Lawrence Retigo."

"Never heard of him," Carson said. "How did you find me?"

"The ferry ticket stub in your shirt pocket when you went to visit Ricky. He remembered what it said."

Carson laughed again, and even more quickly lapsed into a coughing fit.

He finally recovered. "No matter how many times I deal with these people I never seem to appreciate what I'm up against. Let's go for a walk."

He slung the rifle over his shoulder and locked the door, then gestured to a thin path leading to the right.

"You go first," he said.

They followed the trail to a bluff overlooking Active Pass, with a stunning view of the dark blue ocean below. They sat down on a rocky ledge. Carson wheezed for several minutes, exhausted by the exertion.

The air was filled with the scent of salt spray and pine needles. Far in the distance a giant blue and white ferry steamed through the pass.

Carson sat with his rifle on his knees and both hands resting on it, gazing thoughtfully out to sea.

Frank picked up a small twig and twirled it between his fingers. "You faked your own death," he said. "The others were murdered, but you beat them to the punch. You killed yourself off before they had the chance."

Frank flicked the twig out over the edge of the bluff and watched it float to the rocks below.

"Have you ever watched a really talented actor up close?" Carson asked, his voice rasping and thin.

"I'm not sure what you mean," Frank said.

"When I was going to university I worked part-time at the PNE – you know, the fairgrounds."

Frank nodded.

"They had a guy there, a professional actor, playing one of the early explorers in British Columbia. Simon Fraser, I think it was. He sat in front of a tent with a canoe beside him and went through a canned spiel about the life of an explorer.

"I found it fascinating. Not so much the story but the acting. I used to hang out and watch whenever I had nothing else to do, even after I'd seen it a dozen times. I was blown away by the transformation. I *believed* he was Simon Fraser. You watch actors, even good ones, in the movies or on TV and you really don't get what it is they're doing, the magic in it.

"But sitting a couple of meters away, looking into their eyes and listening to their voices – that's when you truly appreciate the actor's art."

For a second Frank thought his host might be losing it, drifting into some obscure youthful memory.

Carson raised his head and looked over at him. "I think that's why I was one of the few people who ever saw through them. Even people who'd worked with them for years had no idea."

"Them?"

Carson's hands tightened on his rifle. "The crowd at Kaffir."

Frank stared at him.

"There's still a lot you don't know, isn't there," Carson said. "I'm talking about the researchers on the Olmerol project. You must be aware that there's a connection between Ricky and Kaffir."

"Yeah," Frank said. "I figured out that much. I'm still not totally clear on the details."

"I first met Carla De Leon, the VP of Research, more than thirty years ago," Carson said, "at Blake Pharmaceuticals – that was the precursor to Kaffir. She was a young researcher just out of university. She was enthusiastic and ambitious, like a lot of the new grads, but right from the start there was something different about her.

Carson shifted his position. He placed the rifle on the ground beside him, on the side away from Frank.

"She had an intensity and drive I'd never seen before," he continued, "in a new grad or anyone else. She expressed an interest in working on the Olmerol research. With her stunningly beautiful looks and brilliant mind, she soon got her way.

"She was a talented actor – brilliant at adapting her persona to get whatever she wanted. I think I was the only one who saw through her. As she matured she got vastly better. If I'd met her later in her life I would never have guessed.

"I didn't think that much of it at the time. I was heavily involved with the Olmerol project, so we spent a lot of time together. Still I never really got to know her. In all the years we spent in the same lab we never talked about anything other than work."

Carson rested for a few seconds, out of breath. He finally recovered.

"Even on the job she wasn't always straight with me. I'd worked with the police forensic team when I first left university. I knew something about sociopathic behaviour, and I was convinced that Carla had all the classic signs of a pure psychopath – pathological lying, manipulation, lack of empathy."

"But she was devoted to her work – she lived and breathed Olmerol. In less than two years she was head of research for the project; she became my boss. When Blake merged with the Anderson Group to form Kaffir, she was promoted to VP of Research."

Carson paused and hunched forward in a coughing fit for almost a minute. Finally he regained control.

"And that's when people started disappearing," Frank guessed.

Carson smiled. "I called it 'the rollover'. I couldn't prove that the resignations and disappearances were part of any deliberate plan, but a voice in my head told me otherwise. As one of the senior scientists, I was still pretty critical to the project, so they hadn't come after me.

"All the replacements were women. I called them 'Carla Clones'," he smiled, "though not to their faces, of course. Carla limited their exposure to the rest of the employees. Since I was still deeply involved in the project, I saw more of them than most.

"They all had the intensity and manipulative nature I'd first seen in Carla. Like her, they were adept at presenting a 'normal' face to the rest of us. If I hadn't seen the characteristics years earlier in Carla I wouldn't have noticed. But an incident got me thinking Carla and her clones were more than just eccentric scientists."

Carson picked up a pebble and tossed it out to sea. Without looking at Frank, he continued.

"A young doctoral student showed up at Kaffir. He was doing a study on Olmerol. The clones usually made a point of accommodating outsiders, but not this time. Roadblocks were placed in the student's path. They contrived to keep research data from him, and I know at least one case where they faked the data he was given.

"Most students would have been intimidated and given up, but this one showed remarkable tenacity. He managed to bypass Carla's crew and got hold of a stack of 'un-filtered' study data. My guess is that he hooked up with one of the few remaining 'non-clone' members of the team, who might have had some suspicions about the drug.

"By this time, I'd developed some suspicions of my own about Carla De Leon and the people that worked for her. I was already thinking about a way out for myself, and I was beginning to suspect there were issues with Olmerol that were being suppressed.

"I had a bad feeling about what would happen to the student, but for a long time I left him alone. 'Look out for number one' had become my motto. Finally I couldn't sit back and watch anymore. I cornered him in a storeroom off one of the basement hallways and warned him about the danger. He didn't believe me.

"We talked about his findings. What he told me knocked me off the packing crate I was sitting on. He'd cross-referenced the prescription of Olmerol to a set of what were thought to be random deformities in newborn infants. He concluded that in about one in a thousand cases Olmerol produced deformities as severe, in their own way, as those caused by Thalidomide, which was first released at around the same time.

"Somehow Carla and her people got wind of what the student's conclusions were going to be. For a few days there was a hush over the whole research wing."

Carson fished a pack of cigarettes from his shirt pocket and lit one up. He offered one to Frank. Recalling the dreadful coughing fits of his host, Frank declined.

Carson continued. "When I saw the news on TV a few days later the hair on the back of my neck stood straight up. Before he was able to release his findings, the student was involved in an 'accident'. His car plunged over an embankment into the river.

"The news report said there was no hint of foul play. The student's work and the impending study were never mentioned. It took up no more than ten seconds of air-time – just ahead of the hockey scores.

"A week later the study was released – right on schedule. When I read the results, my heart skipped a beat – it found no significant side effects in mothers using Olmerol. In fact, it said the drug was remarkably benign. That was when I realized how dangerous the Savants really were, and I figured maybe I better step up my plans to get out of there."

"Savants?"

"That's what I call them. "I think the Olmerol deformity produces a condition similar to what's been found with autistic savants – only without the autistic part."

Frank's eyes widened. "You're saying that Carla De Leon…"

"Has the deformity, yes," Carson stared at him. "Her and all the other clones."

Frank sat for a few seconds with his mouth open. Finally he said, "So the victims of the deformity have taken over production of the drug that produces it?"

"There's no way for an outsider to know for sure," Carson said, "but that's my guess." The old man smiled. "But I don't think the Savants consider themselves victims."

Frank stared down at the ocean below, trying to absorb Carson's revelations. It was too incredible.

Carson picked up his rifle and struggled to his feet. Frank reached out to help him. Carson jumped back, grabbed at the gun, and pointed it at Frank.

"It's okay," Frank said, holding up his hands.

"Sorry," Carson said. "I'm a little jumpy. Let's go back."

"So you've never told this to anybody else?" Frank said as they walked.

"Nope. You're the first – and probably the last."

"Why me? Why now?"

"A few reasons. To start with, you're the first one that's ever asked me. If I'd gone to the cops, I wouldn't have had any proof and they wouldn't have believed me. Carla would have gotten wind of it and I'd be a dead man. I'm pretty sure you believe what I'm telling you.

"Second, I need to get it off my chest. It *is* of some concern to the human race – or it should be, anyway. Third – I'm dying. Lung cancer. They tell me I'll be dead in a few months. If Carla and her gang manage to do away with me before that, well…"

THIRTY THREE

....

RICHARD CARSON

C arson was going a bit stir-crazy out in the boondocks with no company for God knows how long. The old man seemed desperate for somebody to talk to, so when he invited Frank for dinner and to stay the night, he agreed.

"I haven't got much in the way of lab facilities, as you can see," Carson laughed and gestured around his cabin as they shared some of his homemade stew and bread. Frank had asked about the medical basis for the Olmerol deformities.

"I'm no neuro-scientist," Carson continued. "I've got theories based on what I've learned from general research and observation…"

"And those theories are?"

Carson got up and dug around on a shelf in the living room, and returned with a plastic model of the human brain, which he set down on the kitchen table.

"The human brain is actually made up of three separate brains," he said, his hand resting on the model, "that developed at different stages of our evolution."

He dismantled the model and held up the small, club-like, innermost section.

"The oldest and most primitive is what's called the 'reptilian' brain. It's largely unchanged from what it was millions of years ago, and we share it with all other animals that have a backbone. It controls involuntary bodily functions like breathing, and behaviour relating to survival, like sex drive and defense of territory."

He picked up a small, cap-like piece of the model and fitted it on top of the original one.

"Next to evolve was the mammalian brain. It added structures to control digestion, fluid balance, body temperature, blood pressure. It also added the capacity for storing memories, like response to danger based on past experience. Understand?"

Frank nodded.

Carson picked up the much larger, helmet-shaped section, with the whorls and ridges Frank associated with the human brain, and placed it over the original two.

"The modern human brain was formed by adding the neocortex, which envelopes the earlier brains and amounts to about eighty-five per cent of the human brain mass."

He pointed to the deep fissure that split the model down the middle.

"The neocortex consists of two hemispheres interconnected by a web of nerve fibers that enable the two halves to communicate.

"The left hemisphere communicates using words. It has highly developed verbal abilities. It's logical and systematic, concerned with matters as they are. The right hemisphere communicates using images.

It has highly developed spatial abilities. It's intuitive and imaginative, concerned with emotions and feelings.

"Human emotional responses depend on neuronal pathways that link the right hemisphere to the mammalian brain, which in turn is linked to the even older reptilian brain."

Carson smiled. "With me so far?"

Frank nodded.

He picked up the entire model, and drew his finger along the side.

"My guess is that the Olmerol deformities short-circuit some of the neural pathways, cross-connecting parts of the right and left hemispheres, and link the conscious mind more closely to the older mammalian, and even reptilian, brain.

"I suspect they also somehow affect the amygdala, which is a critical component of the human emotional response. Basically, the Savants are all psychopaths in the extreme."

"Ricky said they like to live communally in big mansions," Frank said, dipping his spoon into his stew.

"They're much more driven by instinct than we are," Carson said, "so that makes sense. The same way wolves instinctively run in packs, and lions gather in a pride.

"It's kind of a paradox, but I think the deformities also stimulate the neocortex, particularly the left side, creating what you could class as a new 'species' of beings who are super intelligent but with zero empathy and with primitive animal drives. I came up with a cute nickname. I call them 'VIPs'."

"VIPs?" Frank said.

"Very Intelligent Predators," Carson laughed emptily.

276

They finished the meal in silence.

Not long after dinner Carson showed Frank a spare room with a bed he'd made up for him. Frank had assumed that Carson would go to bed as well, but instead the old man shuffled out the back door. The outhouse was in the opposite direction, so Frank wondered what Carson was doing out there. He waited for a while, out of curiosity, but fell asleep before his host returned.

☼

The next morning, Carson grabbed his axe and shuffled toward the back door. He was almost out of wood for his stove. The old man could barely walk let alone chop firewood.

Frank followed him outside. "Let me do that," he said, reaching for the axe.

"I can look after myself," Carson said.

"You can help," Frank said. "I'll chop, you stack."

There was a pile of bucked logs nearby waiting to be split. Frank hadn't swung an axe in years. Carson sat on the back porch and howled with laughter as Frank sweated, cursed, and barely missed chopping off his right toe, but after twenty minutes or so he started to get the hang of it. He split the wood, while Carson piled it in a covered area beside the shack.

As he chopped, Frank filled Carson in on what Ricky had told him about the 'Arx'. How as a teenager the Matriarch had come to understand that she was different, not only from her parents but from everyone else around her. How she'd divined the nature of her differences, deduced that there must be others like herself, and set about finding them.

The small group she brought together formed the first 'Stronghold', Genesis, where Ricky grew up. Genesis formed the nerve-center for all the others. The group called themselves the Arx – Latin for stronghold. The first three Strongholds were all in Vancouver, simply because the Matriarch was born there, and Kaffir Pharma, so crucial to their survival, was headquartered there. Now there were Strongholds throughout the Americas, Europe, and Asia.

It was vital that the deformities, as the 'Monkeys' would have labeled them, that produced the Arx not be linked to Olmerol. Therefore, no affected child could be allowed to remain in the Monkey world beyond the age of a few years. A sophisticated tracking system located the children, who were then either kidnapped and assigned to a Stronghold or, if necessary, eliminated. The system wasn't perfect – errors occurred, but the few deformities detected by the Monkeys were assumed to be random.

Mentally and physically superior to all but a tiny fraction of the rest of humanity, unburdened by scruples of any kind, and driven by a compulsion to preserve and grow what they considered their 'species', the Arx easily vaulted to positions of authority. They accumulated vast wealth, and infiltrated all the important institutions relating to maternity and childbirth.

Carson sat on a nearby stump, shaking his head slowly as he listened.

Frank also explained the circumstances of Ricky's birth, and how he'd lived in a closet for more than seven years.

"So how did you come to know Ricky?" Frank asked.

Carson smiled. "Remember I said how researchers at Kaffir disappeared and were replaced by 'Carla Clones'?"

Frank nodded as he hauled another log on the chopping block.

"I worked with them every day," Carson said, "but I never really got to know any of them – with one exception. A girl named Miriam Leander. She was about the third or fourth 'clone' to join the team. She replaced a woman who left mysteriously and was never heard from again.

Carson lit up a smoke and continued. "Miriam had the same drive and intense focus as the others, but there was something unusual about her. She had a spark of genuine warmth that I'd never seen before. We actually developed something approaching a friendship.

"She'd been at Kaffir for about three years when she called me at home one evening out of the blue. It was such an incredible breach of clone behaviour I knew it must be something pretty earth-shattering. She wanted me to help her deliver a package in secret. She wouldn't tell me what it was. I was to meet her at night at a location in Point Grey, and drive her where she wanted to go.

"By then I knew enough about the clones to guess that our little outing would be dangerous. I don't know why I agreed. Maybe some part of me suspected she was getting a raw deal and felt sorry for her. I drove to the spot and waited in the car with the lights off.

"She came out of nowhere and knocked on the passenger window – scared the shit out of me. When I saw what the 'package' was, I knew I had a reason to be scared. She was carrying a child. The kid looked sick or deformed. I didn't ask any questions. She didn't say a word except to direct me to the nearest hospital. We cased the place and waited until nobody was around, then she carried him to one of the doors and laid him there. The poor little guy was in such pathetic shape he couldn't run after her.

"I couldn't believe she'd just leave him like that. I tried to talk to her, but she said there was no other way. I drove her back to the same spot in Point Grey and she disappeared into the night.

"She never said another word about it, and not long after that she left the team and disappeared like so many others. She was the only clone that I'd ever seen removed like that. I never saw her again.

"That's when I got really scared. What we'd done was illegal and immoral, but that wasn't what worried me. My gut told me that if the other clones ever got wind of it I'd be up shit creek. If they knew about her… That's when I started planning my own 'disappearance'."

Frank shook his head in disbelief.

"Luckily, I'd been talking about a canoe trip with some buddies of mine for a long time," Carson continued, "so it didn't seem out of place. I felt bad for the other guys on the trip. There was no way I could tell them. I was lucky the clones bought it. They don't miss much."

"But you went to see Ricky a couple of years ago," Frank said.

"I got really sick and I had to go to town," Carson said. "That's when I got the cancer diagnosis. I did some research and found out where Ricky ended up. I guess I was hoping to find he was being well looked after – you know, to let myself off the hook for abandoning him back then."

Frank told Carson Ricky's explanation of the experiments and his birth. "You know," he continued, "according to Ricky, the drug trials like they did with his mother might be obsolete."

Carson sat up in his chair. "What?"

"He says they were experimenting with in-vitro fertilization."

"Christ," Carson said. "They can introduce the deformity at the cellular level?"

"They couldn't when he was living there, but now..."

"So they'd no longer need the rest of humanity..."

"They'd still need eggs and sperm from normal humans. But they probably control God-knows-how-many egg and sperm banks. They'd be able to pick and choose from tens of thousands."

Carson stared at the floor.

"Kaffir are about to release a new version of Olmerol," Frank said. "You know anything about that?"

Carson twitched and looked at him. "Where did you hear that?"

"It was in the papers. It's supposed to come out in a few weeks. Any idea what would be in it?"

"There's no way for anyone from the outside to know," Carson said. "But I can make a good guess. The new version probably has no side effects. If they've perfected the in-vitro thing, they don't need the drug anymore. It becomes a liability."

"Then they must have done it," Frank said.

"It would be like some kind of a Holy Grail for them," Carson said. "Kidnapping children is extremely dangerous. One of their top priorities would be not to have to do it anymore."

Carson sat shaking his head. "I always figured the authorities could just shut down production of Olmerol and that would be the end of it. If what you say is true, the Savants could go underground and reproduce in secret. There'd be nothing we could do to stop them..."

Frank locked eyes with him. "Ricky said their goal was to replace humans on earth..."

☼

Frank realized that he'd stumbled on one of the few places where he could hide from Carson's 'Savants'. They'd trace his movements and find him eventually, but at least out here he had a little breathing room. He felt sorry for the old man, dying alone and friendless in the wilderness. He asked if he could stay a few more days, and Carson agreed.

In addition to chopping the wood, he fixed a leak in the roof, and repaired one of the rotting steps up to the front door. At the same time, he continued to pump his host for all he knew about the Savants.

"This Matriarch Ricky talks about," Frank said as they sat on the bluff where they'd talked the first day. "Do you think he's referring to Carla De Leon?"

"I don't know," Carson said, "She's the first one I ever knew about; that doesn't mean there weren't any before her."

He took a drag on his cigarette. Frank glanced at it.

"Hell, what do I care?" Carson said, holding up the cigarette and laughing. His laugh, as usual, degenerated into a rasping cough. He finally got control of himself. "The one good thing about my diagnosis is that I can smoke as much as I want without guilt."

He blew a perfect smoke ring. "My problems are over," he said. "You're the one that should be worried. I'm sorry to tell you this, but I wouldn't give you a snowball's chance in Hell of coming out of all this alive. They'll catch up with you eventually – if you have any illusions about that, put them away."

Frank's body stiffened. "They were chasing me just before I came out here," he said.

"You got away from them twice?" Carson stared at him wide-eyed. "You're my new hero!"

"It was dumb luck, I think," Frank said. "I jumped down into this abandoned city lot, full of stinking water and rats. One of them was right behind me but he wouldn't follow."

"Somebody up there's looking out for you," Carson laughed. "Remember, the deformities affect both intelligence *and* behaviour. The Savants have some pretty big psychological issues. For the most part they're brilliant at hiding them, but they're there.

"One of the most common is OCD – obsessive compulsive disorder. You've heard of it?"

"Yeah, sure – people that wash their hands every five minutes and stuff like that."

"That's right. OCD is far more common in the Savants than in the general public. In fact, I think it's pretty much universal. I know all the ones I worked with had it, though they went to a lot of trouble to hide it.

"One of their big compulsions is cleanliness. They have an irrational fear of dirt and germs. I think the intensity varies. Sounds like you lucked out and got one that was an extreme case. It's a pretty major weakness, but I wouldn't count on it working every time."

Carson took a drag on his cigarette. "While we're on that point, let me give you some advice. There may come a time when you have to fight one or more of them."

Frank swallowed hard.

"All things being equal," Carson continued, "unless you're the second coming of Bruce Lee, you're gonna lose. Not only are they extraordinary mental specimens, most of them are extraordinary physical specimens as well."

He turned to Frank. "You need an edge. You need more than an edge – you need a chainsaw. You can use their OCD against them. Sometimes they have to do things in a certain order. Sometimes they'll only approach you from one side. Sometimes, like your guy, they're petrified of dirt and germs."

Carson stubbed out his cigarette. He flicked the butt out over the cliff and watched it float to the ground.

"Recognizing those flaws could give you a big advantage, but you're not going to have much time to figure out what they are. If you have any chance of winning against them, that will be it."

Frank nodded. If that was his only hope, was there any point even trying?

"You seem to have an incredible depth of knowledge about these Savants," Frank said, "but you say you only met them at work, and you never really got to know them."

Carson gazed wistfully at a sailboat passing far below. He didn't speak for almost a minute.

Finally he said, "When you first showed up here you said you were investigating the disappearance of some children."

Frank looked up, surprised. "Yeah. That's how all this started. I dug up evidence that babies were being kidnapped, and maybe murdered."

"Did you ever come across a case where a child went missing while his mother was picnicking beside a river?"

"Sure," Frank said. "The body was never found. That was one I actually worked on when I was still on the job."

Carson turned to him with the saddest of smiles. "Well that one was me."

THIRTY FOUR

....

CARSON AND JIMMY

Frank's mouth dropped open.

"I had to understand," Carson said. "I had to know what made the Savants tick. It sort of fell into my lap. I'd just moved into this cabin. I almost never went to Vancouver – too dangerous. But I got really sick; I thought I was going to die. I was wrong – that time," he smiled sadly. "It was appendicitis, but they didn't want to treat it on Galiano. I had to go to the mainland.

"The receptionist at the doctor I went to had to bring her toddler into work. It was one of those emergency situations where no-one was available to look after him. When I looked into the kid's eyes I knew right away. At that age they haven't yet learned to act like us. Nobody else would have noticed, but I'd seen enough Savants to know.

"Trudy Graham was her name. The waiting room was empty and I got talking to her. I managed to steer the conversation to Olmerol. Trudy had a minor heart condition – Olmerol was contraindicated for her, so her doctor wouldn't prescribe it. What she told me next gave me goosebumps. Turns out her sister happened to be pregnant at the same time, and guess what?"

"The sister was taking Olmerol," Frank said.

"Bingo. Trudy was really suffering with morning sickness so she talked her sister into letting her have some of hers. It's like fate had stepped in and handed it to me. Miriam had told me a little about how she'd been 'acquired'. I figured that the Savants tracked the use of the drug by prescription. But Trudy never had a prescription, and from what she told me it didn't sound like her sister's kid had the deformity, so the Savants wouldn't be interested.

"I stalked her for a couple of weeks. I was scared shitless. I'd never done anything like that before. I'd never even had a parking ticket, but I had to know. Every second I spent in Vancouver was an invitation for someone to recognize me. I found out about the picnic and followed her. While she was preoccupied settling an argument between her other two kids I stepped in and grabbed Jimmy. The cops assumed he'd fallen into the river."

He turned to Frank. "He lived here for ten years. He never knew where he came from or why he was with me. I conducted physical and psychological tests, observed his behaviour, interviewed him hundreds of times. In many ways he was like the son I never had."

"What happened to him?"

Carson turned and gazed back out to sea. "What do you think?"

Frank stared at him, horrified.

"You think I'm a monster?" Carson said, with a thin, rasping laugh. "Jimmy was extremely intelligent, like all the others. I was always careful, but by the time he reached thirteen he'd guessed that I was interested in more than just looking after him. He'd also guessed that he was different from everybody else. If I'd waited any longer he would have killed me and run away, and probably located others of his kind.

"He's buried in the back yard behind the cabin. I told anyone who asked that he went off to live with his mother, who they all assumed was my ex-wife. To anyone who knew him before I took him he was already dead, so nobody asked any questions."

Carson tried to rise to his feet but was shaky and almost collapsed. Frank stood and helped the old man steady himself. Frank's mind was numb as they headed back to the shack.

After three days, armed with Carson's information, Frank decided he had to get back and face whatever was to come. Carson assured him that he'd be alright, and anyway there was nothing he could do for the old man. On that final day Carson removed a loose board from the floor of the shack and lifted out a rugged metal box with a heavy-duty padlock. Frank had to help him haul it to a desk in the corner.

Carson used a key on a chain around his neck to open the lock. Inside were several books of notes and a notebook computer. "Everything's in here," he said. I made extensive notes on Jimmy – my observations, interview transcripts, and a few amateur medical tests. I also documented my time at Kaffir and my theories about the Savants."

"You can give it all to the authorities," Carson said. "It'll be a big help convincing them you're not crazy. Believe me, that's going to be a problem. You can tell them everything. I don't care. They might learn something from exhuming Jimmy's body. I preserved his brain in a jar of formaldehyde. It's buried with him. It would be a good idea for somebody to dig it up and study it."

Frank stared at the old man, still stunned by his revelations.

Carson's face was drawn and sad as he spoke. "There are circumstances where one is forced to perform acts that are considered monstrous, for the greater public good. Someday humanity will thank me for the service I've done them."

That night they ate yet another plain but palatable stew. Frank wasn't that hungry, but managed to force some down. They moved to a pair of comfortable chairs by Carson's wood stove. Carson pulled out a bottle of twelve-year-old single malt scotch and insisted that Frank join him in an after-dinner drink, something he hadn't done before.

"Fact is," he said, "I've been waiting for somebody like you to show up for a long time."

Frank wasn't sure what Carson meant by that, but he kept his mouth shut.

Carson held up his glass in a shaky hand and said:

"To the human race – may they not be extinct after all."

They clinked glasses and drank down the golden nectar.

"I know I've said this already," Carson said, "but I want to make sure you get it. Never forget who you're dealing with. These guys are not human, at least not in the way you're used to."

"You know their connection with Kaffir, Olmerol, and the kidnapped children," Carson continued. "You know about Ricky Augustus and now about his mother. You know the leaders of the group and something about where they live.

"Not only that, you're a cop, an authority figure, someone people will believe. Sure, you've got some issues, but you're still going to command a lot of respect. You are the biggest threat the Savants have ever faced. You can bet they'd do anything to get you out of the picture. And if they know about you, they'll know about everyone associated with you."

Rebecca, Frank thought with a shudder.

Carson took another sip of whiskey. "You've been incredibly lucky so far. Don't count on that luck continuing."

"I'll remember," Frank said.

"Stay up as long as you like," Carson said. As he had on previous nights, Carson headed for the back door.

Finally, Frank asked what he was doing out there.

"Oh," he said. "It's a ritual I perform every night. You'll probably think I've got a screw loose. Maybe you'd be right. Before I go to bed I go out and say goodnight to Jimmy." He nodded toward the back of the shack.

"Crazy isn't it," he said, a hacking sound from deep in his chest substituting for a laugh. "I know with absolute certainty that, beyond getting food and shelter from me, Jimmy couldn't have cared less whether I lived or died."

Carson's mouth quivered and his eyes closed. "I loved him, just the same," he said as he turned and shuffled toward the back door.

The shack was silent. Frank sat by the stove, trying to digest all that Carson had told him. The story was so unbelievable, he prayed that the envelope on the desk was enough to convince the authorities, and that he'd be able to get it to the right people before the Savants got to him.

He wasn't sleepy. He got up and wandered around the room, inspecting the books on the shelves and knick-knacks on the window sills. He strolled into the back hallway. He'd only passed through it a couple of times, but he sensed that something was different; something was missing.

He stood with his head cocked sideways, closed his eyes and tried to picture it the way it was earlier.

I'm starting to think like a Savant, he thought, smiling to himself.

That was when it hit him – he realized what was missing and froze. The other times, Carson's rifle had been leaning in one corner.

"Shit," he said out loud. He rushed down the hall to the back door. He'd just put his hand on the latch when he heard the gunshot.

The next morning, Frank found a shovel in the back shed and buried Carson next to the mound that covered Jimmy. He risked becoming a suspect in yet another murder, but didn't dare get the cops involved right now. If he ever convinced them his story was true, he would lead them back to this place. Until then, it would be a while before anyone missed Carson and came out to investigate.

"May God forgive you for what you've done," he said over the grave.

He spent a few hours sifting through Carson's possessions. There was a wealth of information on the Savants. Unfortunately, most of it was in paper form. Frank didn't have time to examine it all in detail, but one file made his heart race: an 'undoctored' copy of the study Carson had told him about, the one the student had died for.

Frank felt like a weight had dropped from his shoulders. The study cited specific cases of deformity that could be linked to Olmerol and included data showing the correlation between prescriptions of the drug and what had been thought to be random deformities. That document alone should be enough to prove his story.

He opened a folder titled: 'Carla De Leon'. It contained scanned copies of journal articles and the scant number of newspaper items in which De Leon had been mentioned. There were records of the corporate hierarchy at Kaffir, De Leon's office number and location, and some of the people that worked closely with her.

The folder contained a fuzzy, badly angled picture of a middle-aged woman. Below it was the caption: 'Carla De Leon – April, 2002'.

Frank smiled when he considered how tough it must have been for Carson to get her picture, especially back in the Neolithic days when every cell phone didn't contain a camera. She was dressed plainly, and looked like the stereotypical research scientist.

But even in the grainy shadows of the blown-up photograph he discerned the blazing light of her intellect, and just the tiniest hint of the primal stare he'd seen in Ralphie's eyes what seemed like years ago now. Something about her face looked familiar. He thought for a minute, but eventually gave up and tossed the picture in with everything else.

He found a couple of flash drives in Carson's desk. He transferred some of the crucial files onto both drives and stuffed everything – the notebook, the drives, files, papers, photographs, and anything else he thought might be useful – into a small suitcase.

In the bottom drawer of Carson's filing cabinet, he found a small handgun and a box of ammunition. He stuffed the gun into a thin cloth bag and slung it around his neck so that it was covered by his jacket.

Still stunned, he chartered a boat to Galiano, then took the ferry back to Vancouver. He didn't feel like lunch on the way back.

THIRTY FIVE

··

SHOWDOWN

"**D**r. De Leon will be with you shortly," Marcie, the pert, young receptionist at Carla's corporate office, smiled. "The meeting is taking longer than expected. Please take a seat."

Rebecca and Carla had agreed to meet there before going on another 'coffee' date. Carla had an important meeting she couldn't get out of, but said she was looking forward to relaxing and talking with Rebecca.

Since Rebecca's confession, the dynamic between the two women seemed to have changed subtly. Rebecca felt uneasy about meeting her friend, even though Carla had insisted that the incident was in the past and wouldn't affect their relationship. Strangely, Carla seemed more concerned about Rebecca's refusal to reveal Frank's name than with her actual lies and betrayal.

Resignedly, Rebecca sat down on a couch in the waiting room. She absently thumbed through a few dull pharmaceutical industry journals, but found nothing of interest.

She got up and strolled around the office, inspecting the pictures on the wall. There was a stunning photograph of Kaffir headquarters, the building in which she stood, and another of researchers at their stations in the lab.

On a far wall was a photograph of several white-coated workers, all young women, holding some kind of award. Rebecca looked closely at the picture. Almost hidden behind the others she could barely make out the face of Carla De Leon. Carla was glancing to her right, as if she'd been caught off-guard.

Something in her expression was familiar. It took Rebecca a few seconds to realize what it was.

Ralphie, she thought, as goosebumps rose on her skin.

She turned back to find Marcie staring at her. Rebecca was relieved when the receptionist was called away on an errand.

Frank's warning came back into her head: *If you go sticking your nose into the head office at Kaffir...*

She thought back on Carla's description of life with her husband. Suddenly somehow it didn't ring true. She considered walking out, thinking what excuse she could use later to explain her sudden departure.

You're letting Frank's paranoia infect you, she scolded herself. *Carla's your friend. She was there when you needed her. DNA doesn't lie.*

Finally Marcie reappeared.

"The meeting's taking longer than expected," she said. "Dr. De Leon says you should go on without her. She'll meet you at the restaurant in about twenty minutes."

Rebecca opened her mouth, about to suggest that they cancel.

"Is something wrong?" Marcie said.

"No," Rebecca said, smiling. "Everything's fine. Tell her I'll be waiting."

☼

The first thing Frank did when he stepped off the bus back in Vancouver was buy a burner cell phone. The second was to rent a car from a cut-rate lot; he needed to be mobile. His top priority in the service of humanity should have been to get Carson's information to the police, but that goal was no longer foremost on his agenda. He'd done a lot of thinking on the trip back, first from Parker Island, then from Galiano. He'd reflected on Carson's words:

They know about you, they'll know about everyone associated with you.

There were two people close enough to him to fit into that category: Rebecca and his sister Janet. He hadn't wanted to phone either in case their phones were bugged, and email was even less secure.

He'd bought a baseball cap and cheap sunglasses at a general store on Galiano. He wore them now as he sat in the darkest corner of a coffee shop at the edge of town, called the receptionist at Janet's work, and asked to speak to her. As soon as Janet answered the phone and he knew she was alright, he hung up. For now, that was all he could do. Speaking to her would put her in far greater danger.

He'd taken steps bordering on paranoia to shield Rebecca from his actions, but he realized that, in reality, he hadn't been careful enough. In fact, it was probably not possible to be careful enough. His plan now was to tell her everything, and convince her to go into hiding.

The knowledge of having put her in danger tore at his heart. If his own life was on the line, then Rebecca's would be also. The Arx probably already knew about their relationship and would find the traces of their investigation.

At least Frank had an idea what he was up against. Rebecca was almost completely in the dark, wandering like a child in the wilderness because he'd withheld the information that might save her life. He shuddered, recalling her trip to the home of the poor researcher who had died. That act alone would guarantee her death if the Arx found out, as he was now certain they would. For all he knew they'd been spying on her all along.

The image popped into his head of Rebecca in front of the Boathouse restaurant in Kits. He remembered the woman she'd been hugging at the entrance. His gut clenched as he realized where he'd seen the face - in the grainy photo at Carson's place…

"Shit!" he said, jumping up from his chair.

His hands shook as he grabbed Carson's suitcase, pulled his cap's brim low and took off for Rebecca's office.

He didn't dare enter through the front doors. Even if the Arx hadn't yet connected Rebecca with his investigation, they would know that he visited her occasionally, and would be watching.

Luckily, she'd shown him a back-way in. He entered the building next door through a side entrance near the alley. An underground hallway joined that building with hers.

An ID card controlled access to the door linking the two buildings, but security was slack. He put away his hat and sunglasses and waited out of sight near the door. When a woman with a card headed for it, he followed closely behind her.

She opened the door and he rushed forward and held it for her. For a moment she eyed him suspiciously. He quickly flashed the back of his credit card, which was similar to the ID card. She smiled and let him through.

He saw no one as he moved quickly down the hall and into Rebecca's office.

"Frank!" Judy said as she hung up the phone. "Haven't seen you around for a while. No offense, but you don't look so good."

"I had a fight with a bottle and the bottle won," he said. "Where's Rebecca?"

"You just missed her. She went out for a couple of hours. She left about twenty minutes ago."

"Any idea where she went?"

"I'm not sure where they went," Judy said, absently shuffling some papers on her desk.

"They?" The hair at the back of his neck stood on end.

Judy flushed, as she remembered something. "Oh, crap," she said, "she told me – sorry Frank, I'm not supposed to say…"

"Who's she meeting?" he asked, dreading the answer.

Judy looked away.

Frank clenched his fists. "Where did they go?"

She turned back to face him. "She doesn't tell me, they just go."

Frank leaned across her desk. "What if there's an emergency or something?"

"No, honestly…"

"Come on, Judy," he shouted. "Her life could be in danger!"

Judy's upper lip quivered, "I don't know... I swear, she didn't tell me."

He rushed out the way he'd come, jumped in his car, and headed for the Kitsilano. His mind twisted in knots as he drove. Rebecca with Carla De Leon? Why? Was it possible she'd been playing him for a sucker all this time? That she'd been in league with the Arx from the beginning? That she herself was...

It was like a deep black well opened up beneath him. "It can't be," he said out loud.

No way, he finally decided. If she was one of them, or had been working for them, he would have been taken out a long time ago. There was no advantage in keeping him alive, and much in arranging for him to have an 'accident'.

If Rebecca wasn't working for them there was only one other explanation: she had unwittingly gotten involved without understanding what she'd done. His mind reeled as he thought about the level of danger she'd fallen into.

He pulled up at the Boathouse restaurant, frantically combed the parking lot, and exhaled deeply when he spotted her car. He fished the gun from the bag around his neck, stuffed it in his belt, and took the stairs up to the restaurant two at a time. Rebecca sat alone at a table near the window. He headed directly for her.

She jumped as she recognized him.

"Frank, what are you doing here?" she asked as he reached her. "Where have you been? I've been worried sick since the news about Grant Stocker."

"Are you alone?" he said, still out of breath.

Her face turned angry. "I meant what I said before, Frank. Gloria and Ralphie are dead, and so is our investigation."

"Who are you waiting for?" he said.

She looked at her hands.

"Carla De Leon," he answered for her.

She turned a bright shade of red as she looked up. "She's really not a bad person, Frank-"

"There's no time. There's stuff I haven't told you."

He quickly tried to explain the highlights of his investigation: the fight with the first attacker, his research into Lawrence Retigo and Arthur Dogan, Ricky Augustus. Rebecca's hands twisted the cloth napkin in front of her as she listened. She didn't believe him.

"Frank... I don't want any trouble," she said when he'd finished. "Please, just go. I'll call you-"

"Look," he said. "You can't meet with Carla. Call her, make up an excuse. Come with me for one hour and I'll explain everything. If you still think I'm nuts and you're worried about what I'll do we can go someplace where there's lots of people."

She glanced out the window and cringed.

"What?" Frank said.

He peered down at the sidewalk below. A handsome middle-aged woman strode purposefully toward the front doors. Inexplicably she paused and looked up. She seemed to be staring right at him. The afternoon sun glinted off her sunglasses. Frank's heart skipped a beat.

He turned back to Rebecca.

"Let's go," he said.

"Please leave, Frank," she said. "I appreciate your concern, but I'm fine."

"It's not a request," he said.

He reached down, grabbed her left elbow, and tried to lift her to her feet.

"Let go of me!" she yelled.

The entire restaurant went silent. Everyone was staring at them.

Several waiters headed in their direction and a couple of men rose from their tables. Frank hauled Rebecca up and started to drag her toward the back door. A bartender at the back picked up the phone.

With his free hand, Frank pulled Carson's gun from under his jacket and waved it around the room, finally pointing it at the guy with the phone. Screams and gasps erupted all around them.

"Put it down!" he yelled at the bartender. The man did as he was told.

"Everybody stay where you are!" Frank yelled. "Don't move and you won't get hurt."

The waiters froze and the men that had stood sat back down. "Let me go, Frank," Rebecca sobbed, tears running down her cheeks. "This isn't the way to deal with your problems."

They reached the back door and he dragged her down the stairs to the parking lot. She struggled as he pushed her inside through the driver's door of his rental and jumped in beside her. He started the car and took off, tearing out of the lot with his tires squealing.

He glanced in the rear-view mirror. A crowd was gathered at the top of the stairs, watching. At the front was the figure of Carla De Leon. She was putting her cell phone to her ear.

"We're gonna have to ditch this car," he said. He shoved the gun in his belt.

"What the hell are you doing Frank?" Rebecca screamed.

"Look, I'm sorry," he said. "I know it seems crazy but everything I've been telling you is true, and I can prove it."

Her eyes drifted to the gun.

"Remember the guy that was supposed to be dead? Carson?" he said. "I met him. He's alive – or at least he was…"

Frank reached into his jacket pocket. Rebecca jumped and pulled away. He pulled out one of Carson's flash drives.

"It's all here," he said, holding it up. "Just let me show you. Give me half an hour. If you still don't believe me I promise I'll let you go."

She stared at him.

"The cops are going to be after us," he said. "They'll have the license plate number."

She looked at the flash drive. Finally her shoulders dropped and she seemed to relax. "Pull the car into the alley there," she said, pointing to their right. "We can go somewhere on foot."

Frank smiled. He parked the car in a dark space behind a wall where it would take time to find. He grabbed Carson's suitcase from the trunk and they got out and walked. Frank kept an eye on Rebecca, but she didn't make any attempt to get away. Police sirens approached in the distance.

They repeated his earlier trick, jumping on the first bus that came along, just to get out of the area. The bus was almost empty. They took a seat at the back, away from any other passengers, and Frank started from the beginning. Rebecca's eyes widened as he told her about

Carson and his analysis of Carla De Leon. He could see that she thought what he was saying had a ring of truth.

He hauled Carson's notebook from the suitcase, plugged in and accessed the flashdrive, and handed the computer to Rebecca.

"Take a look at it," he said. "That's all I ask."

Her fists clenched in front of her as she read. She seemed to collapse from the inside, and sat with her head in her hands. Her image reminded him of Gloria when Ralphie had first disappeared.

"So we're both as good as dead," she said, shaking, as she closed the notebook. The enormity of their situation had finally struck her.

"Not necessarily," he said, putting a hand on her shoulder, and trying to sound more confident than he felt.

"Where can we go?" she asked. "They'll be all over the city."

"Then maybe we better leave the city," he said.

THIRTY SIX

....

SANCTUARY

Rebecca studied Frank as they trudged along the path to Carson's cabin on Parker Island. They'd jumped on another bus, transferred to one that ran out to the ferry terminal, and caught the ferry to Galiano. Frank rented a pair of mopeds, and they caught a charter boat to Parker.

On the bus, he'd told her about his arrest and release, and about Ricky. He described his stay with Carson, all that the researcher had done, supposedly in the name of humanity, and how Carson had finally ended his life. Frank now plodded along like he was on his way to a funeral. It was the only place he could think of where they might be safe, at least for a while.

She sensed the pressure building inside him. The knuckles of the hand gripping Carson's suitcase were white. Frank was unsteady on his feet and stared at the ground as he walked.

"Where are they buried?" she asked, as they approached.

Frank inclined his head toward the back. She imagined the old man's ghost, or the ghost of the murdered child, Jimmy, hovering over them like death.

"How long do you think we'll have to stay here?" she asked.

"*You'll* be here for at least a couple of days," Frank answered. "I gotta go back – not tonight, tomorrow."

"You're kidding," she said, her eyes wide. "You're already connected to a murder. Now you can add weapons and kidnapping. Every cop in the city will be after you. Not to mention that you're being hunted by a gang of psychopathic killers. Have you got a death wish?"

"It's our only hope," he said as they reached the door. "I gotta convince the cops that the Arx are for real, and that what I've been saying is the truth. That's the only way, according to Ricky Augustus. That's not going to be easy. But this time I'll have the documentation to back the story up."

Frank unlocked the door and they walked in. He latched and bolted the multiple locks, and set the security bar. His hands shook as he fished in his shirt pocket for his cigarettes. His knees gave way. He staggered over and flopped into a nearby chair.

"What's wrong?" Rebecca asked.

"Nothing," he answered. "I'm fine; just tired."

"Frank," she said, nodding at his shaking hands. "You're on the edge. I'm surprised you've held it together this long. I'm worried that you're heading for another breakdown."

He tilted back his head and stared at the ceiling. "Come on, Rebecca, not now…"

He leaned forward again and tried to extract a cigarette from the pack. His hands shook so badly he dropped the pack on the floor.

"Do you want me to do that?" Rebecca said. He glared at her, but made no move to get the cigarettes. He hung his head and stared at the floor.

She put a hand on his shoulder. "Look, I know it's ridiculous timing, but maybe you should finish telling me about what happened - before - with Mastico."

He scowled up at her. "Don't you think we've got more important things to worry about right now?"

"I know it sounds crazy Frank, but it works. You open up to someone and it gets it off your chest. It's not a cure, but it might keep you together long enough to finish what you started."

"I already told you what happened."

"Come on, Frank. You met with Mastico, you were about to draw your gun...and then you both went home? We were getting close to the experience that triggered your breakdown in the first place. That's why your sub-conscious is blocking it out."

Frank didn't move for several seconds. Finally he nodded faintly.

"Why don't we continue where we left off," she said.

Frank's jaw tightened and his hands had hardened into fists. She pulled a chair over and sat across from him.

"I'd like to try something," she said. "I'll count from one to one hundred. As I count, I want you to think back on what happened – starting from where we left off last time. You can describe it to me, or not, whichever feels most comfortable.

"By the time I get to fifty, you'll be re-living the worst part of it. By one hundred, it'll all be over and you'll be relaxed. Does that sound okay?"

Frank nodded.

"You got knocked on the head," she said. "You woke up. Mastico stepped out and started walking towards you. You went for your gun."

Frank stared at a spot on the wall behind her.

"But it wasn't just you there, was it," she said.

He shuddered.

"There was someone else," she said.

Frank shut his eyes tight. His body contorted like it was being tugged by invisible cords.

"One," Rebecca said.

Frank waited a few seconds, trembling and breathing heavily.

"Two."

His clenched fists vibrated on the arms of his chair.

"He said I was crazy to even think about going," he finally began, "but I had no choice – a woman's life was at stake."

"Three," Rebecca said.

"We argued for more than half an hour. He insisted I wear a wire. He'd stay in the squad car a few blocks away and call for backup if I got into trouble. I should've said no. I wanted him to see what a hero I was."

"Who?" Rebecca said.

Frank's face tightened. Beads of sweat rose on his forehead. He scanned around him, his eyes wild. He gulped as if he was about to be sick.

"What's happening, Frank?" she said.

"I'm in the alley. There's the stench of rotting garbage. It's dark, but I can see Mastico walking towards me in the shadows. There's a finger of light across his face. He's smiling."

Rebecca continued counting.

"We're going to play the crazy game," Frank shook as he imitated Mastico's sing-song voice. "I've got a present for you."

"Twenty-three."

"I try to grab for my gun," Frank's eyes widened, "but I freeze. I'm terrified. I see the full moon – a blood-red moon – reflected in the water."

"The moon?" Rebecca said. "Are you sure?"

"Thirty-five," she continued. "Who came with you, Frank?"

"Mastico's swinging something in his right hand," Frank said. "Something big. He tosses it right at my chest. I catch it – it's instinctive, like a reflex reaction."

"Forty," Rebecca said.

Frank jumped up and kicked back his chair. It crashed to the floor behind him. His body bent back like he was being swept up in a raging tornado. Rebecca stood and stepped away. Frank straightened. His gaze traveled down his chest. His eyes came to rest on a non-existent object between his outstretched hands.

"Forty-three," Rebecca said.

"It's hairy and slimy," Frank said, his voice trembling, hands shaking. "I drop it on the ground."

He pulled his hands apart. His eyes bulged from his head as he watched the horrifying object fall.

"I still can't see what it is. It rolls into the light."

His gaze followed the invisible object rolling away from him. He stared at the floor, his face twisted into a mask of horror. "It's not the moon..."

"What?" Rebecca gasped. She stopped counting. "Maybe that's enough, Frank."

"His eyes are staring at me," Frank said, his lower lip trembling.

"Who?"

"He's smiling, almost like he didn't mind his head being separated from his body."

"Oh God – who, Frank!"

"Randall," Frank whispered. "It's my partner, Jeff Randall."

He started to shake. His hands were frozen like claws in front of him. "There's ragged edges of red meat and gristle around the cut that severed his neck," Frank's face twisted and his voice broke, "and a white tip of bone that had been the top of his spine."

Rebecca recoiled in horror. She willed herself to stay calm. "Frank, it's time to snap out of it."

"Mastico keeps coming," Frank said, looking up. "The lenses of his glasses glow in the light, like he's got x-ray eyes. I try again for the gun. My hand's slippery with Randall's blood. I almost drop it."

Rebecca fought back tears. "Frank, that's enough for now."

"Stop or I'll shoot," Frank shouted, lifting a shaking right hand like he was holding a gun.

Rebecca moved forward, but she didn't dare touch him.

"That's what I'm counting on," Frank's voice altered, becoming Mastico's chilling sing-song.

Frank's body shook violently as he fought to squeeze the invisible trigger. He wrapped both hands around the non-existent gun, raised his arms straight in front of him, and pretended to fire.

"Please Frank!" Rebecca said. She could do nothing but watch.

"I'm dying! I'm dying!" Frank screamed in Mastico's voice, choking with laughter. "You're killing me!"

Frank pumped six or seven shots into his invisible enemy. His body kicked back with each shot. Drenched in sweat, screaming and shaking, he moved forward and pumped three more shots into the ground at his feet. Finally, he collapsed on the floor.

When Frank woke he was lying with his head cradled in Rebecca's arms. He looked up at her. She was crying.

"Oh my God, Frank," she whispered, her voice breaking. "I'm so sorry."

They lay like that for several minutes, her arms wrapped around him, his head on her breast, his panicked breath gradually subsiding.

☼

That night Frank and Rebecca lay in bed in each other's arms. He stole a glance at her, her hair cascading over the pillow, her gray eyes dreamy, lost in the afterglow of lovemaking. Something felt different. A switch had flipped in his brain, channeling an emotion he hadn't felt in more than a year. It had been so long that at first he didn't quite recognize what he was feeling.

Finally it came to him. It was hope. For the first time since the experience with Mastico he could see a way out of his waking nightmare.

Where only days ago he'd felt like his life was over, suddenly he dared to dream that it might be just beginning. A part of him believed he didn't deserve her. Maybe that was true, he thought, but for now he was just going to accept the treasure he'd been granted and hope he could hold onto it a while longer.

"That Lohengrin guy, from the opera," he said to her. "You said the princess had to promise never to ask him about his past."

She rolled onto one elbow. "What brought this on?"

"Just thinking."

"Well, yes, that's right," she said.

"Let me guess," Frank smiled. "She ended up asking him, didn't she."

"Yep."

"Just couldn't leave it alone."

"That's right."

"So what happened?"

"When she finally asked him?"

Frank nodded.

Her face went dark. "It's very sad. He disappeared and she never saw him again."

Frank was silent.

"That's not going to happen with us, is it?" she said.

"Well... I don't know..." Frank said, joking.

He looked into her eyes. He was surprised to find something like fear behind them.

"No, that's not going to happen with us," he said, wrapping an arm around her. "I'm not going anywhere – unless you want me to."

"Right now, I want you to stay with me forever," she said sleepily, and nuzzled his chest.

THIRTY SEVEN

....

BACK INTO THE FIRE

The wind blew through Frank's hair as he leaned on the railing of the Queen of Nanaimo steaming back to Vancouver. Dozens of gulls circled the ship's wake, gliding in the updrafts generated by its motion. The ferry sailed past rocky islands blanketed with green and the touches of gold marking the coming fall.

The events of the past few weeks had occupied his mind to such an extent that he hadn't had time to think about his life, his condition, where he was going, or even where he was. He patted his shirt pocket for his cigarettes, and remembered he'd run out. Normally a wave of panic would have overwhelmed him and he would have run down to the shop for more. Today, right now, he realized he didn't really care.

He breathed the sea air deep into his lungs and for a moment relaxed. The late summer wind on the water had an edge of biting cold. That was good. He was alive; the wind was being kind enough to remind him. For this brief moment at least, he felt like the Frank Langer of old, the confident Frank Langer, the Frank Langer who knew what to do in any situation and never questioned his own judgment, the Frank Langer who maybe deserved some kind of respect and happiness.

His initial attraction to Rebecca had built steadily from the moment he first saw her. But after last night it had soared to a level he'd never experienced before. In what seemed like an instant she had been transformed from de facto therapist, co-conspirator, and investigative partner to lover, and the most precious thing in his life. In fact, she had become his reason for living.

It was dangerous to leave her at the cabin. He'd caught a break going there the first time, but the Arx would track it down eventually. Problem was, there was really nowhere any safer, and he didn't dare bring her along. After Carson's revelations he realized how incredibly lucky he was to still be alive. His luck couldn't hold out much longer.

The good news was that between his feet rested a suitcase full of information that could persuade his former colleagues that there was something worth investigating. He prayed that Reid and the others at the squad still had enough respect for him to take his claims seriously. The trick would be to get the information to them, and to stay alive long enough for them to follow it up.

☼

The ferry docked at nine-thirty AM. Frank caught a bus into town and made the short walk from the Central Bus Terminal to a Starbucks located under the *Science World* Skytrain station. Every few minutes the ceiling vibrated and hummed as a train raced overhead. He sat in the farthest, darkest corner.

A packet containing one of Carson's flash drives, some crucial pages of information Frank had made copies of, and a note for the police, lay on the table in front of him. He thought about how to deliver it. He didn't dare go himself. The Arx had pulled out all the stops to get him released in the first place. Now that he'd managed to escape, they might well find a way to rescind that decision in the hope that the police would recapture him. Not to mention that he'd kidnapped Rebecca at gunpoint from Kits Beach.

Whatever the priority of his capture was for the cops, it would certainly be at the highest level for the Arx. They'd be watching the police stations, especially the Homicide Squad, which was, in fact, his target. He didn't want to use any form of contact that left a paper trail, like a courier service or even a taxi driver.

He was deep in thought when he heard a shout outside the window. He looked up. A kid on a bicycle was arguing with a guy in a car. It looked like the car had cut the cyclist off, and the kid had nearly bashed into him when he stopped at the light. The kid was in the process of flipping the driver the finger.

Frank studied the cyclist. He had legs like tree trunks, those of somebody that rides a lot, and a large sack slung over his back.

A bike courier, Frank thought.

He jumped up and ran out the door, lugging his suitcase and packet. The courier was about to take off at the changing light.

"Wait!" Frank yelled after him. The kid spotted him, and jumped his bike up on the sidewalk.

Frank rushed over. "You're a courier, right?"

The kid stared at him like he had a screw loose. Finally he nodded.

"How much for an under-the-table delivery?"

"Can't do that," the kid said. "I'd get fired."

"How much?" Frank repeated.

The kid glanced around, then looked Frank up and down. Finally he said: "Fifty, up front."

"Okay," Frank said. "I gotta go to the bank first."

"Five minutes," the kid said. "Five minutes and I'm outta here."

Frank ran to a nearby convenience store with an ATM, sunglasses on and hat pulled down for the inevitable camera. He withdrew two hundred and ran back. The kid was still there.

"I'm a cop," Frank said, "and I've got your license number." The kid rolled his eyes and jumped on the bike to take off.

"Wait," Frank said. "I'm not here to hassle you. I'm just telling you in case you've got any idea of taking the money and not making the delivery."

The kid eyed him suspiciously, but relaxed a bit. Frank handed him the packet. The name 'Sergeant Jack Reid' was written plainly on it.

"Take this to the Vancouver Homicide Squad," Frank said. "You know where that is?"

The kid nodded.

"Give it to this guy," Frank said, tapping the name written on the front. "Him and only him, nobody else. He's a heavy-set guy in his fifties with red hair and a big mustache. If you get it to him he'll give you another fifty."

The kid's eyes lit up.

"Do it first," Frank said. "Before you do any of the others."

"No problem," the kid said, smiling now at the thought of his massive extra tip. He jammed his foot down on the pedal and took off.

"I should have checked that Reid was actually there," Frank said to himself as he watched the courier weave into the traffic.

His cell was dead, and anyway, the Arx might be listening in. To his relief, he found a pay phone. He called the Squad, and asked for Sergeant Reid. The operator tried to slough him off until he said who he was. Suddenly he was immediately punched through.

"You should come in, Frank," Reid said.

"Are the cops still after me?"

"Officially you've been released, but you're still a person of interest in a murder investigation. Everybody here knows the murder thing is bogus. Maybe we can help you…"

"What about the kidnapping thing?"

"What kidnapping?"

"Come on, Sarge, don't shit me. Somebody must have linked me to the kidnapping at Kits Beach."

"Well, yeah, but…"

"Don't waste your breath," Frank said. He explained the circumstances around his abduction of Rebecca, and that in the end she had willingly gone with him. Reid sounded skeptical but went along.

Frank wasn't sure he could believe anything Reid said, but it didn't matter; he had no intention of coming in. He didn't want to spend too much time on the phone either, in case they were tracing the call.

"I'm just calling to tell you to expect a package from a bicycle courier in the next half hour or so. It's evidence of a criminal organization that you guys need to know about."

"The one you were on about before?"

"Yeah, but when you see what I've sent…"

"You sure you're alright, Frank?"

"Just look at it. It's important. I'll call you back later and see what you think. And don't talk to anybody about it – nobody. You'll understand better once you've read it."

"Where are you? I can send a squad car to get you."

"I'm gonna hang up now."

"Frank wait…"

"By the way, I promised the courier you'd give him fifty bucks."

"What!"

"Bye, Sarge." Frank hung up the phone.

He picked up the suitcase and started walking. He wanted to buy some additional flash drives and backup some of Carson's information. He also needed a smoke. The image of Carson hacking up pieces of lung was almost enough to make him quit cold turkey – almost.

He found a computer shop and bought the flash drives, as well as a new burner cell phone. In a dark corner of an out-of-the-way coffee shop he did the backups. A TV nearby had the news on. He watched for a while, mainly to see whether he was on it – he wasn't. Copying the information reminded him how valuable it was. He couldn't haul it along everywhere he went. He needed a secure hiding place. He had an idea, but it would involve taking a long Skytrain ride, and transferring to another bus.

Instead, he took a chance and rented a car. It was probably only a matter of hours before the Arx found him anyway. When they did, at least he'd be mobile.

As he drove he analyzed all Ricky had told him about the Arx, hoping to stumble onto some weakness that might improve his chances for survival. According to Ricky, each Arx Stronghold was dominated by an Alpha male. The Alpha held the power of life or death for all under him, and had his pick of sexual partners. Though a Stronghold might contain dozens of females, the Alpha would tolerate only a handful of submissive males.

The submissives acted as the Alpha's lieutenants, and were granted some privileges, such as sex with females the Alpha had no claim on. Occasionally a submissive would challenge the Alpha for dominance, and win or die. There was a constant shifting of power among the males of a Stronghold; the price of being Alpha was eternal vigilance.

If the males were the muscle behind the Stronghold, the females were its brains. Though as sexually active as the males, they deferred to them regarding sex, and used it to control them. They were rarely required to service aging or unattractive males, since the Arx tolerated no physical defects, and Arx males almost never lived past middle age.

The females managed most Arx affairs and looked after the Arx children. Male children were protected until puberty. After that, if not required as submissives, they either escaped the Stronghold or were eliminated by the Alpha as threats to his power. The purges made no sense in evolutionary terms, since none of the children were fathered by Arx males. The behaviour was wired into the collective Arx psyche by the deformities that defined them.

Expelled males were forced to fend for themselves in the Monkey world. They maintained ties to the Stronghold, and their movements were closely monitored. The goal of these castoffs was to either establish their own Stronghold by attracting Arx females from an existing one, or mount an attack against an existing Stronghold, killing the Alpha male and taking his place.

All knew the importance of secrecy. If they ever forgot and jeopardized the Arx by drawing attention to themselves, they were eliminated.

There was no such thing as mercy in the Arx world.

And these guys have got money and power up the ying-yang, Frank thought, shaking his head slowly. *I'm screwed.*

After a long, circuitous drive and a brief walk he stashed the originals.

THIRTY EIGHT

....

REUNITED WITH THE TEAM

Back in town Frank parked in a quiet alley in the West End. It was now just after three PM. His plan was to find a local library or Internet cafe and fire off copies of the most convincing of Carson's documents to as many newspapers and government agencies as possible. But first he needed to talk to Reid. He called, and once again was immediately connected to the Sergeant.

"You get the package?" Frank said. "I know the whole thing sounds incredible-"

"Frank," Reid interrupted him. "If a tiny fraction of what's here is true, we're looking at the biggest criminal conspiracy we've encountered in my lifetime."

"You mean you believe me?" Frank's entire body relaxed.

"Saying the story's far-fetched is the understatement of the year," Reid said. "But with the weight of evidence this Carson guy puts forward, along with his background, and your corroboration – I think we've got a duty to at least check it out."

Frank exhaled deeply.

"You think these guys killed Stocker?" Reid continued.

"It's possible. All I can tell you is I didn't."

"I don't think anybody here believes you're a murderer."

"So what's happening at the squad now that Stocker's out of the picture?"

"I've taken over the Lead Detective spot until another candidate can be found," Reid said. He chuckled. "Maybe you should come in and apply."

"Yeah, right," Frank laughed.

There was a pause at the other end of the line. Finally Reid said: "After looking over Carson's stuff, we went back and had another look at Lawrence Retigo's journal."

"Yeah?"

"How much of it do you believe?"

"I think Retigo was on the edge, but I think the events he describes actually happened. Of course, I can't prove anything."

Frank picked up his pack of cigarettes, thought better of it, and put it back down.

"Jack," he said to Reid, "maybe you could do me a favour."

"What's that?"

"Get somebody to check on my sister Janet and make sure she's okay. There's no way I can go anywhere near her."

"Sure, Frank," Reid said. "I'll get somebody on it right away."

"Thanks. You guys got any kind of timeline for the investigation?"

Reid said he wanted to pull a few others into the conversation and asked Frank to call back in half an hour. Frank was nervous. It sounded fishy. Reid swore up and down that he was on the level, and Frank had to take his word for it.

"Why don't you come in, Frank," Reid said. "You can even be involved – not officially, of course, but as a sort of a 'Savant Expert'; a consultant."

"Gotta go," Frank said. "I'll call you."

Frank called back at three-thirty.

"Just like old times, eh, Frank," Reid joked, on speaker phone along with Art Crawford, and to Frank's surprise, Terry Hastings, Stocker's former assistant.

"I hope you're not all just getting together to keep me occupied until the men in the white coats can track me down," Frank said.

"We believe you, Frank," Reid answered.

"You've still got friends around the squad, Frank," Art said.

"And at the Academy, including me," Terry put in. "We even studied some of your cases. A couple of the students wrote you off, but I never believed it. You've had a rough time, but you're still a great detective."

"Question is," Reid said, "what do we do now?"

"The Arx, the people Carson calls the 'Savants', have operatives everywhere," Frank said. "They virtually control Kaffir. They've probably infiltrated the force, so be careful."

A shiver rippled through Frank's body as he thought about Ricky in light of Carson's warnings. He made a mental note to call and check on the quadriplegic.

"However big the threat is," Reid said, "we start pissing off somebody like Arthur Dogan without iron-clad proof, the shit's gonna fly. For now, we'll have to treat it like an exploratory expedition."

"We need a way to get inside," Terry said. "Maybe we'd see something to give us probable cause."

"This is a pillar of the community we're talking about," Reid said, "not some stoned out crack dealer. And according to Carson's stuff he's got more brains than the lot of us put together. He's not likely to leave anything lying around that would incriminate him. And if by some chance he does, he's not gonna be dumb enough to let us in. We'll go over there and talk to them. Right now, that's all we can do."

Frank scoured his brain for an alternative to Reid's plan. He came up empty.

"And you're not gonna go anywhere near the place, right, Frank?" Reid said. "I don't want to have to arrest you – or shoot you."

Frank hung up on him.

THIRTY NINE

....

REBECCA RETURNS TO GALIANO

Rebecca had always assumed that Frank's claims about the 'conspiracy' were at best an over-reaction, at worst a symptom of paranoia. Carson's record of his time with Kaffir, and his chilling journal of the years he spent with Jimmy, the boy he finally butchered in cold blood, changed all that.

Now she glanced around her constantly as she pulled her moped up to the dock on Parker Island. There were few people around as she waited in a grassy area nearby for her chartered boat to Galiano. Even so, she interpreted every movement, every glance, every nuance of expression, as confirmation that she was being followed.

As she and Frank had agreed, she'd waited until two to head out, minimizing the time she spent away from the sanctuary of Carson's cabin. There was intermittent cell phone service on Parker, forcing her to travel to Galiano to wait for Frank's call at four PM.

When the boat bumped at the pier on Galiano, the pilot helped her haul the moped onto the dock. She walked it to the gravel road leading from the marina, then took off for town.

She'd only gone a few blocks when a white van turned onto the street behind her, and moved up to within a few meters of her rear wheel. She steered far to the right and waved the driver ahead. A hand waved in response as the vehicle passed her.

She pulled back to the center of the road, now following the van. There was no one else around. When they reached a heavily treed, secluded area, the van jammed on its brakes and skidded to a stop. The brake lights flashed and she hit her own brakes. She lost control and toppled to the ground, sliding to a stop just behind the vehicle's back wheels.

Two men jumped from the van. Before she could scream an arm clamped a damp cloth over her mouth and nose.

Chloroform, she recognized the smell.

One of the men opened the back door of the van. A foam mattress lay on one side. She struggled, but began to lose consciousness, nauseated by the stench. She felt herself hoisted inside and a metal door slammed behind her.

Then everything faded to black.

FORTY

··

A CHANGE OF PLANS

Frank was still hoping to flood the Internet with Carson's information, but it was now three forty-five. Rebecca should have
arrived on Galiano by now and would be waiting for his call at
four. He drove to another location and parked in the darkest corner of
the back lot of an aging strip mall.

There was no point in trying to call early. He'd instructed her to
keep her phone turned off in case it could be traced. Instead he phoned
Mountain View Clinic and asked to speak to Nurse Carstairs. Over the
phone he heard a rush of frantic activity in the background. Carstairs'
voice shook as she explained what was going on.

Ricky Augustus was missing.

"I don't know how it could have happened," the nurse said, her
voice breaking. Frank heard doors opening and slamming, and employees shouting as they rushed up and down the halls. "We've always been
so careful keeping an eye on him."

"He's got that electric wheelchair," Frank said. "Is it possible he
just took off?"

327

"He's never shown any interest in going anywhere before," she answered. "Anyway, the chair is only good for an hour or so, and it's very slow. We scoured the area for blocks around. We couldn't find anything."

"So what are you saying? That he's been kidnapped?"

"I don't know what else to think," she said. "But why?"

The bile rose in his throat as he hung up the phone. If they had Ricky, would they know about Carson?

Frank closed his eyes and tried to calm himself, tried to imagine that it was all over, that the state of terror that had gripped him for weeks now was somehow magically lifted away.

He thought about his life before that night at Janet's: before Gloria, Ralphie, Lawrence Retigo, Ricky Augustus, Richard Carson. It had been a plodding nightmare, a dull gray wash of nothingness: floating in limbo, neither wanting nor expecting anything out of his existence.

That life seemed almost idyllic now, as he cowered in dingy back alleys, jumping at every sound, expecting death at any moment. And now tormented by thoughts of what might have happened to the woman he loved.

He waited the few minutes until four. Finally, his hands shaking, he dialed the number for Rebecca's cell.

A deadpan male voice answered. "Hello, Detective Langer. Good of you to call."

"Who is this!" he shouted into the phone. "Where's Rebecca!"

"You have something we want," it said. "Now we have something you want. Maybe we can make a trade."

"Let me talk to her!" Frank yelled.

328

"We know about your delivery to Sergeant Reid," the voice said. "If we hear you've told anyone else, you know what will happen to her. We'll contact you about a meeting place."

The phone went silent.

"Wait!" he shouted.

He redialed for another ten minutes but there was no answer. He sat back, his mind swirling with images of Rebecca bound and gagged in the darkness, beaten – or killed on the spot? The warning dispelled that idea. Anyway, his psyche couldn't accept that possibility.

Rebecca was the bait to draw him out of hiding. Frank had been involved in enough hostage/ransom cases to know that the hostage rarely came out alive. Since Rebecca knew almost as much as Frank about the Arx, her death was a certainty unless he did something. They would have brought her to one of their Strongholds, and he was pretty sure he knew which one.

They'd be waiting. That didn't matter.

He started the car and took off, tires squealing.

FORTY ONE

....

THE INVISIBLE HAND

A t the same time a drugged and unconscious Rebecca was being loaded onto a float plane on Galiano, a truck painted with
the logo 'Reliable Plumbing and Heating' showed up at Frank
Langer's home in Burnaby, and a pair of workmen wearing coveralls
and tool belts walked to his door. One knocked, then stood blocking the
view from the street as the other picked the lock. They left the house
after about twenty minutes and drove away.

Exactly one hour later, a neighbour reported the smell of gas waft-
ing over from Frank's home. Emergency crews were called, and the
houses in the immediate area were evacuated. Before the crews could
act, the telephone inside rang, and the house exploded in a gigantic ball
of flame, scorching two neighbouring homes, and showering the entire
block with smoking debris.

On Galiano Island, a fire boat had to be dispatched to deal with an
explosion and fire at a cabin on nearby Parker Island.

During lunch hour at the Homicide Squad, when the squad room was almost empty, Deputy Chief Constable Harold Chase flashed his credentials and was admitted without question.

He nodded casually to the one or two detectives present who knew him, and brushed a speck of lint from the sleeve of his jacket as he asked to see Sergeant Reid. Informed that Reid wasn't there, Chase demanded access to Reid's office, claiming that Reid was in possession of some documents that were urgently required for a court case. His actions were highly irregular, but his lofty position in the force was enough to convince the detective in charge.

At Reid's office he dismissed his escort. A few minutes later he had located and opened a small safe hidden in one wall, and found the materials he'd been ordered to remove. Using stolen passwords and security clearances he quickly hunted through Reid's computer for any copies or any mention of Frank Langer's accusations. He found nothing. He broke open a locked drawer of Reid's desk, removed several flash drives he found there, and stuffed them in a pocket of his coat.

He exited the office, and the detectives stood scratching their heads as the Deputy Chief Constable strolled out the front doors and into a waiting car.

FORTY TWO

....

A PRISONER

Rebecca awoke with a splitting headache. Fighting the pain and nausea, she rubbed her eyes and groaned as she dragged herself up on one elbow. The room started to spin and she felt a sudden urge to be sick. She lay back down and closed her eyes. A few minutes later she made a second attempt. This time the contents of her stomach stayed put. Hanging onto some kind of wooden column beside her for support, she surveyed her surroundings.

She was in the exact center of a spacious bedroom. The column she was clinging to belonged to a gigantic four-poster bed on which she sat. The bedding, curtains, decorations and furniture in the room were sumptuous in the extreme, clearly of the highest quality, even to her untrained eye.

Strangely though, there were a variety of styles, many of which didn't go together very well. The aesthetics of the room combined in a way that was surprisingly unattractive. It was as if whoever had decorated understood what constituted quality (through research?) but had no taste whatsoever.

A bottle of ibuprofen sat on the night table. She was leery about taking one, but decided that whoever brought her here could have done anything they wanted to her by now; she couldn't see any motive for drugging her again.

Anyway, the throbbing in her skull was so intense she couldn't think straight. She slid off the bed and stumbled into the equally impressive ensuite, fully laid out with towels and a bathrobe. Again, all were of the highest quality.

She took a long gulp of water and washed down two of the ibuprofen. She looked for her purse, but it was gone. Gradually shaking away the fog enveloping her brain, and feeling a bit stronger, she wobbled unsteadily back out to inspect the room. The windows were all shuttered and the shutters were locked, as were both of the room's doors.

She was a prisoner.

Fifteen minutes later she was brought a meal, by one of the men who'd forced her into the van.

"Where am I?" she asked.

He set down the tray without a word.

"You can't keep me here," she said, and strode confidently for the door he'd entered. He grabbed her arm and hauled her back.

"Don't make me hit you," he finally spoke without emotion.

"What do you want with me?" Rebecca asked.

He said nothing, just turned and exited by the door he'd entered. She heard the click of the latch falling into place. She pulled on the door handle, but it wouldn't budge. She pounded on the door and screamed until her throat was raw. Eventually she gave up.

The presentation of the meal was impressive, but it was surprisingly tasteless. Shortly after she'd eaten, the same man returned, holding a gun. He motioned for her to leave the room and walked behind her.

"So I'm finally going to find out what I'm doing here," she said, though in truth she had a pretty good idea.

She was led through a hallway of what appeared to be a single gigantic home. They passed another bedroom, and a room with shelves filled floor to ceiling with books. So far, other than her captor she hadn't seen another soul. She finally heard voices in one of the rooms ahead. They reached a pair of French doors, and she could see inside.

A group of children of various ages sat on chairs, watching someone at the front. One of the older girls had a baby sitting on her lap. She turned and stared at Rebecca, her eyes black wells of emptiness. Rebecca's gaze moved to the baby and her breath caught in her throat.

"Ralphie," she whispered to herself.

She rushed to the doors and tried to pull them open.

The children turned to her. All had the same distant, animal stare she'd first noticed in Ralphie. She unlatched one of the doors and hauled it open a crack, but it was slammed shut again by her captor. He slapped her face, jammed the gun in her back, peeled her hand off the door handle, and dragged her roughly forward.

"Ralphie!" she screamed, tears running down her cheeks as she continued to watch through the doors. Ralphie stared at her with the same empty expression as the others.

Her captor steered her toward a narrow set of stairs on their left and she was prodded downward, towards the blackness below.

FORTY THREE

....

THE ONLY WAY IN

Frank lost count of the traffic violations he committed on his way to the Dogan mansion, but luck was with him and there were no cops around. He thought about Rebecca, a prisoner, possibly under torture at this very moment by a gang of psychopathic monsters. If she was alive, she'd be at Dogan's mansion. All his research had led him to believe the mansion was the 'Genesis' Ricky had described, the Matriarch's personal sanctuary. If Rebecca still lived, her life would be cut short very soon. Once the Arx had what they wanted...

He pounded his fist on the steering wheel - he was wasting time.

I failed her, just like I failed her sister, he thought.

He was almost overcome with the old paralyzing depression and helplessness. Suddenly he had the overwhelming urge for a drink. For an instant he considered turning the car around, abandoning his quest, and losing himself in the familiar numbness of alcoholic stupor. Inadequacy and failure had been his constant companions for so long now, what difference did it make?

Then he thought back to his time with Rebecca, how she'd stood by him as he battled his guilt and fear. How she'd put up with his

335

belligerence, his childish denial, his panic attacks. How she'd inspired him to be the man he once was.

She had become the most important thing in his life. Now *her* life depended on his actions. Even if he didn't care about himself, he vowed to keep it together for her. He dragged his consciousness out of its mire of self-pity.

On the way over, he'd replayed every scenario open to him. Even when they showed up, his former colleagues would be constrained by law to go through proper channels, with no proof that anyone's life was at stake. Their careers would be on the line if they blew it dealing with someone as powerful as Arthur Dogan. The Arx would have cranked up security at the mansion; sneaking in was out of the question.

There was only one way inside.

He pulled his car up to the entrance, got out, and walked up to the gate with his hands in the air.

FORTY FOUR

....

AN ALLY

R icky Augustus concentrated, focusing all his attention on moving his hand to the control of his electric wheelchair. He accomplished this task, and drove the machine to the window of the upstairs room where he was being held prisoner.

When the Arx had kidnapped him from Mountain View he'd expected to be killed immediately, but then realized that his contact with Frank Langer had created uncertainty. Now they wanted to know who else he might have talked to.

He'd been brought back to Genesis. Coincidentally, he was being held prisoner in the very room where he'd grown up with his mother. He swiveled his chair and inspected the closet that had for so many years been his home. He was unable to wipe away a tear that streaked down from his one good eye.

He felt a stab of guilt that he'd broken under the Arx's torture and told them about the man who had come to visit him several years ago. He hoped for the man's sake that he was already dead, and wouldn't have to endure what the Arx would have planned for him.

His captors had left Ricky alone for almost a day, probably fearing they would kill him before he told them all they wanted to know. Twenty minutes ago, Ricky had heard a woman screaming in a room down the hall, but now the screaming had stopped.

His torturers had returned momentarily. They'd been about to start in on a new round when they'd gotten a phone call and rushed away.

The drip feed of his pain-killers had run dry long ago. He was in excruciating agony, but he wanted to know what was happening. He rolled his chair up close to the window and peered through the slats of the blinds.

In the distance, the front gate had opened and two figures were walking down the laneway towards him. The gate closed again and as they moved closer Ricky recognized the men as the gatehouse guard and Frank, the other man who'd come to see him. The two approached and he saw that the gatehouse guard had a gun pressed into Frank's back.

Ricky reflected that, apart from his own mother, Frank was the only person who'd ever shown him any real kindness. With monumental effort, he swiveled his chair around and inspected the room. He wondered if there was any way he could help Frank out.

He stared for a moment at the electrical outlet in the eastern wall. It was at a height he could reach. With difficulty, he moved his head and inspected the chair in which he sat. One of his drug delivery tubes was held in place by two twist-ties – the old style ones, consisting of a metal wire sheathed in paper. He remembered a trick for lighting cigarettes he'd heard some inmates talk about at Mountain View.

338

A box of tissues sat on one of the side tables. He wheeled his chair up next to the table and managed to knock the box into his lap. He turned and moved his chair as close to the outlet as possible.

It took several minutes to untie both of the twist-ties, and several more to strip the ends of each to bare metal, using his teeth.

With painful slowness, he manipulated the wires with his good hand, working one into each side of the electrical outlet.

He removed a tissue from the box on his lap and worked it into a ball, then held the ball next to the bare end of one wire as he moved the other to touch it and make a spark. It took several tries, but finally a spark landed on the tissue and it caught fire.

Ricky set the flaming tissue on the blanket on his lap. Soon it was burning as well. He added some more tissues, then the entire box. A cloud of thick gray smoke billowed into the air. The automatic sprinkler in the ceiling across the room began to spray, and an alarm echoed throughout the building. As the flames engulfed his body, Ricky smiled. The Arx would never know whether he had anything more to tell.

FORTY FIVE

....

A BATTLE BEGINS

T erry Hastings gazed out the passenger window as the unmarked
police car in which he was riding toiled up the hill on Belmont
Avenue, drilling ever deeper into the realms of the super-rich,
rolling past the most prestigious addresses in Point Grey. The vistas of
English Bay and the North Shore Mountains grew ever more stunning
as each block rose in altitude. The team was headed for Arthur Dogan's
stupendous mansion hidden away in the most distant reaches of a me-
andering lane-way.

There were four of them in the car: driving was Sergeant Reid, the
head of the unit. Reid didn't normally do field work, but had made an
exception this time. Beside him rode Art Crawford, Frank's old poker
buddy. In the back next to Terry was Charlie Hunter, a seasoned detective Frank trusted.

Terry wished Frank could have been with them, but that was impossible. Not only was Frank no longer officially on duty, he was now
wanted on kidnapping and weapons charges, not to mention still a person of interest in the murder of Grant Stocker.

In fact, though the evidence from Carson was compelling, they were risking their careers intruding on the home of one of Vancouver's wealthiest citizens, when by the book they should be combing the city to pick Frank up on his outstanding warrants. They'd be lucky to hold onto their badges if Frank was proved wrong.

Frank had warned them about the danger of confronting Carson's 'Savants', and based on Carson's evidence they believed him, but they'd all signed on anyway. Backup was in place should it be required.

They stopped the car at the gatehouse guarding the entrance and were surprised to find it empty. Sergeant Reid got out and pushed a button on an intercom on the outside wall. Terry listened through the open car window.

"Police," Reid said, holding up his badge to the camera. "We'd like to speak to Mister Arthur Dogan."

A female voice answered. "What is this regarding?"

"Just routine," Reid said. "We're investigating the death of a reporter named Lawrence Retigo."

Terry smiled. *That should get a rise out of them,* he thought.

"Mister Dogan is not here," the deadpan voice said.

"Then I'd like to speak to whoever's in charge," Reid said.

"You can't come in here without a warrant," the voice answered.

"Look," Reid said, "at the moment we've just got a few routine questions about a suspicious death. We can come back with a warrant if necessary."

There was a long silence.

Finally the voice returned: "Mister Dogan is unavailable."

Reid headed back to the car. He was reaching for the door handle when a siren erupted from inside the mansion. Reid rushed to the massive gate and peered through the bars. He ran back to the car.

"There's smoke pouring out of an upstairs window," he shouted. "Looks like we've got probable cause."

He raced over to the gatehouse. "Open the gate!" he yelled into the intercom. Nothing happened. He ran inside the gatehouse and released the gate, then jumped back into the driver's seat.

They tore down the laneway and skidded to a stop in front of the main entrance. The team jumped out of the car, and rushed to the foot of the stairs leading up to the building's sweeping portico. One of the giant wooden doors at the entrance swung open and a young woman appeared.

"It's a false alarm, officer," she said to Reid. "Please leave the premises."

Reid glanced up. Smoke continued to billow out of a second storey window.

"Then what's that?" he said, nodding at it. "You better let us in." He started to climb the steps.

"Please leave," the woman insisted. "Everything's under control."

"We need to see for ourselves," Reid said.

"You have no authority!" the woman shouted. "Do you know whose property this is?" A man appeared behind her.

Reid continued on.

Terry drew his weapon when he noticed the man's hand move under his jacket. The hand emerged holding a gun.

"Drop it!" Reid yelled, reaching for his own weapon. The man raised his gun. Terry fired and the shooter collapsed to the ground, his shot tearing a chip out of a wooden pillar beside Reid's head.

"Art, call for backup!" Reid shouted.

The woman moved aside and another man appeared at the door with an automatic weapon. Terry lay down covering fire as Reid rushed down the stairs and the team dove behind the nearest trees. Terry peeked from behind his tree. Charlie Hunter lay on the pavement. He wasn't moving.

The man at the door stepped out and sprayed the area with gunfire. The three of them returned fire, but the shooter was hidden behind the jamb.

"I'm going for Charlie!" Terry shouted. "Cover me!"

The other two showered the front door with bullets as Terry ran out and dragged Hunter behind a tree. He was still breathing.

"We'll get you out of here, buddy," Terry said.

"Backup's on its way," Art yelled.

Another man appeared on the balcony with a weapon in his hand.

FORTY SIX

....

REBECCA AND CARLA

R ebecca and her captor reached the bottom of the narrow staircase they'd entered after her encounter with Ralphie. She was still stunned by the confirmation that her nephew was alive, and haunted by his animal stare. She was shoved down a short passage and emerged in a cavernous foyer. A curving staircase curled up to the floor above.

Ahead of them, waiting in front of a pair of ornately carved wooden doors, and flanked by two dangerous-looking men, was Rebecca's coffee companion, Carla De Leon.

Her captor took Rebecca's elbow and guided her toward her friend. Rebecca barely recognized Carla. The self-effacing, quiet, thoughtful, scientist persona had disappeared so completely she could hardly remember it had ever been there. The woman standing at the center of the palatial building was intense, charismatic, confident, and indisputably in command.

As they reached her, Carla and her bodyguards fell into step with them as they turned right and headed toward an open doorway. Rebecca scoured Carla's features for any trace of her friend, but saw nothing. They passed through the doorway and into another corridor.

In a few minutes they reached another pair of French doors, leading into a room bathed in green light. The interiors of the beveled glass panels were fogged with moisture. Carla motioned to her bodyguards and they moved deferentially to either side of the doors.

With her own hand on Rebecca's elbow now, Carla led her into a spectacular metal and glass Victorian-style conservatory. Rebecca's guard followed and stood just inside the entrance.

Rebecca stared up in bewilderment at the vaulted glass roof far above her head. The air was thick with humidity and the odour of earth and decay. The late afternoon sun traced prisms of light on the floor, and on the variety of tropical plants and flitting birds surrounding them. They strolled down a stone walkway and over a stone bridge straddling a babbling stream, and sat on a bench beside the walkway.

"Do you like my home?" Carla said, with only the tiniest hint of the voice Rebecca used to know.

"So the apartment in Kerrisdale...?" Rebecca said.

"Merely for show," Carla said.

"It's magnificent," Rebecca said sincerely, gazing around her.

Carla smiled. "I'm glad. You can understand that I would be very unhappy if all this was taken away from me."

"Why would that happen?" Rebecca asked, though she was pretty sure she knew the answer.

"You," Carla said. Her face hardened and her smile faded away. "You and your little friend. The one you refused to reveal to me. The one that was investigating your sister's death – tell me about him now."

"I told you," Rebecca said, "I can't. It wouldn't be…"

Carla put a hand on her shoulder and squeezed until she winced in pain. "Let me make it easy for you. It's that lunatic detective, Frank Langer. You see, I don't need his name. All I want to know is where he is."

"You're hurting me," Rebecca said.

Carla loosened her grip, but maintained a hold on her shoulder.

"Who else knows about your little project?"

Rebecca kept silent.

"It's alright," Carla said, suddenly reprising the comforting friendly voice Rebecca had come to know so well. Even her facial features seemed to soften into the familiar expression Rebecca remembered.

"You can trust me," Carla continued. "It's just important that I know – you understand, legally. Remember, I'm the injured party here. It was you who lied to me and betrayed my trust. That hurt me deeply. I opened my heart to you thinking you were my friend. Maybe you can redeem yourself by telling me. See, we already know about Frank Langer. Is there anyone else?"

Rebecca shuddered at the reference to *we*. She looked up but remained silent. Carla's expression reverted to its original darkness and menace as she stood up and faced Rebecca. Somehow she seemed much larger than before.

"Do you think this is a game?" she shouted.

Rebecca stared up at her but said nothing. Without another word Carla swept back her right arm and backhanded Rebecca in the face.

They were interrupted by the piercing wail of a siren throughout the building.

Carla looked to the guard by the door. He texted someone. "They're looking into it," he said.

They all froze, trying to comprehend what was happening. Rebecca hunted around her for an escape route. There was nowhere to go.

The guard got a call and his fingers moved quickly over the phone keyboard. "Fire," he finally said matter-of-factly.

There was a gunshot, followed by shouting and a flurry of heavy footsteps in the hallway.

Seconds later, gunfire crackled in the distance. All stood waiting while the guard texted again. "Police," he said.

Carla nodded to the guard. He grabbed Rebecca's arm and they rushed out the door.

FORTY SEVEN

....

INSIDE DOGAN`S MANSION

Frank craned his neck and gaped at the ceiling ten meters above his head as he was prodded across the cavernous foyer of the Dogan mansion. When he'd appeared at the gate, the gatehouse guard had frisked him and taken Carson's gun, then trained his own on Frank and propelled him down the winding laneway to the entrance and inside.

Now they stopped and waited as the guard talked to someone on his phone. A few minutes later a new 'escort' appeared and the guard handed Frank over. The new man shoved him towards a door on their left.

They passed through it and were half way down a dimly lit hallway when the fire alarm started to sound. Frank's new handler stopped and held the gun on him as he listened. There was a single gunshot, then more gunfire in the distance.

The man dragged Frank back to the foyer. At the entrance, the gatehouse guard lay in a pool of blood just inside the open door. Another man was standing behind the door jamb with an automatic weapon in his hand, firing at something. Frank couldn't see the man's target.

Police sirens wailed in the distance, approaching. The smell of smoke wafted through the building.

Frank's captor fished a cell phone from his pocket and used one hand to text someone. He dragged Frank back through the door they entered earlier, and they rushed down the same hallway and into a massive living area. Its walls were studded with exotic pieces of art, and antique furniture ringed a luxurious east-India rug in the center.

The space overflowed with the hallmarks of luxury and culture, but the precious objects were placed without design or purpose. They were a collection, strewn around like the spoils from the sacking of some captured city.

Frank glanced to his left at a set of massive plate-glass windows with venetian blinds. He guessed that this was the room Retigo had described in his journal, where he'd witnessed the sex acts and the life and death battle.

They exited the room and soon reached a convergence of hallways. Frank noticed the square outline of what looked like a trap door cut into the floor.

Ricky's tunnel, he thought.

They passed through an open door on their right, and entered a boardroom with a large table in its center.

In the southeast wall of the room, a barely-visible crack defined a rectangular shape. Frank's captor pulled an electronic fob from his pocket and pointed it at a sensor in the center of the shape. A door slid open, revealing an elevator. He pushed Frank into it, then stepped in after him. Again the man waved the fob at a depression in the wall. Frank had expected to go up, but he felt them descending.

They stepped from the elevator into a brilliantly lit, modern space at odds with the ornate mansion above. The guard forced him down a hallway with antiseptic white walls and florescent lighting. They turned right through an open door and emerged in an expansive open-plan work area.

Frank studied the room. The walls were lined with racks of computers and consoles. A few of the consoles were still in use, the operators, all women, frantically typing or clicking their mice. Other workers were crimping bundles of rainbow wire to putty-coloured bricks attached to the unoccupied computer stations. He tensed as he recognized what was happening.

At the far end of the room was a single door, with a sensor similar to the one on the door of the elevator.

His captor shoved him through a knot of workers, and Frank stumbled to within an arm's length of a man in a black business suit, with long graying hair and a thin, intelligent face. Frank recognized him from pictures he'd seen in his research.

It was Arthur Dogan.

He thought back to the descriptions from Retigo's journal and shuddered. Dogan nodded at Frank's guard and he rushed out of the room. To Dogan's right stood a much younger man with blond hair, probably one of his lieutenants – a submissive, as Ricky had described them.

Frank scanned to Dogan's left and heaved a sigh of relief. There, held by another young guard, was Rebecca, her face flushed and bruised, terror in her eyes.

Thank God, he thought. He locked eyes with her, and nodded his reassurance.

Next to her stood a middle-aged woman. Frank had seen her enough times now to know her instantly. There was a quietness, an ease of movement, about her, but at the same time an intensity and strength of purpose he'd never witnessed in another human being. Her body was infused with an energy that seemed to emanate from its core. She was like a wild animal frozen in the act of eviscerating its prey, her deeply-set eyes following the action like a lion stalking an antelope on the African Savannah.

It's true, he thought. *She's not actually human.*

She turned to face him.

"Carla De Leon," he said. "The Matriarch."

"Congratulations, Detective," she answered, "or I suppose I should say ex-Detective. As of this moment you are one of only two human beings on earth who know who I really am."

"I've met at least one other," Frank said.

"If you're referring to Dr. Carson," Carla smiled, "we both know what happened to him."

They'd found out about Carson, Frank thought, *but did they know about Jimmy?*

The disturbing thought surfaced in his mind that humanity was going to have a lot of trouble dealing with the Arx. But that was a problem for the future. For now, his only goal was to get Rebecca the hell out of here.

"How accommodating of you to drop by," Carla said, a thin smile curling on her upper lip. "You've saved us the trouble of apprehending you."

The fire alarm and the barely-audible drone of distant sirens still echoed upstairs.

"Kill them," Dogan said. He waved his hand dismissively. "We've been compromised. They're no use to us now. They'll be in the way."

The one holding Rebecca raised his weapon and pointed it at her head. Frank reacted and tried to rush him, but the blond man grabbed his shoulder and jammed the gun barrel into his back.

"Travis, wait," Carla said.

The man holding Rebecca lowered his gun.

Carla turned to Dogan. "They may still be of use to us."

Dogan raised an eyebrow.

"The copies of Dr. Carson's notes in the hands of the police have already been removed," she said. "The few who have seen them are conveniently present in this building. They can easily be eliminated without implicating the Arx."

"You bastards!" Frank yelled. He lunged for Carla. The blond lieutenant clipped his head with the butt of his gun. Frank collapsed to his knees.

"The only stumbling block is locating the originals," Carla said, ignoring Frank's outburst.

She turned back to Frank, who struggled to his feet. "You can lead us to them."

"I'm not leading you anywhere," Frank said between laboured breaths.

Dogan nodded. "Miles," he gestured to the blond lieutenant. Miles put a hand out, gripped Frank's shoulder, and motioned ahead with the gun. Frank struggled against his grip.

352

Dogan gestured at Rebecca. "Do you want her to live?" he said to Frank.

FORTY EIGHT

....

THE TEAM ENTERS

Terry and the others hunkered down behind several of the massive trees that dotted the mansion grounds, waiting for backup. Terry did his best to staunch the bleeding wound in Charlie Hunter's shoulder. If nothing changed in the next ten minutes, Hunter would die. Moving from behind the tree that protected them would be suicide.

Reid and Art Crawford were locked in a fire-fight with opponents both at the entrance and on the balcony. All they could do was try to hold off the shooters and hope that backup would arrive soon.

As if in answer to his prayers, a blaring police siren in the distance intensified, and within minutes a huge amoured assault vehicle appeared at the front gate. The vehicle tore down the lane-way and came to rest a short distance from Terry.

Seconds later an Emergency Response team, in full battle gear, heavily armed, and carrying ballistic shields, poured out the back and deployed toward the mansion. One of them lobbed a tear-gas canister at the entrance. A cloud expanded in the doorway, and the firing from that position was interrupted. The ER team joined in the firefight with the man on the balcony.

Terry took advantage of the distraction to drag Hunter to the waiting vehicle, where a medic began to examine him. Reid and Art soon joined them. The three of them borrowed some spare body armour and helmets and prepared to enter the mansion.

Terry wondered what had happened to Frank Langer. His gut told him they would eventually find the former detective inside, dead or alive.

By the time he and the others were equipped and had exited the vehicle, the ER team had deployed around the entrance. Terry and the others rushed to join them.

FORTY NINE

....

FRANK FIGHTS FOR HIS LIFE

Frank glanced around as Miles shoved him toward the door of the computer room. All the workers had now disappeared. The bricks of explosive were all wired and in place at intervals along the racks of terminals. Rebecca was ahead of him, being led by Travis. Miles and Frank caught up with them.

"They're going to blow this place," Frank leaned over and whispered to Rebecca.

If he was right, the building was going to go skyward, and anyone still inside when that happened was going to die.

Two guards remained outside the door.

"If they get too close," Carla said to one of them, gesturing upwards, "initiate the sequence. Otherwise, wait for my signal."

The guard nodded. Frank's group – Carla, Dogan, Travis holding Rebecca, Miles holding Frank – entered the hallway and rushed back the way Frank had come, but turned right into a large open space.

At its center stood a column about two meters in diameter. Frank estimated that the column would line up exactly with the tunnel hatch above. A group of armed men was steering a line of workers into an open doorway cut into its side.

Gunfire and shouting from above echoed through the opening. The fire alarm continued to blare. The acrid odour of smoke drifted down to them. In the distance, sirens wailed and a voice crackled through a bullhorn. Frank couldn't hear what it was saying, but he dared to hope it was the cops.

Inside the hollow column, a spiral staircase wound from above. A group of women and children were descending, converging with the workers.

They're evacuating, Frank thought.

He scanned the crowd on the staircase and noticed something else.

A few of the women were pregnant.

Dogan took Rebecca's arm and nodded at Travis, who took off toward the fighting.

"Time to go," Dogan said. He pressed a gun against Rebecca's temple.

"Don't help them Frank," she said. "They'll kill us both anyway."

"But not yet," Dogan said. He tightened his grip until she winced in pain. "Isn't that the irresistible drive of humanity? To stay alive a few seconds longer? And who knows? Maybe God will grant you a miracle. Maybe He'll fire a lightning bolt at us all, or we'll turn into pillars of salt."

Frank stared at the gun against Rebecca's head. Dogan smiled, and cocked the firing mechanism.

Finally Frank said. "Okay, I'll come with you."

"No!" Rebecca yelled.

"He's right," Frank said. "It's our only hope."

Frank understood that once they left the mansion, he and Rebecca were doomed. He scoured his brain for a way out. There was none. All they could do was stall and pray something happened.

By now the last of the evacuees and guards had gone. Dogan shoved Rebecca toward the opening and nodded for her to start walking.

Rebecca's body relaxed, as if in resignation, and Dogan loosened his grip to allow her to step inside. As soon as he let go Rebecca elbowed him in the stomach and grabbed for his gun.

"No!" Frank yelled. He tried to move but Miles held him fast.

The weapon was knocked from Dogan's hand and bounced into a dark corner of the shaft. Dogan gripped her arm again and slapped her hard across the face.

Frank felt the hold on his own arm loosen and he heard a barely audible click. Dogan heard it too. He glanced to his left and a thin smile curled on his lips. Miles had let go of Frank and backed up a step.

He was pointing a gun at Dogan.

"Miles," Dogan said, amused. "Who would ever have thought...?"

"You've had a good run, old man," Miles said, raising the gun to point at Dogan's chest. "But everything has to end sometime."

Dogan shook his head slowly and stared at the floor.

Miles cocked the gun, about to fire.

"This isn't the way to decide succession," Carla shouted.

"Those are the old rules," Miles sneered, his blond hair drooping over his forehead as he sighted down the barrel. "When I'm in charge, there are going to be some changes."

Dogan glanced at Carla. She nodded.

A blur rushed past Frank and Miles fired. Suddenly Dogan was beside Miles, a knife in his hand. There was another blur. Blood sprayed from a diagonal line on Miles's neck and he collapsed to the floor at Carla's feet.

"I'll be the one to decide about changes," Carla spoke to Miles's lifeless body. She cringed as she used a handkerchief to wipe several drops of blood from her sleeve.

Dogan had dropped the knife and was pressing his hand on a patch of red expanding across his left shoulder, where Miles's shot had struck. He was breathing heavily and there was a strange, animal fire in his eyes Frank hadn't seen before.

The gunfire from the west was approaching quickly. Carla stared down the corridor.

She turned to Dogan. "It's too late. We can't get away dragging both of them."

She nodded at Frank. "And we can't take the chance that he'll tell them what he knows. We might still be able to locate Carson's information ourselves."

Dogan studied her, considering her logic. The intense animal stare hadn't left his eyes.

"Better kill them," she said.

Frank glanced over at Rebecca. Dogan was several steps away and she'd been left unguarded.

"Run!" Frank yelled at her. She turned and vaulted for the tunnel. Carla took off after her.

It was Frank's only chance. He dove at the Alpha of Genesis, knocking him off balance. Dogan straightened and turned, his face

framed by his graying hair as he gave Frank a lopsided grin. It brought
back the chilling images from Retigo's journal.

Carla had caught Rebecca and dragged her back.

Dogan glanced at his knife on the floor, then at the gun beside
Miles's body, but didn't move to get them. Instead he sprang at Frank
like a wild animal. Though Dogan was wounded Frank was no match.
Dogan head-butted the bridge of his nose and he nearly passed out with
the pain. He fell to his knees, swaying, moving in and out of consciousness. He glanced down and noticed Dogan's knife, almost at his feet.

"Kill him or take him with us," Carla said.

Dogan seemed oblivious to her, consumed by blood-lust.

"Get up," he said to Frank. He was smiling.

It's a game for him, Frank thought.

Frank stayed where he was. If he could stall long enough maybe the
police would show up, or Dogan would lose enough blood to pass out.
Blood still dripped steadily from his wound.

"Get up!" Dogan yelled. He stepped forward, grabbed Frank by the
collar, and hauled him to his feet.

Frank wobbled in place, the image of Dogan a blur.

If I don't play, he'll kill me, he thought.

"Finish him or I will!" Carla yelled.

Dogan staggered slightly. He was only off balance for a fraction of
a second, but he was losing it.

My turn to win the acting award, Frank thought.

Frank stared ahead blankly, swaying, eyes half-closed, like he was
about to collapse. He guessed that the Arx's predatory instincts would

compel them to deliver the killing stroke to a prey live and struggling, not unconscious and still.

With his good arm, Dogan grabbed him by the shoulder and shook him. Frank sagged, so that Dogan was forced to take most of his weight. Frank kept his eye on Dogan's knife, still less than a meter away.

Frustrated, Dogan transferred Frank's body to his bad arm, and drew back his good one, preparing to slap him awake. At the moment the arm reached its maximum backward trajectory, Frank twisted away, breaking from Dogan's grip, and punched Dogan's wounded shoulder with all his strength. Blood spattered everywhere. Dogan screamed in pain, but recovered quickly and drove a fist into Frank's jaw.

Frank dropped to his knees. As he rose, he turned his body to block Dogan's view, palmed the knife, and slid it into the pocket of his jacket.

Dogan exploded toward him.

Frank had thought he'd understood what he was up against, but he was stunned by the speed of his opponent. Before he even was aware what was happening Dogan's good arm was wrapped around his neck. Dogan squeezed, and Frank felt the air choked out of his windpipe. The blood pounded in his ears.

"Frank!" Rebecca screamed.

Dogan lifted him into the air by his head.

This is it, Frank thought.

He was about to pass out. He heard footsteps close by, and there was movement on the periphery of his vision. He tried to focus. Was it a dream?

"Drop him!" the voice of Sergeant Reid yelled.

Dogan spun around, still holding Frank. Now facing the newcomers, Frank recognized Reid, Terry Hastings, and Art Crawford, in battle dress, followed by what looked like part of an Emergency Response team.

"Do you want me to snap his neck?" Dogan said. He squeezed tighter and Frank almost blacked out.

"It's over," Reid said.

"It's never over," Dogan answered him.

He backed toward the tunnel, his arm still wrapped around Frank's neck, holding him in front as a human shield. Reid and the others stood with their guns trained on him.

Barely conscious, Frank fought to clear his head. The room was awash in red, like blood was being pumped into his eyes. He glanced to his left and could just make out the wound in Dogan's shoulder, still dripping blood. Frank's arms were free, waving at his sides.

He focused his consciousness on one act. If it failed it would be the last act of his life. He replayed it several times in his mind; he would only have one chance to get it right.

He reached into his jacket pocket for the knife, and fumbled for the handle. Drawing on every iota of his remaining strength he threw his right arm across his own chest and jammed the blade deep into the center of Dogan's wound. He felt the wet squish of blood as it hit home. Something gave way and Frank's hand was racked with such excruciating pain he almost lost consciousness.

Dogan screamed. His grip loosened, and Frank dropped to the floor.

Somewhere deep within a blackness that was close to death, Frank heard a gunshot. He dragged his mind back into awareness and looked up.

Reid's gun was pointing at Dogan. The Arx leader had been shot, but was still moving. Reid fired again, and Dogan collapsed at his feet.

Frank lay gasping on the floor. Reid assigned a guard to watch Dogan and he and the others rushed over.

"Are you okay?" Terry said, crouching over Frank.

Frank fought his way back to consciousness and caught his breath. With difficulty, he turned his head and scanned around.

"Rebecca," he whispered.

Terry followed his gaze. "Who? There's nobody else here."

Frank struggled up on one elbow. Terry was right.

"Carla," he croaked. "She's got Rebecca."

FIFTY

···

IN THE HOLY OF HOLIES

Frank struggled to his feet. His right hand was paralyzed with searing pain. He stared down at it. The hand had been driven down onto the knife blade by the impact of the blow, and it had cut deeply into his fingers. The hand was bleeding steadily. Terry tore off a piece of his shirt and wrapped it tightly.

"Carla De Leon," Frank whispered. "The leader of the Savants. She's got Rebecca. We gotta go after her."

"Where?" Terry asked.

Frank hesitated. He glanced at the gaping mouth of the tunnel.

"We've got it sealed off," Reid said. "They couldn't go that way."

Frank's brain was still in a fog of pain and depleted oxygen. He closed his eyes and took a deep breath. Finally his mind was clear.

"I think I know," he said.

He searched the floor for Miles's gun, found it, and shoved it in his belt.

"Follow me," he said.

"You're in no shape to go anywhere," Reid said. "Just tell us and we'll go after her."

Frank ignored him and sped down the hallway back toward the computer room. The guards outside the door spotted them and started firing.

Frank and the others dove behind a corner. The ERT cops stormed the doorway, and after a short firefight the defenders went down. Frank's group rushed to join the team at the door. Frank poked his head around the jamb.

Carla stood against the far wall, holding Rebecca in front of her as a shield, surrounded by several guards. Her right arm was wrapped around Rebecca's neck. Rebecca's eyes bulged as she struggled to get free. One of the guards held a wallet-sized electronic device in his hand.

"Now!" Carla yelled.

The guard started to punch something on the keyboard of the device. An ERT cop stepped out and fired. The guard's body snapped back and the device dropped to the floor. Frank pulled his head in as the remaining Arx fighters opened fire and the ERT man went down.

They were at an impasse. Frank glanced over at one of the ERT cops, who pointed to a stun grenade hanging from his belt. Frank nodded. The man unhooked the grenade and tossed it into the room. A shock wave radiated through the open doorway as it exploded with a blinding flash.

"Wait!" Reid shouted as Frank dashed in ahead of them.

A white cloud of smoke swirled around the room. Through the haze Frank saw the guards lying on the floor. There was no sign of Carla and Rebecca. As the smoke cleared he spotted them, beside the door at the far end. In Carla's free hand was the device the guard had held earlier.

Frank rushed forward until he was almost within reach. Carla tightened her grip on Rebecca's neck and he stepped back.

The team moved in and rounded up the stunned guards. Reid and the others trained their guns on Carla, but couldn't get a shot without hitting Rebecca.

Carla punched a button on the device and the door slid open behind her. She dragged Rebecca through the opening. It began to slide shut. Frank sprang forward, wedged it open with his good arm, and pushed through.

"Frank! No!" Terry yelled as the door thudded shut against Frank's back. The group outside pounded on the hardened steel and fired their weapons, to no effect. Frank scanned around him. They were in a small room packed with antique furniture and art objects.

"Detective," Carla said, slipping the device into her jacket pocket. "Good of you to join us."

With one fluid movement she brought a long knife from inside the jacket and transferred it to the hand at Rebecca's neck. The light from above glinted off the blade as she pressed it against Rebecca's bare skin.

The image of Jeff Randall's severed head exploded into Frank's consciousness, blotting out all else. He staggered back, his body shaking. The room turned dark. The blood thundered in his ears and the walls closed in. A vise clamped down on his chest. His legs started to buckle. He opened his mouth to scream but nothing came out. He sank to his knees, paralyzed, driven into the floor by the crushing weight of fear.

"How pathetic," Carla said, "You really are an obsolete race. It's a wonder you've lasted this long."

"You're monsters," Frank croaked, desperately fighting the crushing terror.

She laughed. "What we are is the future. Like evolutionary dead ends in the past, those afflicted by deformities from drugs like Thalidomide were placed at a competitive disadvantage. Our transformations are something new. We are Homo sapiens: Mark Two, leapfrogging over millions of years of evolution, an advance toward perfection.

"We've watched in amusement as humanity strives to become more like us – leaving behind the silly emotional attachments and relationships, the pointless art and music, the childish quest for pure knowledge.

"You're beginning to understand what's important: competition, advancement, money, and above all, power. You dream of being as we are, but you will always be burdened with your emotional affliction – the weakness.

"History will see you as a stepping stone; an intermediary necessary for the development of our species. Having fulfilled your role in creating Olmerol you've become redundant, doomed to fade away like the Neanderthal or Paranthropus Boisei."

"Perfection?" Frank whispered, still shaking. "You're damaged goods. You're the victims of a scientific experiment gone horribly wrong."

Carla glared at him with contempt. "Victims?" she said. "We'll see who's stronger." She pressed the knife into Rebecca's neck. A drop of blood trickled from the spot where the razor-sharp blade broke the skin.

"No!" Frank screamed.

"Then tell me what you know," Carla shouted, her arm frozen in place. "And tell me who else knows it!"

Frank gazed into Rebecca's terror-filled eyes. He fought to drag his psyche back to earth, to control the irrational terror that gripped him, to focus on how to save her.

Carson had provided him with enough hard evidence to guarantee the banning of Olmerol and expose the Arx for what they were. But what would Carla do if he told her?

He still had Miles' gun in his belt. He couldn't use it as long as Carla was holding Rebecca. He staggered to his feet.

"I've got extensive notes Richard Carson made on his years with Kaffir," he said, battling for control. Carla flinched. "There's detailed evidence of Olmerol's side effects from studies he got his hands on before you could suppress them. Even if the medical community doubts his claims, they're going to be forced to investigate."

"And what have you done with that information?" Carla said. Her knife-hand was trembling.

"Let Rebecca go," Frank said, "and I'll tell you."

He thought back to Carson's words and to Carla's reaction after Dogan's attack on Miles. He had an idea. Blood was dripping to the floor from his injured hand, still wrapped in the blood-soaked cloth. Fighting the intense pain, he twisted his damaged fingers to work the cloth loose.

"You're not in a position to bargain," Carla said.

Frank continued to loosen the cloth, struggling to keep the searing pain from registering on his face.

368

"Give yourselves up," he said, stalling as he worked his fingers. "The deformity isn't your fault. You didn't ask to be this way. We may be able to treat it. Maybe your people can be integrated into society."

He'd loosened the bloody cloth so that it would easily fall from his hand if he let go.

"What?" Carla sneered. "Cure us of our superiority?"

"Superiority?" Frank said. "You're cold-blooded killers." Slowly and painfully, he worked his injured arm into position.

"We do what's necessary to ensure the continuation of our kind," Carla said. "Death is our way. With death comes change and progress."

Frank edged his good hand toward the gun under his coat.

For the first time, he saw something vulnerable, even innocent, in Carla's expression. For a fraction of a second, he felt pity for her. She was like a primeval mother defending her young – in fact, in this case, defending all of the Arx. At some level, she really cared about them; maybe not as individuals, but as a 'Species'.

"Now tell me!" Carla shouted. She clamped Rebecca's shoulder in her free hand and drew back the blade, ready to strike.

It was time to act. Battling the blinding pain, Frank flung his injured arm toward Carla and opened his hand. The blood-soaked cloth flew through the air and landed on Carla's shoulder.

The Matriarch for all the Arx gasped, as the blood from the rag splattered over her face and clothing. She dropped the knife, let go of Rebecca and frantically began wiping the filth from her body.

Frank had almost fainted from the pain. He fought to clear his head. With his good hand, he reached for the gun in his belt.

The leering face of Eugene Mastico swept through his mind as he gripped the cold steel – the stinking alley, the disgusting object lying at his feet, his bloody fingers wrapped around his gun. This was the first time since...

He focused on the pain, reveling in it, willing it to expand through his body and obliterate all other sensations. His arm shook as he lifted the gun and fired. The bullet caught Carla in the left shoulder. She grunted and collapsed to the floor.

Frank rushed forward and grabbed Rebecca. He had to support her; she could barely stand.

He glanced down at Carla. She'd pulled the device from her pocket. She pressed a button and the device beeped. Its numeric display now read three hundred. The value began counting down in seconds.

She pressed another button and a door opened to an elevator behind her.

Frank kicked the knife out of her reach, and wrestled the device from Carla's hands. To his surprise, she didn't resist. Instead she smiled at him. He handed the device to Rebecca.

His hand shook as he trained the gun again on Carla. His finger moved against the trigger but stopped. He couldn't kill her in cold blood. The count was ticking down. There was no more time.

He turned and rushed with Rebecca back to the door they'd entered. They frantically searched for the correct button on the device, and the door slid open. The team was still standing with their guns drawn.

Frank glanced at the display. The count said two hundred sixty. He checked his watch and noted the number of seconds to their destruction.

"The place is gonna blow!" he yelled, supporting Rebecca as they rushed toward the door. "We got two hundred and sixty seconds to get out of here."

The group tore out of the room, down the hallway and back to the evacuation tunnel. The man they'd left guarding the Arx leader lay on the floor. His staring eyes left no doubt about his condition. Dogan's body was gone.

The opening in the column was now sealed. A barely visible line defined its location.

"Two hundred seconds," one of the ERT cops said.

"Blast it," Frank said to him.

"Get back," said the ERT leader.

The group rushed behind a nearby wall and Frank poked his head around. The leader called up one of the team, who hauled a strip of plastic explosive from his pack, placed it along the outline of the door mechanism, and attached a detonator. He joined Frank and the others.

The man activated the detonator. There was a massive explosion, and a shower of metal and plaster flew around them. A huge hole was blown in the column. The leader rushed over, reached out a gloved hand, and threw open what was left of the door.

They ran for the opening and followed the spiral staircase upwards, emerging from the still-open hatch.

"One hundred seconds," an ERT cop said.

Frank nodded to their left. They ran for their lives.

Thank God! Frank thought, as the vast foyer came into view.

The leader radioed the snipers to hold their fire. Frank and the others rushed through the main doors and out onto the driveway. The winding lane was crowded with police cruisers. They dashed across it and had just reached the heavily treed section of the grounds when they heard the first explosion.

Frank glanced back at the building as he ran. Inexplicably, he saw Carla De Leon standing in the topmost window. She was smiling. Seconds later the entire top floor exploded.

Frank led Rebecca behind the nearest tree. They were more than a hundred meters from the mansion, but were still showered with debris. They were knocked to the ground by the shock wave. He got back up and helped Rebecca to her feet. They ran behind a small hill and hunkered down.

Frank crawled to the brow of the hill and peeked over. A massive explosion blew the mansion into a million pieces. Debris and ash flew into the smoke-filled sky and showered on the ground around them as the building collapsed into a heap of smoldering wood and stone.

FIFTY ONE

....

LOHENGRIN

A light drizzle was falling, and Frank stared at a droplet crawling down the blackened wall of what was left of Richard Carson's shack on Parker Island, as a worker drove in a shovel blade and removed the first clump of dirt from Jimmy's grave.

Frank's face, like numerous unseen portions of his body, bore a lattice of cuts and bruises. He wore a plastic brace on his neck, and his right arm was in a sling.

Several uniforms stood by, along with Sergeant Reid, Terry Hastings, and a representative from the Coroner's office. Rebecca had declined their invitation to be there; she was still dealing with the knowledge that Ralphie was lost to her forever.

Frank had resisted coming himself. The horrific experiences of recent weeks were finally fading into a dreamlike past. This was the last place in the world he wanted refreshed in his memory.

In the end, he'd decided that he had to see with his own eyes what Carson had sacrificed much of his life, and finally become a murderer, to preserve.

Two other workers joined in, and the scar in the earth grew more quickly. After about ten minutes, one of the shovels clinked against something hard.

"Wait," Reid shouted.

The workers stepped away and Reid, Frank, and Terry edged up to the grave site. Reid looked at Frank, who shook his head and extended his good hand toward the ground.

Terry climbed into the hole, crouched down, and dug around the object the worker had struck. He uncovered the top of a large glass jar with a sealed lid. Within minutes the entire container was exposed. The workers lifted it to a temporary workbench nearby, scraped off the excess black earth still covering much of it, and finally used a spray bottle to wash it clean.

"Just like Dr. Carson told you," Reid said, bending down and examining the contents.

Inside, floating in a yellowish liquid, was the perfectly preserved brain of Jimmy.

They exhumed the rest of Jimmy's body, and Carson's as well, and got them ready to be transported back to the Coroner's office. Frank exhaled. A massive weight had finally been lifted from his shoulders.

"You okay, Frank?" Reid asked.

Frank nodded and smiled.

"Congratulations," Reid said. "To say we owe you one's kind of an understatement."

Reid glanced over at the body bags being loaded into the van. He turned back to Frank.

"You know, we can provide you with new identities, even have plastic surgery done…"

"From what Ricky Augustus said that won't be necessary. The threat of the Savants themselves, on the other hand…"

"What can they do now?" Reid said. "Their cover's been blown. Olmerol's been banned internationally. The two top leaders are dead."

"You sure about that?"

Reid stared at him. "We saw that Dogan character dead, and you said yourself that you saw Carla De Leon at the window just before the explosion."

Frank shrugged.

"You know something I don't?"

Frank shook his head. "Just a hunch."

"Your hunches scare me."

Frank smiled and slapped Reid on the back. "Let's hope I'm wrong."

☼

"So this is what a Columbarium looks like," Rebecca said the next day, as she and Frank strolled into the ornate building deep within the cemetery proper.

Stacked rows of cells filled each wall. Inside, behind the glass doors, were bouquets of flowers, and occasionally a photograph or war medal.

"It's nice of you to bring me here – I think," she said tentatively, scanning the hundreds of boxes, "but did you want me to see it for a particular reason? It's kind of creepy, but definitely an original place to take a date. And why are you packing?" She nodded at the bulge under his jacket.

"Reid had made some extra copies of Carson's material," Frank answered, "and now they've made more, but the Savants may still be watching me. I didn't want to take any chances."

"But why should they care about your parents' ashes?"

Frank smiled as they stopped at a point near the back of the room. A box just below eye-level had a plaque under it that said: "Edward and Grace Langer."

Frank took a small key out of his pocket, and glanced around the room. They were alone.

"I wasn't sure if the stuff would fit…"

He unlocked the door of the compartment, removed a small vase of flowers, then the urn containing his parents' ashes. Wedged against the back, was a manila envelope and Carson's notebook computer. He pulled them out, and replaced the ashes and the flowers.

"You put the originals here?" Rebecca said.

"I didn't know where else to hide them. I was worried the Savants might find this too, but I was pretty careful about being followed."

☼

A week later, Frank and Rebecca sat holding hands in the reserve seating at the Queen Elizabeth Theatre. From the darkness in a far corner of the stage, a figure approached, standing solemnly in a boat towed by a pair of swans.

"I hate to tell you," Frank leaned over and whispered, "but the swan thing is kind of lame."

"Shhh," someone whispered behind them.

Rebecca rolled her eyes and whispered back. "Just relax and get into the story, Frank. I think you'll like it."

The boat arrived and Lohengrin, resplendent in his shining armour and winged helmet, stepped up to a stone terrace, strode confidently over to the princess, took her hand, and began to sing.

Frank leaned over again and whispered: "He doesn't look anything like me."

Rebecca shook as she tried to keep from laughing. She finally composed herself and jabbed him with her elbow.

"You're not supposed to talk, Frank," she whispered. "You're disturbing the people around us." But she was still fighting to stifle her own laughter.

Three hours later the opera ended to a standing ovation. The performers left the stage, then returned to take their bows.

Frank finally spoke. "That was beautiful," he said, smiling, over the noise of the applause.

"So you liked it?" Rebecca asked, as they strolled through the lobby. Finely dressed patrons crowded around them, discussing the performance.

He nodded.

"Really?"

"Really."

They pushed through the crowd to the bar.

"The constant singing's a bit hard to take at first," he said as they arrived, "but once you get used to it, yeah, it was great."

Rebecca ran a finger under the lapel of his rented tuxedo. "You know, you didn't have to wear this. You could have worn jeans if you wanted. The old thing about opera being just for stuffed-shirts is a bit passé."

"I do feel kind of overdressed."

"I'm impressed that you could get it on over all this," she gestured at the neck brace and sling he still wore.

"You look like the walking wounded," she laughed.

"Thanks," he said.

"On the other hand," she smiled up at him, "there's a new gleam in your eye. You've got some kind of inner thing going I haven't seen before."

They exited the ornate facade of the theater and strolled down Granville Street, headed for Frank's car. Rebecca hooked her arm in his.

"I saw a newscast about the case on TV a few days ago," she said, smiling. "You know, the case that wasn't a case. They never even mentioned you."

Frank said nothing, just kept walking.

"You asked them to leave you out of it?" she said.

"I've had enough of the limelight to last a lifetime. The important thing is that the truth came out about Olmerol."

"Are they at least keeping in touch with you about the Savants?"

"Reid called me a few days ago. They're trying to track them down. Turns out Deputy Chief Constable Chase himself was one. He's disappeared without a trace. Reid said it's like chasing ghosts. They've come

378

up with some kind of medical test for the condition, but they can't force people to take it."

"Any thoughts on what you're going to do now?"

"Reid's trying to convince me to come back to the squad. I'm thinking about it."

"So I won't see you on stage in Vegas anytime soon?"

He scowled down at her.

"Just kidding," she said. "Don't be so sensitive."

His car was parked on the street. He was still nervous around parkades.

He stood by the passenger door.

"As a matter of fact, I think you look incredibly handsome." She moved her hand to his cheek. "I could just eat you up."

"You know, I moved into my new place yesterday," he said, opening the door for her. "There's not a spilled beer bottle or a cigarette butt in sight. You wouldn't recognize it."

"Well, what are we waiting for?"

The colourful menagerie of the city passed them by: street people, bikers, punks with purple hair, couples in evening clothes.

Frank turned and studied the crowd. His body tensed as, for a moment, he wondered if any of them were…he put it out of his mind.

AUTHOR'S NOTE

Thank you for reading The Arx! I hope you enjoyed it.

I know there are millions of books out there for you to choose from, and I'm honored that you chose mine. It's a challenge for authors like myself to reach new readers, and this is where you can help.

If you *did* enjoy this book, and think it would be of interest to other readers, please write a customer review on Amazon.com (http://www.amazon.com/dp/B012P0CTXS). A few words are all that's required. Positive reviews are the best way to attract new readers, and I'm grateful for each and every one I receive.

ABOUT THE AUTHOR

Jay Allan Storey has traveled the world, passing through many places in the news today, including Iraq, Iran, Afghanistan, and the Swat valley in Pakistan. He has worked at an amazing variety of jobs, from cab driver to land surveyor to accordion salesman to software developer.

Jay is the author of six novels, a novella, and a number of short stories. Several new novels are in the works. His stories always skirt close to the edge of believability (but hopefully never cross over). He is attracted to characters who are able to break out of their stereotypes and transform themselves.

He loves both reading and writing, both listening to and playing music, and working with animals. He's crazy for any activity relating to the water, including swimming, surfing, wind-surfing, sailing, snorkeling, and scuba diving.

Jay is married and lives in Vancouver, BC, Canada.

Contact Jay at:

Website: www.jayallanstorey.com
Email: jayallanstorey@shaw.ca

ALSO FROM

JAY ALLAN STOREY

ELDORADO

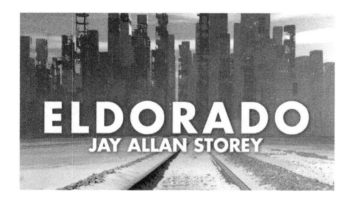

In an energy-starved future, Richard Hampton's world is blown apart when his younger brother Danny disappears and the police are too busy trying to keep a lid on a hungry, overcrowded city to search for him.

What Readers Say About Eldorado:

★★★★★ I was hooked right from the get go, on the edge of my seat throughout the whole thing.

★★★★★ a marvelous page-turner that never stops to breathe.

★★★★★ amazing read of an amazing futuristic journey.

★★★★★ an engaging and thrilling adventure.

★★★★★ Can't wait for a sequel. Very believable – couldn't put it down.

★★★★★ Eldorado, Wow

THE BLACK HEART OF THE STA-TION:THE *BLACK HEART* SERIES

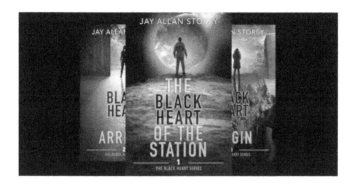

How did we get here? Where are we going? Those are the questions Josh Driscoll, a teenager living in *The Station*, a city built one kilometer beneath the surface of a frozen, lifeless earth, is determined to answer. Josh comes to believe that the *Black Heart*, a computer complex buried by a massive asteroid strike centuries ago, holds the answers to all his questions, and is vital to their future survival.

What Readers say about Black Heart:
★★★★★ 'It's a long time since I've stayed up until 2 o'clock in the morning to finish a book, but I honestly couldn't put it down.'
★★★★★ 'loved all of Storey's books so far, but this is definitely my favorite.'
★★★★★ 'This tops my favorite's list in this genre.'
★★★★★ 'I rarely give 5 Star rating but this book and author

demanded it.'

★★★★★ 'One of the best I have read in a long time.'

★★★★★ 'Loved this story. One of the best sci-fi offerings I have read.'

★★★★★ 'Have no fear, you will enjoy this book!'

★★★★★ 'Wow... what a great read!'

VITA AETERNA

With the fate of the world in the balance, one outlier could tip the scales towards salvation or disaster.

Like all kids his age, on his sixteenth birthday Alex is scheduled for Appraisal, an unpredictable medical procedure with the potential to extend his lifespan. In a world where everything else costs, for some reason Appraisal is free.

Alex has heard of every Appraisal scenario, but none prepared him for his own experience - abducted, imprisoned, and subjected to brutal medical experiments in a high-tech lab.

What Readers Say About Vita Aeterna:
★★★★★ 'I absolutely loved this book.'
★★★★★ 'Never read anything quite like this, read it!'

★★★★★ 'One you have to read!'

★★★★★ 'Awesome plot. Unique! Thank you for writing it.'

★★★★★ 'An excellent dystopian novel with plenty of action.'

★★★★★ 'A must read for anyone who loves a good, original adventure/thriller!'